THE TRAIN FROM PLATFORM 2

Stephanie Steel lives in Manchester, where she was born and raised. After spending her twenties down in London and some time in Sydney, Australia, she moved back home, where she's been settled ever since with her partner and dog, Butter. When not writing she works for a food consultancy, putting her years as a chef to good use, and in her spare time can usually be found reading, hassling the dog, and watching *Law & Order* and *Real Housewives*.

THE TRAIN FROM PLATFORM 2

STEPHANIE STEEL

avon.

Published by AVON
A division of HarperCollins*Publishers* Ltd
1 London Bridge Street
London SE1 9GF

www.harpercollins.co.uk

HarperCollins*Publishers*
Macken House,
39/40 Mayor Street Upper,
Dublin 1
D01 C9W8
Ireland

A Paperback Original 2025
1
Copyright © Stephanie Sowden 2025
Emojis © Shutterstock.com

Stephanie Sowden asserts the moral right to
be identified as the author of this work.

A catalogue record for this book is available from the British Library.

ISBN: 978-0-00-873521-0

This novel is entirely a work of fiction. The names,
characters and incidents portrayed in it are the work of
the author's imagination. Any resemblance to actual persons,
living or dead, events or localities is entirely coincidental.

Set in Sabon LT Std by HarperCollins*Publishers* India

Printed and bound in the UK using 100% Renewable
Electricity at CPI Group (UK) Ltd

All rights reserved. No part of this publication may be reproduced,
stored in a retrieval system, or transmitted, in any form or by any means,
electronic, mechanical, photocopying, recording or otherwise,
without the prior permission of the publishers.

This book contains FSC™ certified paper and other controlled
sources to ensure responsible forest management.

For more information visit: www.harpercollins.co.uk/green

For baby C – we're ready for you (sort of).

One

Warm air rushed at Jess, blowing her hair into her face along with a smattering of grit picked up from the platform floor. Blinking, she spat out strands of her blonde bob and wiped at her eyes with the back of her hand as an echoing screech confirmed the tube's arrival.

Thank God.

It had been an *evening*.

A small bolt of guilt shot through her at that thought, as she stood to one side to let the trickle of disembarking passengers hurry on their way. She boarded the front carriage, having slunk toward the end of the platform, away from the small waiting group that huddled in the middle. It was nearing midnight, the last tube home, and there were only a few other passengers waiting, but still, Jess wanted quiet – a solace usually guaranteed in an end carriage. She sank onto the thin cushioned seat and pulled her phone out of her trench coat pocket, while the doors beeped their alarm that they would soon close. She stared at it and considered messaging Liv, who'd been working tonight and not been able to join the drinks catch-up Jess had just endured. There was that bolt of guilt again. Maybe she was being too hard on Nicole. No one else from work had bothered to try and catch up with her since she'd left the Met last year. Even Liv, her one time best friend, had seemed to forget about her lately as she'd got wrapped up in her new job in the Modern Slavery and Kidnap Unit. Jess was happy for her, of course, but she missed their chatter, their banter. Their banter, often about Nicole. The train began to move, barrelling into the gaping dark, and Jess tapped on her WhatsApp chat with Liv, their last messages sent a week ago – Liv saying she couldn't make the drinks but 'good luck!' with a winking emoji. Their liberal use of emojis, Jess knew from her eldest daughter, aged them as the millennials they were.

She typed out a string of messages and hit send.

Nicole was very *Nicole* tonight 😂

Will fill you in next time.

Hope work's OK!

Jess slipped her phone back in her pocket, trusting the messages to deliver whenever her phone bothered to connect to the patchy Wi-Fi at one of the next stations, and she gazed around the carriage. She didn't feel like music or a podcast tonight. Instead, she wanted to self-flagellate and replay the evening over and over, wondering if Nicole was right. That she looked '*sooo* much like a mum now!' whatever that meant. Or that 'God, you would never tell you used to be a DI!'

Was that true? Had Jess lost so much of her old self?

Nicole had stayed put in their old command, her brash and

no-shits-given personality blending in seamlessly with the boys' club. So much so she would innocently blink her big blue eyes in the face of Liv and Jess's complaints about the unbearable misogyny, as if she had no idea what they were talking about. Nicole had faced it all too, of course, but she'd dealt with it by becoming one of the lads, Gillian Flynn's infamous 'cool girl'. Liv had channelled her rage into a transfer and promotion.

And Jess . . . well, Jess had quit.

She shook herself out of it by pulling her phone back out of her pocket and looking at the lit-up home screen. The reminder of what she'd left to do. Two little girls, nine and four, with gap-toothed grins and their father's penetratingly deep dark brown eyes. They stood either side of a tan Staffordshire Bull Terrier, her panting grin pulled as wide as her human siblings. Jess smiled to herself. It had been worth it. *They* were worth it. This last year of being by their side for every school drop-off and pick-up, every weekend activity, long leisurely walks with Honey in the middle of the day. It had made up for her previous neglect in the face of a demanding job with an unreliable shift pattern.

She put her phone away again, satisfied with her life choices.

But, as she recommenced her gaze around the carriage, she felt a familiar tug. A tug she'd tried to ignore as it had begun creeping in over the last six months, the honeymoon glow of unemployment starting to wane. The tug of, if she was truly honest, *boredom*.

An older man in a suit sitting opposite her shifted uncomfortably, and Jess realized she'd been staring right at him, wrapped up in her own thoughts. She smiled a quick apology and turned away, embarrassed. No one wanted to be trapped on a late-night tube with a weirdo staring at them. He had olive skin and thinning grey hair, and from the bags dragging down his eyes and loosened tie at his throat, she could tell he was only just leaving work. Jess recognized the look of a long day and a late night, and the prospect of, most likely, an early start in a few short hours' time. His brow was damp, and he tugged the knot of his tie lower, stretching out his neck trying to get some non-existent breeze. It *was* stuffy, and Jess rolled her shoulders in her trench coat, feeling damp patches beginning in the armpits of her Reformation dress she'd got second-hand off an app. Nicole's words came back to her, and Jess bristled again. She did *not* look *soooo* much like a mum.

She had a tattoo, for Christ's sake.

She turned her attention away from the businessman and caught sight of a teenaged couple huddled up at the end of her bank of seats, pressed against the curved glass divider before the doors. The boy was white and had a smattering of pink spots along his jawline, his light brown hair worn in curtains, which apparently had come back into fashion at some point. The girl was black, her hair in long braids twisted with bright pink extensions, and she wore platform trainers and flared Lycra trousers – another look Jess had apparently missed coming back on trend. A soft tug of emotion pulled at her somewhere, and she wondered how long it would be before her girls were canoodling with boys on the tube.

Canoodling.

God, maybe she really was *soooo* like a mum.

Leaving the teenage couple to it, intermittently kissing and giggling at their whispered jokes, Jess looked down the other end of the carriage where there was only one other person. A white man on the middle bank of old-fashioned benches that faced into each other, so close together that at rush hour you had to twist your knees at elaborate angles to stop them intimately rubbing up against the person opposite you. He was spread out across a whole bench, leant back with his legs stretched at a wide angle taking up the entire space. Even though this last tube of the night was not busy, Jess had a feeling this man would sit like that even if a troop of elderly nuns boarded and required seats. His face was pink, and he was scowling into a can of Carling. Jess thought about calling out that didn't he know you couldn't drink on the tube anymore, the DI still somewhere inside a stickler for the rules of law and order. But Jess was just a mum now, and she didn't have the energy to get into a slanging match over a can of lager.

The tube pulled to a stop at the next station, Oxford Circus, and a yammering group of what looked like students spilled on. They ignored the seats to stand by the doors, their breathy cadence reliving the apparently exciting events from the evening.

'Did you see that pig's face when Dale shouted at him to go back to the farm?' A girl with thick black curly hair and pale brown skin laughed to her friend, and Jess noticed they were carrying placards. She gave an internal sympathetic tribute to the poor uniforms who'd been put on protest duty. Twisting her head, she tried to catch sight of one of their signs, wondering what the protest had been about. But the group kept moving and contorting around each other, cackling new memories and stories of their night.

Another woman caught Jess's eye as she tried to sate her curiosity about the protest, who – there was no other word for it – *strutted* through the group to claim a seat on one of the benches near the Carling drinker. She was achingly cool with the kind of long and lean figure the body positivity movement said was no longer the ideal, but Jess's warped noughties upbringing still told her to long for. Her hair was a beautiful deep chocolate, faded artistically into bright blonde ends, her face perfectly made up with strong brows and red lips. She was probably only a few years older than the students, Jess considered, but the way she carried herself, with that oversized vintage-looking leather jacket, heavy gold jewellery and nineties-style jeans hung from her hips, made her seem older. She took out her phone and began taking a selection of selfies, her face perfectly framed against the empty tobacco-stained colouring of the Bakerloo train behind her.

A beeping filled the carriage again, indicating the doors were about to close and, just in time, a final woman jumped through before stumbling sideways on her heeled boots.

'Whoops!' she announced loudly to her fellow passengers and pulled herself upright on the rail, her two distinctive yellow Selfridges bags clattering against the glass divider. She seemed to consider the old-fashioned benches for a moment, before tottering with a drunk-looking smile toward Jess's bank of seats, and falling into one a couple over from the tired businessman.

She was wearing a mid-thigh long sleeved black dress that was tailored so well Jess knew it must be designer. She gave Jess a small grin as they accidentally caught each other's gaze, and then flung her long, red hair over one shoulder while she twisted in her seat to root around in the taupe leather Celine tote that had got half caught behind her when she'd sat down. A wallet, crumpled box of tampons, Bobbi Brown compact and accompanying brush were all laid on her lap before finally, digging down into the very bottom of the bag, she retrieved her phone. Jess smiled to herself, thinking this woman had clearly had a good night, to have her phone so forgotten in the depths of her bag. Jess's own phone had been face up on the table next to the wine cooler for the duration of her evening out. Ostensibly to keep an eye on if there was an emergency at home, but Jess knew the girls and Alex would be fine. He'd been their primary carer for most of their lives, he was better equipped to handle them than she was. Really, she'd been praying for an early out, or maybe another message of support from Liv. It had been a long time since Jess had had a night so full of fun and laughter her phone had had a chance to get forgotten and buried.

As if reading Jess's mind, the red-headed woman held the bottom of her phone to her mouth and began recording a poorly whispered voice note. The words had the rasp of effort of trying to keep her voice down, but the volume was not quite as well regulated. Jess smiled to herself.

'Sorry, babe,' the woman half hissed, 'missed your calls. I've had a couple of martinis,' she paused and snickered guiltily to herself and the soon-to-be recipient of her message, 'I *know* I shouldn't, but a few won't hurt, and I've been *soooo* good lately. Ohbytheway,' the words spilled out in a manic, drunken rush, 'I got a present for Sascha and Dan's wedding, Selfridges cookshop had a sale so I got them a Le Creuset set. Anyway, on the tube now, won't be long, I know you're up early tomorrow, so I'll be *super* quiet when I get in – love youuuu.' She elongated the last word with a satisfied flourish and sent the memo. She flashed another guilty-seeming grin in Jess's direction and began repacking her bag.

The group of protesters dominated the carriage with their continued chatter, speaking over each other and breaking off into side jokes and barks of laugher. The tired businessman had carefully balanced his elbow on top of the useless vertical armrest and slumped his face into his hand, eyes fluttering as if threatening to close. The teenage couple could have been entirely alone on a desert island for all the interest they paid their fellow passengers.

The train slowed in readiness for another stop and, as the doors beeped open, a loud scream rang through the train.

Two

Jess's head shot up, her neck twinging with the shock of the movement, only to see the teenage couple wheezing with laughter as the girl held out her phone, filming her boyfriend shriek dramatically, before swinging it around to take in the shocked looks of their fellow passengers. Jess felt her heartbeat start to settle in her chest, the adrenaline having taken her by surprise, and she averted her gaze from the teenager's phone. Was that allowed? Could you randomly film strangers these days? Jess considered that she'd never heard of a law that said you couldn't. She looked up, checking where they were. Regent's Park. One more and then she'd change at Baker Street for the Jubilee line to take her northbound and home.

At first, it seemed like the whole crowd of students had disembarked, some throwing patronizingly dirty looks at the teenagers and rolling their eyes as they pushed out the door, laughing as their placards got in the way, tripping each other over. But when the doors pulled closed again, Jess noticed one of them had remained, hanging back and waving goodbye with a slightly put-out expression. Wherever the friends were going on to, the girl with thick curly hair couldn't, and was already feeling left out. Now the group had filtered out, Jess could read the slogan on the girl's sign, which she had stood up in front of her as she cast about for a seat. *Yes, All Men* was written in black marker, ink stripes visible from where the thick letters had been coloured in. The girl was also wearing a black T-shirt with *I'm Not Asking For It*, printed in clear white text. Jess remembered a rape case she'd worked years ago, back when she'd been a DC. The diligence and hours she'd put into building a rock-solid evidence file, only for the jury to find the guy innocent after the defence had played endless videos and photos of the victim drunkenly dancing with her attacker in the hours before the assault.

Good for these students, Jess thought. Sometimes, despite everything she'd seen in her years on the job, she did have some hope for the world her daughters would inherit.

The loan protester glanced toward the emptiest bank of seats, where the pink-faced Carling drinker was scowling at her sign, mouth slung ever so slightly open as if he had something to say about it. And from the expression on his face, the makings of a snarl in his scrunched-up nose, Jess didn't think his commentary was likely to be positive. The student met his gaze with a defiant expression, but still chose to sit in the more crowded bank of seats occupied by Jess.

The girl plonked herself down two seats away, on the end of the row so there was space for her placard, and opposite the still mirthful teenagers. The train continued its short journey to Baker Street, the canopy of curved brick flashing by, only briefly illuminated by the tube's lights.

Jess had just got to her feet, grabbing at the rail above her head, to go and wait by the doors, when suddenly she was rocked sideways. She swung inelegantly backward as her feet attempted, but failed, to keep balance, and fell across a couple of, thankfully vacant, seats.

The tube had stopped abruptly, and Jess rolled her eyes, her bum smarting where she'd banged her tailbone. *So close,* she thought as she straightened up in the seat, waiting for the train to start again.

Instead, the tinny sound of the tube's intercom buzzed to life and Jess heard the muffled start to the driver's announcement. Instinctively, she turned her head toward the closed door to his cabin – as if she felt it polite to direct her attention to the man behind the wall.

'I'm sorry, folks,' the voice said with practised ease, although Jess thought she could hear a note of frustration in the driver's tone, 'we seem to have come to an unscheduled stop. I'm not quite sure what's going on, but if you'll bear with me, I'll get us some information and hopefully back on our way again as soon as—'

The announcement cut off at exactly the same time as the lights, an ear-splitting screech replacing the driver's professional tone.

The entire carriage was plunged into black.

'What the—' Jess jerked her head around, waiting for her eyes to adjust to the impenetrable dark, for the screeching to stop. But they were thirty metres underground, the weight of London pressing down on them – there was no light to adjust to, and the sound bore into her ear canal, drilling its way into her brain.

Jess didn't panic. Not at first. She felt a pulse of frustration, hoping they'd be in the light and the quiet, and on their way again soon.

The panic took her over slowly. Seconds felt like they dragged into minutes, minutes into hours. Logic told her it could not have been long since they'd stopped, a few moments at most, but without her senses the entire night felt like it was burning away.

And the realization that she might be trapped in this dark screeching tube for God knew how long built inside her until, finally, she let dread take hold.

Three

Jess's eyes were watering from the sound, hands pressed so tightly to her ears she thought she might crush her skull. Pure, instinctive, *chemical*, panic surged through her – nerve endings on high alert as her senses were rendered useless. Time became meaningless, and her only notion of it passing was the feeling of her heartbeat racking through her chest. So, when the screech stopped, as suddenly as it had started, she couldn't have said whether she'd been cowed over in that position for ten seconds or ten minutes. Even with the sound stopped, a ringing in her ears took its place, and Jess wondered if she'd ever hear silence again.

She uncurled herself from where she'd been hunched over her knees and blinked into the multicoloured spots moving across the darkness. It seemed to take her fellow passengers as long as her to recombobulate themselves, but after a few minutes, torchlights from phones lit up patches of the carriage and tentative, scared questions broke through the ringing in her ears.

'Chloe, babe, you OK?' She heard the gentle question from

the direction of the teenagers, a phone torchlight lighting them up from below so their faces were cast in deep, dramatic shadows. The girl nodded silently to her boyfriend, wide-eyed and blinking, and nuzzled into his armpit, her body language stiff and scared. He seemed moderately calmer, but only in a way that made Jess think it was because he thought he had to be. He glanced around the carriage over Chloe's head and caught Jess's eye, as she followed everyone's suit and pulled out her own phone – holding the torchlight up high so it illuminated a larger portion of the seating bank. She gave him a reassuring look, imagining her own girls trapped down here.

'Are you two OK?' she asked, and the boy seemed visibly relieved to have an adult take charge of their well-being.

But still, his answer came with the bravado of wanting to impress his girlfriend. 'Yeah, we're fine,' he said, 'just a shock, in't it?'

Jess nodded in agreement.

'Are *you* all right?' A deeper voice spoke from the other side of that bank of seats, in the direction Jess thought the older businessman had been in. For a moment she thought he was talking to her, and she was about to reassure him, when she realized his phone's light was aimed in the direction of the protester, who had slumped across the vacant seat next to her with her arms over her head. Jess moved her beam in the same direction as the girl unfurled herself, visibly shell-shocked, but nodding.

'What the fucking hell is going on?' A louder, deeper voice came closer, and from the edge of her beam Jess saw it belonged to the staggering Carling drinker, his shadow elongated threateningly across the carriage behind him.

'Obviously none of us know that,' the businessman said with an audibly forced steady tone, not allowing himself to be riled by the Carling drinker's hostility. His worry seemed to still be focused on the student, and he got to his feet and approached her, sitting down on the seat next over but one. 'Are you sure you're all right?' he asked softly. 'You don't look it.'

'Yeah,' the student replied, not sounding convinced of her own response, her eyes flicking up to the imposing figure of the Carling drinker a foot away. 'I'm, I'm fine. I get migraines, I thought that was one coming on.' She shook her head as if trying to clear it. 'It's taken me a minute to realize it wasn't just in my own head.'

'Of course it's not just in your own head,' the Carling drinker snapped. 'The whole world doesn't fucking revolve around you.'

'All right,' Jess said, slipping back into the tone of her old profession with an ease she'd thought had abandoned her. Authoritative, calming. 'Let's not make snipes at each other, that's not going to make any of this any easier.'

'Exactly.' This voice came from the direction of the red-headed martini drinker. She too was directing her beam toward the Carling drinker, so her face was shadowed behind it, but Jess saw her direct a conciliatory nod in Jess's direction.

'Is . . .' Another voice now joined the group from the direction of the old-fashioned benches. 'Is this normal?' She had an American accent, and she came to stand next to the Carling drinker, one hip leant coolly against the pole. 'For the subway, I mean?'

'No,' Jess sighed, raising her eyebrows and closing her eyes as she exhaled slowly. 'Well, it's not happened to me before.' She looked around at her fellow passengers, all now gathered around the final bank of seats in front of the driver's cabin, illuminated in patchy white light and deep, contrasting shadows from the positions of the various phones.

'It'll be a glitch,' the businessman said confidently, with a reassuring smile to the student whose colour seemed to be coming back. 'We'll be on our way soon. These lines are old, these things happen sometimes.'

Jess liked his confidence and didn't want to worry if it was misplaced or not. She tipped her head back on her neck and tried to steady her breathing, feeling the rising humidity of the train build around her. She shrugged off her coat as she recognized the film of sweat that had sprung up all over her body.

'I hope you're right,' the redhead said, 'it's boiling down here, I don't much like the idea of being trapped for too long.'

'Why haven't we heard anything from the driver?' the teenage boy asked, one hand motioning in the darkened direction of the driver's cabin.

'I think that sound' – Jess gestured above her – 'was a glitch in the intercom. He might be trying to figure out what's going on.'

'Hope he does it soon,' the teenage girl said.

And as if she'd summoned it into being, the darkness flitted away as a buzzing yellow light filled the strip bulbs. But it was dull and low, as if it didn't quite have the energy to burn as bright as its potential.

'Ah,' the American said with a smile, 'there we go. All sorted.'

But to Jess it didn't seem like it was all sorted. The lights weren't as bright as they should be, and the train wasn't showing any signs or sounds of starting to move again. She caught sight of the businessman, who was frowning.

'That's the emergency lights,' he said, now seeming deeply worried.

The Carling drinker grunted loudly in frustration and staggered toward the door, pounding on it with his fist in frustration. Jess got to her feet, her hands held up in front of her, that authoritative, calm demeanour shrouding her again like the familiar old hoodie that reminded her of her brief success on a local under-18s football team.

'All right, let's not get agitated,' she said. 'I'll go and ask the driver what's going on, and if he has any updates for us, OK?'

No one said anything outright, but she was greeted by a chorus of accepting mumbles.

She walked the couple of metres toward the driver's door, and as she raised her hand to knock on it, she noticed that the latch was out, holding the door ever so slightly open against its frame.

'Um, excuse me,' she said, pulling it toward her and sticking her head around the opening, 'sorry, but we were just wondering if you had any information?'

Jess frowned, and pulled the door a little wider, stepping over the threshold and into the small cab.

The cab was totally empty.

Four

Jess contemplated what an empty cab could mean, and a wild theory began to develop, the driver abandoning them during the blackout. But why? As she considered this more, she couldn't help but stare ahead out of the wide windows that took over the front of the train. She'd never seen a tube tunnel like this before, from the point of view of the driver. The endless dark, the imposing curved bricks that seemed to be in constant motion falling in on themselves like one of those infinity spiral optical illusions. The tunnel was mostly pitch black. The rails in front, and the walls around were only dimly illuminated from the dull emergency lights that had seeped so half-heartedly through the train. As for the rest of it, she could have been staring out of the International Space Station into deepest space. The hairs stood up on the back of her arm.

She didn't like that thought.

With great effort, she pulled herself back to where she was, which was *not* floating aimlessly through space. She was at home, in London. She was just stuck beneath it for a little bit, that was all. Perhaps this last year had made her soft after all – she'd spent her years on the beat dealing with far scarier things. Jess exhaled slowly, still wrapped up in the void of the tube tunnel, and closed her eyes for a moment to centre herself.

She took in the driver's console, an old-fashioned lever at its centre, and her eyes took a moment to recognize what she was looking at, as unexpected as it was. There seemed to be *blood* splattered across it. She leant forward and looked closer at the window too, seeing that there were dark spots of red also hiding against the blackness on the other side.

Her eyes continued downwards, and then her heart stopped and felt like it would never start again. Directly underneath the driver's console, on his side, curled around the base of his seat – Jess found the driver.

His neck was exposed above his navy uniform vest, but it was not the same colour of pale white skin as his unmoving face. Instead, it was drenched in scarlet, still spilling from a mess of wounds that had been pounded into the right hand side of his neck. Jess allowed herself a moment to understand that she was looking at a series of stab wounds, and then instinct began to move her body. She bent low toward him and, knowing already it was useless, pressed two fingers against his wrist. But there was no pulse. Of course there wasn't.

She stayed over the driver for a moment longer, her fingers still pushing into his lifeless wrist. She closed her eyes and breathed in slowly through her nose, taking in the scent of the dead man's stale sweat and blood. She tried to settle her thoughts, which were careering around her head, questions laced with panic darting through her synapses. A sudden urge told her to let the panic rule, to run out of there screaming to her fellow passengers that someone had been murdered. To flee down the train away from the body and hole up in another carriage and forget about what she'd found. But Jess knew, as she released her grip on the driver's wrist, that she could never leave a scene like this be.

Straightening up and feeling oddly foolish to be doing this in a button-up blue midi dress, she assessed the driver's console again. There was an old style phone to the right of the console, its wire cut through. There were only a few other bits of equipment that had exposed wires, and all of these had been cut through too. But the entire console was dark – even the controls Jess was sure would not have been powered by the cut wires. So, if the tube was down anyway – why bother cutting the wires?

Five

Jess scrutinized the vandalized console for a moment longer. But then she remembered the screeching, and how it had stopped as suddenly as it started. For a blissful moment she forgot the dead man at her feet and concluded that the driver must have cut them to stop the noise.

And then stabbed himself in the neck?

The voice that had asked the acerbic question had not been her own. It had been Nicole's. And Nicole was right, Jess wasn't a DI anymore. She was just a mum now. It wasn't her job to find out what happened to this poor man – *and why*, the old DI in her raised her finger again. Jess forced it back down. But, while that might not be her remit anymore, she could at least keep everyone calm and keep the murder scene clear until the proper authorities did show up. Which surely would not be too long now. The control centre would have a notification of a tube stuck in a tunnel, and the transport police would be on their way to see what was going on if they couldn't get through to the driver. These systems were monitored – the passengers wouldn't be left to their own devices down here for too long.

Giving a nod of respect to the fallen driver as she backed out of his cabin, Jess returned to the carriage proper.

'Well,' the redhead asked at once, urgency splayed across her features, 'what did he say?'

Jess didn't answer but closed the door properly behind her, waiting to hear the latch click into place. 'Give me a minute,' she said, and strode down toward the opposite end of the carriage, through the group of perplexed-looking passengers.

The Carling drinker had returned to his seat and opened another can from his stash in a polythene bag on the bench opposite him, and Jess weighed up what would make the situation worse – allowing him to keep drinking or trying to get him to stop. Sweat patches were now sticking Jess's cotton dress to her armpits and underneath her bra strap as she made her way to the connecting door to the next carriage. They were on one of the old stock of train that only barrelled underneath London on the Bakerloo line. It was all seventies brown, with seventies mechanics to match; these doors operated with only a simple latch to pass through, half the window lowered by the silver catches on either side. Through the open window she peered into the next carriage along and found that it was entirely empty. Jess's mind flashed to the platform at Piccadilly Circus when she'd boarded. Most people had huddled around the centre, immediately where they'd been spat out onto the platform from the escalators, and only a few people, like her, had assumed it would be quietest in the very end carriage.

She turned around from the interconnecting door, the smell of burning rubber in her nostrils coming through the open window, and thought as she walked back. There wasn't enough time for someone to have made their way down two whole carriages during the blackout, into the driver's cabin, kill him and then leave the same way again. Although time had seemed to stretch and knot around itself as she'd been sitting with her hands over her ears in the pitch black, when she'd finally pulled her phone out again it had told her only about five minutes had passed by.

Which meant, she concluded with a sinking in her stomach, one of the group of people she was now approaching at the other end of the carriage was a killer.

'What did the driver say?' the redhead asked again, this time having got to her feet to demonstrate her sense of urgency with the question.

'Yeah, what's going on?' The student looked up from her seat with wide, innocent eyes.

Jess passed through them again and came to a stop with her back to the driver's door, protecting what she had now fully come to understand was a crime scene.

'Look,' she said with a slight exhale. 'I need everyone to try and stay as calm as possible, given the circumstances.' She took in all of their faces, everyone's skin having taken on a slightly greenish tint from the weak emergency lights. 'There is nothing for us to immediately worry about,' she lied. 'The driver is' – she paused and plucked a neutral-sounding word from her DI-life vocabulary – 'incapacitated at the moment.'

'What does that mean?' the businessman asked gruffly, also getting to his feet.

'It means he's incapacitated,' she repeated, and gave the businessman a meaningful look. She hoped that everyone, except presumably the culprit, would interpret it half correctly – that the driver was dead – but not assume that he'd been murdered and that any of them might also be in danger. She wanted to convey the idea of perhaps a tragic heart attack.

'Is that why the tube stopped?' the teenage girl, Chloe, asked, sitting forward now, away from her boyfriend's embrace.

Jess didn't quite know what to say to that. She couldn't conceive of this murder being anything other than premeditated. But – how the hell does someone take down a whole train?

Saul

The woman with the bob seemed to have put herself in charge, despite, evidently, not knowing anything about the situation at hand. She looked flummoxed in the face of the teenage girl's question about why the tube had stopped so dramatically, and Saul almost felt sorry for her. *Almost*. But she had taken it upon herself to take control of this situation.

Saul shifted uncomfortably in his suit and shrugged off his jacket, the heat seeming to rise even more now they were stationary. Logically, he knew, that was impossible, it was only the psychological effect of feeling like he was stuck. Although, it wasn't only a feeling. He really *was* stuck.

And Saul knew something that none of the other passengers did – that they would be stuck there for a good long while. This thought comforted him a little, knowing the length of time that stretched out into the distance before him could allow him to prepare himself, to mentally make the reserves he needed to get through the night. It was how he imagined marathon runners embarked on their race. Not that Saul had ever completed the distance himself, although he had watched the London Marathon a couple of times with his son perched on his shoulders years ago, cheering on the people who had undertaken the mammoth task.

But Saul was not going to tell anyone what he knew.

They did not need to know quite yet that the emergency lights were powered by a backup power station in Greenwich. And that, if that had been activated, they were not going anywhere any time soon.

Especially with an incapacitated driver.

He looked more closely at the woman standing outside the driver's cab, and scrutinized her expression carefully. She seemed calm enough – but worry certainly bled its way through the cracks in her composure. Saul knew she was hiding something from the rest of the passengers.

The truth about what lay past the door behind her.

But Saul was hiding something from the passengers too. Presumably for the same ends. To avert a panic. The last thing Saul needed tonight was a frenzied rampage of people trying to get off the carriage.

No, better to let this woman, whoever she was, take control. She seemed, so far, intent on keeping calm and keeping everyone in place. And that was good, that was what Saul wanted.

Taking stock of his marathon preparation, Saul looked down at his illuminated phone and screwed his mouth to one side, analysing the narrow yellow bar left on the battery icon, telling him he had just 8 per cent left. That would not last long. Saul's gaze floated up to the dull emergency lights. They wouldn't last forever either. At some point the blackness would come again. Dark and impenetrable, laying a cloak of invisibility over them all. Saul would not be taken off guard by that. His phone might not last long enough to light the way, but Saul was always prepared. He had another option. One Nicky had handed him with a proud, gleeful smile one Father's Day morning. Saul couldn't remember which Father's Day, but he knew it must be over five years ago. He sighed to himself as he considered the passed time – the wasted time. Half a decade without even so much as a Father's Day card. Had he really messed it up so badly?

Well, he was making up for it now. He hoped at least.

Saul patted his pocket, looking for one of the last Father's Day presents his son had ever got him. His mind was fuzzy from the stress that had wound itself so tightly around this week – all of it leading up to tonight, apparently. His mouth was dry, and heat and tiredness stung his eyes as he tried to remember where he'd put it.

It was not in his trouser pockets.

He bent over to where he'd slung his jacket on the back of the seat next to him but felt nothing in those pockets either. Frowning now, panicking slightly, he leant forward and unzipped his leather laptop bag, checking every pocket with shaking, sweaty hands. But he couldn't find it.

There was no cool feel of chunky metal, no distinctive flash of Swiss Army red. His penknife, top of the line complete with an LED torch, was not in his possession.

He looked up slowly to catch the eye of their appointed leader, watching him curiously as he'd rummaged so desperately through his bag.

Shit, he thought to himself. *Where the hell did I leave it?*

Six

'I-I don't know,' Jess answered Chloe's earnest question honestly, blinking away from the businessman who had suddenly seemed to need to find something so urgently in his bag. 'Look, I don't want anyone to panic. I'm a detective.' She'd debated whether to say this or not. Her job title usually brought calm to innocent people – and panic to the guilty. And the last thing she wanted was for them to be trapped underground with a panicked killer. But she also wanted to establish her authority, to keep the crime scene clear for forensics, and to keep everyone on board and calm for when the transport police arrived. 'But what I do know is that the best thing is for us all to stay calm, stay in our seats and wait for the authorities to arrive.'

'Aren't *you* the authorities?' the Carling drinker shouted over to her mockingly. Apparently, he'd been listening despite having made a show of trying not to.

'I'm not on duty, but I do know how these things go. And you need to just trust me that the best thing to do is wait for the authorities.'

The Carling drinker rolled his eyes scornfully and shook his head, but he didn't say anything. Instead, he tipped his head back and drained the last of his can down his throat. Everyone else seemed to hover for a moment, as if not quite sure what to do, but eventually, the businessman sat back in his seat, and the others seemed to follow suit and relax a little. Generally, in Jess's experience, most people were happy for someone else to take charge and tell them what to do during difficult times. The redhead also sat back down, folding one expensive-looking leather knee-high boot over the other. The only person who remained standing was the American, who was still leaning against the divider at the end of their bank of seats, her thumb scrolling her phone screen up and down.

'There's no service down here,' she said with frustration, wiggling the screen with even more vigour, as if that might somehow connect her to the outside world.

'You're' – the teenage girl sat even more forward in her seat now, her tone timid – 'you're Jenna Pace aren't you?'

The American looked up from her phone toward the teenager and gave a small smile. 'Yeah,' she said, sounding almost rueful at having to admit it.

'I followed you,' the teenager said, sitting back with a satisfied smile. No more information was exchanged, and Jess waited patiently for some kind of further questioning from fan to idol, but no more was shared. Perhaps that was how it was with influencers, which it now seemed so obvious to Jess that this American was. They weren't *quite* celebrities, not quite worthy of full fawning, just enough to let them know you're one of their cohort who pays their bills with your likes. Jess wondered what kind of influencer this Jenna was. Probably fashion, she concluded from looking at her.

Jess plucked the fabric of her dress away from her again and used the back of her hand to wipe the sweat from her hairline. How long had passed now? How late home would she be? She thought of Alex and the girls, all tucked up in bed by now.

'I won't wait up for you,' he'd laughed as she'd bent low to kiss him goodbye where he was sitting on the carpet getting a glittery purple manicure from their eldest. 'Have fuuun!' She'd laughed and groaned exaggeratedly, though really, she'd been excited to be heading into London on a Friday night for drinks – even if they were with Nicole. The only greeting she'd get when she got back home tonight would be the soft padding of Honey's paws on the wooden floorboards as she came to greet the returning wanderer, tail wagging the whole of her bum, no matter what time it was. She checked her phone again and realized that almost twenty minutes had passed now since the screeching had first stopped. Where the hell were the transport police?

She was not the only person concerned by how long this was taking it seemed; the redhead was glancing agitatedly at her phone, jerking her head around the carriage and allowing her breath to be become shallow – on the verge of hyperventilating.

'Hey, hey,' Jess moved toward her, keeping her voice as steady as possible. 'It's OK, don't worry. We won't be on here much longer.'

The woman gave a few more exaggerated breaths, and turned her attention on Jess, eyes pulled wide, the muscles in her jaw flexing. She was probably only a few years younger than Jess, early thirties, and had a narrow face with sharp cheekbones and a long nose and chin, a thin pink mouth.

'Sorry,' she said, her body language tense. 'I'm not great with small spaces, and . . .' she paused and closed her eyes, shaking her head, 'I've got a banging headache.'

'Too many martinis will do that to you,' Jess said lightly, hoping to relieve some of the palpable tension. The woman looked at her oddly, so Jess explained, 'I heard your voice note earlier. I'm Jess, by the way.'

The woman swallowed thickly, and her eyes darted around the cabin again, before refinding Jess's face and settling a little. 'Amelia. And you're . . .' she paused and nodded toward Jess, 'you're a detective? With the police?'

Jess didn't think now was the time to get into the details of her current employment status, so instead she smiled her best professional smile and held out a hand. 'DI Jessica Hirsch.' Amelia looked at it for a moment and then weakly shook it. 'Do you have any water?' Jess asked, noticing Amelia's hair starting to frizz where the sweat had gathered in her hairline.

Amelia shook her head.

'I do,' the student said, and stepped forward to hand over a Chilly's bottle that she pulled from a cotton tote. 'Here you go. I'm Isa, by the way.'

Jess accepted the water bottle with a smile and handed it to Amelia, who gave Isa a grateful nod.

'Hold on,' the businessman said. 'We don't know how long we'll be down here.' He gestured toward the bottle that Amelia was now glugging liberally from. 'We might need to ration that.'

Jess turned to him with what she hoped was a reassuring smile. 'They'll be on their way soon, we won't be here much longer.' The businessman looked troubled, his brow furrowing, lips pressing thinly together as if he was thinking very deeply about something. 'What's your name?' Jess prompted, remembering her hostage training to personalize yourself as much as possible. Not that they were being held hostage down there exactly, but showing the killer their humanity might not be the worst thing in the world.

'Saul,' he replied.

'Good to meet you,' Jess smiled, and then gestured for the teenagers too to follow suit.

'Um,' the boy said, shifting uncomfortably in his seat, 'I'm Liam, and this is Chloe.' He said the last word at the same time Chloe introduced herself.

Jess turned her attention to Jenna and said, 'Well, we know you're Jenna.' Her eyes slid beyond Jenna toward the Carling drinker, who now had taken to staring at the group with a slightly fuzzy expression through the glass dividers. Jess decided to leave him to it for now.

'Are you feeling better, Amelia?' *Use people's names as much as possible, it calms them, it makes them feel connected to you.*

'A bit,' Amelia answered weakly before the tension tightened around her voice again. 'But I can't stay down here forever.' Her eyes darted toward the doors, and Jess thought she should nip that thought in the bud.

'I can't let you get off this tube,' Jess said, and got to her feet. 'It's not safe. So,' she raised her voice a little and addressed the whole carriage with her repeated message. 'Please, everyone, let's just stay in our seats, stay calm and wait for the police to come and get us.'

Everyone seemed to accept this directive again, albeit perhaps a bit more grudgingly this time. Jess watched Jenna return to her bench and sit with her back up against the window, leg bent and foot resting on the upholstered seat in front of her. She appeared to have something to do on her phone even if it wasn't connected to the internet, and soon, Isa, Chloe and Liam had also turned their attention back to their phones to play games or pick a new podcast. Jess gave an internal sigh of relief and slumped into a vacant chair opposite the still agitated Amelia. Saul leant back in his seat and tipped his head up to the ceiling, closing his eyes.

Finally, Jess let her mind settle, let her tense muscles relax, and tried not to dwell on what lay behind the driver's cab door.

Amelia

Amelia's throat felt looser thanks to the water from Isa. But that was about the only thing that did feel loose about Amelia. Her shoulders had tensed into an uncomfortable shrug, her neck muscles contracted as she felt her body hold itself awkwardly. She closed her eyes and heard Charlotte her Pilates instructor's firmly calming voice: *Imagine a line drawing up through your body, the top of your head moves up, your shoulders fall down into place below it, as if you're trapped between two panes of glass.*

Amelia had instinctively started following the imagined instructions she had heard three times a week for the last four years, drawing her head up and allowing her shoulder blades to slide back into a more natural position. But then she got to the word *trapped*, and her muscles contracted once again, knots tightening achingly into a dowager's hump. Amelia slumped back and gave it up as a bad job. She had enough on her mind tonight to worry about her posture.

The detective, Jess, had been right – the martinis had fuzzed a dull headache to life behind her eyes, the edge only slightly taken off by the water. But still the pain rested there, just above her eyebrows in a halo of guilt, reminding her that she shouldn't have had them at all.

But the alcohol had felt so good going down. It had been six months since she'd had a drink, and my God she'd forgotten how enjoyable it could be. Lawrence wouldn't be happy but, well he'd put her through enough this year too. Everything had piled up at once, bad luck chasing after tragedy. But they were getting through it, they were resilient.

She was resilient.

That was what she'd realized about herself today as she'd sat sipping the ice-cold Grey Goose, the olive bobbing gently against her top lip. She was resilient, and she was strong. She'd got through the hardest year of her life and was now seeing life on the other side. But it was time to stop moping, stop grieving, stop licking her wounds. Now was the time she had to take action for herself.

She rotated her head on her neck and looked around the dully lit interior of the drab tube. God, she hated the Bakerloo line. It was so unnecessarily outdated, like stepping back through a time portal to a land before air conditioning. And now what? She was expected to be trapped on here? Just sit and wait for someone to come fetch her like a child at the end of a school day. There didn't seem to be any evidence so far of anyone rushing to their aid.

Her eyes fell on the doors again. The red emergency release handle hidden under the glass flap. Jess had said it was dangerous – but what did she know? The electrics were off, weren't they? Wasn't that why they were all stuck in this mess? Amelia had not pressed the point, not yet. She didn't want to cause an unnecessary argument, especially not with the mysterious way

Jess had delivered the situation with the driver. *Incapacitated?* That was a consciously vague choice of word. The detective was keeping some cards very close to her chest, that much Amelia knew.

But soon, Amelia *would* press the point. She'd leave it long enough for everyone else to have had enough too. Long enough for them to agree and come with her. Because Amelia had to get off this tube – she wasn't going to waste her opportunity.

Seven

Jess assumed the time was dragging, she could feel the seconds stretching their way across her consciousness. She noticed she was restless, her middle finger tapping a quick rhythm onto her thumb, her heel in her trainers matching the beat. Her hand itched for where her phone lay, face down, on her lap, but she flexed it and brought it back in. Just a little longer. She didn't want to keep checking only to be disappointed by the clock display. She twisted in her seat for the third time, pressing her forehead to the darkened window, trying to see if she could catch any glimpse of the search party that must be on their way to help them. The glass was uncomfortably warm against her skin, and she pulled herself back, not pausing to linger on the driver's cab door as she righted herself in her seat. How long would it be before the open wounds in his neck went putrid in this heat, the stench leaking underneath the door and betraying the truth of what really lay inside to all the passengers? No, she internally shook her head, someone would be here for them by then.

But questions about it all tormented her. Questions bigger than an ordinary murder. Not only the usual question about motive – *why* this tube driver? But questions about the means that were far more complicated than usual. Did the killer somehow stop the tube? How? And if not, what were the odds that the driver just happened to have an enemy riding this tube who struck lucky with the chance to kill him? Opportunistic, heat-of-the-moment kills were the most common form of homicide, but a lot of stars would have to align for this particular grudge to be levelled.

She passed a bit more time by checking on her fellow passengers. *Suspects*, her inner-Nicole corrected her again. Most seemed occupied with their phones, and even Amelia seemed to be glancing through old photographs to keep herself calm. Jess scanned the carriage in an arc, tracking from Amelia to the teenagers, now leaning in opposite directions, Chloe with her legs stretched out and chewing nervously on her bottom lip. Liam was playing some game on his phone, and Jess thought about their parents. They must be worried by now, sitting up wondering where their teenagers were, wondering if their instinctual parental panic had been right all along and they should never have let them go off into London on their own. Behind them in the bank of benches, Jenna was trying her hardest to ignore the Carling drinker, who had now moved over from his side of the aisle to sit on the bench facing her. Jess recognized the tightly polite smile of Jenna's mouth as she glanced up every now and again from her phone to respond to whatever story he was telling. Enough of a signal to show she wasn't interested, but not too obvious a rejection to set him off. Back into her section, Isa had put a headphone in and was scrolling through Spotify, lining up songs, but her expression was furrowed with one nail tapping a similarly agitated rhythm as Jess had been doing on the back of her phone case. Saul had found a crumpled copy of the *Evening Standard* behind his seat and was working his way distractedly through the crossword with a biro he'd fished from his laptop bag. But, just as Jess was, she noticed he was also turning in his seat every few minutes to check if anyone was visible through the windows yet.

Was that suspicious? Jess couldn't decide. On the one hand, she was also keen for the authorities to come so they could solve this mess. On the other, would the killer not also be desperate to get off this train and away from the scene of their crime? Jess turned back to the driver's cabin and thought about going back inside to check out the crime scene again. But no, she wasn't on the job anymore. This was not her remit. Besides, she hadn't investigated anything in over a year, how could she even trust herself to start in the right place? *Secure the scene*. That's what she'd do first – and that was exactly what she'd done. OK, maybe she wasn't as rusty as she thought. It still wasn't her place to poke around in this, she would do nothing but make it worse for the SOCOs.

She eyed the people around her again, wondering which of them could be capable of this. A tingle of curiosity she hadn't felt in over a year began to rise in her, the first spark of adrenaline that there was a culprit to be found, justice to be brought.

Giving in, she blew out a small sigh to herself and turned her phone over in her lap, pressing the side button so the home screen lit up with the time. Nearly 1 a.m.

'What the hell?' She didn't mean to say it out loud, and in doing so, every eye in the carriage snapped toward her.

'What is it?' Saul asked.

Jess smiled up apologetically. 'Sorry, I didn't mean to alarm anyone. It's just, it's so much later than I thought.' All at once those seconds she'd thought had stretched impossibly long had snapped back at her like a released rubber band. 'It's been over forty-five minutes, why hasn't anyone come yet?'

At this, Saul surprised her by giving what seemed like a knowing sigh. 'I've been wondering that too,' he said quietly, not really directing the words toward anyone but himself. He shifted in his seat to look out of the dark windows again. His face was furrowed, distracted, lips pressed tightly together so they all but disappeared into his face. Jess couldn't help feeling that this man was holding something back. 'It'll be big.' The words had come out so quietly Jess had barely heard them, muttered as they were into the face of the black window.

'What'll be big?' Jess asked, now on high alert, taking in Saul's stiff body language, his distracted, troubled expression.

At her question he blinked as if coming out of his own internal reverie and twisted toward her. 'Sorry,' he said, 'what?'

'You just said,' Jess answered, feeling a bolt of frustrated impatience, '"it'll be big". *What* will be big?'

'Oh.' Saul looked briefly down at his hands, which were tensely clasped around each other in his lap. 'I . . .' He paused as if deciding exactly what to say. And then his shoulders slumped a little, and he looked directly at her. 'I can only assume no one has come yet because the problem is not isolated to our line.' He hesitated before adding: 'Or even to the Underground network.'

This statement, delivered with such apparent knowledge, piqued Jess's interest, and she noticed the other passengers sitting up to attention too. Even the Carling drinker and Jenna had stopped their one-sided conversation to listen in.

'What do you mean?' Jess asked.

'I think there might be a citywide power failure.' He gestured up to the low emergency lighting. 'Greenwich Power Station offers backup in times like these, but not enough to get the trains running again – just enough to get the lights on, ready for a safe evacuation.' He scrunched his face up in concern. 'If no one's come down yet, it'll be because the system is in chaos. Mass power failure, probably across the whole city.'

'How do you know all that?' Jess asked, eyes narrowing.

Saul sighed again, as Jenna and the Carling drinker got up and resumed their positions leaning against the dividers by Jess's bank of seats. 'I work for the National Grid,' he admitted. 'We've had a few problems this week, some old equipment that's needed maintenance at key plants.' He gestured upwards toward the city. 'This could be the worst-case scenario I've been working late all week to try and avoid.'

Jess felt a hot spike of annoyance. 'Why didn't you mention this before?'

Saul blinked. 'What good would it have done? I didn't want to panic anyone; we still have to wait here for help.' He gestured around the other passengers. 'Better for us all to hope someone will come soon.' Then he gave a ludicrously optimistic smile around the group. 'Besides, my team is good – they'll have the power up again soon, I'm sure. We have backup, processes, emergency protocols for situations like this, it could come on at any minute.'

Jess wasn't so sure about that but didn't have time to worry about when the power would come back on. Even if it did, they had no driver – they were going nowhere until someone came for them, which, if the city had been thrown into turmoil, could be hours. And she was stuck on a metal tube, deep underground, with a slaughtered body and, it seemed, a murderer. Her stomach flipped, a warm, sickly terror filling her guts.

Scott

Scott watched carefully as the lady detective pressed her lips together tightly, a thick swallow rippling her throat. *Ha*, he thought. *Not so cocky now, are ya?*

He didn't like her, and it hadn't taken him long to come to that conclusion. She was too confident – *arrogant*, to be honest. Putting herself in charge even though no one had asked her to, and ignoring the fact that she clearly had no idea what the fuck was going on. *And* she thought they were all fucking stupid, treating them like primary school kids. Anyone could see there was a problem when she'd come out of the driver's cab – striding down to check out the next carriage, telling them all in her best little miss teacher impression that the driver was 'incapacitated'. Well, Scott wasn't an idiot, and he was no stranger to the looping indirect way the police insisted on communicating. Incapacitated meant fucking dead. She was telling them, without telling them, thinking she was smarter than all of them, that she knew the truth and they didn't.

Stupid cow.

So seeing her rendered momentarily speechless by the business bloke telling her they were going to be trapped for the foreseeable had perked Scott up a bit, even if his current circumstances reflected the state of his sodding bloody day. Nearly an hour he'd been travelling already before the tube decided to lose its mind. All the way from Tooting Broadway. A small snarl flared Scott's top lip as he thought about it. The journey he was now forced to take. His only respite, the offy he'd stopped at by the station, the cool, softening buzz of the canned lager building on the several pints he'd already put away in his old local. That had been a mistake, going back there. He'd seen the way they'd all looked at him, awkward pity behind their stiff greetings. But still, he'd gone and he'd shown his face, taking what little pride in that he could.

He knew the way that lady detective looked at him too. Seen that enough times before. Disgust, judgement, hatred most likely. She thought him pathetic. The way her eyes had caught on the bag of Carlings as she'd passed by him to check out the next carriage. She'd probably clocked the yellowing sheen of his right cheekbone too and made her final decision about his character. It wasn't fair. She knew fucking nothing about him, the judgemental bitch.

The American bird had been nice enough to him though. Felt like he'd really started to make a connection with her.

'Not normally like this, you know,' he'd said, forcing a grunt of a laugh as he'd looked over to her from across the aisle. Thought he should be polite. She was a young-ish girl, all on her own in a foreign country. Well, not *quite* a young girl – he probably had fifteen years on her, she looked in her late twenties, but she *was* an adult, a grown woman. He wasn't some sort of nonce. 'On the tube, I mean,' he clarified, and slid across his bench toward her. She'd looked up from her phone and given him a nice smile. Much more polite across the pond, Scott reckoned. Not like British women.

'Oh, right,' she said with a raise of her eyebrows. She glanced briefly back down at her screen.

Scott hadn't liked that. He was talking to her, wasn't he? Rude. And he'd thought she was more polite than the others.

He crossed the aisle and sat himself down on the bench opposite her, one leg stretched out toward his own bank of seats. He still clutched his can, even though it was completely drained – but it was something to do with his hand, which would hang awkwardly otherwise.

'I'm Scott,' he introduced himself with a teeth-baring smile. 'I do deliveries,' he added, staring intently so she knew he was paying clear attention only to her. Still being friendly despite her rudeness – making her feel welcome. 'All across London.'

'Is that right?' she answered lightly and dropped her hand with the phone in it to her thigh. Scott liked that. Although, she hadn't turned her screen off. He frowned. Why was she making it so difficult for him to just be sodding friendly?

'Yeah,' he said and forced a laugh, shoving his annoyance down. 'So if you ever need a tour guide . . .' He trailed off to allow her to pick up the implied invitation. But she left it untouched, discarded and unwanted like the crumpled Toffee Crisp wrapper shoved between the seat and wall.

She raised her eyebrows and gave another small smile before her big chestnut eyes couldn't help a quick flick down to the screen again.

'All right, love,' Scott said, affronted. 'I was only trying to be fucking friendly. What's so bloody important on your phone?'

She seemed to suck her teeth for a moment before revealing them again in that dazzling white smile.

'Just an Instagram story,' she said, and gave an apologetic

shrug. 'For work, you know. It can be a lot of pressure to get my content done.'

Scott forgave her. She was trying to make it in a new world he hadn't had to navigate. He nodded knowingly, and thought he'd definitely be giving her a follow. He reckoned she posted exactly the type of 'content' he liked.

'All different than back in my day,' he said before correcting himself quickly. 'Not that I'm *that* old,' he snickered. 'Only forty-three – don't be calling the funeral home yet. But all this Instagram stuff' – he waved a hand in the direction of her phone – 'wasn't a job when I was younger. We had to actually graft for everything.' He laughed loudly again, not bothering to see if she joined in or not. 'Not just taking a few pics in a bikini and see the money roll in. Though' – he gave her his friendliest wink – 'can't say I looked quite as good as you. Wouldn't have got paid half as much for flashing the flesh.' He'd roared with laughter again, and she'd tittered appreciatively. Sharing a joke, Scott remembered fondly as his eyes slipped to her, leaning one hip against the barrier next to him. They were off to a great start.

His gaze fell back on the lady detective, who was still staring at the businessman, apparently taking a while to process what he'd said.

Scott felt his throat flex as he imagined again what she'd been thinking about him all this time. The smug, judgemental look on her face. Not half as polite or kind as his new American friend. His hand tightened into a fist by his thigh, stretching the scabbed grazes so they cracked across his knuckles.

What did the lady detective know about anything? Nothing.

Eight

Jess understood on one level that Saul could not know about the body, unless he was responsible, and so technically he'd made the right decision in trying to keep panic to a minimum. But knowing that they could be down there all night changed things. If she *had* known from the start that they could be stranded for hours, what would she have done differently? The answer was an instinct, not a logically thought through decision. She'd have started working the case. Fuck the SOCOs. There was a real and present danger on this carriage. A nervy, clearly violent killer trapped underground was not a mystery she wanted solving by a panicked mass bloodbath. Even she was starting to feel the claustrophobia creep in, convinced every time she looked up that the seats opposite her had inched closer. God knew how the killer felt.

'So, what are you saying?' Chloe asked Saul slowly, leaning over her knees, her braids swinging forward. She had bright eyes despite the late hour, dark amber that shone even in the dull emergency lights. 'That we're stuck down here, maybe all night?' She shot a look toward Liam as she said it, and he sat forward too with a worried expression.

Saul raised his arms out to his sides in a helpless gesture. 'I'm afraid I don't know, and I hope it doesn't come to that.' Jess saw his eyes slide to Isa's discarded Chilly's bottle on the seat next to Amelia. So far no one else had volunteered any water, there was a chance the trickle left in that bottle would be all they had.

'So we get off!' Amelia said, getting to her feet. She had a slightly wild look in her eye, her earlier panic returning in light of this new information. She made to walk toward the doors as she spoke. 'We can't be that far away from the next station, ten minutes tops. Let's just walk to Baker Street.' Jess imagined the overground route between the two stations and knew that technically Amelia was right. If they were stopped in the middle of the tunnel, they were likely no more than a five-minute walk away. She glanced toward the window opposite her, so black it only showed her eerily lit self reflected back at her. In this dark even that journey was not going to be a simple stroll.

'I really don't think that's a good idea.' Saul had got to his feet urgently as Amelia moved toward the doors. 'It's dangerous. We don't know when the electrics could come back on. And if they come back on while any of us are out there, well let's just say we don't want to be on the lines when they turn live again.' He trailed off with a warning look.

'You're saying we'd get electrocuted, mate?' The Carling drinker asked.

Saul nodded. 'That's exactly what I'm saying.'

'What if we walk next to the line not on it?' Amelia asked, her pitch getting higher.

'On another line, maybe,' Jess answered, remembering the story of the passengers trapped on the newly opened Elizabeth line for three hours without rescue before they walked themselves to safety on the legally required evacuation route. 'But the Bakerloo was built way before health and safety – there won't be an evacuation path. It's in the middle of the lines or nothing.'

Amelia looked like she might still be considering it, glancing around at her fellow passengers for support. She seemed to only get a response from the Carling drinker, who had straightened up, shifting his bodyweight ever so slightly toward the doors. Jess imagined he might well fancy the chance to play hero.

'Look,' Jess said with authority, 'it is also trespass to go wandering around these lines unaccompanied. Because it's *dangerous*. It's only been forty-five minutes, no one is getting off this train and risking death for the sake of that, all right?' She eyed them all importantly. 'Or else I'll arrest you.'

The Carling drinker scoffed. 'Oh get off your high horse, *detective*.' The last word was dripping with scorn, and Jess's immediate response was to back down. This man knew she wasn't a real detective anymore, she was a mum who had lost her touch along with her identity.

'Oh, Scott, would you shut up,' Jenna snapped, and Jess saw how the last forty-five minutes of his company had grated her patience down to a spike. 'They both know what they're talking about' – she gestured to Saul and Jess – 'it's not safe, all right? We stay put for now and hope Saul's people get the electrics back on, or Jess's come looking for us eventually. OK? We don't know what's going on up there' – her eyes glanced briefly upwards – 'and I, for one, am not risking my life when I could have saved it by having a nap on a fucking train for a few hours.'

Jess decided she quite liked Jenna. Sometimes you needed that brash American energy to put people in their place. She'd interviewed a witness once, a tourist from Kansas who'd seen a mugging, and taken it upon themselves to intervene and hold the culprit down until the police had arrived. Idiotic, yes, but something about this Kansas mum's confidence in having done the right thing had charmed Jess a little. She'd still read her the riot act though and told her not to play hero anymore on London streets; muggers often have knives. The woman had laughed at that and then said sadly, 'Oh honey, even our teachers have *guns*.'

'Well, when you put it like that . . .' Isa said, holding her earbuds in her hands from where she'd removed them during the conversation. She sat demonstrably back in her seat.

Amelia was looking at Jenna, as if she was carefully considering her words. 'But, you don't understand,' she said, directing her plea toward the American who had made the definitive statement. 'I *need* to get home.' She glanced around the carriage, with awkward, jerking eye movements and when she spoke again her voice was weaker, pleading. 'I'm doing IVF, you have to take the hormones at the same time every day. I'm going to miss my window.'

Jess felt a dart of sympathy, but still wasn't going to let her go. If Amelia died on the tracks out there tonight, missing a batch of IVF hormones would be the least of her worries. No one responded to Amelia's announcement with anything other than sympathetic smiles, including Jenna, who Amelia had been staring hopefully at. Jenna gave her a helpless shrug, visibly conveying the words Jess heard in a New York accent in her own head, *I don't know what to tell ya.*

After a moment, when it was clear no one was willing to accompany her, Amelia obviously decided she wasn't desperate enough to wander the tunnel on her own. She moved sulkily away from the doors.

'All right,' Jess said with a forced calmness she did not feel in her writhing insides. 'Let's all just sit down again and try, as best we can, to relax. Jenna's right, we still have no choice but to stay put.'

After a few moments, everyone settled back into their previous seats, except for Jenna who had obviously decided she was sick of being isolated with Scott and joined the bank of seats the rest of them occupied. Scott eyed her with a curl of his lip but then returned to his original bench.

Jess also sat down, her mind spinning. And then after a minute, her body moved before her brain could catch up. She got back to her feet and strode toward the driver's cabin. If they were going to be stuck down there, she was going to find out who was dangerous.

And who else might be in danger.

Jenna

Jenna narrowed her eyes as the door to the driver's cab swung shut behind Jess. She darted a look across the aisle to Amelia, who, if Jenna was honest, was starting to grate on her. The woman needed to get a grip. But Amelia met her gaze with a similarly curious squint and got up to follow where Jess had gone. She knocked on the door a couple of times, but whatever Jess was doing in there, she didn't answer. She turned back and gave a shrug to the rest of the passengers before sitting down.

'The driver's dead, isn't he?' Jenna said, breaking the silence and saying what no one else had yet.

Saul, next to her, blew out a sigh. 'Probably,' he agreed.

'So why is she going back in there?' Jenna asked, darting a glance around everyone else, to see if they too were unnerved by this. Part of Jenna wanted to get up and demand to know what Jess was doing in there, but if she'd learnt one thing in her two weeks here so far it was that she could not read British people. She wanted to make sure she had the group consensus, before doing anything that might risk suspicion or dislike against her.

Don't make waves, that's what Jenna read in a situation like this. The stress and the claustrophobia would render logic non-existent before long, better for her to just keep her head down and sit it out. Even though she'd already used up most of her reserves of patience with Scott. She'd caught that flash in his eye when he'd seen her dare to glance back down at her phone. It was a flash that asked how *dare* she have the audacity to find something even more enthralling than him? It was the flash that preceded rape or death threats if you weren't careful, endless streams of messages racking up her Twitter and Instagram inboxes for any perceived slight. If she'd had an easy escape, she'd have told him to shove his tour of London up his ass at the first hint of it. But luckily, ever since turning twenty-eight, she'd learnt to mellow out a bit. To stay her poker-hot instincts when she needed to.

Well, maybe not all the time.

And this trip to London so far was wearing her mellow maturity thin. She gave a little shudder of – what? Guilt? Self-hatred? Shame?

All of the above, she supposed, on some level. But really, it was a once-familiar feeling from long ago. It was a shudder at her own weakness.

She'd done this, and she'd put herself in jeopardy as she had. She had cracked the once solid foundations she'd worked so hard to set, and now she was vulnerable. If she did not play this very carefully, she could be destroyed. Everything she'd built – in ruins.

Her brand would never recover.

Nine

Jess had followed her first instinct: *Secure the crime scene*. And now she was following her second: *Assess the crime scene*. Nicole's comments earlier still scratched at the back of her mind, but Jess ignored them too. She knew what she was doing, she'd done this for fourteen years. She'd made DI by the time she was thirty-two. And, despite what her colleagues had laughed loudly over pints at her supposed celebration drinks, it wasn't anything to do with box-ticking. Thinking about her old colleagues sent a surge of furious adrenaline through her, and she almost slammed the driver's cab door behind her, ignoring the questioning looks from her fellow passengers. She heard someone knock, but she ignored them. Her focus was on the situation in front of her.

The smell of blood was potent; trapped in this small, hot cabin, it had nowhere else to flee but up her nose. Acid and rust, from the spilled sticky scarlet that had pooled into the collar of the poor man's uniform and was slowly congealing on the floor next to him. Jess bent down, squatting onto her haunches with her phone torch to get a closer look at the body, being careful not to disturb anything. Now she was closer, she could see the blood had come from three puncture wounds across his neck. They were not very big, and Jess thought the likeliest answer was perhaps a large penknife. She gave a quick scan around the cabin, around the body, getting to her feet and checking all the surfaces, but couldn't see anything yet that might be the murder weapon. The windows didn't seem to open, so the killer couldn't have dropped it onto the tracks. They must have taken it with them.

She bent down again to assess the wounds, and pictured in her mind's eye the force that would be required to drive a blade into someone's neck – not once but three times. This was frenzied. And, Jess was willing to bet, it was personal. The question of the tube stoppage though still confused her. Did the killer ride around on all of this driver's shifts and hope that a blackout might happen one day for them to get the job done? Surely there was an easier way to kill someone? But looking at this scene, Jess was sure it must be premeditated. Unless one of the people she'd spent the last forty-five minutes with was a bloodthirsty psychopath who'd randomly attacked a stranger because the opportunity presented itself. If so, they'd hidden their true nature very well.

Her gaze scanned up and down the driver's body, and she noticed a bloody smear on his pale blue uniform shirtsleeve. It was straight-lined and long down the forearm, as if someone had wiped something clean on it – like a blade. Jess twisted her head on her neck to take in the blood splatter across the console and windows. The neck had a main artery in it, stabbing that would cause a powerful spurt of blood. Why didn't the killer have any on them then? She got to her feet again and tried to picture the scenario. With her back to the door, she imagined that she'd just entered the cabin with the knife – most likely in her right hand, given the position of the wounds. The driver would have been sat facing away from the killer, who would have been unheard in the screeching of the glitching intercom. The driver was likely distracted, frantically trying to work out what was going on, and trying to make the noise stop. He probably didn't even know there was anyone behind him until he felt a sharp pain in his neck, and that sensation had probably not lasted long. Jess imagined the killer stepping toward the stressed driver, raising their arm and driving the knife into his neck. The blood spurted forward – if they'd been careful or lucky enough to stay behind him, then it was possible they'd escaped with no splatter on them. Then, as he'd choked out, grasping at his throat, his mind fading as the blood drained so quickly out of him, they'd lowered him to the ground, hands on his back, wiped their weapon clean and then cut all the wires for good measure.

Why? To keep them down there longer?

Jess lodged that in her mind as a possible lead to follow up, before turning back to the body. The simplest solution was usually the answer. She remembered the old episodes of the American police procedural she'd watched during her early years on the force, oddly soothed by the madcap cases that were easily solved in fifty short minutes, the good guys prevailing, the bad getting justice. 'If you hear hooves in Central Park,' one fictional detective had said to the other, 'you think horses not zebras.' So, for now, she was discounting a bloodthirsty psychopath. This was personal. And if it was personal, then the victim would have the answer.

Examining the body, she saw his name tag declared him to be Matt, underneath a dark droplet of blood. Behind his chair there was a little cubby for his personal possessions. A half-drunk bottle of Lucozade, an open packet of custard creams. Jess reached in and fetched his wallet and his phone, straightening up with a crack of her back to look at them properly in the dull lighting.

She unfolded the leather wallet, revealing little except his work ID badge, a couple of credit cards and a driver's licence. Matthew Donnelly. He lived at an address in Lewisham and was twenty-nine. Jess wasn't sure how relevant that was, but she clocked the information anyway. She tapped on his phone, and a photograph lit up the home screen of a group of guys posing in blue-and-yellow football shirts in front of a pub called the Mason's Arms, the road name sign telling her it was in SE4, which seemed about the right postcode for Lewisham. The name sounded familiar to her, and she screwed up her face in recollection, sure she'd seen that pub before. Had she ever been to Lewisham? Nothing seemed particularly memorable, but she supposed it was not impossible she'd been called to work a case in that area over the last fourteen years. The phone was locked and, with an uncomfortable sickly feeling, Jess's eyes fell to the slain Matthew Donnelly. With a resigned sigh of knowing what needed to be done, but still not particularly liking it, Jess bent over and held the phone in front of the dead man's face. She waited a beat, and then the biometric scan determined it was indeed the owner, and the phone unlocked. She never liked doing that, it felt like a gross exploitation of a dead person to invade their privacy. But, needs must sometimes. The phone didn't give her a lot of information, largely because she didn't quite know what she was looking for. Just enough to get a picture of the victim so that she would be tuned in to anything that might snag against one of her suspects on the other side of the door. She flicked through the screens of apps, multicoloured squares flashing by. The usual culprits were there, a few social media icons, taxis, food delivery. A purple square with a white icon of a hook ending in a heart shape, that Jess recognized from the ads all over London as the latest dating app Hookd. Somehow this one was different from the others, but Jess hadn't bothered to learn how. She'd been with Alex for ten years, her dating app days long behind her. The rest of the apps were more of the same, a couple of games and sport betting apps, and then on the third and final screen, the very last icon for Telegram. Now this was an app Jess *was* familiar with. Telegram, unlike its other messaging counterparts, saved no data on its users, no chat history, and as a result was a favourite of drug dealers, terrorists and anyone else who wanted to make plans that the police would never be able to get access to. But, she also had to admit there was a wide spectrum of users. The majority of people she came across used it for low-level, petty stuff – ordering weed mainly. Logging the information, but knowing it was not enough on its own as a lead, Jess closed the phone for now and put it in the pocket of her dress, wondering if she should bag it for forensics. Well, she'd touched it now anyway, and it had still been in the storage cubby, it wasn't likely the killer had left any prints.

There wasn't much else in the driver's cab that looked likely to tell her anything, and so she readied herself and opened the door.

Isa

The driver was dead. They all knew that now.

Jenna had said it, laid it out there. And Saul had agreed. But why was nobody freaking out more? That's what surprised Isa. Was everyone so comfortable with the idea of disaster? The duration of her lifetime had seemed to be one disaster after another, so perhaps everyone was so exhausted by the concept that when it landed right at their feet, the inertia was too great to respond. Or, maybe Isa was the only person who considered being trapped underground with no electricity and a dead tube driver a disaster. Had she vastly overestimated how people would react to that?

But Amelia certainly seemed to be struggling. She was keen to get off and, if Isa was honest, she'd probably join her if she did go into the tunnel. But it was the claustrophobia that seemed to be getting to Amelia more; her response to the collective recognition of the fate of the driver had been far less dramatic. The other thing no one else seemed, visibly at least, to be worried about – something which was digging a furious nail into the back of Isa's own skull – was the policewoman, Jess, taking herself back into the driver's cab. She chewed the inside of her cheek as she wondered what that meant. Most likely that Jess was investigating whatever had happened to the driver. Isa tapped her foot agitatedly as she thought. Would Jess be questioning them all?

Isa did not need anyone probing into her life right now, and especially not tonight. She looked over at Saul, who had two thick beads of sweat dripping down his cheek, on a trajectory from his temple. He caught her eye and gave her a tired smile.

'How are you holding up?'

Isa shrugged. 'As good as anyone, I suppose.'

Saul scrunched up his nose. 'Not nice though, is it?'

Isa shook her head, and readjusted the hoodie she'd taken off earlier and rolled up behind her into a makeshift cushion. Her body was sore from the protest. She hadn't quite realized it at the time, the adrenaline pumping so hard around her veins, but now she was stiff where her muscles ached from the hours she'd spent standing and marching, her right arm holding the sign aloft, throat hoarse from shouting.

It had been such a rush. The feel of all those bodies together, everyone gathered for the same purpose, the same aim. Showing the Establishment what was right, what was important. Isa had felt truly like she belonged. Like she mattered. Something she'd really only come into since starting university. She was one of six, lost somewhere in the middle of the ranks, and nowhere near the most impressive of her siblings – who counted doctoral degrees, law firm partnerships, countless grandchildren and now even a gold medal from her youngest sister at the European Athletics under-18 championships. And then there was Isa. Perfectly fine, but no more.

But now, now she felt like more. Powerful.

Her mind travelled to the crumpled tote bag next to her. If Jess *was* investigating, would she search their bags? Did she have the authority to? Well, Isa resigned herself. If Jess did, then at least Isa would be the most talked about member of the family for once.

And Isa didn't even care if it was for being a disappointment.

Ten

On the other side of the driver's door, the passengers were sitting up in their seats, no doubt alerted by the click of the door opening, and everyone was staring in her direction.

'What the fuck is going on in there?' Scott demanded, pointing violently at the door as he rose from his bench to approach Jess.

She took a deep breath and made sure the door was closed firmly behind her before speaking. 'I didn't want to alarm anyone before,' she began.

'We've figured the driver is dead,' Jenna interrupted, staring her down with a look that told Jess her explanation better have been hinging on more than that revelation.

Jess had assumed they would have worked out that much, given the cagey nature in which she'd dealt with it. She accepted Jenna's declaration with a nod and continued.

'I didn't want to alarm anyone before,' she repeated. 'But, seeing as it seems likely we'll be trapped down here for a little while, I'm afraid that option has gone. The truth is,' she paused and looked intently at the gathered group, 'and I suppose one of you must already know this, but the truth is it appears the driver was attacked during the blackout.'

The gathered passengers seemed to have gone very still, eyes widening, a few bottom lips dropping open. 'I'm afraid that *that* is the reason for his incapacitation.'

The implication of this took a moment to settle on the carriage, but slowly the realization hit them like the full force of this tube going at top speed.

'Someone *murdered* him?' Amelia shrieked.

'One of you is a fucking psycho,' Scott announced, pointing to each of them in turn.

Isa turned to Jess, eyes pleading. 'He's not been murdered, has he?' she said. 'That's not what you're saying?'

'I'm afraid it is exactly what I'm saying.' At her confirmation another murmur of disquiet began to rumble, everyone looking intently at the strangers they were surrounded by, distrust and panic threatening to break out. 'So,' Jess raised her voice again, 'the driver's cab is *not* to be disturbed. It's now a crime scene.'

'I want to see!' Scott called out. 'I want to know you're telling the truth.'

'Why the hell would I lie about that?' Jess snapped, her patience wearing as thin with him as Jenna's had.

'I dunno, some way to try and control us, to make us do what you want. Manipulate us all so you're the one in charge.' The way he finished his statement with a confident look at Saul, the only other grown man on the carriage, told Jess everything she needed to know. If it had been one of her male colleagues standing here saying this, Scott would happily have taken his worn-out Levi's back to his bench and sat down quietly. Jess dealt with him the same way she had dealt with men like him time and time again – she ignored him. But when she next spoke, it was louder, brasher. Steel rubbing up against steel. If he didn't back down, sparks would fly.

'I need everyone to *sit down*,' she said, raising her hands above her head. 'I don't want to cause panic, but we are in a potentially volatile situation. And I want whoever is responsible' – she paused to look each of them in the eye, ending with lingering scrutiny on Scott – 'to know that I am *very* good at my job. I will find out who is responsible, and I will keep everyone else on this train safe.'

As she finished the sentiment, she realized with a bolt of surprise that she'd been unintentionally channelling Nicole. Jess didn't think she'd ever declared herself to be good at her job before, let alone *very* good at it. Even though she had always suspected it was true. Too trained in life not to boast. 'Stop showing off,' directed at every little girl trying to get attention in a room. It was a trait so ingrained in her and, she remembered with a familiar rising guilt, it had got someone killed. She was not going to make that mistake again. This time she could, quite literally, not run away. And so she had no choice but to back herself. As unnatural as that felt.

'So, this is what's going to happen,' she told them. 'You are all going to retake your seats and continue doing whatever it was you were doing that has been keeping you occupied up until this point.'

'And what are you going to be doing?' Jenna asked with a wry, arched eyebrow.

'I'm going to be questioning you.'

Chloe

Chloe shifted in her seat and pulled one foot up under her bum, her fingers digging into her trousers on the underside of her shin. Liam gave her a smile and leant against the glass divider next to his seat, twisting round again so his back was flat against it. He blew out a sigh and moved his hand to his hairline, brushing the now sweaty strands that usually framed his face back, so they stuck in place on the top of his head. He looked weird with his hair pushed back like that, Chloe thought. Cuter, more vulnerable. He had his hair long to hide the red pimples that gathered around his hairline, something he'd confessed to her during an ill-fated attempt to grow out his stubble to hide the matching complexion on his jawline. But the beard had come in in a patchy, weird consistency, so he'd given it up as a bad job for now. Chloe didn't get why he was so self-conscious about his spots. *She* didn't mind them, and wasn't that what counted? The only other times she'd seen him with his hair pushed back like that was during rehearsals, the bright white spotlights in the college's small studio theatre causing a similar sheen of sweat, but Liam so lost in his role he didn't think to care about hiding.

He caught her looking at him and pulled a face, one eyebrow raised in mock-suspicion. She gave a silent half-hearted giggle and he mouthed, *You OK, babe?* with a meaningful nod. She nodded her affirmation and turned back to look at all the other adults gathered around them, retaking their seats, letting the news of the murdered driver settle on them in their own way.

A murderer.

Was she *really* stuck on a tube with a murderer? One of these people had *killed* someone. Chloe looked back to Jess, the detective, and thought she looked nice enough. Safe, steady. Not quite like a cop though. Her dress was kinda nice – for old-lady style – Chloe supposed, but not exactly what you'd wear to chase down murderers in a tunnel. Although, to be fair, Jess probably didn't know that she'd be doing that this evening.

Chloe turned over her phone and checked the time ticking away, the signal and Wi-Fi displays both still showing nothing. Her dad was going to be losing his mind. But that wasn't what was sending the twist of discomfort through her belly. Her dad was always worrying about her for something or another, at least he didn't *know* she was stuck underground with a murderer.

No. Instead, what was playing on Chloe's mind, sending nervous butterflies slashing their wings against her stomach, was what she knew. Jess had said she was going to question them all – would she be doing it here, in front of everyone? Chloe didn't want the killer to think *she* was onto them – she might be next. She looked over at Liam again and wondered if he was thinking the same thing. Because, surely he knew what she knew – he must have made the same connection. But Liam was looking over at Jenna Pace, trying to do it subtly, through small darts out of the side of his eye.

Chloe rolled her eyes. She didn't like Jenna Pace, not anymore. She used to like her pictures of her glamorous life out and about in New York City, used to fantasize about living the same life. It was weird seeing her here, in the flesh. She was shorter than Chloe had thought, but, she had to grudgingly admit, she was as cool as she came across online.

But then Chloe had found out the truth of Jenna's business, Jenna's *brand*. And now she didn't care how cool Jenna's persona was. Jenna Pace was dark, and Chloe didn't want anything to do with her.

Eleven

The tension in the carriage was as thick as the humidity. Everyone had retaken their seats, but nobody had returned to their earlier activities. Instead, they sat in stiff, stony silence, jerked glances directed toward the driver's cabin door every so often. There were two exceptions. Scott still seemed irate at having to take orders from Jess but had obviously decided he didn't have much of a choice about the situation. He sat on his bench, scowling in her direction, his neck now matching the pink hue of his face above his navy-blue polo shirt. His hair was dark and short, and Jess could see it starting to stick to his scalp from the sweat. The other exception was Jenna, who seemed curiously cool, given the whole scenario. She hadn't returned to her phone but had sat down in the seat right next to the wall of the driver's cab, back leant against it and legs stretched out comfortably across the seats next to her. Her eyes were closed, and it seemed she really was trying to get that nap she'd mentioned earlier.

There were no private rooms or compartments for Jess to take anyone off to, and in the oppressive quiet of the passengers' tense silence every word would carry down the carriage anyway, even if she did take her interviewees down the other end. She considered for a moment passing through into the empty carriage next to them but didn't want to risk leaving the crime scene unattended, possibly giving the murderer the chance to clear up after themselves a bit more. Besides, it seemed that everyone in the carriage were strangers except for the teenage couple, so weighing it up, Jess decided the risks of allowing them to hear each other's interviews were less than leaving the carriage.

Turning to the person closest to her on her left, Jess sat down next to Amelia. Amelia was visibly nervous, with thick swallows and a clenched jaw.

'I just can't believe it,' she said breathily, her eyes on the door behind Jess.

'I know it's a shock,' Jess said kindly, making an effort to keep her body language relaxed, comforting. *I'm someone it's safe to confide in.* 'Let's start slowly. Can you tell me what you were doing during the blackout?'

Amelia moved her eyes away from the door and onto Jess, a slightly incredulous look in her eye. 'I was doing what everyone else was doing, I assume,' she said. 'Covering my ears and hoping that screeching would stop. I *told* you I had a banging headache.'

Jess nodded, accepting the answer. 'And did you notice anything strange?' She gestured to Amelia's position, which was the same one Amelia had sat down in when she'd boarded, a few seats away from the cabin. 'You were closest to the door, did you hear or feel any kind of movement?'

Amelia shook her head. 'I was so distracted. My head was agony, and I didn't know what was going on, and I-I was, I still *am*,' she added pointedly, 'worried about getting home for my IVF hormones.'

Jess nodded sympathetically. 'What have you been doing today?' she asked.

'I don't quite see how that's relevant,' Amelia said, crinkling her brow, 'but I was working and then I went shopping.' She gestured to the Selfridges bags on the seat next to her.

'And did you meet anyone? You mentioned you'd had some cocktails, were they with a friend?'

Amelia gave a small, almost embarrassed sigh and looked down at her lap for a moment. Her expression, when it returned to look at Jess, was sheepish. 'No,' she admitted. 'It's – it's been a difficult time. I . . .' she paused and visibly collected herself, eyes growing wet. 'I lost my sister last year, it's been hard on the whole family – my niece and nephew are only young.'

'I'm so sorry,' Jess said softly.

'And we' – she gestured vaguely down to the diamond ring on her wedding finger – 'we've been trying for kids for ages, and I think the family could do with some good news. But we've not had any luck so far, and the doctor says the stress isn't helping – but what am I supposed to do? I can't bring her back to life, can I?!' She asked the last question frantically, eyes slightly manic as if she hoped Jess might correct her with a way she could, indeed, bring her sister back to life. 'But we're taking it into our own hands, doing IVF, and I really, *really* need to get back for my hormones.'

'I understand that's difficult.' Jess gave a sympathetic nod. 'But there's not much we can do about that now.' Amelia's eyes jumped toward the tube doors again, so Jess quickly distracted her. 'Talk me through your day. Where do you work? Where were you shopping? You were on the last tube home, the shops had closed a while ago – where were you having your drinks?'

Amelia looked for a moment like she didn't want to answer, or that she was offended at being questioned in this way. But she did eventually relent. 'Like I said, I was at work most of the day. I'm a PR consultant, I work for myself, usually from home. But I had a meeting near Oxford Street toward the end of the day, which wrapped up about six. I had some bits to get, a wedding present, and I fancied a browse. Maybe treat myself to something new.' She looked down sheepishly again. 'Have a little look around the baby departments.' She collected herself for a beat and then met Jess's eye again. 'And so that's what I did. Selfridges is open till ten, and that was my last stop. I don't know what time I got there – maybe eight? I did my browsing, found the wedding present and then, well then I decided I needed a drink. It had been a long day. My client is difficult, and I'd been up early perfecting the proposal, which, they tore apart, as it happens.' She took a frustrated inhale of breath. 'And it felt a bit like everything that could go wrong *was* going wrong. I've not been drinking this year, trying to give us the best chance for conceiving. But tonight, I just needed one.'

'And where did you go?'

'Selfridges – the champagne bar, it's right by the cookshop, and I was passing by, saw an empty seat and decided to sit down.'

'And where did you go afterwards?' When Amelia looked a little perplexed at that, Jess reminded her: 'You said Selfridges closes at ten, but you got on this tube around midnight.'

'Oh,' Amelia said, understanding, 'I found another bar. I don't even know what it was called. But I needed something to eat so I got some chips, had some water and tried to sober myself up a little bit. Feeling a little guilty about the martinis,' she added with a small shrug. 'Then I realized how late it was and thought it was about time to get home.'

Jess took in the information, picturing Amelia's daily movements about Oxford Street. Amelia seemed a little more relaxed now, she'd settled into the questions. And one thing Jess had learnt, not only from her days on the job but from navigating awkward party small talk with her low-level, but relatively constant, social anxiety, was that people like to talk about themselves. 'It's easy,' Alex had whispered to her once as they were about to enter his brother's engagement party only a few months into their relationship. 'A top tip from an extrovert – we love talking about ourselves. There won't be any awkward silences if you just keep asking personal questions.' He'd given a cheeky laugh, the top of his nose scrunching up in the way she still loved ten years later, winked and pecked her on the cheek. She'd learnt he was right, and ever since had got through parties without a hitch – and learnt to warm suspects up in the same way.

'How long have you been married?' Jess asked, leaning back a little and resting an arm on the top of the seat so she was sitting sideways, to better face Amelia. The shift in body language was intentional. No official questions, just two women getting to know each other.

'A little over a year,' she answered simply.

'Where did you get married?' Jess probed, offering a piece of her own story as payment. 'We just did the registry office. It was small – but then we all went for lunch at Bob Bob Ricard.' She remembered fondly the extravagant blue and gold interior of the Soho Russian restaurant made famous for its 'Push for Champagne' buttons embedded at every table. 'Alex's parents are from outside of Moscow originally, so we thought that was a nice nod to his heritage. And my *God*, even though there were only eight of us, the amount of vodka we got through! I don't think my parents saw straight for a week.' She laughed, and Amelia joined in. Jess noticed a smile twitch Saul's mouth across the aisle, while the teenagers and Isa looked at each other, ever so slightly perplexed. *Grown-ups and their stories*, was what Jess read in the shared look. Jenna opened her eyes and looked over but didn't particularly respond in any other way.

'We went a bit bigger than that,' Amelia said, not surprising Jess in the slightest. 'Italy, found a beautiful house on the shore of Lake Garda.' Jess raised her eyebrows, impressed, and she noticed Jenna mimic the expression.

'Sounds beautiful.'

'It was.' Amelia was wistful now, and she held a serene expression for a beat before her eyes grew wet again. 'God, sorry,' she said, leaning over to rustle in her bag for a tissue and dabbing at her eyes. 'I told you, I'm a bit of a mess. That was the last big family event with Libby – Theo and Ruby were the *sweetest* page boy and bridesmaid, and everyone had been so *happy*.'

'It sounds like it was a wonderful day.'

Amelia smiled tearfully at her, grateful for the kindness in her tone. She seemed more open now, her mind distracted from the hellish situation they'd all found themselves in. So Jess struck, while her guard was down.

Amelia

'Have you ever met the driver before?' Jess jerked her head behind her, in the direction of the closed door. Amelia blinked into it, surprised by this sudden change in the conversation. Hadn't they just been bonding nicely over their wedding days? This Jess was all about business, Amelia supposed, trying to lure her into a false sense of security. Well, that didn't matter to Amelia, she wasn't hiding a secret passionate fling gone wrong with some tube driver. She didn't even know who the hell he was.

She shook her head and pointed out, 'I don't even know who it is that I should be wondering if I've met them before or not.' Jess might have thought she was being wily, but Amelia was no idiot. She nodded to the closed door. 'You haven't let any of us in there.'

'That's true,' Jess admitted. 'Do you know, or are you connected, to anyone who is a tube driver?'

'No,' Amelia shook her head, answering honestly, 'can't think of anyone.'

Jess nodded. 'All right, thanks, Amelia.' She looked like she was about to turn away, to move her scrutiny on to someone else, but as she shifted in her seat, Amelia noticed her eyebrows furrow, she was thinking hard. Something had obviously come to her, because she turned back and asked one final question.

'Where do you live?'

Amelia thought that an odd question and couldn't see how it had anything to do with anything. 'Islington. Why?'

It apparently didn't seem to be the answer Jess had been looking for. She ignored Amelia's question and lobbied another back at her. 'Are you from there? Where did you grow up?'

Amelia was even more surprised by this. 'Guildford,' she said. 'In Surrey.'

Jess seemed to take it in, but it obviously didn't flag anything with her. Of course it didn't, Amelia thought. What the hell would Guildford have to do with any of this?

'Thanks, Amelia,' Jess repeated. 'I think that's it for now.'

As Jess was getting up to move onto her next interviewee, Amelia placed a soft hand on her arm and shifted her position, so she was fully facing her, making sure her back was to the other end of the tube where that awful Scott was sitting, scowling and huffing to himself. She kept her expression serious and her voice low when she spoke, she wanted Jess to understand the gravity of what she was about to say. If Jess really was police, then Amelia wanted her attention firmly directed toward the person who, Amelia could tell, was trouble.

'For what it's worth,' she said. 'If you ask me, the likeliest culprit to be a killer on this tube is that man behind me. He's drunk, he's aggressive.' She blinked as she remembered his pounded fist on the tube door. She didn't like the thought of being trapped down here with him for much longer. 'And,' her eyes flashed quickly toward all the other passengers in their section, especially Jenna, who had certainly seemed to have a bad time with him, 'I think I speak for everyone when I say he's making us all uncomfortable.'

Twelve

Jess nodded into Amelia's accusation. She'd been thinking along similar lines, but she wasn't going to tell Amelia that. There was no evidence yet, and Jess had nothing else to go on except her instincts. If she voiced her suspicions too soon, especially after declaring herself de facto leader, mob mentality would break out. Her phone display had just flipped to 1 a.m., and the dull light and heat were getting more oppressive by the minute, slowly sanding down any semblance of rationality. They would relish the chance at having someone to blame.

And then God only knew where they'd all be.

Before she moved her attention to the next person, she thought about what she'd learnt from Amelia. Not much, if she was honest. Amelia had seemed, to Jess's professional eye, believable when she'd said she didn't know the driver. Jess had been racking her brain for anything else she had to go on, and it had only been scant information she'd gleaned from Matt's personal possessions, but she had at least got a neighbourhood. A hometown Amelia did not seem to have a connection with.

She parked Amelia in one corner of her mind for now and crossed the aisle to sit down on a middle seat in between Saul and Jenna, right next to Jenna's outstretched feet. She could have stayed where she was and interviewed everyone from the one seat, but something about moving her proximity she felt made clear that she was focusing on someone new. She'd made a connection with Amelia, and she wanted to do the same with each of them – wondering dryly how the attempt would go with Scott.

'Saul,' she turned in her seat to face him with a weary smile, carefully crafted to match his own fatigue. Saul returned it with a kind nod of understanding that he was next. 'Can you tell me what you were doing during the blackout?' She repeated the question she'd opened with Amelia.

'Well,' he said. His voice was steady and deep, the kind of voice that instilled confidence. Jess considered this was a man who got things done, but not in a flashy, arrogant way. She had no doubt he was a quietly hard worker who had grafted his way to a position of seniority in, what she imagined, could be quite a dull job. 'Obviously I was similarly distracted by the noise,' he gestured toward Amelia, tacitly agreeing with what she'd said. 'But also,' he blew out a deep sigh, 'I was worrying about what it meant, and trying to convince myself this was just a simple tube issue. They do happen on these old lines,' he added keenly, evidently wanting to reassure them all that he was not responsible for every delayed commute. 'Now' – he looked around the carriage – 'an hour later, I realize it most likely *is* the worst-case scenario I was dreading.'

'So you didn't notice anything strange? Any movements, anyone getting up?'

'No,' he answered simply. 'I'm exhausted, I've been working late all week, and, like I said, I was distracted by what this blackout might mean.'

Jess nodded, accepting the answer. She wasn't really expecting anyone to announce that they'd got up and killed the driver during the blackout. But she thought she might read something in people's expressions – and in Saul's she'd noticed a tension. But whether it was a tension that could easily be explained away by the stress of his work or not, she couldn't yet say.

'And what had you been doing today?'

'Working,' Saul answered slowly, and Jess thought there was an air of irritation that hadn't he already answered this several times. 'I've been in the office since seven a.m.'

'And where is the office?'

'Charing Cross. I ate lunch at my desk and popped out for some dinner at about half seven.' Then, anticipating Jess's next question, he added, 'I got a burger from a nearby takeaway place. Took it back to the office to eat, and then, when I realized it was nearing midnight, I decided I had to call it a day.'

'Where are you heading home to?' Jess asked.

'Wembley Central.'

'And where are you from originally?'

'Near Watford,' he answered, with an equally confused look as Amelia had had.

'Are you married? Any kids?'

Although he must have heard her question Amelia on similar lines, these personal enquiries sent a ripple of emotion across Saul's face. It was a curious expression, one that combined guilt and pain and fear all in one.

'Ah, um,' he stammered, suddenly unsure of himself, and Jess internally sat up to take interest. 'No, not, um, not anymore.'

'Better off without her, mate,' Scott called over from his bench with a cackle. Jess shot him a warning look. Scott ignored her, huffing another laugh to himself.

Saul's head snapped around to face Scott, a quick flash of

anger driving the movement. 'She's dead,' he barked. 'Died of cancer five years ago.'

Scott didn't look particularly apologetic – he just shrugged, bored, and let his head slump back.

'I'm so sorry,' Isa said softly, seeming to break the spell of Saul's anger.

His face softened and he gave her a sad smile. 'Oh, that's not for you to be sorry about,' he said kindly, and Jess noted that they held each other's gaze for a beat before he turned back to Jess.

'I'm sorry, that must have been very hard,' Jess added to Isa's sympathy and waited a moment before continuing. 'And you're not in a new relationship? You live alone?'

'Yes,' Saul replied, something straining his voice as he finished the sentence. 'I live alone now. My' – he paused long enough to swallow thickly – 'my son is away at university.' His gaze returned kindly toward Isa, her placard still leaning against the glass divider at the end of the seats. 'He's quite into all these protests and activism too.'

Isa gave an important nod. 'There's a lot that needs changing about the world.'

'Well, it's nice that one generation is on it,' he said softly. 'Mine never seemed to find the time, too busy being told that work was the most important thing. That, and you never seem to want to do what your parents did, I suppose. Growing up, there was a photo in our house of my mum pregnant with me at the London march against the war in Vietnam. I grew up thinking protests were a bit passé – my parents had done it, so now was the time for me to carve a new priority out of the world I assumed they'd fixed.' He finished with a small smile, which both Isa and Jess returned.

Jess allowed the moment to linger for a little longer before returning to the matter at hand.

'And did you know the tube driver? Had you seen him before?'

Saul raised a finger toward Amelia. 'As she said, I don't even know who it is I'm meant to know if I know.'

'Do you know anyone who works on the tube? Through work, perhaps?'

Saul shook his head. 'No, the tube network isn't my area at all. Not at all.'

Jess thought Saul seemed keen to want to clarify that fact. That he could in no way be held responsible for the situation they all found themselves in. Was he protesting a bit too much? So far, he seemed to be the only person who had expressed any kind of knowledge about the workings of the tube. A thread in Jess's brain spun off in a wayward direction, away from the reason and simplicity she normally prioritized. Could Saul have *caused* the blackout? She dismissed it. She was getting nervy, allowing the surroundings to press in on her, mess with her logic. The National Grid would not be vulnerable to the whim of one man. And besides, that would be a hell of a lot of trouble to go to just to kill one tube driver who, so far, Jess had no evidence was even connected to Saul.

'You know,' Jenna cut in as silence lapsed around them, 'there isn't anything wrong with working hard. Not everyone needs to save the world.'

Jess turned in her seat, curious that this was the point Jenna had seemed riled to speak out on.

Taking in the confused looks of the people around her, Jenna swung her legs from where they had been outstretched and righted herself in her seat. 'All I'm saying is it's not *bad* to have wanted to focus on your career.' She seemed to be directing the words toward Saul, but to Jess they sounded more like a defence to an accusation that hadn't been thrown.

'Oh.' Saul seemed as surprised as everyone else at Jenna's

sudden interjection into the conversation. 'I suppose, maybe, I—'

'Not everyone cares about money,' Isa snapped. 'Some of us actually want to leave the world a better place than we found it.'

'And a couple of placards is going to do that, yeah?'

Jess saw Isa readying herself for a defence, for an argument that Jess didn't need breaking out right now. 'OK, OK,' Jess said. 'That's not really important right now.'

'Protests show people that—' Isa was continuing anyway, leaning back to look at Jenna along the row of the seats behind Saul and Jess.

'Isa,' Jess said softly, 'please. I understand it's important and I for one think it's great what you're doing—'

'No surprise there,' Scott scoffed, and Jess rolled her eyes and ignored him.

'—but now is not the time, I'm afraid.'

Isa considered for a moment, but then relented, sitting back and letting her sentence hang, unfinished in the air.

Isa

Isa had learnt, since getting involved in activism, when to let a point drop. And the middle of a murder investigation, she recognized, was not the time to stand firm on her platform. Even though it sent a hot ball of anger rising up her oesophagus to let it lie. Especially with Jenna Pace. Isa didn't follow the woman herself – she wasn't exactly the target demographic for Jenna's brand of glamourised hustle culture, but Isa did know who she was. Mainly for her record of problematic posts and collaborations – and there had been some exposé podcast on her business too. Although Isa hadn't listened to it.

What really riled Isa about Jenna's attitude though, was that this woman had a platform – a hell of a platform – and she didn't seem bothered about doing anything with it other than using it for her own financial ends. Even one post from an account like Jenna's would go a long way. Calling out the statistics of unreported sexual assaults in the UK, or telling one girl's story of what had happened to her. Or even just acknowledging that the world is simply set up differently for men than women, and that was before you even got into women of colour, and that Jenna's 'hustle' wasn't enough to solve the discrimination and dismissal and pay gaps that ordinary women had to contend with every day. Isa remembered that Jenna hadn't even posted anything when Roe v. Wade had been overturned in the States. She'd headed up a listicle titled '12 female influencers keeping their complicit silence' that had been sent round Isa's group chats with a frenzy.

And then there had been Jenna's most recent collab with Hookd. She'd even hosted a party for them when she'd first touched down in London. Isa had remembered seeing it all over the dating app's social media. Videos of a grinning Jenna in a tight gold mini dress, hair perfect, as she laughed into the camera, 'Work hard girls need to play hard too', and winked. Isa had been scrutinizing Hookd's social media for a while by this point, outraged by the audacity they had to keep going despite the endless scandals. The founder, some cheesy bloke who always wore a black suit with no tie, white shirt open around his faux-tanned chest, kept ploughing forward, refusing to acknowledge the muck his app was trailing around the cities it launched in. Hookd's successful launch in London, Isa thought, showed you all you needed to know about the amount of attention the constant fight for women was getting. People might be getting sick to death of hearing about it, but didn't they think she was sick to death of complaining about it?

Isa pressed her lips together, trying to contain her annoyance, which had at least been a distraction from the situation she currently found herself in. She tried not to let the anxiety wash over her. But the more Jess seemed intent on questioning everyone, the more convinced Isa became that it was all leading to searching their bags. Isa felt her insides tremble at this, not used to tiptoeing on the wrong side of the rules, let alone the wrong side of the law. Instinctively she brought her tote bag closer into her person, hoping the movement would be blocked by Saul who was sitting between her and Jess. Plus, it was just a simple, innocuous move, nothing for anyone to take note of. Or so she hoped.

Without the water bottle, the bag felt mainly empty, the soft canvas folding around the sheets of paper, stickers and scarf still inside, all weighted down at the very bottom. Isa's throat tightened as she surreptitiously slipped her hand into the floppy bag and closed her fingers around the cold metal inside. Then she looked up, to see if anyone was watching her. But they weren't. She wasn't doing anything noteworthy, after all. Positioning the canvas over her thigh, she slowly withdrew her hand, straining to keep her face relaxed, nonplussed as she did. Then using the tote as cover, she quickly slipped the heavy metal into one of the deep pockets on her baggy cargo pants. She jerked her head up again, waiting for someone to ask what she'd just done. But no one did. No one was paying her any attention at all.

She'd done well so far to keep a migraine at bay, but as the night wore on and after her brief dalliance with an adrenaline spike, she was beginning to regret handing her water bottle over to Amelia. Especially because . . . Isa considered, as she turned to the redhead for a new distraction, taking the attention away from the new weight in her pocket – Isa was sure she recognized her. She frowned as she thought hard, trying to place that distinctive red hair, that narrow face. She could see it drawn and stressed, even more stressed than Amelia seemed to be tonight. She could picture her in a grey suit, hanging back in a photograph. That was it, Isa had seen her in the background of a press conference – she could picture the whole scene now – a cluster of microphones, flashes snapping away. But Isa couldn't remember what the conference had been about. She'd kept up to date with so many news stories this year, mining each one for content and statistics for the campaign – either fodder for the university newspaper, to build their fundraising portfolio, or to print on postcards which they handed out around campus and tucked under car windshields. Amelia had said she worked in PR, Isa remembered and gave an internal eye-roll. God, she was probably defending some terrible company for their pay gap or letting a struggling single mother go for missing too much work or complaining that her boss had felt her up.

Amelia and Jenna, Isa concluded, shifting more comfortably in her seat, were cut from the same bloody cloth.

Thirteen

'Has he been bothering you?' Jess heard Saul ask Jenna in a low voice, nodding his head in Scott's direction. He was bending low to fish out a torn copy of the *Metro* that had apparently been languishing under his seat. 'I saw him, shall we say *flirting*, with you before. While we were waiting for the police. Before we knew.' His eyes flipped first to the driver's door and then to Jess. 'Well before we knew the fullness of the situation.'

'He's nothing I can't handle,' Jenna answered with a slight stiffness to her tone. 'Believe me,' she added, loosening up with a roll of her eyes, 'I've learnt in my two weeks here, your men aren't exactly the romcom princes I was expecting.'

Amelia gave a bark of a laugh, and Jenna looked over at her with a comradely grin. A few seats over, Chloe yawned loudly and leant her head on Liam's shoulder, closing her eyes.

'I'm just resting them,' she said to no one in particular. 'I'm not asleep.'

Liam looked down at her and smiled gently, and Jess was

struck by the tender teenage love they shared. First love really did flame warmer than any other.

She stifled a yawn herself, catching Chloe's, and felt the tiredness sting against her eyes. It was now well after 1 a.m., and she'd been up since seven. Taking the girls to their various school and nursery drop-offs, then to the supermarket to stock up for the weekend on the supplies she'd inevitably forgotten from the weekly Monday delivery. Then a long run, followed by a walk with Honey, and then, while the dog snored contently in the corner, her Friday afternoon ritual of deep-cleaning the kitchen. When she'd worked, she'd never understood what unemployed people did all day – she'd been managing to hold down seventy hours a week with kids and housework and a social life, hadn't she? What would someone do to fill all those spare hours? Alex was a cartoon illustrator, filling his days with drawings for children's books around the school run and after-school activities. He'd lucked out in the early days of his career and partnered up with an author who'd gone on to become an icon of children's literature, the royalties for those books giving them the much-needed breathing room to raise the girls without the financial pressures Jess saw constrain most of her friends. They weren't rich exactly, but comfortable enough that Jess had known, when the time had come, that they could survive for a little while without her income.

But after a few weeks of unemployment, Jess had learnt that she hadn't really been managing before at all. While she'd been distracted chasing justice across the streets of London, she hadn't noticed her social life had fallen by the wayside, or that the house was not quite as orderly as she'd always assumed through her tired, stressed eyes. And she'd found that the empty days do indeed fill up. Without even trying, before she knew it, it would be three o'clock and she'd have to rush to get out the door to be on time outside the school gates. Today's Friday routine had been spiked with an extra, nervous tension about the evening she knew lay ahead of her. Readying herself for battle, preparing silent snide comebacks in the face of the barbs she knew Nicole would throw so effortlessly her way. Snide comebacks that, when it had come to it, Jess had not used – nodding silently instead, sipping on her warming wine.

'I mean, the thing is,' Nicole had said, returning from the bar and putting two wine glasses down on the sticky-topped table and pulling the wine cooler from where she'd trapped it underneath her armpit. She unscrewed the bottle and sloshed two large portions into the waiting glasses, which Jess reached for quickly, taking a mouthful while Nicole was still screwing the lid back on and replacing the bottle in the cooler. 'You absolutely made the right decision in leaving.' Jess had felt a physical weakness spread through her bones that they had turned to her failed career so early on in the evening. 'This job, it's not simple, you know?' Nicole continued with the air of explaining it to someone completely unfamiliar with the police. 'You have to fight for every last thing, use that gut,' Nicole gestured down to her stomach with a clenched fist. 'And that's not for everyone.' Jess's face must have responded involuntarily, because Nicole's eyes had widened in that way they did, half-recognizing that she'd offended someone, but completely missing the point of what that offence might be. 'I don't mean that as a bad thing!' She nearly shrieked. 'Only that, like, after what happened – it was good, it was *great* in fact, that you recognized what your strengths – and your weaknesses – are. We all need to do that. Like, I definitely need to learn to chill out.' She took a gulp of wine and gestured to Jess. 'I mean, look at you! I don't know what I'd have done without work for a full *year*, but you – you're transformed, aren't you?' She finished with a grin and gave a satisfied nod. 'You definitely made the right decision,' she confirmed as her final conclusion on Jess's life, and career.

Jess had felt every sentence like a white-hot whip against her ego. As if Jess had been struggling all those years before, not understanding how the Met worked, floundering under the weight of her own weaknesses. *Not* that she'd had one of the highest solve rates on the team, or that she'd made DI at an almost record young age of thirty-two. Something which Nicole, who was a few years younger and had recently celebrated that birthday, had not yet achieved.

Although, when she thought back, it had been making DI that had begun nailing together the coffin of her career. Jess and Liv had joined their command together as DCs and muddled along OK with the boys' club. They generally kept their heads down, did a good job, and gave no one any reason to complain about them. They both took the sergeants' exam together a few years later, and when Jess had fallen pregnant with Mia, not quite part of the plan, but happy news nonetheless – she'd rushed back to work, abandoning her six-week-old infant. She'd got a couple of snide comments about whether she'd enjoyed her holiday, but generally they'd recognized that she'd come back as early as she could – enough of their team were fathers themselves and so seemed to understand. Penelope had been a different matter. A more difficult pregnancy, one that Jess had struggled through, never once daring to complain or take a sick day, and a complicated birth that had seen her in the hospital for a week afterwards. But still, three months later she was back at work and hauled into a meeting with her CO hinting subtly that if she did plan on having any more children, she really should think about the team before doing so. Jess wasn't sure that a third child had been on the cards anyway, so it had felt a small sacrifice to promise her boss that of course she was done with her maternal instincts. And so, to prove herself, to prove that she was truly dedicated to her job, she had doubled down. Worked harder than everyone, taken more exams, extra courses in extra skills than anyone else, and she'd begun to see it pay off.

When she'd been up for DI, she'd been up against Darren Sutherland, a fellow DS nearing his forties. But Darren was lazy and slapdash and to anyone paying attention it would have been no surprise when Jess had got the job. Darren had left soon after to take up a DI job at a small station out in the sticks. Jess had been relieved at that; she'd wanted him to do well too, so no one could possibly accuse *her* of holding back anyone's career. But that wasn't the way it was received by most of the rest of the team.

'Worst thing to be these days,' Jess had heard one of her colleagues say to Darren at his leaving drinks, which Jess had noted had been far better attended than her celebration drinks, 'just a bloke trying to do right by his family.' He'd paused and taken a sip of his pint before guffawing into it, 'Maybe if you'd taken a couple of months off to push out some babies, you'd have had the leverage to stay and lady high horse would be off to the countryside.' The group had given a low rumble of laughter, cut through by Nicole's higher pitch. Nicole had joined them only a few years before and had soon learnt where her allegiances best lay. Jess couldn't even have the energy to hate her for it, not really. She was petite and blonde, and Jess was sure had been dismissed as just a pretty face for most of her career, and so she'd had to hone her survival instincts.

Liv had been next to her as they stood with their backs to the group at the bar, waiting for their drinks. Liv had squeezed Jess's elbow and muttered softly, 'Ignore them. They'll settle down.'

But they hadn't. Jess had never felt less welcome at a work's drinks than when she and Liv had turned back to rejoin the group and asked with faux-innocent expressions, 'So what's the joke then?'

'Nothin',' the group had grumbled in return.

Jess had stayed long enough to finish her drink so it didn't seem like she was running away, and then made an excuse about having to get the last train home. She'd bolted just in time to let the hot tears that had been threatening to work their way free burst out of her.

Liv had called her as soon as she'd got home, and they'd ranted into the early hours about every single one of their colleagues. Jess had scratched Honey's head as she lay on the sofa talking to her best friend and found that soon the tears had dried in caked streaks on her face, cracking as she laughed at Liv's impression of Darren blundering around the office, not understanding how to work the printer.

'The hi-tech world of printers probably hasn't made it to the arse end of nowhere,' Liv ended with a cackle, which Jess matched. Then Liv's tone had changed. 'Look, babe, we know what we're doing – we're good detectives. You're doing great. You deserved the DI job, which is why you got it. And Darren deserves to be shipped off to *Midsomer Murders*, which is why he has been.' Jess laughed again and had felt such a warm surge of affection for her best friend, she genuinely did wonder what she would do without her. Unfortunately for Jess, that was a reality she'd come to reckon with eighteen months later when Liv had sat her down in the canteen, slid over an apologetic four-finger KitKat and told her she was leaving for a new job in the Modern Slavery and Kidnap Unit. And without her buddy, her support, without one person who was on her side, Jess had crumbled.

In the moment with Nicole though, earlier this evening, Jess had said none of this. She had withered, agreeing with Nicole's testimony, and allowed the reminder of her last case to burn forever as a beacon of her unsuitability to the job.

But now, a few hours later, the night descended into a nightmare she could never have imagined, Jess felt surprisingly emboldened. Liv had been right then, and she would say the same thing to her now. Jess was going to find this killer and keep everyone else safe. Her instincts were right, her experience was good.

It was not *her* who was the problem. It was the system itself that needed to change.

Saul

Saul was glad the spotlight was off him. He'd felt the tightening screw of scrutiny on him as he'd described his day, his work week. No doubt they would all be wondering if he had anything to do with this. But running the electrics to a city like London was not something that fell on the head of one man. He seemed to have got away without too much accusation though, which sent a wave of relief through him. He was no good at confrontation, always managed to seem like he was lying. If this Jess really was a police officer – although he had to admit she'd offered nothing in the way of credentials or proof – she would no doubt want to finish her questioning of everybody before throwing accusations around. Besides, where were they all going to go? Saul thought he had successfully scared anyone from disembarking the tube for the time being – they really were all trapped there. Jess, whatever her motives were – whether professional or something more untoward, had her pool of suspects right where she needed them.

Why *had* she suddenly decided to start investigating this

murder? Why was she no longer content to sit back and wait for the authorities to arrive? Saul considered this. And thought that if they were exactly where she needed them to be, then she was in turn exactly where Saul needed her to be. If anyone tried to get off the tube again, *then* Saul would act. But for now, he was happy to allow her to continue her interviews around him. There was nothing she could find out about him, after all, and he decided it would be useful to get to know more about these people he might be trapped with all night. Useful for what, he didn't know yet – but Saul was a careful man who paid attention to the finer details. Often, his late wife Linda used to say, to the detriment of seeing the full painting. But Saul was who he was, and his obsessions with the littlest things and how they could grow to affect something bigger had served him well in his career so far.

Less so in his personal life.

He thought of Nicky, up in Manchester, enjoying university. From what Saul could see on Instagram, he was living a bright, colourful life Saul could only have ever hoped for his son. It was just a shame that Saul couldn't be a part of it with him.

But over the last few months Saul had set in motion something he hoped would bring them back together. Nicky had thawed toward him, and now Saul was doing something he could never have imagined of himself. But he was doing it for Nicky. It was time to make amends.

Fourteen

Jess blinked away the tiredness in her eyes and turned her attention to Jenna. 'So, you've been here two weeks?'

Jenna nodded coolly. 'Yup,' she finished the word with an elaborate *pop* over the 'p'.

'And where is home?'

'New York,' Jenna said, shifting in her seat, so she leant into its corner, her head resting unbothered back against the wall to the driver's cab. 'The city,' she clarified. 'Manhattan.'

'How long are you staying for?'

'Another couple of weeks,' Jenna asked with a non-committal shrug. 'Then I might take a vacation, go see Europe maybe.'

'Are you here on holiday?'

Jenna's brow furrowed at that, offence etched in the movement. 'No,' she said pointedly. 'I'm here for *work*.'

'Oh,' Jess said, blinking a genuine apology. 'And what do you do for work?'

'I have my own business,' she answered proudly. 'I work

damn hard at it, and I encourage – I *inspire* – other women to work hard too.'

This was the kind of answer Jess had heard on podcasts from influencers trying to explain their empires. It wasn't an answer Jess fully understood. 'And what is your business?'

'Scented candles. Burned. You might have heard of it,' she added with a non-committal shrug and, as it happened, Jess was surprised that she *had* heard of it. Glossy, relaxing Instagram adverts showcasing three- and five-wick candles in ever-changing scents and patterned wraps around their glass jars. *Burned* written in a thin-lined rounded lower case font. The prints and smells seemed to change every few months, new 'drops' advertised on constant rotation.

'I have,' Jess said with a smile, hoping this might warm Jenna to her. 'I haven't bought one yet, but they look lovely.'

Jenna took the compliment graciously. 'Well, we're growing a lot over here, it's my fastest-growing market now. We've taken on more distributors here than in the US over the last year. I'm doing a conference at the end of the month, so I can meet all my amazing saleswomen and thank them for bringing Burned to the UK in *such* a big way.' It sounded like a spiel Jenna had ready to go in her back pocket, although she'd probably been expecting to whip it out for press interviews rather than as a potential murder suspect. 'And a conference takes a lot of planning,' Jenna added. 'So, I wanted to come over for the whole month so I can finalize everything with the venue and the speakers myself.'

'And that's what you've been doing today?'

'A little of this, a little of that,' Jenna answered evasively.

'Can you be a bit more specific?'

Jenna gave a small grunt of annoyance. 'I dunno, I guess I got up at like eleven' – Jess heard Amelia give a snort across the aisle, and guessed that Amelia, who had been up early herself to work on her own business, had bristled at Jenna's insistence on being a hard worker but still having such a lie-in – 'went to the gym, had a smoothie in my room. Did some work, approving final designs for the next drop, then I went into London and did some touristy shit.'

'What touristy stuff?'

'I don't know,' Jenna said, now audibly frustrated. 'Bond Street, Regent Street, Oxford Street . . . shopping and walking around. I don't exactly know this city, I don't really know where I went – I just explored.' Then she added defensively, 'I work hard, but I also tell my distributors not to forget about themselves. We *are* allowed self-care too.'

Amelia gave another poorly stifled snort, and Jess looked dubiously around Jenna. 'You don't have any bags, if you went shopping.'

Jenna looked at her pityingly. 'They sent them to the hotel for me.'

'Right,' Jess said, suitably abashed. How ordinary she felt, having to carry her own shopping bags around. She clocked Amelia's incredulous expression too, a slight scrunch to her mouth, a narrow look in her eyes. Chloe and Liam though looked in awe. Chloe had opened her eyes as Jenna's interview had started, and both had watched with fascinated interest. How successful was this Burned, Jess wondered to herself. And why the hell was Jenna riding around on the tube at midnight instead of some luxury car?

'What were you doing during the blackout?' Jess abruptly brought the conversation back to the issue at hand.

'Like everyone else said' – Jenna gestured vaguely around the group – 'head down, hands over my ears. Wondering what kind of rickety old trains you've got over here, and wishing I'd got a cab instead.'

'Why didn't you?' Jess asked, pleased Jenna had brought it up herself.

Jenna shrugged. 'I dunno, wanted to pretend I was a real Londoner, I guess.'

'And where are you headed?'

Jenna didn't answer at first and, Jess noticed interestedly, her eyes flicked toward the teenagers. 'Back to my hotel,' she answered after a few beats with a vapid smile. And if Jess had ever doubted her instincts before, she did not in that moment – Jenna was lying.

Scott

Scott wasn't really reading his *Metro*. He'd fished it out as cover so the rest of them wouldn't think he was listening in. B he was, how could he not. It wasn't like they were a milli miles away from each other – sound carried in a narrow met carriage, and there was no background noise to drown them ou

So that American didn't think he was a romcom prince? B deal. He'd gone off her anyway when he'd found out what sh did. 'Inspiring women'. Fucking nonsense these days. It w types like her who had convinced Mel she could do bett Breaking up families, ruining lives, that's what all this shit w about. And that student's sign – *Yes, All Men* – didn't that s it all? No one cared about a fair trial or the truth of a situati anymore. One woman's word was all anyone needed. Like t lady detective: soon as she starts demanding answers fro everyone, guess what? They all roll over and start answering h questions. Imagine if he tried doing that? No one would gi him the time of bloody day.

Scott exhaled a deep breath that rippled the thin paper of t

Metro he was holding close to his face, trying to avoid attention from the others. He didn't want any part of this investigation, any part of this farcical situation. He should have bloody known some meddling woman would make a bigger deal out of this than was needed. Should have known he'd never be allowed to sit there in peace till he could get off.

As if his day hadn't been bad enough.

Seeing that smug, pathetic face staring at him through a murky windscreen. Watching him, knowing Scott had lost. And there was nothing Scott could do about it. Scott felt his hand flex unconsciously and remembered the feeling of causing blood to be released. The sight of it spurting out of where it was supposed to be neatly pumping. All because of *him*. A warm tingle of satisfaction worked to calm his rising anger, a reminder that he'd done something real, something concrete and physical with his bare hands. Like men used to.

Not that Mel would ever see it that way. She'd never appreciated or respected him for what he was capable of. Always nagging at him, moaning, complaining. He forced the thoughts away as they threatened to kill his flush of contented calm, and stretched out his neck where a painful knot was starting to gather from keeping his head cowed. He caught sight of the posh bird, the redhead, through the glass panels as he did. She was not pretty exactly, but striking. Her profile showed off a strongly cut jaw and cheekbones, and she had an air about her that Scott liked. Maybe it was simply knowing the type of woman she was that sent the blood surging through his body. She understood how marriage worked. She had respect for her man. She'd stood by her husband, hadn't she? Even if he was a creep. Scott was sure he was remembering the story correctly. He squinted in her direction again, trying to work out if it was the same woman.

Yeah, he thought to himself, he was pretty sure it was.

Fifteen

Jess allowed Jenna to think she had accepted her answers at face value for the time being. Jenna was not the type to crumble under a barrage of direct accusations. She was keeping her cool, her body language relaxed, her expressions natural, almost daring Jess not to believe her. Jess was not forgetting Jenna's lie about where she was headed, she was just letting it be for now – she'd come back to probe the truth out of her at some point. She asked her next few questions – did Jenna know the tube driver, did she know anyone who might be a tube driver – and she got the answers she expected, the same denials as Saul and Amelia. Jess made a show of nodding acceptingly, and then turned to the teenagers.

'Chloe, Liam,' she said with her warmest smile and got up to cross the carriage and sit in between them and Amelia.

'We don't know the tube driver either,' Liam said quickly, before Jess had even had a chance to ask a question. She raised her eyebrows.

Chloe elbowed him. 'He means,' she said, 'like everyone else, we haven't seen him either because we haven't been in there.' She pointed to the cab.

'I get it,' Jess said, and she did. Of all the people on this tube she suspected these teens of committing a brutal murder the least. That wasn't to say she didn't know what young people could be capable of. She'd seen bullying cases gone too far, jealous romances and rival estate brawls in her years on the force, but violence with teens tended to be more emotional and hotheaded, their guilt splashed all over their face in the aftermath.

But this murder . . .

Well for starters Jess couldn't see how two teenagers could have taken down the tube network. Then to have been playing up the way they had been, kissing and filming each other doing pranks, only to go and cold-bloodedly take a human life and sit back down for the next hour without so much as a panicked glint in their eye – it didn't track. But that didn't mean they didn't know something.

'Where have you been today?' she started with a laid-back smile, wanting to make them comfortable.

'We both have Friday afternoons off—' Liam started.

'Are you at school?' Jess interrupted, realizing she couldn't quite peg their age. 'College?'

'College,' Chloe confirmed. 'Started this year.'

So, they were sixteen, possibly seventeen.

'Yeah, but neither of our subjects have classes on Friday afternoons,' Liam insisted, as if worried he was about to be accused of playing truant.

'So, you came into London?' Jess prompted.

Chloe nodded and knocked her head back toward Liam. 'He's doing theatre A level. They're doing *The Crucible* for their project this year and I saw there was a new production on this week.'

'Just a small theatre,' Liam said, now visibly excited. 'But it was *so* cool, what they did with the space.'

Jess couldn't help but be endeared by this unexpectedly cultural teenage outing.

'Dad would never have let me be out in London this late otherwise.' Chloe shook her head with a wide-eyed expression. 'But Mum said the arts are important.' After a moment she gave a small groan and pulled her mouth down at its corners. 'Dad's gonna be *stressssed*,' she elongated the middle sound dramatically. 'He's picking us up from the station, he'll still be waiting for us.'

'Calling the cops or MI5 or somethin',' Liam agreed.

'Where are you heading home to?'

'Willesden Junction,' Liam answered. 'Mum'll have probably gone to bed by now, she won't know to worry,' he added with a shrug. 'She's up early in the morning for work. She's a nurse,' he provided after another beat.

Jess took a moment, thinking of Chloe's poor dad waiting in a parked car, the usually vibrant city around him uncharacteristically black, wondering where on earth his daughter was.

'Well, I'm sure you'll be home safe and sound before she has any need to worry,' Jess told him with a confident smile she hoped beyond all hope was honest. 'And Chloe, I'm afraid there's not much we can do about your dad now, but maybe if he can kick up enough fuss,' she added with a reassuring smile, 'they'll hurry up with the evacuation of the tubes.' She didn't really believe it, a hysterical parent in the face of a citywide blackout – if that was indeed what the trouble was – was unlikely to make any real waves, but Chloe seemed comforted by the thought anyway. 'Did you two notice anything during the blackout?'

And she was surprised to see something shift between them.

The air thickened, their eyes darting a brief, uncertain glance toward one another.

'No,' Chloe said after a beat, the wary smile on her face forced.

'Nothing,' Liam confirmed, pulling his own smile that looked to Jess more like a grimace.

'Like everyone else said,' Chloe added and looked back over her shoulder toward Liam, 'we had our heads down because of the noise.'

As with Jenna before, Jess's instincts flared in the presence of the blatant lie. She paused, weighing up the options ahead of her. She could call them out, tell them she knew they were lying, demand the truth – but, at this early stage that would most likely cause more harm than good. If they were shifty because they knew something, had somehow seen or heard the culprit, that could put them in danger. Or if they were shifty because – and this idea seemed genuinely unthinkable to Jess – they were the guilty party, then she had grossly underestimated what these teens could be capable of. So, as with Jenna, she decided it best to let the untruths rest undisturbed for now. She would probe them gently later, perhaps trying to separate the couple first.

'Of course,' Jess said kindly, but as she was readying herself to turn her attention to Isa, another question sparked in her brain. Not one she thought likely to have anything to do with the driver's murder, but one that her curiosity wanted sating, nonetheless. 'What was with the screaming and filming thing?' she asked. 'Before we got stuck, when the doors opened at the last stop' – she pointed to Liam – 'you screamed and you' – her finger tracked to Chloe – 'were filming it. Filming *us*. What was that about?'

Their body language loosened a touch, the tension replaced with a bite of embarrassment instead.

'Oh that,' he said with a small shrug, a flush creeping up on his cheeks, 'it's just a thing going round on TikTok. This one guy got like millions of views from it on the subway in New York.' He glanced unconsciously toward Jenna for a beat. 'You can make real money from that. You don't need A levels or uni or anything.' He shrugged again, relaxing into his explanation now. '*And*, if I can get a decent following, then agents will definitely look at my showreel and stuff. That's how you get noticed these days.'

Jess had no experience of the world of acting or fame but thought that Liam was probably right.

'And you're serious about your future career?'

Liam nodded importantly. 'Oh yeah.' Then his sheepish smile returned. 'Gonna buy Mum a big house in Hampstead one day.'

That endearing tug pulled at her again and for a moment Jess forgot about the matter at hand, a well of emotion rising in her at the thought of this teenager so dead set on his dreams for the sake of his mum. An image flashed to her mind of Penny, her youngest, presenting her with a bouquet of picked dandelion flowers when she'd returned from work one Saturday afternoon, Alex explaining as Jess had fought back tears that Penny had insisted because yellow was Mummy's favourite colour. It wasn't, but Jess had worn a yellow dress to her third birthday party a few weeks before and Penny had latched onto the memory.

'Is it just the two of you?' Jess asked Liam, swallowing down the tears that threatened to resurface completely inappropriately, given the circumstances.

'Yeah,' Liam said. 'She was only young when she had me, but made it all the way through her nursing degree and everything on her own.' Jess noticed Chloe slip her hand over Liam's arm and squeeze it. 'Said I'd take her to the Maldives too,' he added with another grin. 'Get one of those huts over the sea.'

'I'm sure she'd love that,' Jess said, their earlier dishonesty momentarily forgotten. As she turned toward Isa though, it rushed back at her like a slap in the face. Liam seemed convinced his plan of TikTok fame would change his, and his mum's life, forever. She shifted again and surveyed them one last time, wondering what would a misguided kid do for that fame?

Jenna

Jenna had listened to Chloe and Liam's answers with interest. They were sweet enough kids, and reminded Jenna of her and her high school boyfriend. They'd been inseparable, until he'd gone off to an Ivy League school on an athletics scholarship, and she'd been forced to forgo college as a middling student with no scholarship prospects and not willing to sign on for hundreds of thousands of dollars' debt when she was only eighteen. It had all worked out though, her life, but still, she felt that tinge of her old jealousy when she thought about Steve and his frat parties, his slow introduction to adult life for four years, while she'd waited sticky tables for demanding tourists.

Jenna pulled her attention back to the grimy London tube she was on, a dead body just beyond the thin wall to her right. And Chloe and Liam – they'd lied to the detective. That really *was* interesting. What were they hiding? It was something about the blackout that they'd stiffened up on, something they weren't willing to say. What did they know? Had they seen something, heard something? She shoved one hand deep into her jeans pocket, her fingers twisting and contorting against the soft worn cotton inside. It was a nervous flex she had, a kind of stiffening fidget – her fingers the very extremity of her body she could push her anxious energy into, God forbid it rest inside her for too long. Seeing Chloe and Liam lie so brazenly, so ineffectively, had trickled a stream of unconscious worry that her own lies had been as easily detectable. She thought back, going over and over her words, her delivery, Jess's reaction. No, she was OK, Jess had not responded as if she didn't trust her, and Jenna had said nothing too outrageous to garner attention. She'd passed it off well.

Since when did lying well become something to be proud of? She heard her grandma reprimand her with her cawing, nasal New Jersey twang. Jenna stifled a smile to herself. Gramma Lois always had had a knack of skewering Jenna's worst instincts. But Jenna couldn't feel guilty now about her lie. She had built too much, she had more to protect than most people. And the more you have, the more you have to lose. She watched the teenagers again and wondered what they would think if they knew her plans for the night? They wouldn't care, as long as she kept posting pretty, glamorous pictures, they would still give her their follows and their likes and shares. But that wasn't the empire Jenna had built. Social media engagement was a tiny fraction of her income, keeping easy-to-please teens happy was not her priority.

She turned her head instead toward Amelia, who was periodically glancing down at her phone and listening with polite interest to everyone's answers. No, it was the women like Amelia who held Jenna's fortune in their hands – and the ones who could snatch it away at any moment. Jenna knew her audience well and treated them like a wild wolf chained in her backyard. Happy to receive the affection paid her in return for her scraps of food, but wary that the relationship was not quite even. Not quite symbiotic harmony. The wolf was liable to turn at any moment.

And bored housewives could be so quick to bite.

Sixteen

Isa and Saul were only sitting one seat away from each other, so, rather than squeeze into that intimate space, Jess remained where she was and made a show of sitting forward to direct her attention firmly at Isa. Isa was striking with a square jaw and a heavy brow, and a small nose balancing out from the centre. Her face was free of make-up, skin naturally clear and soft, eyes framed by heavy dark lashes, which she blinked several times as Jess put her focus on her. Jess noticed her dark eyes slide toward Saul for a moment, as if searching for comfort from the fatherly figure to her left.

'Isa,' Jess said.

'I, er, I also don't know the driver,' Isa answered quickly, like the teens had. 'Or I mean, I don't know who he is,' she rushed to clarify. 'I haven't been in there, I haven't seen him.' It was a frantic spill of words. 'And I don't know anyone who could be a tube driver – at least, I don't think so. I mean, loads of people *could* be a tube driver, but I think all my friends are too young, or still at uni, and I don't know how old you can be actually, but—'

'Isa,' Jess said again, more loudly this time and holding up her palm to stem the flow of the nervous student's ramble. 'It's OK, I understand. You don't know him, or anyone else who's a tube driver,' Jess summarized, and Isa nodded jerkily with wide, staring eyes. 'And what were you doing during the blackout? Did you notice anything?'

'I,' Isa blinked, 'I thought I was having a migraine. I get them sometimes, and I panicked. I've never had one come on so quickly before – normally I get a warning, which I' – she gave a small shrug – 'which I need because, when it takes hold' – she blew out a loud exhale and shook her head demonstrably – 'I'm completely out.'

Jess nodded sympathetically, she'd had a couple of mild ones while she was pregnant, and even they had rendered her completely useless for the afternoon.

'So,' Isa continued, 'I didn't really notice anything – I was too focused on that really.'

'Understandable,' Jess said and gave her a smile, which seemed to relax Isa a touch. Her shoulders slumped a little from their previously tense stance. 'Talk me through your day.'

'Um, well,' Isa glanced around at everyone, registering that their attention was all on her. Jess got the impression of someone uncomfortable with the spotlight. 'I had lectures most of the day.'

'Which university are you at?'

'Imperial, I'm doing biotech.' Jess didn't really understand what that was, but she did know Imperial was a university solely for science and engineering degrees and that Isa must be a *very* bright spark to be attending. Jess raised her eyebrows, impressed. 'I'm in my second year,' Isa clarified and then paused uneasily. Jess gestured for her to go on describing her day. 'Oh, um, so I had lectures most of the day,' she repeated, 'and then when I'd finished I went to my friends' house – they're all living together in Camden. We were making the signs' – she gestured to the placard – 'and then we went to Trafalgar Square for the start of the protest at like eight-ish?'

'Did you organize the protest?'

Isa gave a modest nod and waggled her head to either side. 'Sort of,' she said. 'I helped organize the Imperial branch. There's a whole committee of us though, not just me. And we joined up with groups from all the other unis around London.'

'And was it a success?'

Isa scrunched her lips to one side in visible thought. 'I guess that's hard to tell. Loads of people showed up, which is good. But it's still a fucking *fight*. Did you know 63 per cent of sexual assaults are not reported to the police? Because we get treated like it was our fault for flirting, or going back with them, or being drunk. And then you have to relive every single godawful moment over and over again just to get your statement down, and that's before the legal system is even involved.' Isa spoke with a passion that was personal, her earlier shyness in the face of the spotlight eradicated. 'It's like built into our whole culture, our whole *society*. And if we protest then yeah, sure' – she gestured to Jenna, signalling she was returning to their earlier argument – 'one protest might not make a concrete change. But *loads* of protests, loads of people gathering and saying *this isn't right*, well, eventually it seeps into society and people *do* start sitting up and taking notice, you know?'

'It's fucking seeped in, all right,' Scott catcalled from his seat. 'Gone too fucking far; men can't do fucking anything these days. Can't do anything right, and women get away with fucking murder. Ruining families, that's what your lot do!' He finished with a raise of his voice that threatened to break at the top.

'Oh, will you shut up!' It was Saul who had snapped, straightening up in his seat and directing his words over Isa's head toward Scott.

Scott looked for a moment like he didn't know what to say, but then a disappointed snarl fell across his features as he shook his head, muttering something about *snowflakes*. He slumped back in his seat and a thick silence descended on the carriage again.

Isa swallowed and waited a couple of beats before forcing her chin up to make her final declaration. 'See? The reality isn't changing quickly enough for women out there. We need more attention, more eyes on us. The more it's talked about – the more it will *get* talked about.'

'Well, you're clearly very passionate about a' – Jess moved her gaze purposefully toward Scott for a moment – 'very important cause.' Isa nodded proudly. 'Your friends,' Jess continued, 'they all got off at Regent's Park. Where were they going?'

Isa's face fell, an instinctive reaction Jess didn't think she'd had control of. 'Oh, to get the bus back to Camden. Heading to the pub, to celebrate the protest. They all said they'd get on the tube with me for a stop rather than walking, which was nice of them. I'm going back to Kensal Green,' she finished with a shrug.

'And you didn't want to go to the pub?'

'I had to get home,' Isa said, a shiftiness taking over her demeanour for the first time.

'What for?'

Isa's eyes narrowed and Jess sensed a block rising between them at the question. 'It's not exactly relevant, OK?'

Jess disagreed, but as with the others before, she didn't push it. Not yet. But the little details were racking up in her brain, the tiny nuances of a case that she knew would eventually build to the answer.

'All right, Isa,' Jess said, making an effort to keep her voice level, friendly. 'Thanks.' She added a grateful smile which, after a moment, Isa returned.

Isa

Jess was friendly enough, Isa thought, for a pig anyway. But then, maybe that's how they lured you in. Well-practised at being your mate, good cop with no need for bad cop. Isa had actually had no previous interaction with the police in her life. Even during the protests she'd attended in the last few years she'd always managed to avoid arrest or avoid antagonizing them too much. She couldn't help herself, she just couldn't quite push beyond the boundary of the law. It was an innate respect, or fear, of authority that she couldn't escape. So ingrained in her were the teachings of her youth – strict parents to whom it would never occur to side with Isa over a figure of authority. Even when a primary school teacher had accused her of bullying, when Isa had done nothing except got too wound up in a game of Stuck in the Mud and accidentally knocked another girl in her class over. Her parents had punished her for a week instead of believing her pleas and questioning whether they thought their meek little daughter could possibly be capable of bullying.

Her instilled respect for the police was not something she relished.

All her new friends had wild stories to tell – from simple ASBOs for breaking into abandoned buildings, to being caught up in raids on illegal parties and one had even been charged with trespassing for climbing onto the roof of his school on GCSE results day. But despite their flirtations with rebellion, Isa couldn't help but recognize with disappointment that they'd all still ended up with top grades, at exactly the same university, and with the same prospects as her. All her parents' promises of ruining her life if she stepped out of bounds had proved to be completely unfounded.

And so Isa had made a vow. She was going to be more free, more reckless. She was going to live her life and fight for the things that mattered.

That included tonight.

She'd never broken the law before, and the very thought that tonight would change the trajectory of her character so radically sent a tight, sharp pain through her chest. After tonight, would she always live on that boundary, uncertain whether she'd get caught? She was by no means a professional; she was foolhardy and unthinking, if she was honest with herself, and she knew the chances of leaving evidence that pointed in a neat arrow directly back at her were high. But it had to be done. She'd been driven to it. And not just by what she believed in. She'd told none of her friends her plan for tonight. She knew they'd try to talk her out of it, to tell her it was a step too far. That they all wanted as many eyes as possible on the movement, but there were better ways to do it. But they didn't understand, not all of it, there was so much more to this than the movement.

So she'd lied and told them she had to go home.

Because she had her own personal revenge to enact.

Seventeen

Jess closed her eyes for a beat, blowing out a half-hidden sigh through her nose, as she readied herself for her final interviewee. Scott seemed intent on making an already shit situation even worse. She got to her feet and walked past the doors, to settle in the bench that Jenna had previously occupied, sitting on its edge so she faced Scott.

A smirk appeared on his face, but he didn't look at her when he spoke. 'My turn is it with the lady detective?'

'You can just say detective,' Jess answered coldly.

He turned his head slowly toward her with a roll of his eyes and blow of a mocking laugh. 'Go on then,' he said, pulling his eyes exaggeratedly wide, 'let's get this over with. Ask me if I killed him, just because *aaaall* those other people don't like me. Just 'cause I'm an English bloke, enjoying a drink, and being myself.'

'So you know you've been making everyone uncomfortable?'

'I can fucking hear, you know.'

Jess accepted that and gave a tilt of her head to show she

recognized that he'd heard everyone's concerns around him. 'But you're not surprised by it?'

'Listen, love,' he said, turning in his seat so he was facing her properly, his doughy face contorting into a snarl. 'I know what you lot think about blokes like me. We don't even need to do nothin' and you start puttin' your little lasers on us, tryin' to catch us for any old thing. Tick them boxes so you get another English white man off the street – that's what everyone hates now, isn't it?'

'Have you ever stopped to think about your own behaviour?' Jess lobbied back. 'Do you not think anyone might have a reason to feel uncomfortable around you tonight?' She purposefully brought the conversation back to their circumstances – she wouldn't allow him to distract her with a pointless argument about how terrible it was to be a straight white man these days. She'd come up against that tactic before – deflecting attention away from themselves by throwing out a wider, controversial statement they knew their opponent couldn't resist being riled by. But Jess wasn't going to rise to it. It was late at night, she was tired, they were stuck underground in a metal tube with a temperature inching up the mercury, and she had a murdered body less than ten metres away. Now was not the time to let Scott draw her into an argument. She gestured over to the other passengers who were all watching the interaction with interest. 'You've physically separated yourself from everyone, only to shout aggressive comments about Isa's protest and Saul's wife, and you made Jenna so uncomfortable she's moved seats. We're all in a very stressful situation, and you, I believe, haven't even tried to make it easier for anyone – including yourself.'

Scott rolled his eyes again, like a kid being told off for breaking a rule they knew existed. 'Whatever,' he muttered. 'Go on then, get it over with. No, I don't know the fucking tube driver or anyone else who's one. I'm going home – to the end of the line before you ask – and today I've been minding my own fucking business is what I've been doing.'

Jess watched him, and then gave an accepting nod. 'All right then.'

'But you don't really care about any of that, because you're just gonna believe any old shit thrown at a man, as if women are so fucking perfect.'

Jess did not answer, not immediately. Instead, she assessed him carefully under the dull lights. The attempt at an interview had gone about as well as she had expected. His body language was combative, chest puffed up, shoulders broadened, and his hands fidgeted – not quite sure what to do with themselves now he'd apparently finished his cans of lager. Sweat dripped down his temple, and he wiped it angrily away with the back of a large hand. As he raised it up, Jess noticed a ruddy patch of grazes across his knuckles, a yellowing bruise spreading down toward his wrist.

'What happened there?' Jess asked, pointing at his hand. He looked down at it in surprise, and now she looked at him with more attention, she could see in the low lighting he had a healing cut across one eyebrow and another yellow tint across his left cheekbone.

'Nothin',' Scott said, tucking the hand out of sight by his side. He used his other one to gesture around. 'Nothin' to do with any of this. Anyway,' he added, looking carefully at Jess, a quick look toward the other passengers, 'you need to use your brain more, *Detective*. How the hell do you think *I* could do any of this? I'm a delivery driver, for God's sake, just 'cause you lot all hate me doesn't mean I could stop a fucking tube in its tracks. If you ask me, it's that bloke over there you want to be looking at. No further.'

He pointed over to Saul, who scrunched his face into a defensive scowl.

'You're being ridiculous—' Saul began, starting to get to his feet.

'Saul,' Jess interrupted, getting to her own feet first and moving to the standing section in between the two banks of seats. 'Let's not start throwing random accusations around, OK,' she said, twisting her head to look at everybody. 'We don't know anything for certain. We don't even know if the tube stopping has anything to do with the driver's death.'

'As much as I hate to agree with *him*,' Amelia piped up, tipping her head in Scott's direction, 'it does seem a bit like it *must* be connected. Not that I mean it's you, Saul,' she rushed to correct herself with a brief flash of an apologetic smile. 'I mean – otherwise, why would someone take the chance to kill a person behind a door when they don't even know who it is?'

Jess noticed the question land on everybody and felt the threat of a wider conspiracy slick over the carriage like an oil spill, suffocating any of the previous camaraderie that had begun to emerge.

Eighteen

Everyone was sitting in silence, which on the one hand was allowing Jess to think. On the other, she was afraid of the divisiveness that had permeated the hot, thick air. Jess had taken herself off to the very back bank of seats, behind the old-fashioned benches. She needed to think everything through, and the added heat of extra bodies seemed to weigh on her. Down at the other end of the train she couldn't breathe easily exactly, but it felt like there was more air, more freedom. She glanced every now and again back along the carriage, keeping an eye on the door to the crime scene, but no one seemed interested in checking it out themselves. Whenever she looked up, she usually caught someone's eye as they cast a nervous glance in her direction, keeping an eye on the authority figure who had separated herself.

Jess knew what was on their minds: the stopping of the tube.

It had been the thought percolating throughout all her own questionings, but it was not one she wanted the other passengers to dwell on. Because if they did, she knew the finger would point to Saul.

Her phone was on less than 10 per cent battery now, that last-minute boost from plugging it in before she'd left not quite stretching to the early hours of the morning. Wanting to save it as much as she could, knowing how quickly those last grains of power faded away on an iPhone that dared to be older than two years, she was refraining from tapping up any notes. She wanted to be able to keep an eye on the time, now ticking depressingly closer to 2 a.m., and, if the lights went out again, she wanted her torch. But it meant she had to keep everything straight in her own mind, which was proving more difficult than usual. She was tired and groggy and a dull headache had started, radiating somewhere from the centre of her brain, telling her it was dehydration taking hold. Her mouth was dry, lips sticking uncomfortably to her teeth, and she wished she'd taken Saul's advice on rationing Isa's water more effectively. Even a mouthful.

Saul. It all *did* come back to him. How had he known to suggest rationing the water? Because he knew they'd be down there for a long time. But was that because he'd caused it? Because he knew how much damage he'd done and how long it would take to fix? Jess knew nothing about the National Grid, or what managing it would even entail. Maybe there was a soft spot, a vulnerable opening ready to be exploited by one man with decades of experience and knowledge. She thought of what she knew about Saul, what she'd read in him so far. He was conscientious, every word carefully thought through. If he did have murder in mind, it would be pre-planned, every detail lined up over a long period to ensure nothing went wrong. She pictured him working late every night, doing whatever he did to manoeuvre things into place to cause citywide power failure exactly as the last tubes completed their final journey.

All that to kill Matt Donnelly?

Who was Matt Donnelly? Who was he to *Saul*? Because if Saul really had gone to all that trouble, they must have a connection. And a personal one at that. Jess cast back to what else Saul had told her about his personal life. A widower. A grown-up son away at uni. Could Matt and his son have a connection? Parental protection was a force to be reckoned with, she knew that herself. If Matt had done something to Saul's son, having already lost so much, would Saul exploit every ounce of power he had to take revenge? Would Jess do that for one of her girls? She thought of losing Alex. Of someone wronging Penny or Mia, and she knew that the answer was yes, she could be capable of that. The image of Matt's butchered neck flashed back in her mind. Those injuries were the result of anger, of passion. Matt must have done something *really* bad to warrant such an end to his life.

She pulled Matt's phone out of her pocket again and considered going back into the cab to unlock it, to search for more clues of a connection between him and Saul. His WhatsApp and emails probably held some answers. Maybe he'd been receiving threats from Saul that would clear the whole thing up once and for all. No one knew that Jess had Matt's phone, so Saul wouldn't know to worry about it.

She stared down at the black-screened rectangle for a moment longer and then returned it to her pocket. She was following a winding trail that only led to one destination, and that was no way to run an investigation. She needed to consider the others, other motives, other means, so that when she did look for more evidence, she wouldn't be blind to anything of use just because it didn't fit in with one theory.

She'd seen people make that mistake before. Her stomach churned with the memory of it. Jess had let it happen. And she'd seen the consequences of those kinds of mistakes.

Next, she turned her attention to Scott. The most obvious

suspect in terms of his temperament. He undoubtedly had rage, and barely suppressed rage at that. It was true he was not a likely culprit to have the means to stop the tube, let alone the whole city of London, but – her thoughts returned to her imaginings of a bloodthirsty psychopath – was he angry enough to seize the opportunity of a blackout to physically express some of that rage? Jess decided she needed more from him. No one behaved the way he did without a reason – there was a back story there and she needed it. She eyed the back of his head. He must be suffering by now, a headache, dehydration and on top of that the buzz from his earlier beers settling into the fuzzy start of a hangover. Maybe he'd soften soon.

Jenna had money, that much was clear. And, Jess supposed, a lot of money could buy a lot of things. A lot of ways into getting what you want. A thought struck her, and she turned her attention to the other passengers, to Jenna and Saul, sitting a few seats away from one another, ignoring each other. Could Jenna have paid Saul off? But why? She'd only been in the country two weeks; how on earth could she have selected a random tube driver as her target and found a willing shill at the National Grid in that time?

Isa, the teens and Amelia were a different story. None had displayed any characteristics of someone who had just exacted a well-planned revenge, and she also wasn't sure about how they could have orchestrated the power cut. Amelia clearly had money, and possibly influence or contacts too, so Jess didn't immediately rule her out either.

But. There was something else that was niggling at her.

Where was the murder weapon?

The entrance wounds in Matt's neck were small, and she'd guessed a penknife. So where was it now? Presumably the killer still had it on them. She assessed the other passengers again, reminding herself of their outfits, their bags. Jenna had no bag but baggy jeans and pockets in her jacket that could probably fit a small knife. Saul was wearing a suit, the jacket of which he'd discarded behind him as it had got hotter. Could there be a penknife hidden safely in one of its pockets? Isa had a thick bomber jacket with pockets, also discarded in the face of the heat, cargo pants and her tote, from which she'd produced the water bottle. Amelia had no jacket and no obvious pockets on her tightly tailored dress, but she had a handbag. Liam was also wearing cargo pants with plenty of room to hide a murder weapon. Only Chloe, in her Lycra trousers, crop top and cropped pocketless jacket, didn't seem to have anywhere obvious to put it. But, she supposed, if the teens were in on it, they were in on it together, so Liam's cargo pants came back into play. And Scott – well, Scott was wearing jeans and had no jacket, his only baggage the polythene bag discarded on the seat opposite him. If he had a knife hidden in his jeans pockets, would Jess not have seen the outline pressing against the denim when he'd stood up and moved about the carriage? She bent over in her seat, scanning the tube floor underneath his benches, but couldn't see a knife obviously discarded. Jess considered her options of trying to successfully conduct a search of the passengers' possessions and persons, and concluded that at the moment that was a step too far into invading a group of strangers' privacy. Besides, she could already imagine how the suggestion would go down with Scott, and just the thought of his reaction sent a wave of visceral exhaustion through her. That time would come, and when it did, it would be done by the real police whenever they eventually got there.

'Amelia, is there any water left in there?' Jess heard Isa break the silence with the innocent question.

'There's a bit, yeah,' Amelia replied, and Jess saw her lean across the aisle to hand Isa back her bottle. 'Thank you for letting me have it. Obviously, if I'd have known' – she gestured around at their current circumstances – 'I wouldn't have had so much.'

'It's OK,' Isa said kindly and took a gulp of the water. 'Does anyone else need any? There's not much, but enough for a mouthful.'

Jess wanted to get up, to accept the offer of a mouthful of water, but she wasn't ready to face them yet. To face their questions or accusations of one another that would inevitably break out when she returned to the group. She'd put herself in charge, so now it was her they expected answers from. But, she was pleased to note, the sharing of the water did seem to have dissipated some of the earlier tension. Bits of small talk broke out, Saul asking Isa what music she'd been listening to, Isa responding and in turn asking Liam what game he'd been playing. It was bland and unimportant talk, but it was a lifeline of normalcy Jess knew they must all be craving.

She waited a few beats for them to settle into their conversations. And then, with everyone suitably distracted, she moved to get to her feet. It was time to revisit the crime scene and delve more into Matt's phone. With a bit of time passed too, maybe she'd find something she missed first time round in the cab itself. Some clue she could read more clearly now she had more of an impression of her fellow passengers. But as she was about to move back through the carriage, heading for the driver's door at the very end, someone else got to their feet and broke away from the chattering group, heading right for her, a tense expression on her face, white teeth gnawing at her bottom lip.

'I just need a bit of space,' Chloe called back over her shoulder to Liam's questioning expression. 'I need a breath of air for a minute – it's getting too hot.'

'I'll come with.' Liam stood up.

'No,' Chloe insisted, stopping in her tracks and turning to face him. 'Honestly, I'm fine. I need a bit of space, that's all,' she repeated. Liam accepted it and sat back down, waiting a beat for Chloe to continue walking down the carriage before he leant forward again across the aisle to show Saul and Isa the game on his phone.

Jess stayed where she was. Something in Chloe's expression told her that the teen was not merely seeking some space or non-existent air. She waited until Chloe drew level with her.

'Everything all right?'

Chloe jerked a nervous look over her shoulder, back toward the group. 'Um, I don't know,' she said, taking pains to keep her voice low. 'But I think I know something that might help you.'

Amelia

Amelia kept turning to her phone, as if it was going to offer her respite. An instinctive reaching for a comfort blanket that had nothing to offer except barbs. She still had no signal or internet, no contact with the outside world, not even an updated Instagram feed to keep her entertained. In the void of anything else to do she had turned to scrolling through old pictures, each one a glowing memory tarnished with a sheen of hindsight across it.

She had been looking at photos from her hen do, the month before her wedding, not much over a year ago. They'd gone to Brighton, Libby as her maid of honour going all out on every little detail. A beautiful rental house right by the beach, a private chef and barman to greet them on arrival. A treat, she later found out, Libby had not asked anyone to pay her back for – Amelia's school, university and Pilates friends showering Libby in praise and gratitude for her generosity. Amelia had remembered thinking Libby had glowed under the attention, the golden-hued aura around her shining even brighter when she'd presented

Amelia with a Louis Vuitton Neverfull tote, the iconic LV logo printed against the chocolate brown leather, and Amelia's new, soon-to-be married initials – A.M.K. – monogrammed in gold and pink in the middle of the bag.

Amelia's friends had cooed and Amelia herself had squealed with excitement – Libby graciously accepting her hug before modestly batting away any continued professions of thanks. But, Amelia had thought that in giving her that tote in front of everybody – well, at the time she'd thought it had meant more to Libby than it had to herself. Now the bag sat barely used in its official dustbag and bright orange box at the bottom of her wardrobe. Unreturnable, thanks to the monogram, but too shrouded in guilt for Amelia to ever use. She continued scrolling past a quick succession of pictures of her and Libby, smiling and holding up the bag, before the photos descended into blurs – posing with lime-topped shot glasses and penis unicorn headbands.

Amelia clicked back to the main camera roll and scrolled down further, past her emerald green and azure blue backed wedding photos, and settling on a honeymoon shot of Lawrence sipping an Aperol Spritz on a pebbly beach of the Amalfi Coast, the recognizable mismatch of crooked roads and hotels rising up the hill behind him. She thought about him now, probably asleep with his noise-cancelling headphones in the spare room. He always did that when he was working weekends, not wanting to risk a bad night's sleep courtesy of Amelia's noisy bedtime routine. Their first year of marriage had not exactly been smooth, and Amelia couldn't deny that she'd thought about packing up and escaping halfway across the world – leaving Lawrence to clear up his own mess. But she hadn't, because she was stronger than that – and *they* were stronger than that. She'd stood by him despite everything, and had held her head up falsely high as she'd done it. She wondered how many people in this carriage had heard of Lawrence's case. Probably all of them would have seen it, gossiped about it in an *Ohmygod did you hear about that doctor* kind of way. Would anyone recognize her? A slick of embarrassment slid through her at the thought. But then she corrected herself. *She* had done nothing wrong. And Lawrence had been under an inordinate amount of pressure, something she understood all too well. Pressure had a way of slowly crushing you without quite realizing the weight of it, until all too late you noticed the tiny hairline fractures that had cracked into your very soul – one tap and you'd shatter.

Nineteen

Jess gave a single nod, keeping her face as expressionless as possible. She didn't want to spook Chloe by overreacting in any way, but curiosity had raged through her as Chloe had spoken.

'Come on,' she said, guiding Chloe down to the back of the bank of seats, right by the dividing door to the next carriage. She saw Chloe glance up at it in interest, as if she'd only just considered other people might also be on this tube. 'It's empty,' Jess said. 'There wouldn't have been enough time for anyone else to have made it down two carriages and back again.'

Chloe seemed to understand the implication of this and shot a brief look over her shoulder toward the other passengers, including her boyfriend. Was it Liam that Chloe wanted to talk to Jess about?

Jess sat down, and Chloe followed suit, sitting next to her.

'What is it you think you know? Did you see something during the blackout?'

At the mention of the blackout Chloe shook her head, a quick, flustered motion. 'No, no, it's not that I saw anything. O even,' she paused before admitting, 'that I know anything about what happened to the driver.' Jess frowned at that, wondering what on earth Chloe wanted to tell her then.

'OK,' Jess said slowly. 'So what *do* you know?'

'I saw this YouTube video, right?' Jess frowned again, but stayed quiet to allow Chloe to keep speaking. 'I dunno how I ended up seeing it, but you just go down rabbit holes, you know?' Jess wasn't quite as enamoured with YouTube herself, but she'd seen Alex follow endless trails of recommended videos, each one Chinese-whispering a slight alteration so that where he might have started out watching new car reviews, he'd end up on an instructional video on how to pick locks. She nodded that she understood, gesturing for Chloe to continue. 'So, I saw this video, only a couple of weeks ago probably, about EMPs.' She ended dramatically on the last acronym, as if she expected Jess to immediately respond with recognized concern. 'About how to build one yourself. It's actually not *that* hard, if you could be bothered and got the right stuff. The video really breaks it down for you. So,' she said again with finality, 'my point is, even if *I've* seen a video on how to do that, then surely anyone else' – she turned and looked over her shoulder again – 'could have.'

'I'm sorry,' Jess said, shaking her head, completely lost. 'What's an EMP?'

Chloe looked at her with an expression of pitying acceptance that of *course* adults didn't know anything about anything. Jess remembered plastering a similar look on her own face when she was young, the kind of expression you grow out of in your early twenties, when life hits you with full force and you understand for the first time how little you truly know of the world.

'An electromagnetic pulse,' Chloe clarified. 'It disrupts electrics in the vicinity of where it's activated. I also saw one on EMP weapons, so I guess this could be an attack by Russia or whatever.'

Chloe casually waved the possibility of global catastrophe away. 'Anyway, I thought you should know, given . . .' She stopped and looked back toward the driver's cab. 'Well, given what's happened. That *anyone* could have disrupted the tube service.' Jess paused to try and take this in, wondering briefly how her simple commute home had ended up in the middle of an underground murder investigation, a possible Russian attack, or at the very least a killer with some kind of futuristic device that could take down the city. While she thought, Chloe continued: 'I'm not trying to place the blame on anyone, but it's just, I know what Amelia said. And it makes sense, right? The killer had to have caused, or known about, the tube stopping so they could make their move. And right now, everyone's looking at Saul because of his job.'

'But you don't think it was Saul?'

Chloe shrugged. 'I don't know if it was Saul, but I didn't want you to get fixated on one person, only for the real killer to get away with it.'

Jess smiled. 'That's a good investigative instinct you've got there.'

Chloe gave a nervous grin. 'I, er, I want to do criminology at uni. I'm doing that and psychology for A level.'

'You want to work for the police?' There were not many young girls inspired to join the Met, for understandable reasons, which only kept the status quo ticking along quite nicely. Jess thought a girl like Chloe would be a hell of an asset to the future of London's police. But then she got a flash of sadness, thinking of this bright, ambitious girl being beaten down by the institution, having to fight for every last thing. Jess knew better than anyone that living in a constant state of struggle was no way to thrive, and that, really, without Liv there to lighten the load, to share a joke or an eye-roll, it was no surprise that inertia had slowly taken her over.

She'd felt it beginning to creep in even before Liv had left. Something so innocuous as the collection for Liv's leaving present – organized by Jess, of course. She'd got her a beautiful set of Japanese knives; Liv's love of cooking well documented by the freshly baked loaves and leftover casseroles she'd bring in for the staff kitchen after her days off. She'd put up with enough jokes about 'belonging in the kitchen' for it, but she loved it, and Jess had spent hours researching the very best present for a budding chef. But as if they could sense her impending weakness at losing her partner, half the team did not bother paying her back for the collective gift. Even after Nicole had jokingly chided them one lunchtime that it was only fair they cough up. When they still hadn't paid, Nicole had given Jess a half-hearted shrug that said *I tried*. Jess had taken the hit on the present, finding herself surprised that the principle of being taken advantage of in such a clear, obvious way, had not riled her into more action.

'I can't be arsed,' she'd told Alex as she'd rolled over in bed after Liv's leaving drinks, where she'd let their CO hand over the knife set as if he'd picked and paid for it himself. Alex had asked her why she hadn't at least told Liv the truth, a secret giggled whisper like he'd seen them do so many times before. 'She's got a new command to worry about now, she doesn't need to be stressed about me being owed eighty quid for her present.' Alex had given her a sympathetic look and leant over to kiss her cheek. The gentle way in which he'd done it had made Jess wonder later if he hadn't recognized that moment as the beginning of the end.

Chloe seemed to consider Jess's question about working for the police. 'I dunno – maybe. Or I might do a law conversion after; I like the idea of working for the Innocence Project London. Greenwich uni actually has a programme where you can work for them while you're studying.'

Jess gave an impressed nod. 'You've thought a lot about your future.'

Chloe shrugged. 'Gotta have a plan.'

Jess allowed the moment to settle before returning to the matter at hand. 'OK, so these EMP things,' she said waving her hand over the unfamiliar acronym, 'you're saying anyone could make one and carry it with them, and it would be strong enough to take down a tube and all the comms and everything?'

Chloe twisted her mouth ruefully. 'I mean I don't know *loads* about it, I'm not really science-y. But someone who *was* science-y could definitely use those videos as a base. And the one this guy built was like this big' – she held her fingers apart about the length of a 15cm ruler – 'so it could fit in someone's pocket or bag or something.'

Jess thought briefly for a moment about this device nestled snuggly next to the wiped blade of a knife, in someone's possession somewhere on this carriage. It still seemed far-fetched, if she was truly honest, but at the same time she couldn't claim to be at the cutting edge of technology, or the latest skills anyone willing could learn online. She thought back to all the panicked reports of forums teaching swathes of people how to make at-home explosives during the early noughties War on Terror. Hysterical hyperbole from newspapers desperate to sell copies, she'd always assumed, but she couldn't deny it must have at least been based on a couple of true case studies.

She blew out a long sigh.

'You don't believe me, do you?' Chloe asked, half correctly reading Jess's hesitation.

'It's not that, Chloe,' Jess assured her. 'I'm glad you told me. I just— it feels so *far-fetched*, you know.' She sat back in her seat and gave an exhausted laugh. 'I only wanted to get home after having a few drinks.'

Chloe smiled too and slumped against her own seat. 'Tell me about it.' She seemed more relaxed now she'd imparted this information. It was for Jess to now do with that what she will, overlay it onto her suspects and hunt out the right one.

Chloe's job was done.

Chloe

Chloe felt relieved to have got it off her chest. To have told someone who knew what they were doing and have them believe her – not dismiss her like she was just some kid. Even if Jess did think it was far-fetched. Chloe thought it was far-fetched too, but so far the world she'd grown up in seemed to be full of far-fetched things. She'd not even really paid much attention to the EMP video while she'd been watching it, letting it play on in the background while she scrolled her phone on her bed in the early hours of the morning. She had stopped every now and again to look up and see what the nerdy American guy was saying, rolling her eyes at his hysteria, the claims that weapons like this were going to be vital for the war that was coming to fight the New World Order. She did like conspiracy nuts sometimes, they made for good content, whether they knew they were doing it or not. She hadn't thought about an EMP at first when the tube had stopped. How many times before had she been on a train that stopped randomly in the tunnel? Even when it became clear the power was off, the significance of the emergency lights, the lack of police coming to their aid – she had believed Saul, who seemed like another sensible grown-up, that there was a citywide power cut. It was unusual, and she'd never experienced it before, but she wasn't going to jump immediately to a late-night YouTube video.

No, it was when Jess had revealed the tube driver had been attacked. Murdered, Chloe thought, the word sending a shiver through her. Coincidences happened in life, sure, but everyone could see that this would be a hell of a coincidence for the driver to have happened to have a murderous enemy on board exactly when a power cut hit. So, she'd worked out that surely, in order to kill the tube driver, the murderer *must* have caused the blackout. And suddenly that little sparked memory had unravelled a waterfall of agitation inside her that she, aside from the killer, might understand more about the situation than anyone else. And that knowledge she'd needed to impart.

Jess had said she had good investigative instincts, and the compliment had made Chloe glow a little with pride. She rarely got compliments like that for her work; Liam's chosen career of performance lent itself much more readily to spontaneous declarations of his brilliance. High marks on essays tended to get forgotten. Chloe thought again about if she'd like to be in the police. It had once been her childhood dream, to be a detective like on TV, engrossed as a kid in the puzzles and mysteries of Holmes and Poirot. As she'd got older she'd come to understand real life was not exactly like the satisfying trails of fiction, but something else had come over her in the face of that realization – the feeling of wanting to make a difference, to do something tangible that affected the world every day. And yes, joining the police was one way to do that. But growing up in the world that she had, it was perhaps not a surprise she'd become disillusioned with that particular establishment.

'You can change it from the inside though, chicken,' her dad had told her once when she'd voiced her newfound reticence at joining the police. But that had been before what happened to Jason, her cousin's friend. No one would have claimed Jason was an angel – he had a record, and from what her cousin said, it was a record he deserved. Shoplifting from a young age, car theft when he was only twelve, and just before everything that happened, he'd been bragging in the pub about slipping through the net for a string of burglaries. Not someone her dad would ever let her hang out with, and he berated his sister about letting her son have such friends. But even Chloe's dad had been horrified by the way Jason, only a year older than Chloe, had been hounded by the police for murder. They'd had no evidence or witnesses – just a hunch from one of the detectives.

That had been when Chloe had decided against the police and had started researching the Innocence Project London. If she was going to make a difference in this world, then *that* would be how she'd do it.

Twenty

Jess watched Chloe as she exhaled slowly, the relief she felt at having imparted her load palpable.

'How long have you and Liam been together?' Jess asked with a smile. Jealous of the mild small talk the others had found respite in.

'Nearly two years,' Chloe replied with a small grin.

'He seems nice.'

Chloe nodded. 'Yeah he is, I'm lucky. Most of my friends have been fucked over, you know, but Liam wouldn't do that to me,' she added proudly.

'Sounds like he's got big plans too,' Jess said, thinking of him buying his mum a mansion and taking her to the Maldives.

Chloe laughed. 'He's gonna be famous, that much he knows.'

'Sounds like Jenna could give him some tips,' Jess said lightheartedly. But Chloe's face scrunched into a small scowl at the sound of Jenna's name. Jess raised her eyebrows and thought that perhaps she'd misplaced the fascination with the influencer at the teenage girl's feet. 'You don't like Jenna?'

Chloe shrugged. 'I mean maybe *she's* fine, but her business is *dark*.'

Jess was intrigued. 'Dark how?'

'There was a podcast on it, some of her sellers who left blew the whistle on what it was like working for Burned.' Chloe nodded dramatically. 'It was a good podcast though, I love stuff like that.' She turned in her seat and gazed down toward Jenna. 'Kinda cool seeing her tonight, I suppose. Kinda like meeting the Tinder Swindler or Fyre Festival guy.'

Jess laughed and allowed a comfortable silence to beat for a moment longer between them, and then her mind wandered to her earlier concern of what a misguided teen would do for fame. She eyed Chloe carefully, a suspicion forming. Had Chloe told Jess about the EMP to point her in the direction of Liam? Was the implication that they'd watched this video together? Was the teens' shiftiness in the face of questions about the blackout because Chloe knew Liam had got up and left her side? Jess's brief moment of craving normalcy and small talk passed, her curiosity burning it into a dusting of ash.

'What happened during the blackout?' Jess asked Chloe again, and she saw by the way Chloe blinked several times quickly that she'd been taken by surprise.

'What? Huh?' she said, visibly trying to buy herself some time. 'Nothing. Like, er, like we said, just trying to block out the noise.' It was a bald-faced lie, and not well delivered.

'Chloe,' Jess said meaningfully, raising her eyebrows.

'That's it,' Chloe said with a stiff shrug and got to her feet. 'Anyway, I, er, wanted to tell you that, about the EMPs. So you know.' She was backing away as she spoke. 'I'm gonna go back now.' She pointed with a thumb over her shoulder. 'I think Liam has a film downloaded on his phone, gonna try and block all this out for a bit.'

Jess watched her go, her footsteps hurrying back toward the safety of the group. Chloe's instincts were right – Jess was not going to call out a seventeen-year-old for lying in a murder investigation in front of a group of trapped, panicked people whose rationality might well abandon them at any moment.

Jess sat with her new information for a bit. Reconsidering each of her suspects. The possibility of any of them having a device to cut out the power to the tube *did* widen the frame. If this was personal, as Jess strongly suspected it was, perhaps it wouldn't be difficult to find out Matt's work schedule. Make sure you were on the last tube and strike. Maybe the culprit had made their device much stronger than they thought, they hadn't expected to cause so much disruption?

Pressing her hands to her knees, Jess pushed herself up to her feet. It was time to go back to the victim himself and see what else he could tell her.

She walked down the tube, accompanied by her ghostly-lit reflection in the black windows on each side and stifled a shiver. Scott ignored her as she walked by; he now sat low with his head resting on the back of his bench. As she'd said, Chloe was looking over Liam's shoulder at his phone, trying to persuade him to watch whatever he had downloaded. 'I don't think my battery'll last though, a whole movie'll *rinse* it,' he was saying with a worried twist to his mouth. Saul and Isa were deep in conversation, and Amelia was still scrolling through her phone. But Jenna was watching Jess carefully and got to her feet as she approached.

She stood facing Jess, a defiance to her stance with her back to the driver's cab door. Sweat had gathered in her stylishly coloured roots, giving her previously perfect blow-dry a drab, deflated quality. Foundation had creased in orangey caverns on her face, and smudges of black mascara blurred from the bottom of her eyes. She'd shed her leather jacket and the thin white tee underneath stuck to her in damp patches, exposing the hint of a purple lace bra underneath.

'Everything all right?' Jess asked, confused. She pointed to the door behind Jenna. 'I need to go back in there.'

'You know,' Jenna said slowly, performatively for the benefit of the whole carriage. 'I've been thinking. How do we know, it's not *you*?'

'*Excuse* me,' Jess said, incredulous.

'You *say* you're a detective, but we've not seen any evidence of that. Not shown us your badge, have you? *You're*' – she jabbed a finger toward her – 'the only person who's been in that cab, from where I'm standing. And you're the only person who's come out and accused one of us of being a murderer.'

'I haven't accused anyone of—'

But Jenna cut her off. 'You've questioned *us* all, why the hell can't we question you?'

Jess didn't have time for this, and it flashed through her mind that Jenna was purposefully, in fact *physically*, barring the way for Jess to continue her investigation.

'She's right.' Jess heard Scott's voice from behind her, and turned without surprise to find him roused by Jenna's words to move closer to the group again. 'We don't know who the hell you are!'

It was with a tightening worry that Jess noticed the realization land on the other passengers too. Saul and Isa shared a shifty glance, Chloe and Liam paused from their debate about the movie, and Amelia looked up from her phone, biting her lips tensely between her teeth.

'I've *told* you who I am,' she said with forcible calmness. 'DI Jessica Hirsch.'

'Can we see some ID then?' Jenna asked, her head cocked to one side, as if she already knew Jess didn't have any.

'I . . .' Jess faltered, feeling strangely guilty even though she knew she wasn't lying, not completely. 'I don't have any on me. I'm not on duty.'

'How convenient,' Scott snarked from behind her.

'Well, no actually.' Jess twisted toward him. 'Evidently, it's not.'

'Jess,' Chloe said softly and from the furrow of her brow Jess knew she was worrying if she needed to regret what she'd just divulged. 'You *are* a detective, aren't you?'

'Of course I am,' Jess snapped, harsher than she meant to.

'But you can't seem to prove it.' Jenna remained firm. 'And I'm sorry, but I'm not letting you back in there until you can.'

Jess rolled her head on her neck to indicate Jenna was clearly being ridiculous. But as she looked around the others, hoping to find something, even a grain of support, she was met with nothing but tense, worried gazes.

'I'm sorry Jess,' Saul said. 'But Jenna's right. We can't let you in there unless we know for certain you're not destroying evidence.'

'Destroying evidence?' Jess spluttered and turned to appeal to Amelia instead.

Amelia gave a one-shouldered shrug and gestured to everyone. 'They're right,' she said. 'We don't know that *you're* not the killer.'

Twenty-One

Jess had no choice but to stand down. She shook her head in sharp, jerking movements and rolled her eyes as she reluctantly took a seat next to Amelia with a loud, frustrated exhale. She wanted them all to know she thought they were being blatantly ridiculous. But of course, if she was truly honest, she knew they weren't being ridiculous. She'd offered them nothing to prove her authority, and in a way she was surprised it had taken this long for one of them to call her out on it. As much as she wanted to get back inside that cabin and root deeper through Matt's phone, she couldn't help but have a modicum of respect for Jenna. Respect that didn't quite negate her lodged suspicion at Jenna's efforts to derail the one person searching for answers though.

Jess's choice not to battle the point any further seemed to be enough to defuse the tension. Jenna looked satisfied to have made her point, but not actually interested enough to question Jess properly as she sat lazily back down. An awkward silence settled on the rest of the group for a few moments after the stand-off, no one else apparently wanting to step forward to take Jenna's place as Jess's interviewer. Eventually Scott slunk away back to his seat, looking half satisfied, as if he was pleased to have knocked Jess down a peg or two, but also like he might have been hoping for more of a fight. Next to her, Jess saw Amelia return to her phone, evidently unsure what else to do. Jess noticed that what she'd been passing the time doing was flicking through photos, pausing every so often with a sad smile.

Jess wondered if the small talk would break out again, or if her presence had ruined the camaraderie the others had started to build. The answer came from the last person Jess expected. Liam, leaning forward to rest his elbows on his knees, said in Jenna's direction, 'Do you mind if I ask' – Jenna caught his eye and gave a little nod of curiosity for him to continue – 'how did you manage to grow your following so quickly?'

Liam's expression was earnest, his brows pulled together as if waiting for a very important and complex answer he was ready to take note of. Jess noticed Chloe sit back in her seat with a small frown, demonstrably not interested in listening to what Jenna had to say.

Jenna smiled and pulled the edges of her mouth down in a falsely modest expression. 'I work at it every day,' she answered, adjusting in her own seat to face more directly toward Liam, settling into the interview. 'When I first started, I had like *nothing*. I was a server – and I saved up all my tips and bought my first candle-making kit, right? I started to experiment with the different smells and knew I wanted to sell them. Obviously, there was no way I could ever afford a store in New York, and even a website would cost money – but Instagram, it was this free platform, a free shop where I could do whatever I wanted and scale however I wanted. If I only had time or money to make thirty candles, I only needed to advertise enough for that, right? But' – she held up a finger, indicating she was about to get to the most fascinating and genius part – 'you can't smell on Instagram, right? So it was super-hard at first to get traction. My page looked exactly the same as a million other pages selling candles. Why would you follow me? So, I had to think about how I could set myself apart. What did *I* have to offer that was different to everyone else? I'd always loved art class at school, so I bought some glass paint and started painting my patterns onto the jars – and it really took off. I made something that's not visual, *visual*. And because I was doing it around working full-time, I kind of accidentally created this exclusivity around it. I had people waiting and begging for the newest designs, asking if any of their favourites would be coming back, that kind of thing.' Liam was nodding intently, and Jess could see his cogs whirring at how he could apply this to his own pursuit of fame and riches. 'But crucially,' Jenna added, with an air of coming to the crux of the matter, 'I was doing something *different*. Sure, I'd started out the same as everyone else, but then I made it my own, played to my strengths. And that's how you get people's attention.'

To Jess it sounded like bland meaningless advice. But Jenna continued her TED talk, responding to the enthusiastic nodding of her audience. Liam was taking in every word.

'Now, how you *keep* people's attention is a different matter,' she continued. 'The business started to take off and through it I was able to help and inspire so many women to take charge of their own destiny, you know?' Next to her, Jess saw Amelia put her phone down in her lap, her attention homing in on Jenna with an incredulous, narrow look. 'So as well as the business account, I started to build my own brand, posting every day with advice for women in business, inspiration to keep going and keep working hard. You've got to be able to respond quickly.

When videos took over from photos, I moved with them early on and the algorithm rewarded me. I expanded to other social media, making sure to keep all my content curated differently for each platform. If you want it all, you have to follow me on everything. It's hard work.' She nodded to herself. 'But success *takes* hard work.'

'Yeah, yeah,' Liam was nodding enthusiastically.

'Sorry,' Amelia cut in, that incredulous expression still on her face. 'I don't want to be rude, but how exactly do you inspire women with *candles*?'

If Jenna was offended, she didn't show it. In fact, she looked like she was used to disbelieving jabs being thrown in her direction. She responded coolly and calmly.

'When I was first starting out, I'd sell through Instagram, but I didn't have the budget for a delivery service – I didn't have enough stock and for such small numbers it would have added so much more onto the price. So instead, I got a stall at a market on Saturday mornings for people to come and pick up their orders. Anyway, I had this one girl who came for pretty much every drop, and one day I asked her how she was burning through these candles so quickly. And she laughed and said she was picking them up for friends who couldn't make it to the market stall, and they were paying her. She was like my age and I liked her so I started chatting about what she was doing. Turned out she was in college, bartending to make ends meet, so I said, "I'll give *you* a 15 per cent discount on the candles you pick up for other people and then you can take the extra as your service fee." It wasn't long before that 15 per cent loss was cancelled out by the number of candles she kept buying in order to sell them on to her network of friends – making her own profit at the same time. So as the business grew, that model just sort of expanded. That girl introduced me to another of her friends who was heading home to Florida for the summer and wanted a bulk order to sell to *her* friends and family down there. I kept getting women who wanted to sell for me, and my distributers kept growing and growing. And now' – she glanced briefly around the carriage – 'I have them over here too.'

'Yeah, but how exactly is that inspiring women to change their lives?' Amelia, it seemed, was not buying it.

'Because I'm giving them the opportunity to start their own business,' Jenna said simply, as if Amelia was stupid. 'Like a franchise. They have brand recognition and a good quality product, so all they need to worry about is running their own empire.'

Amelia didn't look particularly convinced but let the point lie.

'It shows you what your hustle can get,' Liam piped up toward Amelia, as if he felt she needed more explanation. 'You know, that you really can make it if you put in the work.'

'Hustle culture isn't everything,' Amelia said with a grunt.

'It's easy to say that when you have money.' Liam's response was quick and landed heavily in the carriage. Jess felt Amelia shift uneasily next to her.

Jenna had an impressed smile on her face. '*You* get it, Liam. My mom raised me alone too, and all I ever saw was her worrying about paying the bills, working two, three jobs. And I said to myself, "No. If I'm going to put in that many hours, I'm going to make sure I'm not still stressing about the bills at the end of the week."' She looked toward Amelia again. 'And the only way to do that is to take control of it yourself. Not let yourself get walked over by a boss who won't pay you above minimum wage. My mom had me and my brother, she would never have had the time to set up her own business. But now I've done it – and I can give the opportunity to women like my mom to take that control for themselves and actually get damn well paid for it.'

'Money doesn't solve everything,' Amelia snapped, her lips pursing tensely so a ripple of dimples appeared on her chin. Jess noticed her hands flex in her lap, fingers stretching exaggeratedly upwards so the tendons stuck up in high ridges. 'Even if you think it could. It doesn't'.

'I'd rather give life a try with it though,' Liam said.

'Ask my sister if you don't believe me,' Amelia replied, a dull, faraway curtain falling over her gaze. Her voice dropped. 'Better yet, ask her husband and kids what they would say about it.'

'Amelia,' Jess said softly, placing one hand gently on her forearm. 'Are you all right?' It occurred to Jess that Amelia had spent the last couple of hours trapped and scared and looking through old photos, picking at the fresh scab over her grief through stress and boredom. She'd already been anxious before, and all this time she'd been silently tormenting herself.

Amelia blinked a couple of times and turned toward Jess, as if surprised to find someone directly asking after her welfare. 'Yes, yes, I'm fine.' She did not sound particularly convincing. She turned to Liam, and Jess noticed she specifically avoided Jenna's eyeline in the motion. 'Sorry, I didn't mean to – to make it sound like you shouldn't try and do whatever you want to do. It's just' – she gestured briefly to Jenna, still avoiding her gaze – 'all this talk of only working hard for success – it, it makes you feel like if you fail it's your fault for not working hard enough. And that, that can be a dangerous spiral. You need to be careful, you're still so young,' she added with a maternal smile. 'Don't ruin your childhood because you feel all this pressure.'

Liam didn't say anything, but gave an awkward nod, visibly uncomfortable with being given such emotional life advice from a relative stranger. Amelia seemed to understand this and turned away without waiting for a response. 'Sorry,' she told the carriage at large, 'that's my own personal shit. I didn't mean to make it any more' – she hesitated over the next word – '*difficult* down here than it already is. Just ignore me.'

Jess breathed out into the thick silence that fell again as everyone followed Amelia's instructions to ignore her. The exhale was louder than she'd expected, and she saw Jenna's eyes flick interestedly toward her, as if she expected her to start speaking again. They held each other's gaze for a moment, and then Jenna tipped her head back and closed her eyes.

Next to Jess, Amelia recommenced her scrolling through old photos and, sensing that she didn't really want anyone to ignore her, Jess asked softly, 'Is that your sister?' and gestured to the photo on her screen. Amelia was standing in a blooming garden wearing a summer's dress, posing with a glass of fizz next to another woman who had very similar features but bright blonde hair in place of Amelia's red.

If Amelia was surprised or even annoyed at Jess looking at her photos over her shoulder, she did not show it. Instead, she answered simply, 'Yeah, that's Libby. This was a week before she died. She looks happy, doesn't she?'

Jess assessed the photo with a little more attention. And, despite the broad smile stretched on Libby's pink mouth, Jess actually didn't think this woman looked very happy at all. If you covered over her mouth, you'd be left with tense, sad eyes, heavy bags bruised beneath them – giving the look of a woman with the world on her shoulders. But Jess did not say this, she did not want to tarnish one of Amelia's last memories with her sister. Instead, she nodded with a murmured agreement.

Amelia shook her head. 'You really never can tell, can you.' Her thumb pressed down on the screen and swiped to the left, bringing the next picture in the camera roll up. It was of a polished oak funeral casket, a cascade of dark purple roses falling from the arrangement on top. Jess blinked in surprise and felt her shoulders tense. Amelia seemed to feel, and recognize, the movement. 'I know it's morbid,' she said. 'But I took it to remind me that you never know what someone's going through.'

'What happened?' Jess asked, feeling it was the right time.

'She killed herself,' Amelia answered simply. 'Got into a lot of debt, couldn't see a way out of it and was too embarrassed to ask for help. Even though we all would have in a heartbeat.' Amelia added the last sentence with a sudden, urgent look up at Jess, as if Jess had been about to accuse her of abandoning her sister in her time of need. 'It wasn't the money,' Amelia clarified, 'it was the shame that killed her.'

Jess didn't have much to say to that, so instead she put her hand back on Amelia's forearm and gave her a gentle, brief squeeze of support.

Jenna

Jenna had always liked the feeling of control, of people listening to her. She supposed that came hand in hand with being a CEO, while her therapist said it was a response to feeling like she had no voice as a child – her mom always running from job to job, her brother in and out of trouble demanding the rest of her attention. Jenna had decided they were probably both right. Only Gramma Lois had ever had the time to listen to what Jenna had to say, what movie she wanted to watch, what she wanted to eat for dinner. Little decisions that Jenna made, that only Gramma Lois would listen to. So, it was no surprise for Jenna that Jess giving up on her mission to return to the crime scene had sent a familiar dart of pleasure through her that, even now, Jenna Pace commanded authority. Jenna knew Jess had not killed the driver. One look at her could tell you that woman had always lived by putting too much stead in the rules. But Jenna hadn't liked the way Jess had declared herself in charge – demanding information and details from them, offering scant little of her own in return.

Even now, simply sitting among them, Jess had somehow managed to probe a personal story from Amelia. Although, if Jenna was being truly honest, it hadn't seemed like something Amelia had particularly wanted to hold back. Jenna felt like Amelia had spent the last couple of hours on the edge of hysteria, waiting for someone to ask her what was wrong. And Jess had finally obliged. It was a sad story, and Jenna had not been able to help but listen in as Amelia spoke of her sister's fate. The carriage was narrow, there was no such thing as a private conversation, but she'd taken her cue from everyone else and acted like Jess alone had heard the story. Jenna had stared down at her phone, uselessly adding videos to her stalled Instagram story that wouldn't upload, and pretended she wasn't eavesdropping on Amelia's pain.

The thing was, Jenna thought to herself, self-aware enough that her opinion would be considered too callous by most people to voice in public – people like Amelia's sister were, to be frank, weak. Not that Jenna would ever dismiss someone's struggles with mental health; if anything, discussing her own inner battles was a large part of her brand. Jenna knew how hard it was. But Jenna had also got *through* it – she'd had therapy, she took pills when she needed to, and she was not just living but *thriving*. So, if she could do it, she didn't understand why other people made such a fuss about it. It was the same as the complaints from people who said Burned fostered a toxic work environment, too much pressure, too much blame when they failed. From where Jenna was sitting, that was the reality of working in sales. So many people just didn't *get* it – you have to work for every little thing in life, and if you *do* that work, then goddamnit you'll succeed. But people like Amelia, and presumably her sister too, had never had to work for anything, so they didn't get it, and they never would. The first sign of an obstacle to overcome, and the sister had tapped out. Weak people, Jenna supposed, made weak decisions.

Now, Jenna, her grandma reprimanded her again. *That's not fair. We all have our demons.* Jenna felt suitably chastised, but her grandma wasn't done, it seemed. *What if I'd have called you weak when I found you in the bathroom with a razor to your wrist?*

Jenna sucked in her teeth and hated Amelia in that moment for somehow unknowingly rooting through all of Jenna's history and trauma and poking one of those peach-painted fingernails directly into her deepest wound.

Yeah, Jenna rebuffed her grandma, *I was weak. But I became strong.*

Jenna straightened herself up and rolled her shoulders back, feeling every iron-willed fibre in her body tensing with determined pride.

Twenty-Two

Amelia accepted Jess's squeeze of support and flashed a small, grateful smile before returning to continue scrolling on her phone. Jess glanced toward the cab, wishing she could get back inside without causing a scene. She still didn't know who she could trust on this train, and the idea of someone taking out the electrics of possibly the whole city just to kill one tube driver would not stop scratching at her brain. What could this Matt possibly have done to warrant such dramatics?

Jess shook her head, and decided she needed her own distraction. Taking Amelia's cue, she put her hand in her pocket to fish out her own phone, thinking that looking at some pictures of the girls and Alex and Honey would soothe her. She absentmindedly pulled the rectangle out of her pocket and out of habit, squeezed the side button to bring the home screen to life. It took a moment for her to blink into the screen, the brightness jarring suddenly against the dullness of the carriage.

Next to her, Amelia gave a small laugh, and Jess turned her head to find that Amelia was looking down at the screen in her hand. Jess supposed it was fair – she'd been looking at Amelia's photos after all.

'Didn't have you down for a football hooligan,' Amelia gave another small hiccough of a laugh and gestured at the phone.

'Huh?' Jess responded to Amelia with a small, confused sound, and then followed the direction of Amelia's finger to look at the home screen. She found that she'd accidentally pulled Matt's phone out of her pocket instead of her own.

'Is one of those your husband?' Amelia craned her neck toward the phone, her brow furrowed as if trying to work out the relationship between this mid-thirties woman in a nice dress and the group of twenty-something lads on the screen. Jess didn't know what to say. She didn't want to admit that she had pocketed the victim's phone. Given the distrust Jenna had spawned against her, even Jess had to admit that would look suspicious.

'Oh, um, no,' Jess faltered, trying to find a suitable explanation. But Amelia continued speaking.

'Isn't that the pub from that brawl the other week? The Mason's Arms?' she asked, her frown now deepening as she looked up at Jess, as if everything she thought she'd known about this new acquaintance was crumbling around her.

'Brawl?' Jess asked, still staring at the photo, the recognition of the name the Mason's Arms suddenly coming screaming back to her.

'Yeah, it was all over the papers,' Amelia said, suspicion rising in her tone. 'You must have seen it. A huge fight broke out after some football match – some local league, small teams, but it basically became a riot.' She pointed back to the phone. 'And it all started at that pub.'

'Yes,' Jess said, the story now firming up around the fuzzy edges of her memory. She *had* read about it – that was why the name of the pub had snagged some recognition. There had been over seventy people involved, a couple of dozen ended up in hospital. News of arrests had spilled out across the following few days as the police trawled through CCTV trying to identify whoever they could. She couldn't remember the names of the teams involved, but clearly, one of them was based in Lewisham.

'Yeah, I remember.'

'Didn't you know your husband was there?' Amelia asked, now confused more than suspicious, a slight tone of sympathy as she watched Jess apparently realize her husband might be a violent football rioter.

'That's not my husband,' Jess said distractedly, her mind whirring, wondering what this meant — if anything. Could it be the first stirrings of a motive for this victim, that perhaps one week ago he had made a very dangerous enemy?

Jess unconsciously thought of the grazes on Scott's knuckles, the fading bruise on his cheek, and her head snapped up toward him.

And she found him staring directly at her through the glass dividers, a snarled, defiant look on his face.

Jess felt threat prickle against her skin alongside her sheen of sweat, as Scott narrowed his eyes at her through the glass. How much had he heard? Presumably, from the look on his face, all of it. He must have heard Amelia bring up the football riot, but could he know that they were looking at the driver's phone? That Jess had made a mental connection between the two of them? Jess held his gaze for a beat longer, she wasn't going to be intimidated, even though all her instincts screamed at her to be. She straightened her head on her neck and closed her eyes, trying to get it clear. To work it out. Scott and Matt had possibly been involved in the same brawl a week ago, presumably on opposite sides. Scott was holding a grudge for reasons Jess didn't yet know and decided that he needed to take Matt out. She raised her eyebrows as she opened her eyes. It still felt a fairly dramatic way to retaliate over a football brawl.

Unless—

She'd become so wrapped up in this idea of conspiracies and EMPs, she'd forgotten the possibility that Scott was merely an opportunist. That when the tube had pulled into the stop as Scott waited on the platform, he recognized the driver through the front windows. He spent his journey drinking lager and becoming more and more riled by the memory of the previous week. So, when the tube stopped in the blackout, Scott snapped. Some people live on the cusp, knock one thing out of balance – say taking out your key senses of sight and sound, add in claustrophobia, fear and a beer-induced headache, and it might not take much for the inner monster to come out. The timings were still tight. He'd have to have got up from his seat the moment the tube had stopped. Scott was the furthest away from the cab – he'd have to have passed by them all on his murderous mission. And he'd have to be confident that the glitch would last longer than a few seconds, or not be thinking straight enough to worry about such things. So far though, this seemed the likeliest explanation. As if she was finally inching closer to an answer.

A sudden streak of terror sent a cold dart down her spine as she remembered Matt's butchered neck. If Scott could do that in a matter of minutes, with only adrenaline and anger driving him, what could he be capable of after nearly two hours of cabin fever?

Scott

Scott frowned toward the lady detective, trying to work out what was going through her mind. He knew she had no real authority over them, but Christ he also knew she could cause enough trouble for him if she wanted to. A female police officer trapped on a tube with a body and someone she now had in her sights as prime suspect? There was no way her old buddies wouldn't just take her word for it when they eventually got here.

As soon as he'd heard the posh bird mention the Mason's Arms, his attention had shifted from where he'd been dazing unfocusedly at the crumpled newspaper on his lap. Almost napping, but not quite, the day's lager now having dropped a fuzzy down duvet over him in the boredom of being stuck there. He'd been sure he heard her say Mason's Arms, and had blinked himself back to full consciousness and brought his head up to see what they were talking about. The redhead seemed to be looking at the lady detective's phone, and then she'd asked if her husband had been there. He hadn't heard her response but a moment later she'd snapped her head toward him like a magnet finding its opposite pole – staring at him with a definite air of threat.

Oh, here we fucking go, Scott thought. That fucking pub had already caused him enough trouble. He wondered what side her husband had been on, and dropped his eyeline down to his grazed knuckles, unable to stop a small smile playing on his mouth that maybe they'd landed on her husband's face, given him a black eye to take home to his copper wife. The smile didn't last long though as Scott thought about the repercussions of that damned brawl. It had already cost him so much, and now – what? Would it cost him even more? He'd managed to avoid being rounded up so far, he'd not been visible on CCTV and besides, he'd barely been involved. Not like some of them – fucking animals, throwing chairs and bricks. That was mainly the other side though. He was only defending himself, defending his honour. He'd thrown a couple of punches, taken a couple of punches and then been on his way before anything had got too out of hand. Nothing for the police to take note of. At least, that's where it should have ended. But it didn't, did it? Because of *him*. Scott felt the muscles in his face contract unconsciously, pulling his top lip into a scowl as that smug fucking face swam into his vision again, staring at him from behind the windscreen. Unspeaking, but his expression may as well have been screaming *You lose!* at the top of his voice.

Twenty-Three

'When can we get off and walk to find help?' Amelia cut into Jess's silent panic about Scott. She'd evidently given up on looking through her old photos, that scab thoroughly picked, and now she was returning to her earlier anxiety. 'How long has it been now? It must be hours!'

Jess subtly moved Matt's phone back into her pocket and retrieved her own out of the other one. No one seemed to notice the switch. She lit up the home screen and saw that it was nearly 1.55 a.m. 'It's been about an hour and forty-five minutes, maybe two hours,' she told the group, as apparently the only person who'd kept track of what time the tube had gone down. Her eyes slid to the top-right corner of the screen, where the battery icon had dwindled down to a thin sliver, telling her she had only 2 per cent left. *Shit*. That was not going to last much longer than another five minutes.

'Saul, what do you think?' Isa asked, looking up at him imploringly.

Saul looked uneasy. 'I still think it's too much of a risk. If anything, the longer it's been out, the more likely it is that it'll come back at any point – if everyone has been working away all this time.'

'Yes, but how long do these things usually take to fix?' Amelia snapped.

Saul gave a helpless shrug. 'How long is a piece of string?'

'Very helpful.' Sarcasm dripped from Amelia's voice.

Jess couldn't concentrate on the back and forth, thanks to the tangible tension coming from Scott's direction, hot waves pulsing at her as she made pains to avoid his gaze and not let on how her suspicions had contorted in his direction. She still needed more evidence to connect him and Matt, and she didn't like her chances of getting a straight answer out of Scott about the riot. Not to mention her worry that it might well set him off again – this time toward her. She *needed* to get into Matt's phone, see if he had more pictures of the fight, emails, chats about who was involved.

'Guys, someone *will* come for us eventually,' Jenna cut in. 'Let's just wait it out.'

'Well, if you have nowhere to go and no one to get home to, that's easy for you to say!' Amelia's voice was high-pitched now, her earlier hysteria cloaking her like a familiar blanket.

Jenna narrowed her eyes. 'Who's to say I have nowhere to go?'

Amelia puffed out an annoyed exhale.

'Saul,' Isa cut in, 'do you *really* think it's dangerous out there? Because' – she gestured vaguely toward Amelia – 'I get it. I have somewhere to be too.'

Jess remembered how shifty Isa had been about where she was heading tonight, instead of going out with her friends.

Saul blew out a non-committal sigh. 'I don't like the idea of it,' he answered honestly.

Jess looked toward the teenagers, who seemed to be sharing their own tense glances, as if they too would be willing to join the party going out into the tunnels should there be one. Jess knew they were both thinking about Chloe's worried father. She also knew that she could not stand to have his grief on her conscience. If Saul was right about this being a citywide power cut, then it was possible he was also right about the power coming back at any minute. And Jess couldn't take any more bodies on her soul. It briefly flashed through her that perhaps they'd all be safer taking their chances out in the tunnel, rather than cooped up on this carriage with a killer. But if the murder was indeed a grudge settled on impulse by a half-drunk football lout, she at least knew now to keep an eye on Scott. He'd held himself in check so far, but if he made a move toward anyone, she would throw herself in harm's way rather than let him get to any of the other passengers.

Amelia got to her feet and strode toward the doors.

'Amelia,' Jess appealed, getting to her own feet and following her. 'Please. We've already got one person dead – we don't need another.'

'I'm only looking at the mechanism,' Amelia snapped back, her impatience now woven seamlessly into her panic. 'So I know.'

'What is it?' Liam asked, getting up and peering over her shoulder as Amelia inspected the emergency door handle. Chloe hesitated for a moment and then followed him, slipping one hand into his as they peered together.

'Will this still work?' Amelia turned to Saul, pointing at it. 'Even if the power's out?'

Saul pulled an unknowing expression and stood up to lean over and take a closer look. 'I don't know for sure, but I would imagine it's designed to. It'll probably be a manual release mechanism.'

Amelia nodded and seemed to be considering flipping up the metal covering and yanking it down. Isa had got to her feet now, also wanting a closer look.

'Isa,' Saul said, 'I really don't think it's a good idea.' He said it with such paternal care in his voice, Isa couldn't help but stop and look up at him.

'But Saul,' her response was quiet, on the verge of pleading. It reminded Jess of Mia, pleading with Alex to let her go parasailing on holiday the previous year because the dodgy-looking guy in the excursion shack had insisted she was old enough. Jess had stayed silent and then played the good guy by buying her a shell necklace from a woman on the beach, Alex pouting later that she owed him one for making him the villain. 'When she comes to us wanting a tequila slammer tomorrow,' Jess had promised with a grin, 'I'll take that one.' Alex had laughed and then thrown the wet towels she'd left on their bed before dinner at her and told her to be useful for once and put them away. The happy holiday memory was wiped quickly away by the desperation in Isa's voice.

'I really need to get off.'

Jess found it interesting that Isa, this confident activist twenty-something, was deferring so heavily to a man she'd only just met. There seemed to be a vein of trust between them that ran deeper than Jess would have expected. But before Jess could take any more note of the interaction, it was cut short.

The emergency lights flickered, sending a brief strobe across the carriage before blackness crashed down on them again with the weight of a collapsing tunnel.

'Oh *fuck*,' Jess heard Jenna say, an uncharacteristic tremor to the words as the American drew closer to the group gathered by the door. 'Again?'

'Saul,' Chloe asked with a reedy inflection, 'is this normal? Will they come back?'

'I-I don't know,' Saul's earlier calm, collected demeanour sounded shaken now. 'The backup generators must be overrun.'

'What does that mean?' Amelia demanded from where she stood, still by the doors.

Saul audibly floundered. 'I-I can't say anything for sure, but it's not a good sign for the backup generators to fail.' He paused and Jess thought his face was probably twisted in thought. 'Without knowing what's happening up there, I can't say anything more,' he finished weakly.

Jess did not like this dark. It was so impossibly black, there was not even the smallest semblance of a shadow for her eyes to catch on to. It had fallen so quickly, with the shock of a cold bath, it was a struggle to orientate herself. She suddenly felt like she was spinning through space, being suckered into the black hole of the tunnel she'd seen through the driver's windscreen. She could feel the bodies around her where the group had congregated to look at the door release handle, but she couldn't place herself among them; it felt like a giant crowd crushing and pressing in on her, although she knew it was only six people, seven at most. She couldn't explain it, but she felt both exposed and constricted at the same time, as if her body was ripe for the taking, a knife could be forced into her flesh at any moment and there was nowhere for her to go, nowhere to run. Someone knocked into her, and a voice said, 'Shit, sorry' – maybe Isa.

'What?' Another voice said from next to Jess, very close by, which Jess thought might be Chloe.

'Nothing,' Jess thought she heard Liam answer from an indeterminable position that seemed both next to her and in front of her and behind her all at once.

'Hey, watch it!' That time it definitely was Chloe, and Jess felt her stumble and fall into her, Chloe's long braids tickling Jess's arm.

Another body seemed to have stumbled over their feet too, because a second weight pressed against Jess, who was about to open her mouth to ask if anyone had their phone to hand for a bit of light before they all trampled each other to death, when a new feeling took her by surprise, stopping the words cold in her throat.

It was not a sensation she'd ever felt before, but she knew at once what it was.

Cold metal, followed by a warm rush, before, finally, pain ripped through her.

A scream caught in her throat as she staggered back, doubling over, knowing for certain that what she'd felt *was* a knife through her flesh.

Twenty-Four

'Who screamed?' someone asked, and Jess thought through her confused senses it was Amelia. But she couldn't focus on that now, the pain tore through her, and all she could feel was blood seeping from her arm. Blindly she groped for her dress and lifted the skirt to press the thin material against the source of the pain – without being able to see, she couldn't be sure where the wound was exactly because her whole arm radiated in agony, but the pressure seemed to relieve a little as she desperately pressed against it. Her mind was swimming, going blank for anything else to do except try to keep focus and avoid bleeding out. The girls pressed forward to the front of her brain, Honey wagging her tail and playing with them in the garden, Alex handing her a glass of pale white wine.

This was not where Jess was going to abandon them all. Bleeding out in the dark on a dingy tube carriage.

Suddenly her vision seemed to change, the blackness faltered, a hint of light washed over the oppressive dark.

'Did you lot forget about these?' Scott said, closer than where Jess thought he'd been. 'What's going on?'

Jess blinked as she adjusted to the new light source, recognizing the beam of torchlight that was falling on them from Scott's phone. She could just about make out his shadowy figure pressed among the group, between Isa and Amelia. When had he joined them by the door?

'Oh my God, Jess!' Chloe was the first to notice her, bent over, almost on the floor. 'Are you all right?'

'Is that blood?' Isa's voice was strained with horror.

Saul dropped to his knees, taking hold of Jess's arms, supporting her injured one with a firm grasp, and clasping his large hand over the wound, applying pressure to stem the flow of blood. Jess blinked away watery tears and tried to focus on the whorls of greying hair that carpeted Saul's olive-skinned hands.

'Come on,' he said softly in her ear, 'can you step backwards a few paces so we can get you sitting down?'

She somehow managed to nod and felt much of her weight relieved as he moved his arms to cradle her as she staggered, still bent low and double, over to the nearest seat. It was the seat that had been Isa's, and her tote bag and hoodie were scrunched up next to it.

'What happened?' Amelia asked, her voice weak, catching in panic.

'Think I was . . .' Jess gasped and pressed down harder on her injured arm, but she felt her senses slowly returning. 'I was stabbed.'

There was a collective inhale among the passengers forming a close arc above her, and Jess was sure if she looked up she would see them exchange suspicious, terrified glances.

'Who was it?' Saul asked, his tone serious, businesslike. He knelt down so he was eye level with Jess.

She took another moment to collect herself, feeling the cold thrill of shock wearing off, and blinking the focus back into her sight. She looked at him, and then up at the others, before returning her eyes to Saul to answer his question.

'I don't know,' she answered honestly. 'It was pitch black, I couldn't *see* anything. Everyone was so crowded together.' She swallowed thickly before throwing down the gauntlet. 'It could have been any of you.'

No one seemed to have a response to that. Even protesting their individual innocence would be a waste of breath. Instead, everyone exchanged thick, meaningful glances, the earlier mistrust that had spread between them returning with a vengeance.

'Right.' Amelia broke the silence, her matter-of-fact tone struggling to conceal the underlying frenzy. 'That's it then, we need to get off. I'm not staying on here when one of you is a *psycho*.'

That accusation seemed to break the spell. Suddenly they were all clamouring that *they* weren't a psycho, how dare she suggest that, they hadn't had anything to do with it, maybe *she* was the psycho.

'Guys,' Jess said weakly, the pain dulling to a constant, distracting throb. 'Guys!' She raised her voice with evident strain, and they stopped their squabbling, as if to acknowledge the effort she'd put into demanding their attention. 'Does anyone have any painkillers?' she asked, lowering her voice to a level that didn't require so much exertion.

'Shit, sorry,' Amelia said, sounding genuinely apologetic. 'Yes, yes of course, I've got some co-codamol in my bag, hang on. Only thing that takes the edge off my period pains when they get going,' she rambled as she used Scott's thin torchlight to find her way back to her Celine tote and rooted around inside it. She pulled out a box of medicine and handed it to Jess, at the same time retrieving her phone from her seat and turning her torch on. For lack of any water, Jess swallowed two of the pills down dry, and coughed as the sweet, claggy coating caught on her throat.

'Can I have a look?' Saul asked, gesturing to Jess's arm, as Chloe, Isa and Jenna also located their phones and turned on their torches, helpfully directing them down to where Saul was crouched in front of Jess. Scott hesitated and then he too added his torch beam to the collection to help Saul inspect Jess's wound. Only Amelia seemed incapable of keeping her torch beam trained steadily on Jess's arm, her light jerking up every now and again to land on a different passenger or abandoned corner of the train, as if she hoped she might catch the culprit out with her wandering spotlight.

Carefully, Saul removed Jess's hand from where it had remained clamped against her forearm and peeled her now blood-soaked dress away. Her arm was a mess of scarlet smears so the wound itself was almost impossible to see. Saul reached over a couple of seats to his abandoned suit jacket and pulled out a small packet of tissues, extracted one and wiped very gently down Jess's bloody arm. She winced at his touch, but he had been incredibly gentle, so it was more in anticipation of pain rather than a reaction to it. The small tissue turned immediately ruby red, the blood soaking with ease through the fibres. It didn't do much to clear the spilled blood, but it did remove enough to show a slash below the inside of her elbow. It was about three inches long, uneven and ragged where it had torn through the honeypot tattoo she'd had done when they first brought a bouncy, excitable Honey home from the rescue centre.

'I don't think it's too deep,' Saul said, tilting his head to inspect it. He pulled out another tissue to wipe away more spilled blood. Jess thought that must be an impossible task, given how much blood she was sure had seeped out of her, but as she looked closer, her mind getting clearer by the moment, she realized he was right. It wasn't that deep; possibly she'd need some steri-strips or a stitch or two, but the damage seemed relatively superficial. There was no bone exposed, and when she went to wiggle her fingers, she was confident no important nerves had been slashed. 'We need to try and keep this bleeding at bay,' he said, and then began looking around for something of use.

'Hang on,' Isa said, manoeuvring around the group to Jess's side so she could reach into her bag. 'I might have something.' She dug one hand in the soft, cotton tote and pulled out a black scarf, tangled up with several other possessions that spilled onto the seat as she tugged it. Jess thought the scarf looked unseasonably warm for this time of year, but if Isa was willing to sacrifice it to get ruined by Jess's blood, she wasn't going to complain.

'Yeah,' Saul said with a nod, accepting the scarf, 'this will work. Thank you.'

As he set about making a pad of tissues to secure at the centre of the makeshift dressing, Jess averted her gaze. She wasn't squeamish, she didn't mind having her blood taken or having doctors prodding, but she didn't necessarily like to watch. Instead, she turned her head toward where Isa was hurriedly repacking her bag, the last thing retrieved from the seat a stack of circular stickers that looked like a classic forbidden sign of a circle with a slash through it, but instead of the usual red it was purple. Inside were the words *Hookd THEN Fookd!*

'Those for the protest?' Jess asked with a wince and a thick swallow, as Saul pressed down on her cut inordinately hard and began wrapping the scarf tightly around the pad of tissues.

'Huh?' Isa said, looking up with a mindless blink. She glanced back down to the stickers in her hand, as if surprised to find them there. 'Oh yeah,' she said, and stuffed them back in her bag.

'That's a dating site, isn't it?' Jess asked. 'Hookd?'

'Oh, we're protesting dating now, are we?' Jenna said in a dry, arch tone.

Isa seemed like she wanted to respond, but then decided she didn't have the energy. Instead, she answered Jess with a tired sigh. 'Yeah, just some stupid trend going round to do with it,' she finished and rolled her eyes. Jess glanced toward Jenna to see if she was annoyed Isa hadn't risen to the bait. But Jenna only eyed Isa for a moment with a narrow expression before she lowered her gaze to the floor, her long lashes fluttering down, a muscle flexing in her jaw.

Saul

Saul finished wrapping Jess's arm and brought the two ends of the scarf together to tie in a chunky knot. It was not elegant, but it would do to stem the flow of bleeding temporarily. His eyes ached from concentrating in the dark with the bright white lights of the torches pointed his way, burning into his retinas. He blinked a few times as he sat back from Jess and smiled up at her.

'Thanks for this, Isa,' he said. 'It'll do the job for now.'

'No problem,' she mumbled in return, seeming ever so slightly abashed as she slumped back on her chair and clutched her bag close to her.

Jenna, Saul thought with a dart of frustration toward the American. She seemed so intent on picking on every little thing Isa found important, why was she so bothered about protesting some dating site? Why couldn't she see the girl was trying to make the world better. Like his Nicky was.

'It's important, *Dad*,' Nicky had said when he'd stomped out of the house to his first protest. He'd joined an anti-fascist group who were doing a counterdemonstration to an EDL march.

Saul was by no means in support of the EDL, but throwing his fifteen-year-old son in their path hadn't been his idea of good parenting. But there had been no one else there to back him up by that point; Saul had been floundering on his own as a widower and sub-par father for the best part of two years, and any respect Nicky might have once had for his father had long since evaporated. Nicky had left the house, deaf to Saul's admonition, and had not returned home till the following day, refusing to say what had happened but sporting a cut on his forehead. Saul had been glued to the news all night, watching as the two protests had turned nasty, but he'd pushed down his fatherly instinct to go out himself, run into the fray and save his son. That would, he knew, push Nicky even further away. But it had turned out doing nothing had pushed Nicky away anyhow. Saul really hadn't figured out what to do for the best without Linda there to guide him.

'Are you OK, Jess?' Chloe asked as Saul pressed his palms to his knees and hoisted himself up with an audible grunt.

'Yeah,' Jess answered weakly. 'This feels a bit better now.' She blinked up at Saul and gave a half smile. 'Thanks.'

A thick tension fell over the group as the reality settled on them again that one of them had pulled out a knife and slashed Jess. Everyone who had trained their phone lights on Jess's arm now stepped away from each other, shining them around the carriage instead. Everybody seemed intent on blending into the mostly innocent crowd.

Jess reached her good hand into her pocket and pulled out her phone, flicking her torchlight on. It lasted only a few seconds before evidently proving too much for her waning battery.

Looking at the black screen, Jess raised her eyebrows and gave a shrug. 'Guess that's no use then.'

'I've only got 5 per cent,' Liam said, and Saul thought he

heard regret in the young lad's voice that he'd wasted so much playing his game earlier.

Saul gave a sigh and ran a hand over his thinning hair, feeling every bump of his almost bald head press against his palm. 'Mine died a while ago,' he admitted. 'Although,' he added, muttering to himself, 'I'm sure I do have a little torch somewhere.' He patted down his pockets, already knowing it wasn't in there from his earlier search, then stepped toward his jacket where it lay abandoned on the ledge behind the seats, and patting down those pockets too. Isa moved her torch as she shifted, and Saul caught a glimmer of metal from something on the seat below his jacket.

'Oh there it is,' he said to no one in particular, and stuck his hand in the crease between the seat and the backrest, fishing it out. It must have fallen out of his suit pocket. He clicked it and a weak beam of light emitted from the end of the thick red casing. 'It's not much, but it's something, at least.'

It took him a moment to realize that everyone had stopped their fidgeting and turned to stare directly at him, horror etched onto each one of their faces.

'Is that . . .' Jess began before trailing off and restarting. 'Is that a *knife*?'

Saul looked down at the Swiss Army knife in his hand, his own sense of horror now falling into place. How could he have been so stupid? His eyes met Isa's, her face creasing into disappointment.

He hadn't been thinking, he'd just wanted his own source of light. This dark, it was playing tricks on him, and he didn't like other people being in control of when he would be cast into blackness or not. He hadn't thought it through. But as he looked at Isa, he saw the same look of betrayal he'd seen on Nicky's face so many times before.

How could he have been so stupid as to bring his knife out?

Twenty-Five

Jess felt like she was going mad. A sudden, visceral urge to jump up, flip the emergency door release and sprint down the tunnel away from the situation surged through her. She'd lost complete track of this investigation, if anyone could even call it that, and every action and statement had lodged itself in her mind as evidence – whether it was or not.

Everyone was staring at Saul, the penknife in his hand. His own expression seemed shocked when he recognized what he was holding.

'*You* did it?' Jenna said, not an accusation – a declaration. 'You slashed Jess?' She gestured vaguely down to where Jess was sitting, still cradling her cumbersomely dressed arm.

'No!' Saul replied, wide-eyed and startled. 'Oh my goodness, no, of course not!' He flailed around and gestured to the seat Jess had seen him rooting in underneath his discarded jacket. 'I didn't even have this on me, I just found it again on the seat there.' He gestured wildly to the spot. 'It must have fallen out of my jacket pocket.'

'That's true,' Isa said fairly, 'he did just find the torch on that seat.' She gestured with her phone light to the seat a couple over from the one where she was sitting next to Jess. 'I saw him.'

'It's not a torch,' Amelia spat, eyes narrowing on Saul, 'it's a *knife*. You must have stabbed the driver too! And then wanted to scare Jess off from finding out it was you!' Her voice had grown wild, her tone undulating over the accusations. But, Jess had to admit, they were accusations that made sense. But why would Saul be so foolish to then parade the so far missing weapon in front of everyone?

'No, no!' Saul's voice had now abandoned the calm sensibility Jess had grown used to from him, catching desperately on his denials. 'Look, I *didn't* have it on me!' he insisted. 'And, and' – he looked frantically down at the penknife and began to scrabble with the attachments, the torch's weak white beam bouncing jarringly off the ceiling and windows of the carriage as he jiggled it in his unsteady hands. From Saul's expression, Jess thought that even he didn't know what to expect when he pulled the largest blade free, pinched between his thumb and forefinger. A look of palpable but pleasantly surprised relief flooded his face as he inspected the blade in the beams of phone light that had zeroed in on him. 'Look!' he declared triumphantly, holding it up. 'The blade on this knife is perfectly clean, and there's no blood on the handle or anything. Surely, if I'd used it to attack someone, I couldn't have got it so perfectly clean in the dark.' He gestured down to himself, his white shirt and blue suit trousers free of bloodstains.

Jess held out her hand, gesturing for him to give her the penknife so she could inspect it more closely. Saul obliged and handed her the weighty tool. Jenna shifted her torch so Jess could see more clearly, but Amelia kept hers trained on Saul and Jess thought she might have seen one too many old cop films where they got a confession from someone by shining a light directly into their eyes. Jess turned the knife over and over in her hands, picking out a few more of the attachments, but Saul was right – there didn't seem to be any blood on it at all. She thought back to the wiped smear on the driver's shirtsleeve. The killer had already made one effort to clean off the weapon, so they would probably have done the same thing following Jess's attack. But this knife was thoroughly clean; it was possible the SOCOs could take it apart and see if any blood had dripped down into the mechanism, but as Jess examined it under the light, squinting down into the gaps, she was sure there was no blood visible to the naked eye.

She frowned and then looked back up at Saul, taking in his sweaty and dishevelled – but blood-free – appearance. He had produced a packet of tissues to clean and dress Jess's wound, so she supposed he could have one extra crumpled in his pocket, streaked with bloody smears. She turned her head to the seat where she'd seen him rooting around and tried to picture the chaos of the dark. He *could* have had it in his pocket, slashed her and then tossed it onto the seat. But would he have had time to clean it so thoroughly?

It was one more murky detail of this case that looked so temptingly like concrete evidence but relied too much on conjecture.

'It is clean,' she admitted to the group, then blew out a weary sigh. 'I don't know if this is the knife that cut me or not, but I have to say, it would have been quick and impressive work to get it *this* clean in the dark.' She heard Saul give a relieved exhale. 'I'm going to keep this for now,' she said, looking up at Saul. 'It still might be evidence. Besides, seeing as we know there's someone violent on board, I don't think it's the best idea to have a knife lying around.'

She stood up and moved over to where she'd originally been sitting, her crumpled trench coat and evening bag still on the seat. Reaching into her bag, she fished out the string of dog-poo bags she knew would be languishing inside. Jess was always surprised at the dog paraphernalia she could locate on herself at any given moment – spilled treats, poo bags, even the odd ball turned up in pockets and bags she had no recollection of ever using on a dog walk. But in this case, the connected crinkled green bags would work very nicely for holding evidence. She secured the knife inside one, tying it in a tight knot, and zipped it back in her evening bag, before dropping it on top of the nest of her trench coat. Then she straightened up and scrutinized the group of people now staring at her.

She could feel the darkness pressing in from behind her, as if it could climb in through the windows, seep around the edges of the door frame and suffocate her in its embrace. The lights pointed in her direction from the remaining five phones were too bright and sent purple splodges pricking across her vision. Everyone's face was cast in a dramatic shadow of clean lines between the light and the dark where the patchy beams glanced off the gathered group. They were looking at her like they expected her to say something, but she did not know what she could say. Her arm throbbed, although Amelia's co-codamol did seem to be kicking in to take the edge off.

Before she said anything, she wanted to get some things straight in her own brain first. So she allowed the silence to grow thick as moss, and mentally took herself back to the drawing board. What did she know for certain, what concrete facts did she have?

Twenty-Six

Jess knew the victim had three wounds in his neck caused by a small blade. She knew that Saul had been in possession of something that matched that description.

She knew that Matt had been in attendance at a pub that had had a riot last week. She did not know for certain that anyone else on this tube had also been there.

She knew . . . Jess paused and racked her brain for anything else she'd seen or found. She replayed her search of the driver's cab and snagged on something curious she'd nearly forgotten. The cut wires. She still couldn't place the reasoning for that, especially if the culprit had orchestrated the whole blackout. And if they hadn't, why would an opportunist want to delay them getting to freedom any longer than they had to?

Those were the only three concrete facts Jess had about this case so far. It was not enough. She needed more. Back in her days on the force, once she'd determined what she definitely *did* know, she would list any potential leads that might bulk out the evidence. She didn't have any leads down here per se, but she did have suspicions and unanswered questions – any one of which could hold key information.

Saul had access to a potential murder weapon, and through his job he could perhaps have had the ability to cause the blackout to facilitate the murder.

Scott was volatile, angry and with the marks of a physical altercation in the last week or so – an altercation the victim was possibly also a part of. Scott was an opportunist, taking advantage of a genuine citywide electrical fault. But why cut the wires? Why did he want them stuck down there even longer? His whole demeanour made Jess want him as the culprit, but she couldn't escape the fact she had nothing but conjecture. If Scott had done it, she still needed a lot more to prove it.

What else did she not yet know? Three lies so far tonight had been told to her, and Jess was well trained to recognize and remember lies. Jenna had lied about where she was headed, and Isa had been shady enough to also not answer the same question. The teens had lied about what they did, heard or saw during the blackout. Another memory poked her – a crossed look from Jenna to the teens before she'd told her lie. Were they all somehow in on it together? Some strange ploy for fame and followers?

Every scenario at once felt ridiculous but also true, and Jess worried about what the tiredness and stress was doing to her faculties. Would any of these theories hold muster in what she now thought of as the outside world? Nicole seared into her thoughts again, that fist pounding toward her stomach. *Use that gut.*

Jess had failed to fight for her gut feeling before – on her last case. And that had led her right there, taking the tube home after drinks as a regular civilian, her investigative mind rusty having not been used in a whole year. But that hadn't been just down to *her*. Her whole team had played their part. Ignoring her instructions, so sure her leads were misguided. And then, when she'd reprimanded them for disobeying direct orders, they'd appealed to the higher-ups. Her CO instructing her informally over a 'casual coffee' to drop it. That, yes, they shouldn't have disobeyed, but wasn't it better to have coppers with *good* instincts rather than those that blindly followed orders? The not-so-subtle implication was clear: Jess's instincts were bad, and she should allow her subordinates to keep following their own noses.

The case shouldn't have been a complicated one. The body of an elderly woman found beaten to death in her front room. Some signs of forced entry, and the SOCOs determined it was likely she'd answered the door and the culprit barged in. Her team had immediately set their sights on a string of burglaries that had swept the area, the culprit a teenager known to them, but who had so far managed to keep slipping from their grasp. Now he'd turned violent, killed somebody – an innocent old woman at that – and her team were going to nail him for it. Jess hadn't bought it. She'd had run-ins with the teenager before and he was a little scrote, but he was no killer. Instead, Jess wanted them to pursue the victim's daughter, whose reaction to her mother's death had been both overdramatic and dry-eyed. Subtleties Jess had picked up during her statements and interviews had told her there was a strained relationship, a resentment that the victim had started giving money directly to her grandchild, cutting her daughter out of the transaction. The twelve-year-old grandchild had passively revealed this to Jess while sitting hunched up on the sofa next to her mum. 'I miss my nan,' she'd said, teary-eyed. 'She was always doing nice things for me. She'd just given me three hundred pounds so I could go on the French exchange next term.'

'That was my mum, wasn't it,' the girl's mother had replied, tight-lipped. 'Always thinkin' she knew best about what we could do with money.' She'd blown out a frustrated sigh. 'You don't even need a French exchange trip,' she'd added, turning on her daughter.

Jess had asked her team to look into their financials, look into the victim's daughter to see if she had any history of violence, to interview the little girl alone to see if she knew anything. But they'd all ignored her, unable to register any nuance in the case, seeing it only as a violent – *male* – attack. Her CO had told her she was overthinking it, and Jess had backed down. Already so tired of the fight after fourteen years on the force, having to fight twice as hard for her ideas to be heard, and now her one ally was gone too. She'd found herself growing wearier and wearier with the prospect of each new case that threw up anything other than a simple solution, her patience rubbing thin at home, unintentionally blowing up any time she sensed Alex and the girls weren't listening to her. She now knew, having spoken to Liv since she'd transferred out, that they had been trapped in an unfortunately toxic command. Their CO had come up in the eighties when women on the force were a novelty, tasked with paperwork or fingerprinting, perhaps the occasional – safe – patrol. He was overdue for retirement but was clinging on by his brittle yellow fingernails.

So she'd allowed her team to pursue the wrong culprit while she worked alone. The day she finally got the granddaughter to admit her mum had been furious when she'd found the stash of twenties in an envelope in her school bag. The day she tracked down her suspect's three previous arrests for assault, and found conclusive footage from a video doorbell across the street that her team had not even bothered to check – that same day, a struggling seventeen-year-old kid who'd spent his life in foster care only to be spat out at sixteen, alone with nothing – had been found hanging in a holding cell, brought in for an endless interrogation over a murder he hadn't committed.

That was the day Jess decided to leave. She'd done what she could, but the system didn't want to change – even if she was trying to do it from the inside. In those first few weeks after leaving, she had beaten herself up for being too weak. If she'd been more like Nicole, she'd have stared down her CO, broadened her shoulders and defended her ideas with loud, brash words. But that wasn't how Jess communicated. She was a product of a society that had told her to keep quiet but then changed the rules on her, accusing her of keeping too quiet. And after those first few weeks, her internal anger became external. Toward her CO, toward her team, toward Nicole. Why couldn't she be a strong and respected woman without having to pretend she was a man?

She'd been reprimanded for overthinking, and here she was, in the early hours of a Saturday morning on a trapped tube, doing it again. But when lives were at stake, Jess considered that overthinking was far better than under. Her instincts had turned out to be right on that previous occasion, and on many more before that. And as Jess tried to organize and prioritize her suspicions, to make a plan for her next steps – Amelia decided to take things into her own hands.

Amelia

'That's it,' Amelia said, directing her phone light toward the panel next to the doors and flipping up the cover of the emergency handle. 'I can't take it down here anymore. I need to get home.' She pulled the red handle down and a *pop* and *hiss* sounded as the doors loosened their grip on each other. Amelia pried her fingers between them, easily pulling them apart. She turned back to the group and gestured vaguely to Saul. 'I still think he did it. And if he did, then I don't believe we're in danger of the electrics coming back on.' Saul began to protest his innocence but she interrupted him, holding up a hand. 'Even if you didn't do it, the power's obviously not coming back on anytime soon.' She turned her attention to everyone else. 'We can't be far from Baker Street. I'll send back help if . . .' She hesitated and forced an intake of breath. 'Well, if no one else wants to come with me.'

Amelia had had about enough of the whole situation. There was a murdered body, an attack on someone else and now, *now*, another person revealed to have had a weapon that could have done it all and *still* people wouldn't listen to her about getting off! Amelia knew she carried her emotions close to the surface, especially after the last year, and she knew the thin film that kept them in check had worn through in several places tonight. She'd seen the exchanged looks dismissing her as a drama queen; the way Jenna had pressed her mouth thin and barely suppressed an eye-roll when Amelia had been on the verge of a panic attack. But the danger of staying on that train was clear, and if no one else could see it, then she would point it out and hope she could persuade *someone* to come with her.

She stuck her head out of the door and assessed the space between the carriage and the damp curved brick of the tunnel, then turned her gaze toward the gaping dark at the front of the train. An unconscious swallow shuddered down her throat as she realized the black was denser than she had imagined it would be. For the first time, her plan of wandering into the tunnel did not seem as simple as she'd imagined. She'd been so blinded by her desperation to get off, she hadn't allowed herself to contend with the reality. All the same, she was not going to be put off now. Her body stiffened a touch and then, with one last look toward the rest of the passengers, she climbed down off the tube.

Twenty-Seven

Amelia looked like an unsuspecting deer on a country road about to be ploughed up by a Land Rover as she stood frozen in the narrow gap between tube and tunnel – illuminated by four torch beams that sent long black shadows off in different directions on the brick wall behind her. Jess could tell the realization was settling on her that even a five-minute walk in this solid dark with only a phone torchlight would not be an easy stroll.

'Urh!' Amelia gave a sudden yelp and hopped backward as two rats the size of chihuahuas scurried across her path to escape the beams of light. She shuddered and looked appealingly up at the passengers now crowded in an arc around the doors. Her gaze seemed to land first on Jenna, then Jess, then back to Jenna. Jess considered that they were the likeliest peers for Amelia to cling on to. She certainly wouldn't want to be wandering alone in a dark tunnel with a strange man, and Isa and the teens were young, they'd probably be even more spooked than she was.

'I'll – er,' Isa began to speak, but with less confidence now she'd also seen the reality of the walk down the tunnel. 'I'll come with you.' Saul gave a worried murmur, but Isa nodded determinedly to herself. 'Yeah, no, I'll come too.' She seemed to be convincing herself as much as anyone else that she was capable of this. She took a deep breath and stepped towards the edge of the carriage, lowering herself down to the ground with one hand on the bar. Amelia looked less than impressed, and Jess saw her eyes flick pleadingly at the gathered group, where Jess and Jenna stood next to each other.

'I mean, I'd go too,' Scott said with a nasty tone, 'but I wouldn't want to be accused of rape or anything, being alone in a tunnel with two birds.'

'Well, don't rape anyone then,' Isa snapped.

'Not as simple as that, is it though?'

'All right,' Jess said, a weary snap to her voice.

'Yeah, Jesus,' Jenna said with a drawl, 'I can't hear this *again*. I'll go.' She held her palms up in a surrender motion and Jess saw Amelia's body language immediately relax. Her shoulders slumped, and she gave a relieved smile in Jenna's direction. Amelia didn't wait for Jenna to get down off the carriage before taking a couple of exploratory steps toward the front of the train.

'Besides,' Jenna said under her breath to Jess, 'I don't think Isa should be alone with Amelia out there. She's already an anxious mess.' She rolled her eyes unsympathetically. 'What's Isa going to do if she has another breakdown?'

Jess thought Jenna had a point, although it seemed cruel to hold someone's understandable anxiety against them. 'And what are you going to do?'

'Tell her to sort herself out,' Jenna answered simply, and Jess thought that probably Jenna *was* best suited to delivering Amelia some tough love should it be needed.

Jess knew there was nothing she could do to stop them from

going out there; they were adults – they knew the risks. At least, with Jenna gone, she would have more chance of getting back into the driver's cab to look for evidence on Matt's phone. But a voice in her head kept arguing that they should all be going together. Jess felt a throb pulse through her arm at the thought of what had happened the last time they'd all been plunged into blackness. *She* especially did not want to be out in the dark tunnel, waiting to fall victim to the next knife attack. But then would her chances of survival be any better if she remained in the carriage with the killer?

Panicked thoughts shot through her mind in bright streaks like the multicoloured lights on a long-exposure photo of a cityscape. The killer had taken pains to hide their identity so far; if they had chosen to remain in the carriage with her, she could only hope that they wouldn't make a second attempt on her life in plain sight and with everyone on high alert. She hovered in the doorway, watching as Jenna climbed down to the tracks. After a moment's hesitation, she followed.

'Are you going too?' Chloe asked, eyes flashing toward Scott and Saul, her voice catching. Jess understood the role she'd come to occupy for Chloe – proxy mum, even if Chloe wasn't being 100 per cent honest with her.

'No,' Jess said as she stepped down from the tube. 'I'll be back in a minute – I just want to see what they're dealing with.'

Chloe gave a tight nod of understanding, but chewed her lip uncomfortably in that way Jess had come to recognize.

'I promise,' she told the girl earnestly, 'I'll only be a minute.'

Chloe

Chloe felt a little bubble of blood pop on the inside of her lip where she was chewing it too hard. She didn't want Jess to go – Jess was the only person, other than Liam, she could be certain wasn't a knife-wielding-EMP-setting-off maniac. She took a step back from the tube door, leaning into Liam, who was behind her. She groped for his hand, found it and slipped hers into his sweaty grasp. As she looked up at him, he gave her a little frown, questioning if she was OK. She didn't answer but stepped back toward the seats cast in inky blackness and dragged him with her as she plonked herself down. Scott and Saul half turned in the direction of their movement, but Chloe kept her head down, ignoring them. She wanted to be far away from anyone's grasp, so she'd have enough time to see them coming. Liam slumped back in his chair and yawned, and Chloe envied him. She was sitting upright, her phone light trained in a halo around her so she could keep watch.

She was not going to be left vulnerable in the dark again.

'Babe, you OK?' Liam asked softly through a yawn, noticing

her stiff position on the edge of her seat. Chloe didn't answer, but gave a quick, stiff nod in his direction. 'Don't worry,' Liam said with a faux-calmness she recognized from when he'd been reassuring her the night before their GCSE results. She knew his own impending grades would have been playing on his mind too, but he'd put that aside for the night and done everything he could to distract her in the face of a near panic attack. 'No one wants to kill *you*.' He'd said it with a jokey lightness and put his hand on her back in a move she knew was meant to be comforting, but she couldn't stop herself flinching away from him.

'Sorry,' she said, blinking. 'You took me by surprise.'

Liam looked hurt, but nodded acceptingly and removed his hand to tuck it back under his armpit.

He didn't understand.

Someone *did* want to kill her. Chloe knew that *she* was the intended target of the knife attack on Jess.

Ever since they'd got some light back and discovered Jess's injury, Chloe had been replaying the movements of the second blackout over and over again. She was sure she wasn't misremembering, hadn't distorted the memories in a daze of panic and confusion. They'd all been huddled together, Jess behind Chloe's shoulder, although Chloe didn't know it was definitely her until afterwards.

Someone had lunged toward her, although at the time Chloe had thought they must have stumbled in the dark. She'd called out 'Hey, watch it!' and stepped back, falling into the person behind her – apparently Jess. But the figure had carried on lunging, although Chloe had naively assumed they were falling. As she felt them land on Jess, Chloe had scooted out of the way so she wouldn't get crushed. A few blissful innocent moments had passed where she'd been able to breathe freely in her newfound space away from the confused group. But as she fumbled for her phone to get some light, she'd heard Jess scream.

That was the moment she knew: it wasn't Jess the killer was after. They'd been aiming for her.

And Chloe knew why.

Twenty-Eight

Jenna had already followed Isa and Amelia to the front of the tube by the time Jess climbed down, and she could see the tunnel illuminated by their phone torches, doing little to penetrate the black more than a few metres ahead. Without a light of her own, she groped for the side of the train, reaching her good arm over to run her hand along the metal as a guide, her feet tentatively sweeping the blackness around them for obstacles before taking a step. She felt like they were entrenched in some deep bog, wading through the unknown and wishing her ankles and shins weren't bare as she imagined the scurrying of rats prickling her skin.

She came to a stop next to the three others at the head of the train. 'Are you all sure about this?' she asked, following their gaze out into the black hole ahead.

Isa gave a small jump of surprise at Jess's voice and stepped back to illuminate her with her torch.

'Sorry,' Jess said. 'Didn't mean to startle you.'

'Are you coming too?' Amelia asked.

Jess shook her head. 'No, I'll stay. I don't think Chloe wants to be left alone on there.'

'Scott,' Isa said tightly.

Jess didn't confirm or deny her assessment, although she thought it was probably accurate. Instead, she said. 'Look, the stations aren't far apart – a ten-minute walk above ground. But we don't know where we've stopped, how far it is in either direction. And in this' – she gestured to the blackness – 'a few minutes will feel like a lifetime, and could be dangerous. If you're in any doubt, come back to the train.' She gestured to the city above them. 'They'll get to us eventually.'

'I'm not coming back to the train,' Amelia said determinedly. 'I'm going home.' She paused and added quickly: 'But we'll make sure to send help – there must be officials around the stations, police on the street. We'll tell them the situation with . . .' Her voice trailed off, reluctant to say the words; instead, one hand flicked vaguely in the direction of the driver's cab behind them. 'Well, the situation with the driver. Then they'll definitely prioritize you.'

Jess nodded, but she wasn't sure Amelia saw her, all three torch beams having now been turned toward the tunnel ahead and the route the three women were about to take. Heavy silence settled on them. Something had shifted, being out there, off the carriage that had contained them for the last couple of hours. Jess felt it herself. Not relief, that was too strong a word. But the reminder that perhaps they were not the last people left on earth, that *something* connected them to the lives they had all been trying to get home to.

'I'm . . . er . . .' Amelia broke the silence with a quiet voice, keeping her light directed away, so she spoke from the shadows. 'I'm sorry if I've been a bit, um, *hysterical*.'

'Don't use that word,' Isa said kindly. 'You've been rightly anxious.'

Jess saw Amelia's shadowed mouth twitch affectionately. 'It was seeing that knife!' She flung her arm out behind her. 'How is no one else worried about him?' She turned her attention earnestly toward Jess. 'Are you *sure* you want to stay on that train, given what he's already *done* to you?'

Jess opened her mouth to give assurances that she was on high alert, and that she really did not think Saul's penknife had ever seen blood let alone slashed open her arm or killed a man – but Isa responded instead.

'Saul didn't do anything,' she said, her tone confident, unwavering. 'He's not the kind.'

Amelia blew out an annoyed sigh but gave Jess one last meaningful look before deciding to drop the argument. Jess figured Amelia thought she'd done her best; the important thing was that *she* was out of there, and if Saul went on a murderous rampage in the carriage at least she wouldn't be caught up in it. Instead, she said with a frustrated exhale, 'What a *fucking* year.' She shook her head. 'This is the last thing I need.'

To Jess's surprise, Jenna gave a small laugh, her usually brash tone softening. 'I hear that,' she said comradely, then turned her head toward Amelia. 'And Isa's right, don't call yourself hysterical. Grief doesn't just go away, and in a situation like this . . .' She left the sentence unfinished, but they all knew what she meant. Isolation and fear – it pushed the darkest moments, the darkest memories of your life to the surface. Amelia had her grief. Jess had her guilt.

'You lost someone?' Isa asked intuitively.

'My grandma,' Jenna said. 'Not recently or anything, and she was old, it wasn't . . .' She paused to glance at Amelia, who was staring ahead, her thoughts lost in the tunnel. 'It wasn't a tragedy or anything. But she helped raise me, and I still miss her. And tonight, I keep hearing her' – she moved her hand to her ear and opened and closed it like a feeding bird – 'yapping away in my ear. Do—' She stopped herself, considering for a moment before ploughing on: 'Do you guys think the veil is thinner down here?'

Jess saw Amelia turn to Jenna with a curious frown on her shadowed face. 'Veil?'

'You know, between the worlds.' Jenna had answered so confidently, it took Jess a moment to understand what she was saying. Jenna suddenly laughed, breaking the confused tension between Jess, Amelia and Isa, who clearly had had no response to this. 'Sorry, didn't mean to freak you out. I don't mean *ghosts*, not really.' Her torchlight wavered as she gave a shrug. 'I dunno, I guess I just feel her sometimes, like she's really there. And it's been super strong tonight.'

Jess thought it was understandable to imagine your lost loved ones at a time like this, for the memories to be so vivid that they felt real. But she didn't say that. If it gave Jenna comfort to think her grandma's spirit was down here in the tunnel with them, then who was she to take that away from her?

'I feel Libby too,' Amelia said quietly. 'And everything comes flooding back like a punch in the stomach. Like I've only just got the phone call. Like for one brief moment I'd forgotten she'd gone.' Quiet lapped at them for another beat, then Amelia readjusted her stance. 'Right, let's go.'

'Be careful,' Jess said, turning to return to the tube. 'Would one of you light my way back? My phone died,' she added with a shrug.

Jenna turned her beam on her for a moment, then she flipped it around and handed it to Jess. 'Take mine,' she said. 'My case has a battery pack in it, it should hold charge for a couple more hours.' She gestured to Isa and Amelia. 'They can light my way to the station, and you don't know how long you guys will be down here. Chloe and Scott's phones won't last forever.'

'No,' Jess said, holding her palm up. 'You need it.' She gestured to the tunnel.

But Jenna shook her head. 'We have two already, and I guess the idea is we'll be outta here soon. But you're gonna be stuck in that carriage.'

Jess gave an internal shudder at the thought of being stuck on the tube, all sources of light diminished, sitting in the penetrating dark, her mind taunting her with knives in her flesh and rats on her feet.

'All right.' Jess accepted the phone with a grateful nod. 'Thank you. I'll get it back to you as soon as we get up there. Or if you guys end up coming back.'

Jenna gave a nod, agreeing that it was a likely possibility.

'Jenna,' Jess said, feeling the question rise up inside her – the gesture of handing over her phone thawing something between them. As if Jenna was admitting that she didn't really think Jess was a likely suspect, fraudulently posing as a police officer. 'Where were you headed tonight?'

Jenna gave a curious smile, her brow crinkled in surprise at the question. 'On a date,' she answered easily. Then lowered her voice, but it had a playful lilt. 'But don't go telling everyone I have late-night booty calls in foreign countries. I have young fans.'

'Are we going or not?' Amelia snapped, and took a few tentative steps forward into the tunnel, lowering her beam to illuminate the ground ahead as she navigated between the raised lines.

'Be careful,' Jess told them again, before lighting her own way back with Jenna's torch. As she slid between the curved metal of the train and the brick of the tunnel, she considered how easily Jenna had delivered the answer this time around. Had it taken her this long to craft a believable response?

Jess made her way back to the doors and hoisted herself up by the brown bar. As she straightened up, she came face to face with Saul, illuminated by the weak bluish glow coming from Chloe's phone. There was a deep line between his brows and his jaw visibly flexed under tension.

'You shouldn't have let them go,' he said.

And Jess felt a bolt of fear scream through her.

Twenty-Nine

Forgetting for a moment the torch in her own hand, Jess's eyes frantically sought out the other sources of light and positions of everyone else – half expecting to find a bloodbath and three brutalized corpses. But despite the nervous adrenaline that had surged through her, she felt her breath steady as she made out Chloe and Liam now back in their seats behind Saul. Perfectly fine, albeit tense. Scott was leaning against the divider panel, head against the glass, lit-up phone hanging down by his thigh. Jess pulled herself back from her instinctive fear, the remembered feeling of a blade tearing through her flesh, and centred herself in the facts. Saul's knife had been clean. Everyone else was OK. Saul was not a threat.

'We should have gone with them,' Chloe said, although she sounded uncertain. She turned her head briefly to look out of one of the useless blacked-out windows as if she could see whether they were already too far away. 'All of us should go together.'

Saul spun toward her. 'No,' he said firmly, and Jess heard the disciplinarian in his tone. 'I've told you, if the electrics come back on you don't want to be out there. The tunnels aren't lit, so it'll still be dark and all it would take is one stumble and your feet could hit the live line.' He turned back to Jess, a thick swallow rippling his throat. 'Shit,' he said, before repeating, 'we shouldn't have let any of them go.' He looked for a moment as if he wanted to chase after them, drag them back. Jess thought of the sensation she'd had of wading through a bog, disconnected from her senses, every step a tentative exploration of the ground in front. And she realized Saul was right: if the electrics did come back on, it would be all too easy to come in contact with a live line.

'Saul,' Jess said calmly, her earlier authority returning. 'For what it's worth, I think you're right to be cautious.' She turned to Chloe and Liam. 'It's dark out there, darker than you have probably ever seen, especially living in London. But' – she turned back to Saul – 'they're all adults. They understand the risks and they've decided to go. We can't stop them.'

'Isa's barely an adult,' Saul said.

'But she still is one,' Jess reminded him gently. 'You two, however,' she added, indicating Chloe and Liam, 'aren't. And I won't let you take an unnecessary risk and have to explain to your parents why we let you go.'

Chloe and Liam looked at each other but accepted it, relieved to have someone else be responsible for their decisions. Jess glanced at Scott, who didn't seem to be making any moves to leave the train or even put up a fight. Remembering Jenna's torch, she raised it high to illuminate the carriage. Scott looked exhausted. His shoulders were slumped, head lolled forward from where it had been resting on the glass, and his chest rose and fell in deep, deliberate breaths. When the light hit him, he moved his head up to find its source, and stared at Jess with a drawn face, heavy bags creasing the thin skin under his eyes. She wondered for a moment if he was about to start another argument with her, but instead he met her eye for a brief moment and then hung his head again, chin returning to his chest.

Jess raised her eyebrows at Saul, checking if they had any other problems – anything else he wanted to discuss. He stepped back, his body language slumping in similar exhaustion to Scott's. He raised an arm to his forehead and wiped away at the sweat that had gathered there with the back of his hand, but he did not say anything more.

She waited for him to retake his seat, stretching his long legs out across the aisle and leaning back as if hoping he could really relax. Jess strode down toward the driver's door, lifting her feet clear of Saul's shins, feeling the drying blood on her dress scrape crustily on her bare legs as she did. She passed by Jenna's crumpled leather jacket and Amelia's abandoned bags, forgotten in the stress and desperation of the last few hours. No one said anything as she reached the door, not even Scott, and Jess did not turn back to see if they had moved to acknowledge what she was doing.

She got into the cab and closed the door behind her, leaning back against it for a moment to take a breath, which she immediately regretted as she tasted rust on the air from the spilled blood. She was pointing Jenna's phone straight ahead, the white spotlight reflecting back at her with a disorientating halo on the windows. The bright light spiked a headache somewhere behind her left eyebrow, a familiar twinge from her pregnancy migraines. Jess did not have the time for one of those right now. She stepped forward off the door, and directed the torchlight down toward where she knew the driver was lying, slain. As she did, she adjusted her grip on the phone, her thumb slipping from the side onto the screen, which immediately lit up, unlocked. Jenna must have changed her settings to the maximum time before it automatically locked, something which Jess supposed made sense if you spent your days recording yourself. Jess had remembered in lockdown, Mia – then only five – had been determined for Jess to learn a dance from TikTok with her, but Jess's phone had annoyingly shut itself down every few minutes, demanding a face or pin code to continue its use.

Jenna's phone had opened on a draft Instagram story she must have been curating to distract herself, a frozen white circle in the bottom right corner telling Jess it had failed to upload in the void of signal. The first picture was of Jenna in front of the sign for Bond Street tube station, something Jess supposed would look glamorous to her American followers who didn't know of the burnt-oil fast-food smell or stalls selling plastic light-up tat. Jess kept tapping, professional curiosity piqued, wanting to see photographic evidence of what Jenna had done with her day. She flashed through a few more pictures and videos. Jenna shopping in a well-lit designer handbag section, the on-screen text reading *When the hustle pays off*. Jenna drinking a glass of champagne at a bar, a plate of sushi in front of her. Jess got bored as she kept tapping through the near identical images, which finally ended on the selfie Jess had seen Jenna take when she'd first boarded the tube. A perfect pout, and wide 'smizing' eyes worthy of Tyra Banks, the grim Bakerloo line carriage framing her from behind. This caption read *Livin' like a local*. Jess struggled to understand how this type of content could keep over a million followers glued to Jenna's account, but so far this Instagram story did at least seem to prove Jenna's account of what she'd been doing all day had been truthful. Jess closed Instagram, the home screen popping up with the usual mix of multicoloured tiles. Jenna seemed to have an inordinate number of photo-editing apps, all the social media platforms and, Jess stifled a small smile, the familiar purple square for Hookd. Maybe Jenna really had been heading out for a one-night stand in a foreign country.

Jess propped Jenna's phone up in the driver's storage cubby, against the bottle of Lucozade with the torch facing out so it provided something akin to light for the whole cab, albeit uneven and too bright, with black patches of shadow gathering like mould in unreached corners. She pulled Matt's phone from her dress pocket and, feeling uneasy again, bent over to unlock it using his unmoving face. When the home screen successfully popped up, Jess straightened her spine and stepped back, leaning against the door to take some pressure off her tired feet. She hadn't realized until now how sore they were, how swollen and sweaty from the heat, the smarting of early blisters on the tops of her toes. She stared into Matt's phone, momentarily blank as to what she'd even wanted it for. So much had happened since Amelia had first reminded her about the football brawl. Jess's mind was spinning that only a short time ago she'd thought the answer might simply lie in connecting one football hooligan to another.

She stared down at the now unlocked key to this stranger's life and wondered where to start. Thinking she may as well do this methodically, she moved her thumb to the first icon on the top left of the screen, a blue square with a white envelope. Matt's emails popped up. Maybe he'd been sent a death threat that would clear this up nice and easily.

The first screen held nothing of any use, just spam and payment reminders, order confirmations and a few login notifications on other devices. She kept scrolling, still not catching anything of use, until she saw an email from TfL, Matt's employer. She opened it up and found it was his schedule for the month, the details of his shift pattern. Scrutinizing it for a moment longer, she wondered how difficult it would be to hack into someone's emails. Presumably not very difficult, considering the many stories of fraud and constant warnings of the importance of having strong, ever-changing passwords. She kept scrolling down the emails, well past the six-month mark, but found nothing else that snagged her attention, no death threats or warnings, no long-standing feuds being hashed out. In fact, the only emails he seemed to receive that weren't from a company were either his employer, or his sister, who had apparently moved to Australia to be a bush nurse and only had intermittent access to the internet. Matt's replies to her were too bland to read anything into, enquiries after her partner and updates on his days off, which seemed to be spent either watching football, going on a boys' night out, or the occasional visit to their granddad.

She closed the emails, giving them up as a bad job, and tapped instead on the WhatsApp icon. His top chat was with Damo, and Jess opened it to a stream of consciousness between two evidently very close mates. There were memes and impenetrable inside jokes between them, complaints about work and a countdown to an upcoming stag do in Prague. She kept scrolling up, the amount of content these two sent each other every day prompting sympathy for Damo, who didn't yet know that this chat would get no more updates. Finally, she stopped on a photograph Damo had sent Matt about a week ago. It showed Matt in a blue football shirt, one hand holding up a pint in cheers, the other in a thumbs up, his face beaming as blood poured from a cut by his hairline, streaking scarlet smears all the way down his face.

Showing Bec how we do in SE 😂

Then there was a gif of a street fight from some film Jess didn't recognize. So, Matt definitely had been in the Mason's Arms brawl that had hit the papers. Now she'd been reminded, Jess knew it had been against a group of Tooting Bec fans, who'd been making their way to the station en masse after a bad loss in the play-offs that saw Lewisham promoted. She didn't need to remember the specific details of how this one had started; it would have been the usual chants and taunts, one irate fan deciding to make it physical, the others quick to follow suit. She kept scrolling back to before the brawl but couldn't see anything that proved anyone else from the tube had been there. Closing the chat with Damo, she scanned down Matt's other recent chats, where her gaze landed curiously on one called *Hookd & Fookd*.

She opened it up and felt a shiver of ice slide down her spine.

The chat was full of photographs of unconscious naked girls, some partially covered in a sheet, some with a bra skewed around the waist. Each photo was accompanied by a caption along the lines of needing to get them out.

Uber already on the way

Promised her breakfast, I'll put a cereal bar in her bag.

As she kept scrolling up, she felt sick. There were dozens of pictures of vulnerable naked girls in this chat, all being shared without their knowledge to a group of six strangers. Feeling that these poor girls had had their privacy invaded enough, Jess closed it down and let the phone hang by her leg as she thought.

And something came back to her, a throwaway comment she hadn't known to pay attention to before. What had Jenna said? *I've learnt in my two weeks here, your men aren't exactly the romcom princes I was expecting.*

Jess's head snapped up, a new concern flooding her.

Had she just let the killer make an easy escape into the night?

Isa

The tension was thick as they made their tentative way along the tunnel. The curved brick felt closer than Isa had thought it would, the high raised lines bunching them close together as they walked three abreast down the centre. The light from two torches did not go very far down here, Isa soon learnt. And it seemed like they were working their way to nothing. She'd assumed, or hoped, that there would be a literal beacon at the end of the tunnel, Baker Street station lit up and ready to guide them home. But now she understood how stupid that had been, a citywide power cut meant lights off *everywhere*. Even when they got back to the surface, there would be no respite. Scurrying and scratching sounds seemed to bounce at them from all directions and Isa could only imagine a sea of writhing rats in the black areas untouched by their light.

She wondered if she should make conversation as they walked together. They'd all seemed to have a tender moment before, but that note of camaraderie had been lost as they'd embarked on their slow, nervous journey. Neither Amelia nor Jenna were making moves to continue the chat, and so Isa decided she didn't need to either. Besides, she didn't even like either of them. Jenna with her social media following, and Amelia with her PR business – both had these vast platforms and used them in a way that was blatantly wrong. Sometimes Isa felt like she was pushing against an endless tide in her hopes of progress, why couldn't everyone see it the way she did? As she walked in the continued silence, her thoughts and frustrations continued to wind tighter and tighter through her, imagined conversations she'd start with them, perfectly honing her monologue to make them shudder with embarrassment for the way they'd lived their lives. But then she imagined their responses, both women laughing patronizingly at her that she was just a little girl who didn't understand the ways of the world, one day she'd need to *grow up* and those principals would fall by the wayside. It was exactly Isa's family's attitude to her, her vast array of successful siblings rolling their eyes as she launched into another speech at family dinners. The worst had been her dad, who'd smiled indulgently in the same way he had when she'd shown him her gymnastics routine at age seven and told her he was happy she'd found 'a hobby' she was passionate about.

Her frustration started to burn hotter through her, until, eventually she realized it had turned into full-blown rage. But Isa didn't want to calm it. She wanted to use it – that's what tonight had been all about, acting on that rage, using it for something productive, something *real*. Because Isa did agree with Jenna on one thing – protests weren't enough. They fell into the news for half an hour before something else pushed them out again, unless of course, they turned ugly. *Peaceful* protests got nothing done.

'*Shit*,' she hissed to herself, suddenly realizing something.

'What?' Amelia's response was quick, terse, on the edge of panic.

'Nothing,' Isa said, her lip curling into an annoyed snarl with herself. 'I realized I forgot my fucking bag on the tube.' Isa needed that bag, and she certainly didn't want Jess the detective to go rooting through it – she'd already seen the stickers and the scarf. But Isa felt the metal weight jangle against her knee in the low-slung pocket of her cargo pants, so at least had the most important thing she needed for tonight. She could improvise the rest.

'I've left everything too,' Amelia said, as if only just realizing it herself. 'I wasn't even thinking.' She gave a small sigh of annoyance. 'Oh, I hope I get it back, that wedding present wasn't cheap.'

Isa rolled her eyes but Jenna gave a murmur of agreed sympathy.

'I left my jacket,' she said. 'Got it at a vintage store in Brooklyn. I loved that jacket.' She stopped talking and twisted her head on her neck, back in the direction they'd just come.

'Are you thinking of going back?' Amelia sounded incredulous and stopped her walk to look back over her own shoulder into the blackness they'd journeyed through.

'Nah,' Jenna said, turning with a small shudder. 'Not worth it.'

Isa though, who had also stopped and turned to follow the direction of Jenna's gaze, was still considering. 'We've not been walking for that long,' she said, musingly.

'Feels like we have,' Jenna said. 'I hate it out here. I feel like someone's about to grab me from behind. It's too dark.' She gave another little shiver. 'Wonder how far away we are now?'

'I've no idea,' Amelia said, her tone musing. She looked back again in the direction they'd come from. 'Maybe it would have been quicker to go back to Regent's Park.'

Jenna gave an annoyed hiss. 'Are you saying we should turn around?'

'I'm saying,' Amelia snapped, 'I know as much as you about where exactly we are in this dark tunnel. But there's a chance Regent's Park is closer.' Silence fell between the three of them while they thought it through. 'Should' – Amelia broke the silence, her tone unconvinced but throwing her idea out anyway – 'should we split up?'

Isa thought quickly. If she volunteered, that would give her the excuse she needed to finish the job she'd set out to do tonight, make headlines. And without two chaperones. Plus, they *had* been walking for over five minutes; if they'd been closer to Baker Street, they would have hit it by now.

'No,' Amelia answered her own question. 'Ignore me, that's ridiculous. Let's keep going, we can't be far now. We should stick together.' She began walking again, her light bobbing in rhythm with her steps.

'Well I don't have a light,' Jenna said, stepping forward to catch up to Amelia's pace, 'so I'm stuck with you lot.'

'I'll go back,' Isa said, making the decision quickly, instinctively. She had unfinished business tonight and this could well be her chance to do it – without raising any suspicion. She thought through her plans and realized that, yes, it would be much easier if she was on her own. She could slip into the shadows, with nobody keeping an eye on her. Although she was willing to martyr herself for her cause, in an ideal world she could succeed *and* keep out of the grasp of the police. She did still have plans for her own future too, plans that wouldn't exactly flourish in prison.

'Isa, don't,' Amelia called back, 'come on, stay with us. It'll be safer for everyone – and you're only young, I couldn't have it on my conscience.'

'I'm not that fucking young,' Isa retorted. 'And I don't see what advantage being middle-aged is down here.' It was a cruel barb designed to sting as much as Amelia's unintentional swipe.

Amelia's bobbing torch stopped and she swung back to face Isa, still a few feet behind her. Isa had her phone pointed in their direction and saw Amelia's expression was not quite hurt, but more surprised confusion. 'All right,' she said in what Isa recognized as an infuriatingly amused tone, 'no need for that. Do whatever you please.' And then she turned back and continued her walk again, this time with a noticeably quicker step. Jenna didn't immediately follow and looked like she was about to say something. But Isa didn't give her the chance. She turned into the darkness and took a few steps, until she heard Jenna blow out a sigh and head back to Amelia with hurried footsteps and a breathy, 'Hey, wait up!'

Isa stopped walking and twisted to watch them leave, slinking back into the black shadows.

Thirty

Every new development or clue seemed to send Jess off into a spiral of even more unanswered questions. One apparent step forward in this case was like fifteen back. If Jenna was one of the girls photographed in that group chat, she certainly had a motive to want to kill Matt. Especially given her status – if a nude like that got out, her brand would surely be rocked. So now the questions beckoned: how did she find out that Matt had taken such a picture and shared it with his friends? Did Jenna have enough tech know-how to hack into his emails to find his shift pattern? And did she have enough money or influence to somehow cause a mass power cut?

Jess supposed Jenna probably did have enough money to settle a score if she wanted, and money bought influence. Or at least an EMP device. Jess frowned. Just because Chloe had only seen videos of home-made pocket versions, it didn't mean that professionals weren't selling more powerful ones – most likely on the dark web.

Jess didn't have much experience with the dark web, but

she'd worked with the cybercrime team over at the National Crime Agency on one case and knew that all it took was downloading a browser called Tor to access a million putrid corners most internet users could never dream existed. It was a lot to organize in the space of less than two weeks, Jess thought, but desperation could often yield the quickest of actions. She thought of Jenna standing guard over the crime scene, rallying the other passengers to stop Jess from investigating any further. But then she thought of her handing over her phone, a moment of solidarity between them. If Jenna really was the killer, why would she hand over something that possibly had incriminating evidence on it?

Jess's brain whirred. She had a potentially victimized one-night stand with a lot to lose out for revenge. A violent football rival. And a man who had the means to have caused everything that had happened tonight, but no obvious motive. Jess felt her trust in her instincts start to slip.

She let out a loud groan and brought her good arm up toward her face, pinching her thumb and middle finger tightly on the bridge of her nose. All she wanted in that moment was to go home, slide into bed next to Alex, and wake up to her usual Saturday routine of swimming lessons and kids' parties. She was out of her depth. Why had she decided to investigate? She should have just sat quietly back and waited for the real police to arrive.

But—

If she had done that, if she did that now, would that not give the killer – whether it was Jenna or not – a greater chance of getting away with it? These first few hours were crucial, and Jess had utilized them as best she could. She had three solid suspects, and maybe the answers weren't all figured out yet but that was at least something to go on. Something to hand over.

Unsure of her next move, Jess put Matt's phone back in her pocket and rescued Jenna's from the storage cubby. She let herself back out of the cab, her mind feeling like it was wrapped in a thousand indistinguishable wires, all needing unpicking and laying neatly out. It took a moment for her to realize in the patchy torchlight that Liam, Saul and even Scott were gathered around Chloe, who was leaning forward on her seat, head in her hands, elbows on her knees.

'Chloe,' Jess said, taking a beat to take in the scene and then hurrying her pace toward the teenage girl. She flashed a concerned look toward the grown men lurching over her. 'Are you all right?'

'She's OK,' Liam said uncertainly. 'I think.'

'I'm sorry,' Chloe hiccoughed and sat upright, wiping her eyes with the back of her hand. 'He's right, I am OK. I don't know, it just, it all came out.'

'It's been quite a night,' Jess said kindly.

Scott walked away from the group and Jess inwardly rolled her eyes.

'Do you think they'll have got to the station by now?' Liam asked, and Jess saw his eyes were creased in a similar worry as Chloe's. 'Reckon they'll be sending someone down soon?'

Jess pressed her lips together as she thought. 'It's only been five minutes or so,' she said. 'I think it'll take them longer than that in the dark. And we don't know how far away we are either.' She forced a smile. 'But hopefully it won't be much longer.'

Liam nodded but didn't seem too comforted.

'Here—' Scott had returned and was gesturing to Chloe with a can of Fanta. 'It's not cold anymore, but the sugar will make you feel better.' Chloe looked up at him with wide, surprised eyes. 'At least,' Scott continued with a shrug, 'that's what my mum always said. If I was upset, she'd give me a can of pop.'

Jess blinked into this very unexpected display of softness and Chloe hesitated for a moment before accepting the can with tentative hands.

'Thanks,' she said quietly, sitting back and popping the cap so it gave a small hiss. 'That's really nice of you.'

'Yeah well,' Scott brushed it off with a shrug. 'My girl's not much younger than you, and she'd hate it down here.' He rolled his head on his neck, looking around at the dark tube. 'Needs to sleep with the lamp on, door open, and hallway light on.' He stopped and gave a tense laugh. 'I used to lose my nut on the cost of the leccy bill.' He exhaled, casting a sideways glance at Saul and Jess. 'But you do what they want in the end, don't ya?'

When no one else said anything, presumably as blindsided by this turn in direction from Scott as Jess was, Scott gave a slow nod and walked away, returning to his seat.

Jess waited a moment before asking Chloe, who was sipping on the Fanta, 'Are you feeling better?'

Chloe shrugged. 'I dunno,' she said, and offered the can to Liam, who accepted it and took a swig before handing it back. 'I just want to get out of here.'

'I know,' Jess said kindly, and put her hand on Chloe's knee. 'I'm sure it can't be much longer now. It's been hours. Even if the others haven't made it to the station yet, we must be getting to the top of the list of people who need assistance.'

Chloe nodded, accepting the answer, and leant closer into Liam, resting her head on his shoulder. He turned his face to her and gave her a gentle kiss on her forehead. Saul seemed uneasy at invading this tender display and stepped back before folding his long body onto his seat, his leg jiggling a nervous rhythm on the floor.

Jess stood up and straightened out her back with a crunch that made her feel like a decrepit old lady.

'Um, Jess.' The words were so soft, Jess had barely heard them. But Chloe had lifted her head from Liam's shoulder as she'd spoken. Jess frowned and bent back down to her. Chloe kept her voice quiet, so quiet, Jess had to strain to hear what she was saying. 'I think . . .' She paused and chewed her lip. 'I think *I* might have been the person who was meant to get that . . .' She gestured to Jess's wrapped arm. Jess frowned down at her injury.

'What do you mean?' she asked, keeping her voice as quiet as Chloe's.

'I, I felt someone lunge for me,' Chloe said. 'I thought they'd fallen and I moved out of the way, and you were behind me, and then, then you screamed and . . .' She trailed off and nodded meaningfully down at Jess's arm again.

Jess considered this, thinking hard. She did remember Chloe falling into her and then stepping away. The movements were so confused, but she supposed it *could* be true that Jess was a mistargeted attack.

'Chlo, what?' Liam sounded confused, hurt. 'Do you really think that? *Why* would anyone want to hurt you?'

Chloe's shadowed expression, patchily lit up in the torchlight like a kid telling a horror story, looked like it had an answer. 'What if they heard what I told you?' The words came out in the quietest whisper yet.

Jess thought. Saul had said the second blackout wasn't normal, the backup generators weren't supposed to fail. Had someone knocked the tube's electrics out *again*? She thought back to what had happened before the second blackout. They'd all been gathered around the doors, Amelia spearheading the party to leave the carriage. She pictured a thumb hovering over a button, waiting to collapse them all into darkness again as people tried to leave the tube. But why? Well, the answer to that was buried underneath Isa's scarf, now crusty with drying blood.

To launch a second attack.

Much easier to do it with everyone gathered in one place than moving along in the tunnels. It made sense that the killer would want to keep people on the train if they had their sights on more victims.

But why go for Chloe? She'd already imparted the information about the EMP, there was nothing to gain by silencing her now. Unless it was revenge? Pure anger that she might have provided the clue that led to their identity. Jess added this new thought to the tangle of wires in her brain, unable to lay any of them straight – or even connect them together – at that moment.

'Don't worry, Chloe,' Jess whispered, offering her a reassuring smile. 'I really don't think that's likely,' she lied. 'You'd already told me your information, there was nothing to gain by targeting you.'

'What information?' Liam asked, his brow wrinkling into three deep creases as his confusion splayed across his face.

Neither of them answered him, but Jess continued. 'We were all pressed close together, and it was pitch black, there's no way of knowing who they were aiming for. But for what it's worth,' she added, 'I'm glad it was me who got the blade rather than you.'

Chloe gave a small smile and nodded, not quite reassured, but visibly better than she had been. She took another swig of Fanta and Jess got to her feet again.

As she walked away, a thought snagged her, one she'd almost forgotten. Chloe and Liam's unwillingness to talk about the first blackout. Did Chloe know something else about the killer that she hadn't yet told Jess?

Jenna

'So you're over here organizing a big conference?' Amelia was asking Jenna while they walked. She'd barely shut up since Isa had left them, and Jenna was starting to get seriously irritated. She was close to wishing the presence of the awkward, judgemental student was still there to cast them in a silent shroud of accepted dislike toward one another.

'Yeah,' she answered wearily. It was the early hours of the morning, she was hot, she was tired and the last thing she could be bothered to do was delve into work discussions.

'You have a big team over here then?'

'Yeah,' Jenna answered again, hoping the one-word responses would discourage the conversation.

'What have you got planned?'

Jenna was glad she was in complete blackness so she could close her eyes and physically gather herself to reply. 'Motivational speeches, awards for our top sellers, sessions on how to grow their own business, some cool street food and bar sponsorships, and Justin Timberlake's playing. Most of my sellers are sort of your age, maybe a bit older – stay-at-home mums mainly,' she added with a shrug. 'They love the nostalgia.'

'Sounds like quite the production,' Amelia said, and Jenna thought she would be ideal for the Burned community.

'You should check it out,' Jenna said. Even when exhausted, her mind could flip automatically to business. 'I can get you a pass. We've got a waiting list of people wanting to become sellers, but we do a raffle at the conference and the winners get to jump the list. You could do it around your own business already, you do PR right? You'd be great with Burned.'

Amelia gave an indistinguishable murmur. 'Maybe,' she said, and then added a little more enthusiastically, 'You do make it sound like a good event.'

'Well yeah,' Jenna said, 'come along anyway, no pressure. Just enjoy the free wine and concert, if you want.'

'Sounds fun.'

But Jenna couldn't get her usual satisfaction from signing up a new recruit for Burned. She used to relish every single sale. *Take care of the dimes and the dollars take care of themselves*, Gramma Lois always said. Jenna knew that one sale could lead to ten thousand sales – if she slacked on one, she may as well slack on the whole business. But Jenna understood now that her own efforts for Burned were not as intertwined with its success as she'd kidded herself. Her investors and business managers were anonymous people in suits, and even without her they would continue hawking the candles she'd lovingly first created in her tiny studio apartment. It had grown far beyond her, so it was not the fate of Burned itself she worried she'd destroyed on this godforsaken trip to London. It was the fate of Jenna Pace the brand. She was a face, a name. She had photo shoots in *New York* magazine, hordes of followers who recognized her wherever she went – even apparently on a late-night subway in a foreign city. No, the problem that faced Jenna was not the fate of Burned the business. She needed to worry about the fate of herself. Whatever her next move would be, Jenna would have to play it very carefully.

Amelia seemed satisfied by Jenna's answers and she allowed a silence to fall again as they continued walking, but it was comfortable, more friendly now. Jenna thought she should ask Amelia something about herself in return, but she was too distracted. Now she was off the train she found she was desperate to be back up on the surface. Her earlier plan of quietly waiting the night out was discarded in favour of action. She still had her personal phone hidden in the baggy pocket of her jeans, the battery draining quickly away without the cumbersome battery pack she used for her work one. She wasn't going to waste that on a torch, not when Amelia had one to light the way. Plus, she needed as many grains of power as she could to make her calls when she got back up to the top. Get ahead of the events of tonight before they got ahead of her. It was easy enough to cancel her work phone and wipe it remotely, she'd always had that set up in case she ever lost it and didn't want any old stranger getting access to her accounts with the follower count she'd worked so hard for. Tomorrow she'd buy a new one, get it set up exactly the same from the cloud and the phone she'd handed over to Jess would just be collateral damage from a very odd night indeed.

The night hadn't exactly gone as expected, but hey, Jenna was nothing if she wasn't adaptable. Go with the flow, turn herself around at a moment's notice. That had always been her secret to success. One last thing niggled at her though as she thought about getting back up to the top. Amelia. She'd been making noises about being desperate to get home, but Jenna sensed her vulnerability and, more worryingly, instability that meant that she might not go willingly on her way. How long would Jenna be tied to the frantic Amelia as she insisted on searching for a police officer to send help down to the others and possibly even demand an escorted ride home? Because Jenna didn't really care about getting help for the others, they'd be OK. It was like she'd said before, have a nap and ride it out. And she'd have done that too, but then she'd got off the tube and a new plan had formed.

One she did not need Amelia hanging around to ruin.

Thirty-One

Scott was back on his bench, sitting in the dark, his phone torch now turned off. Jess illuminated her way with Jenna's phone but averted the glow toward the back of the train as she came to a stop by his bench and leant one hip against a brown pole. She didn't want him to feel like he was literally in the spotlight of her scrutiny.

'That was very nice of you,' Jess said, nodding back toward Chloe to indicate she was referring to the Fanta gesture.

Scott barely acknowledged her presence, just gave a grunt and another shrug.

'You have a daughter?' Jess probed, hoping that the wall he'd built around himself had crumbled enough by the interaction with Chloe that he wouldn't get aggressive at her questioning. He was still a suspect for her, but, she knew, people contained multitudes. And so far tonight Scott had managed to successfully hide his, until this moment.

Scott nodded but didn't say anything. His jaw flexed a little.

'How old is she?'

He waited a beat as if deciding whether to answer. 'Eleven.'

Jess nodded. 'Mine are nine and four.'

'Good ages,' Scott said gruffly.

Jess gave a small laugh. 'They have their moments.'

Scott raised his eyebrows and his mouth tightened into a sad smile, recognizing Jess's sentiment.

'What's eleven like?' Jess continued, straining to keep her voice light, as if they were simply two parents who'd met at a drinks party, trying to find common ground. 'What have I got to look forward to?' she added with a wider smile.

'Couldn't tell ya,' Scott said, his own smile twisting into something more strained. 'Don't get to see her much these days.'

'I'm sorry,' Jess said genuinely.

'She's with her bitch of a mum,' Scott elaborated, and Jess noticed his anger return. 'Look, I know you lot think I'm just some woman-hater,' he said, gesturing vaguely, 'but some fucking women deserve it.' Jess didn't quite know what to say to that, so stayed quiet. 'And everyone assumes that because I'm the bloke, it's all my fault. Like I wasn't a good husband, wasn't a good dad. 'Cause let me tell you, I gave fucking everything to those two. And what did Mel do? Fuck some bloke from her work, steal *my* house and move him in to play happy families with *my* daughter.'

Jess let the moment settle. 'That's really shit,' she said. 'A *really* shitty thing to do.'

Scott looked up at her, as if reassessing what he thought he knew of her. 'Yeah, well,' he said, 'not many people see it like that.'

'Do you have joint custody?'

Scott gave a bitter laugh. 'I did. Till she used whatever she could to get the judge to strip me of that, so now I only get one supervised visit a week. Supervised,' he spat. 'By her and her new fella. Watching *me* and my daughter. No wonder Lily's so confused, doesn't know who her dad is meant to be.' Jess was not surprised to see angry tears creasing at the corner of his eyes. 'All over something that was *nothing* to do with them.'

'What happened?' Jess knew that for a revised custody hearing, there must have been an incident to prompt it.

Scott waved his hand as if it was unimportant. 'Like I said, it was nothing to do with them.'

'Is it to do with the bruises on your face and hand?' Jess was feeling bolder the more Scott was opening up.

He looked at her curiously for a moment, before rolling his eyes. 'You really are a copper, aren't you?' Jess gave a *guilty as charged* look and Scott sighed before deciding to answer. 'Look,' he said, his tone already defensive. 'I had to move out of my home, move back in with my mum up in bloody Kenton, *miles* away from my life. At forty-three years old. Fucking embarrassing. All I wanted was to go see my team, with my mates, have a laugh, see them get promoted.'

Jess felt her heart beat a little faster in her chest. 'Who's your team?' she asked, already knowing the answer.

'Tooting Bec,' Scott answered. 'Yeah, yeah, I know you'll have seen the news. I was there, all right?' He gave a *Happy now?* raise of his eyebrows and flare of his hands. 'But fuck me, it felt good for one moment to just' – he extended his hands and curled them back into fists again a couple of times – 'feel like a fucking bloke again. Satisfying you know? Knuckles against my face, not lyin' and cheating behind my back.' Jess did not know, but she did not say as much. Instead, she let Scott continue to talk. 'Anyway, that bitch and her new namby-pamby boyfriend jumped on it. Told the judge I was volatile. I never *once* raised my hand to my girl or to Mel, and Mel knows that. Just wanted any excuse to get me out of the picture once and for all.'

So, Scott's wife had used the football brawl to take Scott's custody rights away from him. One of the tangled wires around Jess's brain tightened against the grey matter, as she imagined how Scott would feel coming face to face with one of the men responsible for that as he drove a tube directly toward him. Before Jess could figure out a response to Scott, he stood up.

'Look, I need some air,' he said, gesturing to the open tube doors.

Jess thought of Amelia, Jenna and Isa out there in the dark tunnel. Even if Scott's attack on Matt had been thoroughly personal, he was clearly still angry and this pressure cooker situation seemed to have eroded the line between logical revenge and desperate reaction. She imagined him lunging for her in the dark with a blade clasped in his sweaty hand, aiming for the woman who'd been questioning and undermining him all night. Not caring that a teenage girl might have got in the way of his attack.

'There's not much air out there,' she said, trying to deter him. She wanted to keep him on side for as long as possible. He was already wound so tight cracks had started to show; she needed to treat him delicately lest he shatter completely.

'Yeah, well, it's a change at least. Stretch my legs, get off this fucking thing.'

'Scott,' Jess said slowly, a warning tone creeping into her voice, 'I really don't think that's a good idea.'

He eyed her for a moment, and Jess could almost see the cogs turning in his brain, calculating how much he wanted to fight this. His body language sagged, and he bent over to the polythene bag on the bench opposite him. He rustled in it and pulled out the last of its contents, a crumpled pack of Lucky Strike.

'Look, I just need a fag, all right? Now I can light up on here if you want me to, or I can take myself off and save you all from my second-hand poison. Besides, there's not really anything you can do to stop me, is there?' The question verged on a dare, one Jess had to decide whether or not to take.

She looked between the pack of cigarettes and Scott's face. Crumpled and sweaty, spiky stubble pricking his drawn jowls, heavy lines dragging the whole expression to the floor. She thought of his cracks and stepped reluctantly to one side, thinking that at least the others would hopefully be a little way away by now – maybe even already at the station. She watched him climb down into the tunnel, light up his phone and move toward the front of the train – and wondered if she'd come to regret her decision not to pick this particular fight.

Scott

Scott hadn't expected Jess to let him off without so much as a complaint. But then again, she'd also surprised him when she'd agreed that what Mel had done was fucking shitty. He'd had her pegged as one of those who'd assume Mel must've had a good reason to cheat on him. Then again, maybe she did think that, but was keeping her cards to her chest, trying to get him on side, trick him into something. Well, that wasn't going to work. Scott was too savvy for that, he knew how to spot a woman's lies a mile away, Mel had given him enough practice. He blew out a half grunt, half sigh, and flickered the blue plastic lighter to life and held it to the cigarette clamped between his lips. He'd moved to the front of the train, the gap between the brick and the metal outside the doors was so narrow he'd felt he was being squashed like in that Indiana Jones film where the booby-trapped walls start pressing together.

Scott half-heartedly wandered as he smoked, keeping his torch off, sort of enjoying the feeling of being completely lost in the world. In that moment no one knew where he was, no one could see him, he was alone in the blackness, no one nagging him or yelling at him or telling him he wasn't good enough. He took another lungful of the cigarette smoke and felt the nicotine rush through his limbs, calming after so long holding on without. He'd felt his way over the high raised lines, kicking one painfully with his toes in doing so, and now he walked up and down, a few metres in one direction, a few back in the other, the occasional figure of eight.

Whenever he turned with his back to the train, he could see light bobbing ahead and assumed it must be the three birds. He pressed his lips together as he thought, how long would it take him to reach them? Why did they get to get out of here, go back home before all the others? Although, all Scott had waiting for him was his eternally disappointed mother, who'd berate him for being so late, tell him no wonder Mel left him and then remind him it was her grandchild he'd ripped away. Then he thought about what awaited him back in the carriage. A lady detective who was playing mind games and trying to trap him, and a dead body. Neither option held much promise.

Scott thought maybe he'd just stay right where he was, smoking in the dark and wait for the train to start moving again and plough right into him. Everyone would be happier for it.

For the first time that night, the cigarette clearing the last of his lingering beer fuzz, Scott felt ashamed. He'd acted on instinct earlier, let the rage take over him, thought that if everyone thought him a violent fucking monster anyway he might as well be one. Anyone would have done the same in his position. The bold prick staring at him from the driver's seat, knowing what he'd done and proud of it. That rage threatened to surge through Scott again, but it was doused by the realization of the reality of the situation, how he'd fucked everything up even more. Mel would never let him see Lily again.

He closed his eyes for a moment and considered how his life had collapsed all over again. Opening them, he stared ahead of him, toward the light in the distance that signalled the three women making their escape. Fuck it, he had nothing left, what was to stop him from following them and getting the hell out of there too? Stop off at his mum's and pack a bag, head to the airport before the coppers inevitably came knocking tomorrow. Or at least to the train station, go north, Scotland or something. Scott reckoned he could probably start a new life again quite nicely there. The thought of not seeing Lily again ripped through him, but perhaps it would be easier knowing she was hundreds of miles away, rather than waiting at the other end of the tube line, playing happy families with Mel and her new fella. So close, but out of reach.

Thirty-Two

'Where's he going?' Saul asked, sitting upright in his seat and twisting to watch the progress of Scott's torch along the dark windows.

'For a cigarette,' Jess said. 'Didn't think it would be good to light up on here.'

Saul narrowed his eyes a touch, but slumped back again.

'He's not as bad as he seems,' Jess said with a sigh, feeling that in defending Scott she was also defending herself against blame for letting him go so easily.

'No,' Chloe agreed, 'he didn't need to give me that.' She pointed to the now empty can of Fanta on the vacant seat next to her.

'Sounds like he's had a tough run of it lately.'

'Hasn't everyone?' Saul blew out a sigh.

Jess looked at him with interest. 'You have too?'

Saul hesitated but decided to answer. 'Things are a little strained with my son, that's all. Ever since we lost Linda, it's been hard. She was, you know, the glue that kept our little family together.'

He shook his head. 'I could never quite get on with Nicky in the same way.' He looked up at Jess and shrugged with a strained grunt that gestured toward a laugh. 'Kids, eh?' Jess nodded sympathetically, but stayed quiet, hoping Saul would continue. He obliged and filled the silence, as Jess had learnt people are often wont to do. 'We had a bit of a blow-up before he left for uni, I don't even know what it was about. The previous five years, I think. I never really grieved *with* him – I, I thought it would be better to try and brush over it, convince him it wasn't such a terrible thing that his mother had died.' He pulled a face that told Jess he now understood his mistakes in bright technicolour detail. 'Well, all that had to come out in some way, and it did. I've been trying to make amends, but it's hard. We're taking slow steps.'

'At least you're doing something about it,' Liam said, surprising Jess with a level of maturity in his tone. 'It might not seem it to you now, but he'll appreciate it in the end.' He gave a confident nod. Saul gave him a grateful smile. 'My dad's always been a waste of space,' Liam confirmed. 'Never bothers with anything. Last time I saw him he turned up pissed to my fifteenth, not even a card. Insisted on sitting down with me and having a tinny and telling me I was a man now so I'd understand how a man can't be tied down.'

Chloe pulled a face. 'He was a pig,' she remembered. 'And he dropped in you have a half brother and sister.' She looked up at Jess, incredulous. 'Who drops a bomb like that at a birthday party and then fucks off?'

Jess nodded in agreement and Liam rolled his eyes, before looking back to Saul. 'So, yeah, at least you're doing something now.'

Saul accepted the sentiment with a kind smile.

'Ah fuck,' Liam said softly, 'I hope I'm back before Mum gets up.'

'We will be,' Chloe said confidently, and squeezed his hand. 'Don't worry. Your mum'll be fine.' The familiarity with which Chloe said this told Jess that Chloe knew deeply how much Liam worried about his mum. Their closeness sent a dart of affection through her. They were good kids. For all the worry she and Alex had spent on the upcoming teenage years, reading horror stories in the press, remembering the very worst of the cases she'd worked, it was easy to forget that actually most teenagers were normal, sweet kids trying to navigate the world from child to adult as best they could.

But they *had* lied to her.

They had both been shifty about what had happened during the blackout, Chloe actually walking away the last time Jess had confronted her about it. Jess knew she needed to find out what they were hiding and, if Chloe really *was* the target of the second attack, she needed to find out sooner rather than later.

Isa

Isa was panting, her chest burning from the adrenaline, fear, and the pace her feet were trying to keep. She kept stumbling over the tracks, the thought of a sudden jolt of electricity ending her sending new waves of panic every time she made contact. She had to fling her arm out to catch the grimy cables that ran along the curved brick wall, to stop her from falling over completely. Isa needed to keep going, make that distance between them, get back to the carriage, that was the easiest thing. She'd get back on and pretend nothing had happened, block it from her mind, and wait for the authorities to come and rescue them like everyone kept saying.

Forget the rest of the plan for tonight. She hoped she'd done enough already, no doubt set in motion *something* that would garner attention, spread the word. Even if she couldn't fully execute it as she'd wanted. Maybe it would be better to wait a bit anyway. She didn't want to be linked to it – a criminal record, *prison time*, was not exactly in her future plans. But it was worth the risk to get something done, to change society one strand at a time. Maybe other people thought it was just a stupid trend going round, but she knew *Hookd & Fookd* was more than that. She recognized it as the insidious slip back to women as property, as sex objects for men to trade as they pleased. The culture of fear that fucking trend had fostered on campus when word of it first began to spread. Every girl Isa knew, including herself, lived in a state of constant panic and shame at what pictures might be out there of them, circulating on strangers' phones. Because *everyone* had been on Hookd dates. They were young, free, single, at uni – and wasn't that what uni was all about? Slowly the app had waned in popularity on campus, the girls becoming warier of it, but the damage had been done. Pictures lasted forever, and that lingering threat over the head of almost every girl on campus struck Isa as one injustice too far. It was ironic then, that her friends had said her plan for revenge was 'too far'. Isa didn't think there was such a thing when you were trying to change a culture so ingrained in centuries of patriarchal rule. Sometimes 'too far' was how you won wars.

But tonight had got out of hand. The rest of the plan would have to wait, but she knew she'd get to it one day.

The dark played tricks on her as she stumbled between the train and the wall, catching her shoulder roughly as she staggered through, her phone light swinging as she tried to keep up her pace. She could feel hands reaching out to grab her from the shadows, half expecting to feel a grip around her ankle at any moment to trip her up. Finally she saw the open doors to the black carriage, illuminated only by the glow of a single phone inside. Adrenaline and panic surged her forward, so close to what she was surprised she now considered safety.

Thirty-Three

Before Jess could dwell any more on what she thought Chloe and Liam knew, her attention was caught by a panting breath and a clumsy stumble behind her. Jess swung around to find herself staring into white torchlight, smarting her eyes. She squinted, waiting for her eyes to rectify the bright torchlight against the rest of the dark background and for the swimming blotches to fade away.

Saul's eyes obviously got there first. 'Isa!' Jess took a step to one side and blinked away the last of her spots as Saul got to his feet to guide Isa toward a seat. Her chest was rising and falling in deep, racking breaths, and she sat down heavily.

'What happened?' Jess asked, as her vision finally cleared. 'Are you OK?'

Isa shook her head dismissively and waved a hand. 'I'm . . .' she stammered and then seemed to collect herself, 'I'm fine, I'm fine.' Although Jess noted she didn't seem convinced by her own assertion. She stared for a moment at the floor and then looked up and gave a shudder. 'It's just, out there it's . . .' But she trailed off and didn't seem to be able to find the word.

'Where are the others?' Jess probed. 'Did something happen?'

'No, no,' her voice wavered as she took another steadying breath and moved her thick curly hair out of her face, tucking it behind her ears. 'At least, not as far as I know.'

'What do you mean?'

'We'd been walking a little while, and it seemed further than we thought – we don't know where we've stopped, so I said I'd go back in the other direction to see if Regent's Park was closer, and then I could get help there.'

'You split up!' Saul sounded outraged.

'You went on your own?' Jess said at the same time.

Isa looked between them for a beat. 'Yeah, well we only had two phones, so it made sense for Jenna to stay with Amelia so she could light the way for her. And I figured it was going to be just as creepy on my own or with people.' Isa paused and gave another shudder. 'But I was wrong. It's *so* dark. I felt like time, I dunno, it wasn't passing like normal.' Jess remembered how she'd felt it stretch and snap around her perceptions earlier. 'I felt like I'd been out there *ages* but my phone said it was only like five minutes. Anyway, I got to the end of that empty carriage,' she gestured at the carriage connected to them, 'it's really tight between the train and the wall,' she clarified, 'and I felt like I was tripping over my feet all the time, so I had my phone pointed at the ground so I could see where I was going and then . . .' This time when she paused she shook her head in a few fast, jerking movements as if trying to shake free a memory, 'Then I stumbled onto a rat nest. There were *so* many of them, squirming all over each other and there was no way I could get past them. So, I freaked out and came back here.'

Jess nodded understandingly and Chloe gave a disgusted sound and an elaborate shudder of her own.

'Ugh,' Chloe groaned. 'I hate rats.' Then she looked up with wide eyes. 'They won't get *on* the tube, will they?' Those wide eyes darted quickly to the open doors.

'No,' Jess said with forced confidence. 'I don't think they'd come on here, they'll hear us talking and the vibrations of us moving about. They're more scared of us than we are of them.' It was the same sentiment she'd soothed her own daughters with before, but it didn't make it any less unsettling to think about a writhing nest of rats just down the tunnel.

'Well, I'm glad you came back instead of keeping going on your own,' Saul said with a gentle smile.

Isa nodded and returned the smile back to him. 'I hope the others get someone soon.'

'Tell me about it,' Liam said, sitting back and sliding down in his seat with a sigh.

Silence dropped around them, not uncomfortable or tense, a soft return of everyone to their own thoughts. Jess stayed standing for a minute longer, stilled by indecision of her next move. She watched Isa blow out a tight sigh and tip her head back on her neck for a brief moment before it fell back to look at her phone, which she'd tapped agitatedly to life. The lit-up home screen cast a bluish glow on Isa's face, which was tense, her lips twisted tightly together, jaw slightly flexed. Jess considered Isa's tension. It wasn't a residual panic or disgust from her interaction with the rats, or even an understandable flood of adrenaline from her journey into the tunnel. Instead, it read more like strained annoyance. Annoyance that she hadn't made it to freedom?

Saul opened his mouth as if he was about to say something but was interrupted before he could by a desperate gasp from the open doors.

'Someone help me up!' Amelia whelped into the carriage, and Jess spun around in shock and hurried toward her.

She was a state.

Blood was smeared across her temple and into her hairline, her body shaking all over. Jess bent low and held her arms out in a frame for Amelia to grab onto and pulled as Amelia raised a bloody leg and planted it on the carriage floor, hoisting herself inelegantly up and sliding into a slumped seated position on the floor, back leaning against the glass divider. She was breathing heavily.

'Oh my God,' Chloe said, moving closer.

'Where are you hurt?' Saul asked, striding toward them, his face crumpled in worry.

'What happened, Amelia?' Jess asked urgently, her mind only on a killer loose in the tunnel, as Liam and Isa joined the crowd in an arc around her.

It took Amelia a moment to answer, raising her hands to her forehead and pressing tightly down against her hairline. Her eyes were closed, and they stayed closed while she tried to settle her breath and force the words out between pants.

'I—' she breathed, 'I think I was attacked.'

Chloe

Now Amelia had been attacked too? Chloe felt the world swim before her eyes, a rush of light-headedness she had to blink away to try and focus. What was happening tonight? *Why* was it all happening? She looked up to Liam, who looked as horrified as she did, his cutely handsome face furrowing so a deep vertical line appeared between his brows.

Jess was bent in a low crouch in front of Amelia, who was still breathing deeply, the whites around her eyes visible in strained sockets. Chloe thought she should get up, go and offer her help, or support, or at least *do* something – but her legs felt like they weren't attached, like she couldn't have controlled them with all the will in the world. Instead, she leant forward, her elbows on her knees, hands over her face. She felt Liam's hand fall tenderly on the middle of her back.

With her eyes closed, she tried to relive the second blackout again, when Jess had got slashed, when Chloe had been so sure the culprit was aiming for her. She tried to rethink their positions, what exactly had happened. She had been certain that someone had lunged for her and she'd slipped out the way – she *still* thought that, even now. But maybe she hadn't slipped out of the way, maybe she'd *got* in the way instead. They'd all been so close together, it was impossible to tell which direction anyone was coming from. And why had she been so convinced that she'd be a target of a deranged killer? Because she'd thought she was so smart. That she'd figured out how they'd stopped the tube – that she'd taken the attention off Saul and revealed it could have been literally any of them. But why attack Amelia? She had posed no threat to the killer, hadn't claimed to know anything, and hadn't even been bothered with anything except her own damned business. But she'd been targeted too.

Now, Chloe wasn't convinced she'd figured anything out at all. What did she even know about EMPs? She had no idea if they could be powerful enough to knock out a whole tube, let alone the entire underground system. What had she been thinking, going to Jess with such half-arsed information? She'd been thinking, she reprimanded herself, that *she* was going to be an investigator too. That *she* knew things the real-life detective did not. A flush of embarrassment prickled all over her. Who had she been kidding? Chloe didn't know the first thing about investigating anything real, and tonight was nothing if not real. She didn't know what to think anymore. Her EMP theory seemed ridiculous and childish, but surely the killer must be behind the power outage? They *had* to be, nothing else made sense. But the only person on that carriage who even came close to having the ability to do that was Saul. She moved her hands off her face and straightened up a little, opening her eyes and turning to look at where Saul had gone to join Jess in standing over Amelia. He'd not once got off the carriage. There was no way he could have hurt Amelia.

Chloe decided to give up. Stop trying to work out what the hell was happening and instead focus on surviving it. That thought sent a thick lump down her throat. Jess seemed competent, she'd work it out, she'd keep them safe. Unless . . . a terrible thought slashed through Chloe's confidence in Jess. What if she'd sent Jess off course? On a wild goose chase expecting to find some kind of futuristic device that tied it all together. The next time she got a chance, Chloe was going to talk to her. To tell her she didn't think she was the target of the second attack anymore, and to forget all about EMPs.

Thirty-Four

'What do you mean you were attacked?' Jess asked. 'By who?'

Amelia shook her head, visibly trying to straighten out her thoughts. 'I don't know, I don't know. Maybe I wasn't.' She blinked a few times and pressed the heels of her hands into her eyes. 'I'm not sure what happened.'

Jess felt her instinctive response to Amelia's first statement unwind a touch. Amelia had already shown herself to lean into hyperbole.

'OK,' Jess said slowly, endeavouring to keep her tone as steady as she could. 'Tell me what you think happened, or what you remember.'

'We . . .' Amelia pressed her lips together, thinking hard. 'We were walking down toward Baker Street.' Her eyes flicked quickly up toward Isa. 'Isa had already gone in the other direction, so it was just the two of us. I was lighting the way because Jenna didn't have her phone, but then . . .' She paused again, trying to recall. 'I lost my footing and I fell over.' She gestured down to her bloody knee, which Jess now understood to be the source of the red streaks on Amelia's hands and face, presumably from having pushed her hair back with bloody hands. 'My phone scattered away and I think it must have smashed or broken because the light went off. So, I was on the ground, and my leg was hurting so much. And I said to Jenna I needed help back here because I didn't want to keep going in the dark with an injured leg if I didn't know how long it was going to be for.' She looked up, another dart of alarm shooting across her face. 'You don't think I could get an infection, do you? Whatever I cut it on, it could have tetanus or rat wee or something!'

Jess had no real medical knowledge beyond the first aid course she'd taken a while ago for work, and it didn't seem like anyone else in their party was qualified to make a judgement either. 'I'm sure it'll be fine,' Jess said and bent lower to investigate the cut below Amelia's knee. Her tights were slashed and blood had pooled in the top of her expensive leather boots. 'We'll get it cleaned up best we can, and soon as we get up top, you can go straight to A & E for a jab or whatever else they think you'll need.' Amelia still looked worried, so Jess prompted her back on track with her story. 'Where's Jenna?' She glanced toward the doors. 'Did she not help you back?'

Amelia shook her head. 'No, she said she wanted to keep going, to get back to the surface. She *insisted*. She said it would be better anyway because if I was injured she should definitely go and get someone. She was gone before I could really argue with her – so I had no choice, I had to limp all the way back here in the dark.' She stopped and gave a shudder. 'I managed to find my way with one hand on the wall, running along these thick cables.' She pulled a slightly disgusted face. 'It's all damp and grimy.' She flexed her palm out in front of her and Jess saw mucky smears across it. 'I don't know if Jenna made it to Baker Street, it took me ages to get back here on my leg.' Then she frowned a little. 'At least, I think it did. I have no idea what time it is. But it *felt* like ages.'

'Amelia,' Jess said calmly, 'why did you say you were attacked?'

Amelia took a deep inhale and nodded, preparing to explain herself. 'I was thinking as I walked back, I'm sure I remember feeling hands on my back – like, like I was pushed. And then I'm *sure* I heard footsteps near me while I was on the ground.'

Jess considered this answer. She remembered how she'd felt in the dark, so viscerally certain that she was soon to feel a knife slide into her neck. She could have almost convinced herself she *did* feel it. Isa and Scott had both been out there at the time, the sound of their footsteps would have echoed and carried in the tunnel. But . . .

For all the logical explanations Jess could come up with to explain away Amelia's fear, she could not deny that even she had worried that the killer would strike again. Jess stepped back from Amelia, thinking. The only thing she knew for certain was that she, Saul and the teens could not be responsible for the possible attack on Amelia. Jess's mind filled with the images of those unconscious naked girls and she wondered if Jenna was buried somewhere in that group chat. Had she pushed Amelia to get her out of the way, so she could make a quick escape, not have to bother with calling the police down for any of them left behind – just disappear into the night, her revenge complete?

It was certainly possible, but as Jess ruminated further on the complications of that theory, Isa cut in, looking around and sweeping her phone's torch across the carriage.

'Where's Scott?'

Amelia blinked and sat up straight, suddenly alert.

'He . . .' Jess hesitated before answering, almost embarrassed about what she was about to admit. 'He said he was going to have a smoke.'

'And you let him go!' Amelia shrieked. 'Knowing we were all out there on our own in the tunnel!'

Jess shared an uneasy look with Chloe, wondering if they had indeed been taken in by a vulnerable act, all part of Scott's plan to slip into the night and get away with murder. But why attack Amelia? Jess's gaze landed on Isa's phone and she thought she understood. Amelia had the only source of light – get rid of that and Scott could sneak past unseen.

Shit.

Had she really made such a rookie error? Jess didn't know what to believe anymore. She had read genuine emotion in Scott's story, his kind gesture to Chloe seemingly backing it up. But she felt worn down, exhausted and running on empty. As she looked around at the gathered passengers, she realized she didn't know who she could trust. It was not a feeling she relished. Even the teens were hiding something from her.

Jess retreated from the group and, finding her way by the edge of the pale light from Isa's and Chloe's phones, she headed to a seat at the front of the carriage, the same one where she'd held vigil outside the crime scene when Jenna had blocked her entry into the cab. She exhaled loudly through an 'O' in her lips, a technique that reminded her of the breathwork she'd used to get through her labour contractions with the girls. She leant forward, resting her elbows on her knees, and let her head drop so her sightline was in between her two scuffed trainers. She could feel the gaze of the group settle on her, but she ignored the feeling of being watched. There was so much they didn't know, so much she wished *she* didn't know – it might well make this whole thing much easier. She tried to imagine looking at it through their lens, for most of them were undoubtedly innocent in this whole fiasco, but she couldn't reframe it without her mind twisting her existing connections and suspicions around each of them.

Jess wasn't quite sure how long she sat like that, staring down at her feet, taking in the muddy stain of the laces where she'd had to traipse through boggy ground to retrieve Honey's abandoned frisbee. She'd been so annoyed that she'd worn her nice trainers for that walk, and the brown tinge had remained ever since. She felt a hand on her shoulder and tipped her head up to find Chloe looking down at her with concern creased at the corners of her eyes. She squatted low on her haunches so she was at Jess's level, and Jess couldn't shake the thought of the role reversal between them. Chloe now the adult, come over to see if Jess was OK.

'Are you all right?' Chloe asked, her voice soft.

Jess gave a tired smile. 'Yeah,' she lied through an exhale. 'I just,' she twisted her hand around on her wrist in a vague gesture at everything, 'I don't know what to make of anything or who to trust.' Chloe gave a sigh but didn't say anything. Jess eyed her carefully. 'Even you've lied to me.' Chloe blinked and stared at Jess, waiting for her to elaborate. 'What did you and Liam see during the blackout?'

Chloe dropped her eyes to the floor, averting them from Jess's direct gaze. 'Oh,' she said. 'That. I, er, I thought you might have forgotten about that.'

'I can tell when someone's lying to me,' Jess said. 'Comes with the job, unfortunately. And in a situation like this' – Jess raised her arms either side of her in a shrug, her injured one smarting with the gesture – 'I can't really afford to forget about anything.'

'Look, it's not what you think,' Chloe said, glancing back up at Jess but unwilling to hold her gaze. 'It's not anything to do with the driver or the tube stopping or anything.'

'I think you need to let me be the judge of that.'

Chloe looked shiftily at the ground and when she spoke her voice was even lower than before. She mumbled something and Jess had to lean closer to try and make it out.

'What?' she asked.

'Um, we were sort of, um, taking the opportunity to, I don't know, mess about a bit.' It took Jess a moment to understand what Chloe was saying and she felt a hot flush rise on the teenager's behalf as Chloe continued to explain, gaze intent on the geometric moquette of the seats visible in the glow from her torch. 'We don't get loads of time together, Dad's strict and he won't let me stay over at Liam's especially if his mum's working. We were messing about, taking advantage of just the two of us and the dark and,' her voice fell despondently, 'it was only meant to be a bit of fun.'

'God, Chloe, I'm so sorry.' Jess sat up and felt awful for probing so far into Chloe's personal business. She thought too of Scott explaining about his nasty divorce. Saul and his estranged son. Amelia's grief over her sister. Jess had wheedled these most personal of details out of all these strangers, and for what?

To find a killer.

The sight of Matt's butchered body did a lot to wipe her guilt away. But not enough that she didn't wish Chloe could have been spared winding up as collateral damage. The last thing a teenager would want to do was publicly confess sexual experimentation to a group of strange adults. Jess felt like she should offer up something personal of her own in return. Her apathy at managing her team that had caused a guy, not much older than Chloe, to take his own life in a cold and horrible cell. But her throat constricted over the words, as it always did. As it had done when Alex had implored her to talk about it. As it had when her new therapist had said she should open up. Because if she verbalized it then everyone would know that that young boy's life was on her conscience.

'It's OK,' Chloe said gently. 'You have to ask, given everything that's happened.'

'What?' A loud voice came from the doors, Chloe and Jess both cricking their necks to the middle of the carriage to see what was going on. Scott had climbed back on board and was eyeing Amelia, now on her feet. Saul and Liam, who seemed to have taken a step back from the door, were scowling at him warily. 'What am I supposed to have done now?' Scott demanded. He looked over to Jess, pointing his torch ahead of him. 'I ain't even been here!'

'Yes, well,' Saul said calmly but authoritatively. 'That's one of the problems.'

Saul

Saul scrutinized Scott, who had returned to his so far default position of angry defensiveness, his body language stiffening, shoulders broadening ready for a fight. Jess had said he wasn't so bad, but so far Saul had seen little evidence of that. Aside from giving Chloe a can of Fanta, his attitude had been nothing but argumentative and aggressive all night. Which was not what anyone needed in the face of the situation they all found themselves in. Saul knew nothing of the intricacies that might have led to the events of tonight, but in his mind Scott was the likeliest culprit. Saul didn't need to worry about conspiracy theories as to why the tube had stopped, or whether the killer had done it – Saul had known from the start what had happened: the code red scenario he'd been dreading but half-expecting all week. It was no one's fault, just one of those things. A combination of budget cuts, overworked staff and small problems ignored until they gathered momentum like a tumbleweed, one mammoth cluster of spiky brambles, hurtling through the city. No matter how many of the thorns he'd spent the week removing, he knew there were still enough tangled in there to cause damage.

He'd told them all this from the start and all he'd succeeded in doing was landing suspicion on himself. Well, he hadn't left the tube once, so no one could accuse him of attacking Amelia. But Scott, now he *had* slipped out, and Jess, despite all her protestations of being good at her job – had let him go.

Scott clearly had a red-hot rage swirling inside him, and no idea of how to deal with it appropriately. How to calm himself before he took things too far, how to find an outlet for his troubles before it got to this tipping point. But hadn't Saul been just like him until recently? Torn up about Linda's passing, grief and anger and confusion knotting him up until he couldn't even recognize himself. And even worse, until Nicky couldn't recognize him either. It wasn't until one phone call a few months ago, late at night, that Saul realized how badly he'd messed up. Let his own grief overwhelm him, and ignoring Nicky's pain because he didn't know how to deal with it, how to watch his son suffer. But in that moment, as he had groggily answered the phone, he knew that his son was as muddled and disjointed as he was.

'Dad,' Nicky had said breathlessly, and Saul thought that he sounded like he'd been crying. An alert shot through him, sending him bolt awake. 'I've been arrested.'

Something dropped out of the bottom of Saul in that moment, feeling like he was in freefall, spinning wildly into the abyss. How could his son, his smart, caring, loving son who had loved to sit the family down to put on dance shows for his parents – be sitting in a jail cell?

'What . . . what happened?' Saul asked, hoping his tone showed no signs of disappointment. He knew then that Nicky only needed him to understand, to be there for him. Not to reprimand him, in the way Saul was sure Nicky was already doing to himself.

'Assaulting a police officer.' The reply had come through strangled and scared, his voice breaking over the words. Nicky was only nineteen, still a child, regardless of what the legal system said.

Nicky had been at a march that night, it had got out of hand, and the sign Nicky was carrying had collided with the head of a police officer. Nicky claimed it was an accident, and Saul chose to believe him. But privately, he'd wondered. Wondered if Nicky had got so lost in his emotions he'd seen an opportunity to channel them all into one more person who seemed intent on stifling him. Saul had paid for a good lawyer, and with no previous record, and Nicky's insistence on it being an accident, he'd got away with community service. The next step had been to convince the university not to chuck him out, and it had been the day they'd heard the result of that hearing that Saul and his son had spoken, properly, for the first time since Linda had left them. Across a sticky pub table, Nicky victorious in being allowed to continue his studies, but none of it feeling much like a victory, Nicky had told Saul how lost he'd been. How his mum had gone and then he'd been all but abandoned by his dad. And guilt had seared through Saul as he'd realized everything he'd done wrong.

But now they were on the right track. They were in therapy both together and solo, and slowly their relationship was healing, knitting together one stitch at a time.

Saul pressed his lips together as he considered Scott. Was he being too hard on a man who he himself could have been a few short months ago? But Saul would never have *killed* anyone, never have attacked anyone with a knife, no matter how desperate he'd become. But Nicky had turned violent in one moment of madness . . .

As Saul thought this, his gaze slid unconsciously toward Isa. The girl stood stiffly to one side of the group, biting a fingernail, eyes narrowed toward Scott. He'd recognized so much of his son in her, felt that parental urge to protect her. But now he wondered, he feared, how much Isa and his son really did have in common.

And what would Nicky have done if he'd had a knife in his hand instead of a placard?

Thirty-Five

Jess and Chloe approached the rest of the group, Scott's gaze now settling on Amelia's blood-streaked appearance.

'What the hell happened to you?' he asked, eyebrows arching in alarm.

'You tell me,' Amelia replied haughtily.

'Oh here we go again!' Scott stepped back with both arms outspread in a wide performative gesture to the rest of the group. 'Gotta be my fault, whatever the hell it is that's happened.'

'Scott,' Jess said carefully. 'We're not accusing you of anything.'

'I am,' Amelia muttered under her breath and Jess shot her a look.

'Well,' Jess continued, 'as you can see, Amelia had an accident, or was pushed, out in the tunnel. She's been injured and her phone was broken in the fall.'

'And what's that s'posed to do with me?'

'Did you push her?' Isa cut in, and Jess could see how quickly everyone's preconceptions of Scott would turn this accusation into firm fact if she wasn't careful. Tried and sentenced in an underground kangaroo court.

'Why would I want to push a random woman over?' Scott asked. 'No offence, love.'

Amelia didn't seem to appreciate Scott's attempt at levity and scowled in his direction. No one seemed to have a firm answer for that, and even Jess could only come back to Amelia being the one with the torch. But why would Scott want to take that out? To stop them from getting help. So why come back? If Scott had killed Matt, he had to know that the police would be coming at some point. Surely his best chance of getting away with it would be to make it to the station and slip away, get a head start – line up his story for when the police came knocking.

Exactly like Jenna had done.

Jess tried not to let her suspicions run away with her. She needed cold, hard facts and explanations to ground herself in first.

'Scott,' Jess said, attempting to keep her voice reasonable. 'You *were* just out in the tunnel weren't you? Having a smoke?' Scott nodded suspiciously and Jess knew he was deciding whether she was on his side or trying to trap him. 'Did you not hear Amelia coming back? She must have passed right by you.' Having another thought, she turned to Amelia. 'Actually, did you not see Scott?'

'I was a bit distracted with my leg and the dark,' Amelia answered shortly.

'I moved round to that side,' Scott jerked his head to the opposite side of the train to the open doors. 'There's a little signal box thing that I was perching on while I smoked.'

Jess nodded, so far so believable. She turned back to Amelia. 'Did you not smell smoke?'

Amelia rolled her eyes and gave a shallow exhale as if

wondering why she was suddenly in the spotlight. She made a show of thinking and then frowned. 'Actually,' she said, 'I did smell smoke.' She waggled her head. 'I didn't think much of it at the time. I-I was so distracted, I don't think it registered that that was an odd thing to smell down here.'

Both of their stories seemed to line up, but neither really told Jess much about the truth of what had been going on.

'Isa' – she turned to the only other person present who had got off the tube so far that night – 'you didn't see or hear anything?'

Isa shook her head. 'I told you, I was off in the other direction.'

Jess nodded. It wasn't impossible for Isa to have hung back in the shadows, pushed Amelia when they all thought she was safely off back to Regent's Park. Isa had clearly run back to the train and wasn't injured, so would have easily beat Amelia back. But why on earth, as Scott had said, would Isa want to push a random woman over? It made no sense. As much as she tried not to pin too much on circumstantial evidence, Jess found the only way the jigsaw pieces slotted together was to form a picture of Jenna's beautiful face. Jenna had killed Matt, wanted to get away on her own – and Amelia was the only thing standing in her way.

'Amelia,' Jess said, thinking out loud. 'Seeing as you had the torch, does that mean you were ahead of Jenna in the tunnel? Lighting the way?'

Amelia nodded. 'I suppose so, yes. Sometimes we were walking next to each other, but sometimes I definitely moved ahead.'

Jess turned to look out at the black curved wall of the tunnel through the still-open doors. A realization dropped inside her, one that felt like molten lead. Jess needed answers. And currently, the only person who could give her those answers was Jenna.

She contemplated the thought of making her way through

that dark, rat-infested tunnel and felt her stomach turn. At least she still had Jenna's phone, she would have a source of light which Jenna didn't. That might well let her move at a quicker pace and maybe catch up with her. And if she didn't . . . then at least she would be at Baker Street and could get help for everyone else, while immediately alerting the authorities to everything that had happened and everything that she knew, hopefully stopping Jenna before she had the chance to make a proper escape.

Jess glanced back over her shoulder, not loving the idea of leaving the crime scene unprotected. Even if she did think Jenna the likeliest culprit, she couldn't be 100 per cent sure that she wasn't leaving the killer access to interfere with their crime scene. Considering the rest of the passengers again, Jess decided Chloe and Liam were the most trustworthy.

'Chloe, Liam,' she said, looking between them both. 'I'm going to go after Jenna.' There was a collective murmur from the group, shock and confusion creasing everyone's faces. 'I want you two to make sure no one goes in there'– she moved a finger, first between the two teens and then reached her hand over her shoulder, extending her thumb to gesture to the driver's cab.

'Why are you going after Jenna?' Amelia asked, looking stricken. Her mind seemed to be racing as she spoke, slotting things into place. 'You don't think—' She halted for a second before completing her sentence. 'You don't think *she* did that?' Her eyes flicked past Jess to the driver's cab, and Jess thought that perhaps Amelia was imagining her lucky escape out in a darkened tunnel with a killer.

Jess gave a tight shrug and when she answered she addressed everyone. 'The truth is, I don't know for sure. But I have reason to believe she *could* be the culprit. And seeing as she's the only one who's tried to make a run for it so far tonight, I want to make sure that if she *is* responsible, we have the best chance of getting justice.'

'Why on earth do you think *Jenna* is responsible?' Saul sounded genuinely perplexed.

Jess did not deign to give him an answer. Now was not the time to get into the nitty-gritty details she'd learnt of everyone's life so far. 'Chloe and Liam,' she said again, 'are you two happy to watch the crime scene?' They looked at each other for a beat, and then nodded solemnly. Jess addressed the group at large again. 'Look, the truth is, if it's not Jenna, then it's one of you. So, it doesn't really matter who is "in charge"' – she formed air quotes with her fingers – 'of the crime scene. If someone tries to get into that cab, then the rest of you' – she lowered her hands to indicate the gathered passengers – 'will know why.' She eyed them all meaningfully, and everyone gave stiff nods to show they understood the situation.

'All right,' she said and glanced back over her shoulder toward her abandoned trench coat, scrunched on a seat with her bag on top. She went over and retrieved the bag, happy to forgo her coat which would only be a burden in the oppressive humidity.

'Are you not coming back then?' Amelia asked as Jess slipped the long chain strap over her shoulder.

'I'm taking it just in case,' Jess said. 'If I do get all the way to the station, then after I've spoken to the police, I'd at least like to be able to get back into my own house after all this.' Everyone seemed to accept that answer, and Jess cast a glance at Amelia's own abandoned bags. Evidently she had not thought that far ahead in her desperation to get off the train. Jenna's leather jacket was also cast haphazardly along the back of the seats, but Jess noticed now there was no bag accompanying it. Had Jenna even had a bag to begin with? Jess couldn't quite remember.

She made her way to the doors and climbed down onto the tracks.

'Should someone not go with you?' Scott asked.

'I think,' Jess said with a sigh, looking out into the black route that lay ahead of her, 'in the circumstances that would only complicate things.'

'Why are you so keen to go out with her?' Isa asked, her tone verging on accusatory.

'I didn't say *me*, did I?' Scott answered impatiently.

'Try not to kill each other while I'm gone,' Jess said wearily, channelling her parental frustration with her squabbling daughters, but then she stopped and realized what she'd said. The words had settled on the rest of the passengers too, and they fell silent, shooting tense glances toward one another.

'Jess, if you do get to the station,' Chloe piped up as Jess fumbled with Jenna's phone, scanning the light up and down the narrow gap between the train and wall ahead of her, 'can you try and get a message to my dad? Let him know we're OK? Edward Nnadi,' she added with a nod. Then scrunched her face guiltily. 'I'd give you his number but I don't know it by heart and' – she held up her once-illuminated mobile – 'my phone died.'

Jess nodded. 'I'll see what I can do.' She considered for a moment that now they only had Isa and Scott's phones for light. She wondered silently how long the remaining phone batteries would last, but didn't raise the point. She didn't want to panic anyone. 'Right,' she said with a nod and took a step forward. 'See you all maybe on the other side,' she added with a forced smile she did not feel and that no one else returned.

Jess held Jenna's phone as high as she could to illuminate the path for her feet, convinced she could hear the squeaking and squirming of Isa's rat nest. She made it to the front of the train and stared out into the impenetrable tunnel. Moving to the centre of the lines, she decided that was the least likely position for her to hit one if it were to become live again, and began her journey.

It did not take long for Jess to realize that Isa and Amelia had been right. Time felt endless out here, as if the only world that existed was Jess and her halo of torchlight. Her arm ached as she held Jenna's phone high above her shoulder, trying to illuminate as much as possible of the dank tunnel. She ploughed on, quickly losing all sense of time or distance, the world she'd retreated from no longer existing, as she focused only on putting one foot in front of the other.

Suddenly, she stopped.

She'd heard something. Had she?

She tried to steady her breathing, to quieten the sound of it in her ears, to listen beyond the beat of her pulse that thudded through her skull. The feeling that a knife was about to slide into her exposed neck shuddered through her again and she instinctively moved her good hand to cradle the bare skin. Swinging round, she scanned the torch into the tunnel behind her – reassuring herself there was no one else out there with her. She could see the front of the train was not far, less than a hundred metres away. She turned forward again and recommenced her walk into the unknown.

A rat squeaked across the track in front of her, and Jess flinched instinctively. She wasn't normally squeamish about mice or rats, usually she found them quite cute to watch scurrying around the tracks as she waited at a station. But out here, with her shins and ankles exposed, she couldn't rid her mind of stories of giant rats pulled from sewers, rat bites sending a poisonous fever racing through your bloodstream. She kept walking though, pausing every now and again to reassure herself that she definitely couldn't hear footsteps or breathing behind her.

After a few more minutes, something caught Jess's eye.

A glint, as she swept the torchlight across the ground ahead of her. It was not far, perhaps a couple of metres, and came from the left side of the track. Jess hurried forward and, focusing her beam directly onto the ground, she found a phone. Lying face up, the shattered screen having picked up the glancing light.

Hoping that the electricity hadn't secretly come back on, Jess tentatively reached forward to retrieve the fallen device, half-expecting to be thrown back by an electric jolt as she made contact with the rail.

She straightened up, holding the phone out and flipping it over to see the leather monogrammed case confirming it was indeed Amelia's. She turned it back over and inspected the dead, shattered screen, frowning at something she couldn't quite put her finger on.

The shatter pattern looked odd.

It radiated out in a concentric circle from the middle of the screen. Way too neat to be caused by a random throw. There were scuff marks along the top, that Jess could match with being flung out of her hand as Amelia hit the ground. But it seemed that the phone would have survived being skittered along the floor like that.

This full destruction of it – well, it looked deliberate.

It looked like it had been stamped on.

Thirty-Six

Aware that she was now apparently guardian of four phones – her own, Matt's, Jenna's and now Amelia's – Jess decided to empty out her dress pockets and redistribute the weight. She slid her own, dead, phone into her handbag, and retrieved the string of dog-poo bags from inside. Holding Amelia's phone carefully between her thumb and finger, she dropped it into a bag and wrapped it carefully around itself. She didn't expect prints off it – phones were always a mess of smudges with enough reasonable explanations of how other people could have handled it – but there might be something the techs could do with the shatter pattern. She was always amazed at the details they could pull from the most innocuous-seeming things: a fleck of dirt transferred into the cracks from the bottom of a shoe, perhaps, that only came from the very narrow geographical region right outside the culprit's home. It was unlikely, but Jess wasn't going to risk losing a single grain of hard evidence in a case which so far lacked so much of it.

She secured Amelia's phone next to her own in her bag and

began walking again. A little way ahead she could hear scratching and squeaking, the sound of creatures moving over each other, unseen in the shadows. She thought of Isa's description of the rat's nest in the other direction and tried to will herself to move forward without looking. But as she continued slowly, the fear of the unknown began to grip her with increasingly tight needling fingers, the rats looming larger in her mind's eye than they could possibly be in reality. She needed to see them. Firmly planting her feet, she swung the torchlight to her left and toward the sound of the rats. It took a moment for her to understand what she was looking at – her instinctive revulsion at the long, wormlike tails sliding over each other as a dozen or so rats swarmed. She blinked into the horrifying sight and realized that the rats were swarming all over *something*.

She took a step closer, ignoring every instinct that told her to flee.

No, she realized. The rats weren't swarming over something.

They were swarming over some*one*.

Jess didn't need to get any closer to figure out who. But she did anyway, professional due diligence overriding her fears. She held the torch directly on them and hurried forward with loud, shuffling steps and a *shoo*-ing sound. The rats scattered, revealing Jenna's artistically dyed bronde hair, now a matted, tangled mess. The white T-shirt that had hung so effortlessly off her model-like figure was now bright red, blood having seeped through the thin fabric from a source buried underneath the mass of hair.

Jess closed her eyes for a moment and turned away. She could feel the breath rising in her, a tightness starting to burn in her chest. This felt different to the driver. This felt different to any other murder scene she'd attended during her years on the police. She'd *known* Jenna. Not well, but enough that she could still hear the tone of her voice, picture her mannerisms, the way she'd held herself with a cool nonchalance even in the face of a nightmare. She now understood why victims' families would wail incredulously, 'But I'd *just* seen her! She was *fine*!' As if the sudden act of violence that had taken them should have been evident earlier. It felt incredible that Jenna had, not long ago, been asking Jess if she thought the ghost of her late grandmother was down in that tunnel with her. That this body, lying unmoving and blood-soaked, could ever have walked or talked or created an empire felt impossible.

Jess forced herself to turn back to Jenna and let the comfort of ordered regulation wash over her. She let her training, her years of experience take control of her and, as she had with the driver, she set about assessing the scene and gathering whatever solid evidence she could. She pushed her questions, suspicions and theories into a tight corner of her mind; they had no use in this moment. Jess needed to work this case afresh. She'd come across a body, and she had to forget everything else that had happened so far that night. Including the fact that, up until a few moments ago, Jess had thought she was hunting this woman as a killer. She forced her attention back to the body and bent low.

Sitting on her haunches and leaning in close, Jess could see the slim hilt of a knife protruding out of the bush of Jenna's thick hair. Not wanting to disturb too much of the crime scene, and secretly fearful that a small rat might have burrowed inside, Jess carefully moved the two sections of hair around the knife out of the way. The knife was buried deep into Jenna's neck, but unlike with Matt, there was only one entrance wound. It would have required a hell of a force of strength to drive a whole knife blade through the muscles and tendons of the neck, especially on the first try. She imagined Jenna, walking blindly in the dark, feeling the very thing Jess had been convincing herself all night was about to happen to her. Jess was not a doctor, but she had seen and read enough reports of post-mortems to know that this was unlikely to have killed Jenna straight away. Jess looked up and moved the torchlight to the wall above her. There was a sticky dark patch just below head height that looked to Jess like congealing blood. As she had with Matt, Jess took a moment to envision what had happened.

From the position of the knife in Jenna's neck, it was clear she had been attacked from behind. Jenna would have staggered forward while her attacker . . . what? Watched? No, that didn't make sense, unless Jess's earlier theory of the bloodthirsty psychopath was about to rear its ugly head again. Most likely the attacker had bolted. Maybe they panicked, hadn't thought it through as they were trying to make their escape through the tunnel, saw Jenna and wanted no witnesses. They still had their weapon and so instinct, desperate, protective instinct took over. And then, realizing what they'd done, they panicked. Returned to the train.

No. Jess was getting ahead of herself again, her suspicions were running as wild as the Dartmoor ponies she'd loved as a girl. She needed to establish the facts first.

Jenna had staggered forward, gasping for breath, gurgling blood most likely. She'd rested against the wall for a moment, feeling weaker, feeling agony, but not understanding how – or why. And then as the consciousness slipped out of her, she fell, face forward onto the ground, one arm across the track, ready to be sliced off when the tube started up again.

Jess's brain felt frazzled as she swung the torchlight around, but she couldn't see anything else in the surrounding area that could constitute a clue. She zeroed back in on the knife, scrutinizing it carefully. It looked to be a kitchen paring knife, and from the size of the handle she imagined the blade underneath could well match the small-ish incisions in Matt's neck. Saul's penknife seemed to be innocent of the crime. There was something else she knew she should take in about this knife, about this scene, but her head was throbbing. A combination of dehydration, stress and exhaustion. She couldn't think as quickly or clearly as usual; she was accustomed to her synapses working for her – firing off decisions and conclusions at the speed of light. She didn't want to do anything more to disturb the body, and she certainly wasn't going to remove the knife, so instead she slid Jenna's home screen to the left and pulled up the camera. She snapped several photos, glowing eerily in the dramatic white flash, and then stood up to take a few more of the scene as a whole from a distance.

Jess stood in the middle of the tracks, gazing at the scene of Jenna's demise for another moment. Then she turned her head in the direction of Baker Street station, no one yet having made it any further than the point at which she stood. She yearned to forget all this, to run down the tracks to home.

But something turned her head back the other way. Toward the carriage. She could pretend it was the professional hunt for justice still so ingrained in her. Or even professional curiosity. But the truth was it was something more visceral. Someone was lying to her. Someone had been hiding this darkest corner of themselves all night. And Jess, so far, had missed it.

But not now.

She turned away from Jenna and strode back toward the carriage, rats and darkness be damned. She walked toward the strangers she'd spent the night with. One of whom was a cold-blooded killer.

Jenna

It had not taken long after she'd felt the sharp agony radiate out of her neck for Jenna to understand what had happened. And it had not taken long, after she'd fallen to the ground, feeling her focus swim, the last grasps of consciousness slipping away, for her to understand that she was going to die down here – in a disgusting, dark tunnel, only the company of rats to witness her last moments. Even resigned to her fate, surprised at how she could literally *feel* the lifeblood seep out of her, Jenna's instinct was to stay alive. Even for just a moment longer, she wanted to keep her mind sharp, to prove that she'd lived as much as she could right up until she couldn't muster it anymore.

Those final moments of her life must have only been that, mere moments, the blood gushing too quickly from the well-placed knife doing the job it was intended to do. But to Jenna they swooped and flew over the course of her whole life. *How clichéd*, she'd thought.

Her earliest memory, a day out to Coney Island. Mom, Gramma Lois, Jenna and her brother.

Later memories, elementary, middle and high school. Her days waiting tables and waiting for her big break. A lot of waiting back then. The sear of desperation to make something of herself, to make Burned everything she'd known it could be. How it had got out of hand. Turned into something she could no longer control – partners and investors pushing, moving the direction away from her candles and toward the business model that was driving the most revenue. Her distributors. The candles had got worse and worse, scents cheap and galling, gawdy designs that could have been churned out by a team on Clip Art, peeling and wearing off even before delivery.

But what was Jenna supposed to do about it? She was the success she'd always known herself to be, the money was rolling in, the *respect* from her peers near endless. Except that one podcast that had put a small spanner in the works. But Burned devotees were exactly that, devoted. And the business had quickly recovered, a firm denial issued.

Burned began from two things – my love of scented candles and my love of design – and those two things are still the foundation of my business today. Any suggestion of a pyramid scheme is uncalled for and untrue, the candles are the product and they draw in the customers – and our sellers. Women want to sell for me because of the support and inspiration I provide. I take accusations of bullying or pressuring tactics to purchase more stock than a seller can offload very seriously, and will be looking deeply into those individuals named on the A Burned Empire? *podcast. That being said, I stand by the women in my company, the sellers who have put their passion and hard work into creating their own success, and I am confident that this 'culture of toxicity'* is a mere work of fiction to flesh out a podcast with little other content.

And then this trip, the conference at the end of the month. Her announcement. She was stepping aside, giving it all up. Let her partners have it. Let them run whatever corrupt, unethical pyramid scheme they wanted. She was taking her name off it. She'd started from scratch once, she could do it again. And this time she would not be starting from scratch. Her plan was to get out before she could become too tainted with that brush. Burned had been her life's work, but lately she'd understood it had only been the first step. Jenna Pace was bigger than the company, and tonight she'd even created the perfect storyline as she'd walked through the tunnel, risking her life to escape from a killer underneath London, only to get help for the people who couldn't make the journey – well, that was an excuse ready to go. She wouldn't even need to do the conference. She could claim trauma, needing time to spend with family, to re-evaluate what was important to her. It was a ready-made cover, and no one could accuse her of doing what she'd really been planning – a captain abandoning her sinking ship. Brand Jenna Pace would remain intact, a traumatized hero, refocusing her business endeavours. She had pictured herself on *Good Morning America*, maybe even a self-help book about turning trauma into success. It had all been such a neat plan.

This whole, hellish trip to London would be reframed, both in history and in her own mind. Delete that first night, that fucking app, how she'd slipped, she'd let too much of her polished persona fade to show someone – strangers – her true self. Jenna had never been able to hang on to a relationship, her pathological need for control was too great. But she still wanted to *feel*, and late-night booty calls had become part and parcel of her life. No man seen twice, no man even treated to her presence still there at breakfast. A couple had turned nasty when she'd told them she didn't want to see them again, threatened to reveal to the world what a slut she was, but they'd all been bluffing. They always were. And even if they did say something – who the hell would be listening? These were normal guys, a few hundred followers getting lost in a newsfeed of people who released content for a living. Sure, there might be a few rumours spread around friendship groups in certain boroughs of New York, but not enough to make waves for her.

But then she'd fucked it up. Let herself be seduced by the founder of that goddamn dating app at the party she'd hosted. She'd been off her game, feeling insecure and uncertain about spending a month in a city she didn't know, with no friends, no one who knew her, and organizing a supposedly career-defining conference. She'd been vulnerable and weak. She'd outstayed her welcome, long after he'd been desperately trying to get her out – something she'd finally understood when his model girlfriend returned home and caught Jenna still in her underwear in the bathroom. This was not some anonymous man, this was a man with influence, a girlfriend with a public profile – a story like that would turn her cohort of stay-at-home mums against her in an instant. They'd managed to placate the girlfriend, manipulate her into understanding they would all be as embarrassed by this scandal as each other, the girlfriend only twenty-one and just booked her first fashion week – not willing to risk losing her big break. Jenna had been going to repeat her mistake tonight. She didn't even know why. But his message had popped up, promises that the girlfriend was away on a shoot for the whole weekend, and her body had responded on instinct – two weeks of loneliness could do mad things to you.

Well, Jenna thought as she felt the first brave rat sniff around the bloody mass below her hair, no energy left to try and bat it away, lonely was how she'd lived and it seemed that lonely was how she'd die.

As her mind faded she could see the thin veil she'd felt wafting around her all night, Gramma Lois waiting to greet her on the other side. Jenna hoped she'd be proud. There might be no real friends to mourn her passing, no kids, no partner – but she'd left behind *something*. A legacy. And Jenna was proud of that at least.

Thirty-Seven

Jess climbed back onto the train and saw two torch beams swing toward her. In the time she'd been gone, it seemed everyone had sat back down in their various self-assigned seats.

'Are you OK?' Chloe asked, and although Jess couldn't see her clearly in the dark, she heard the concern in her voice.

'*I'm* fine,' she answered pointedly.

'What's happened?' Scott asked, sliding over on his bench and standing up, holding his torchlight on Jess as he approached.

'Who says anything happened?' Jess bristled.

'Because last we heard from you, you were chasing after Jenna and heading to the station. But now, less than ten minutes later, you're back.'

Jess nodded, and turned to address the rest of them, gesturing for Scott to follow as she moved to the head of the bank of seats, and pointed for him to sit down. He surprised her by obliging.

In an ideal world she'd deliver this news with enough light to allow her to scrutinize everyone's reaction in turn. But as she gazed out into the darkened half of the carriage, blurry flares of pale white light contrasting against deepest black, she knew the killer would be able to hide their reaction easily enough. She held Jenna's phone up as high as she could to cast them all in its glow before she spoke.

'Jenna's dead.' She delivered the news simply and bluntly. They'd come too far tonight to bother pussyfooting around the issue.

She watched the news settle as if in slow motion. Saul's forehead creasing in shock, his mouth gaping a little. Isa's eyes widening, displaying the whites criss-crossed by a spiderweb of tired red veins. Liam made some sort of grunt of shock, and Chloe gasped a half-formed 'What?' Amelia jerked her head upward from where it had been gazing at the floor, meeting Jess's gaze with shocked, pinched eyes that seemed to bulge from her head. And Scott remained unmoved, except for a slight, almost disbelieving, shake of his head.

Jess waited a beat to see if anyone would say anything, but nobody did.

'OK,' she said, squaring up her stance and addressing them all from the standing area by the door, everyone gathered on the bank of seats in front of the driver's cab. The adrenaline sent the blood pumping through her, making her injured arm throb. She ignored it. 'Given these new developments, the way I see it, only myself, Chloe and Liam, are in the clear,' she said.

'And me!' Saul called out. 'I've not left this carriage either.'

'I'll get to that,' Jess said, making a plan for her speech as she went. She had an irresistible flash of herself as Poirot, her suspects all gathered together, awaiting the denouement. She gave a small sigh, feeling out of her depth – this was not how investigations were concluded in the Met. And she didn't even *have* a conclusion, just enough evidence to be wary of basically everybody. 'Chloe, Liam, me and Saul,' she added with a conciliatory nod toward him, 'have not left this carriage. We are the only four that cannot be physically responsible for Jenna's death, or whoever pushed Amelia.' Again, no one made any attempt to defend themselves, a spell seemed to have settled, as if they'd decided that Jess was speaking and there was little point in interrupting her. 'I am still trying to work out the exact details of how any of this is connected to the killing of the driver, and how or even if the tube stoppage has anything to do with it. What I *do* know is the following.' She glanced toward Saul, feeling she may as well start with him and explain the only reason she'd still got one eye on him.

'Saul, I appreciate you have not stepped off this tube. However, I can't ignore the fact that you work for the National Grid, and that the attack on the driver feels not only personal, but premeditated. Given the circumstances of his killing, the power cut feels too relevant to ignore – so I'm afraid I do have to keep that in mind. Also, you have, so far, been the only person in possession of something that could be the murder weapon, even if it does, at first glance, seem clean.' As Jess said this, she thought of the knife still buried in Jenna's neck. There was nothing to say *two* knives hadn't been in play tonight. Two knives, which meant – Jess felt a chill at this thought – two killers. 'But, that being said, I can't see any connection between you and the driver at this stage, although I'm confident a more thorough investigation would unearth one when we get out of here.'

'But Jenna . . .' he said weakly. 'And Amelia—'

'I know, but I can't rule out that you're not working with somebody else.' Her eyes slid unconsciously to Isa. 'Or,' she added with a weary sigh, reluctantly voicing the worry that had just come to her, 'that there are two separate culprits.

'Isa, you say you turned back in the tunnel, but we have only your word for that. It would have been easy enough for you to hang back in the dark, push over Amelia to take out the source of light and then attack Jenna.' Isa seemed ready to mount her defence, but Jess continued, raising her voice to talk over the potential interruption. 'It was obvious to everybody here that you didn't harbour much respect or liking for Jenna Pace. And you *have* hidden things tonight – where you were going, why you stayed on this tube when all your friends got off. I can't help but think those details could well be relevant in light of the attack on the driver.'

The fight seemed to seep out of Isa at the mention of her plans for the evening, what she had chosen to do instead of celebrating with her friends. She slumped weakly back in her chair, leaving Jess to continue her monologue.

'Amelia.' Jess turned to the redhead, who looked silently incredulous at being included in this line-up. 'I'm sorry, but you *were* out in the tunnel and, as with Isa's insistence she turned back in the other direction, we only have your word for it that you were pushed over, leaving Jenna to continue on her own.'

Amelia sat up to protest, but got no further than a muttered 'Ridiculous' before Jess carried on, ignoring the interruption. 'However, I've found no evidence that would connect you to the driver.'

Turning to face the others, Amelia nodded, satisfied she'd been exonerated.

'And Scott' – Jess turned to him, letting out a breath. 'Unfortunately, I *have* found a connection between you and the driver. You were both present at the Mason's Arms riot a week ago – and on opposite sides.'

Scott's mouth dropped open in surprise. 'How the hell could you possibly know that?'

'That's not important now, but I do have hard evidence that I will be passing on to the authorities. *And* you were alone, out in the tunnel when both Amelia and Jenna were attacked.'

'Right, so I kill a bloke, manage to escape and attack two birds on my way, and then I, what? Come back here for shits and giggles to wait for the fuzz to turn up and cart me away?' He held out his arms invitingly. 'Search me, see if you can find even so much as a toothpick. I got nothing.' One of his outstretched arms extended into a chubby pointed finger in Saul's direction. 'He has a sodding knife, *and* you just said it – he could have done all of this!' He rotated his head, taking in the patchily lit cabin.

'No, I couldn't!' Saul insisted.

'Right, 'cause he's all nice and put together and wears a suit, you like *me* for it better than him.'

'That has nothing to do—' Jess began, but Scott's argument had broken the spell, and everyone began shouting at once. They called out defences of themselves, accusations of anyone and everyone. 'Please!' Jess pleaded with the group, who were beyond listening to her now. 'This isn't going to help anything!'

She could feel the tension rising, the heat in the carriage intensifying alongside. This wasn't what she'd wanted, but perhaps what she should have expected. When she'd re-boarded the train, Jess knew she didn't have enough information to firmly accuse just one person. But she did have four solid suspects all contained in one place, and a cornered culprit could well be a dangerous one. The reason the killer had returned to the tube was most likely panic, and now their only choice was to blend in with the innocent and hope for someone else to take the wrap. And so, Jess had wanted them all to know that there were four people in the frame for this, and the safest course of action for the killer was *not* to act again. She'd wanted them to point their fingers at each other, to confuse themselves all so readily that everyone would be inclined to believe anything of the people they'd spent the night with. Keep them contained, keep them distracted, until the police finally arrived. But their reaction was threatening to get out of hand – and she'd given them the ammunition for desperate mob mentality to break out. She heard an inner barb from Nicole that she'd been naïve to think her plan would cause anything other than chaos. Now, she realized with a rush of tight prickles across her skin, it was not only the killer she needed to be wary of.

Thirty-Eight

Jess felt her body sag back against the central pole, her mind blurry, her muscles aching from where they'd been braced all night. She stared into the dark carriage and thought she would never be able to see the underground in the same way again. Her perception of it had distorted around her. No longer a mundane way of rattling around London, so familiar and ingrained in her consciousness she never gave it a second thought. Now it was a metal prison, a source of cabin fever she couldn't escape. Claustrophobia settled in, something she had never before suffered from that now threatened to become a lifelong affliction triggered by this one night, assuming she survived.

She tuned back into the melee and heard Amelia call out, 'Isa you've been on edge all night, it's so obvious.'

'That's nothing to do with this,' Isa defended herself. 'And if you want to see someone on edge, take a look at Scott!'

'Oh yeah yeah, here we go again.' Scott made a yapping gesture with his hand as Isa continued talking over him.

'Scott, you *are* the only person with a previous connection to the driver,' Chloe said reasonably, her voice demanding more attention thanks to her previous quiet. She was also the only person who had managed to keep the accusatory tone out of her voice, phrasing it as a plea for him to explain himself. 'And you *were* really hot-headed before – that was why Jenna moved away from you.' Again, her tone was reasonable, an invitation for a calm defence. Jess realized with a bolt of hope that Chloe might well help her plan succeed after all – the teenagers were the only ones not to have made any jibes or barbs toward any of the other passengers. And when Scott opened his mouth to reply, the answer that came out was not, for once, laced with aggression.

'It's all a coincidence,' he said weakly, as if he could hear how feeble it sounded. 'There were so many people at the Mason's, I didn't *see* anyone's bloody face. And how would I know he was driving this tube? You think I've been following him round all bloody week, waiting for a power cut so I can kill the bastard?' No one responded, it sounded a reasonable defence, but Jess knew there were holes. She'd already built her own explanation for Scott as the culprit and, she couldn't deny, it was the one that made the most sense. It required no grand conspiracy, just a man on the edge, knocked off by a bad run of circumstances.

The others listened in silence as Scott continued his defence, which was now directed toward everyone, not just Chloe. The deference he'd previously afforded the teenage girl was audibly wearing thin. 'And Jenna? I couldn't give a toss about that stuck-up bitch – I wouldn't fucking *kill* someone just because she couldn't stand a bloke trying to have a nice conversation with her.'

'Was it really a nice conversation though?' Isa snorted, and Scott rounded on her, getting up from his seat to loom across the aisle.

'Hey!' Saul matched the movement, sliding in front of Isa so he and Scott were face to face, pressed close to one another in the confines of the narrow aisle.

'Oh, playing the hero, are we?' Scott snorted.

'Better than playing the villain,' Saul responded quickly.

'Look, *mate*, I ain't done nothing to anyone.'

'Then start acting like it.'

'I don't need to prove myself to you.'

Jess could read the body language, primal instinct visibly working its way through their muscles. She stepped away from the pole, readying herself for what might come next.

'That's not what the court will say.'

And that seemed to have done it. Scott launched himself forward, aiming a fist at the side of Saul's head. Saul was about half a foot taller than him, so had time to lean back to avoid it connecting, but the thrust of Scott's attack knocked him back, so he stumbled and fell back on top of Isa, who let out a wail of surprise. Jess reacted before Scott could steady himself and throw another, better-aimed, punch. She leapt forward, gripped Scott's shoulders and shoved him hard, glad to discover that her strength hadn't abandoned her. During her years on the force she'd made an effort to stay fit, even though it was considered less relevant for a DI; she'd never liked the idea of a suspect getting away because she couldn't be bothered to keep up. Surprise was also on her side – Scott clearly hadn't expected a woman to intervene. His eyes glazed over, his focus on nothing except anger and instinct, and he fell back, landing sideways across a couple of seats, his shoulder banging into Amelia, who gave a disgusted look and leapt out of the way.

'This is why everyone needs to calm down!' Jess shouted into the cabin, her voice hoarse where it caught in her throat as she raised her volume to that of a near-scream. 'Stop making it harder than it has to be!'

'He's dangerous!' Isa shouted, now free from underneath Saul, who had moved over with profuse apologies.

'He's clearly violent,' Amelia agreed with a wide-eyed expression from where she now stood in the centre of the aisle. 'We need to make a citizen's arrest – it's legal if we have enough to reasonably suspect him, which we clearly do. He needs to be restrained,' she added, looking around at everyone. 'Before someone else ends up dead.'

Jess did not like the idea of that at all. Innocent until proven guilty. Enough of her colleagues might not have followed that most basic rule of the law, but Jess had always ingrained it into every case, every day at work. Find as much evidence as possible, build a case that could stand up to scrutiny, that no defence lawyer could tear apart. It wasn't always easy, or even possible, but that was always her aim. And tonight, she knew that it *would* be possible. She had enough leads on everybody to hand over, and some proper, professional investigation with the right resources would surely bulk out that file. But this wasn't the moment for Jess to mount a lecture on the rule of law, and Saul had already taken off his belt and was approaching Scott who, now the film of rage had fallen from his eyes, looked defeated. He shook his head and allowed Saul to loop the belt around his wrists in a figure of eight and then buckle it to the nearest handrail by the glass divider panel, the teenagers moving aside to make way for him.

'This is fucking ridiculous,' Scott muttered under his breath, and Jess was inclined to agree. But silence had finally fallen. A calm that Jess didn't trust but fell into willingly anyway. She needed to think, to try and sort out exactly what she was going to tell the police when they, eventually, turned up.

The teenagers found new seats near the driver's cab, where Jenna's leather jacket still lay crumpled. Amelia sat down opposite, pressed as far against the wall as she could, leaning away from Scott at the other end of the bank of seats. Between them her once-forgotten Celine tote and distinctive yellow Selfridges bags formed a kind of luxury goods barrier.

Jess remained standing for a moment, unsure what to do with herself. She gazed down at Scott, the light from her phone now the only illumination in the carriage. Everyone else had seemed to abandon their own attempts at providing light, happy for Jess to take responsibility of the task. In the deep shadows, a glow only tickling him from the sides, Jess thought she had never seen a more defeated figure. Head back against the window, arms pulled uncomfortably together by his makeshift shackles at the pole. And she noted, with surprise, a glistening on his cheeks. An unexpected wetness that he was trying to keep contained in his determinedly shut eyes.

Scott

Scott knew what was waiting for him. Prison. A long fucking stint too, if he was going down for murder. He'd never see Lily again. Never see her grow up, get a job, maybe go to university, he'd never get to take her on holiday again, never get to walk her down the aisle. It had been that thought that had brought the tears on. *He'd* probably do it in Scott's place. The thought left him defeated, the anger that had consumed him replaced with a helpless listlessness. Maybe Scott did deserve prison. He'd lost it in front of everyone, brought all this on himself. All because he let everything run away with him, acted without thinking, wanting to *feel* the physicality of action, of *doing* something

Mel leaving him had unleashed something. He'd spent years trying to keep those dangerous emotions cooped up inside, desperate to make their marriage work. And Scott had a lot to keep cooped up. His useless, gambling addict dad, always nicking Scott's paper-round money for the bookies. His eternally miserable mum, barely able to muster a warm smile even on Christmas morning, and who seemed to blame Scott for their constantly shitty family circumstances. That one fucking bully who'd take Scott round the bins after school and smash his face into the cold, clanging metal pretty much daily. 'Pathetic,' his dad would mutter with a brief glance away from the horses on telly, eyeing his twelve-year-old son with blood pouring from a broken nose. 'Letting them do that to ya.'

And Mel had repaid his efforts to be a good husband, a good dad, by walking out on him. The one upside was that it left him free to finally let loose. To show the world that he wasn't going to let anyone push him around anymore.

But he hadn't killed anyone, even though there'd been moments when he'd felt like he could. The thought of Lily, with her curious, frightened little face, had stopped him. Not that anyone on here knew, or cared, about that. Scott didn't even know who the damned driver was, so how was he supposed to know the guy had been at the Mason's Arms? It wasn't like he'd been taking in everybody's faces, sitting down for a nice chat about what they all did for a living. Besides, Scott held no ill will toward anyone at the pub. He wouldn't *kill* someone over a sodding football match. They'd got everything out on the day, moved on with their lives. Wait for next season, believe they'll do better then, because that's what football fans do.

Now it looked as though he'd be going down for murder anyway, he wished he'd given in to the temptation that afternoon. Mel's new boyfriend, *Neil*, fucking weak name if you asked Scott, insisting on supervising Scott's already supervised visit with Lily in the park. Sat in his shiny red Honda, pulled up at the kerb, and staring out at them through the windscreen from the driver's seat.

'Does he have to fucking do that?' Scott had muttered to Mel as Lily spun wildly on the roundabout he was pushing. A playdate they all knew the eleven-year-old was too old for, but activities and locations for supervised visits that were free were more difficult to come by than Scott had anticipated. 'Can't he leave us alone to be a family?'

'We're not a family, Scott,' Mel had retorted from her position a few steps behind him. Arms folded tightly across the jacket Lily had shrugged off after getting too hot on the domed climbing frame earlier. 'Neil wants to make sure we're safe.'

'Course you're fucking safe,' Scott had spat.

'Well, show us that with your actions then,' Mel had chastised him. 'Stop getting into trouble. Set a real example for your daughter.'

Scott had stepped away from the roundabout then, leaving Lily to spin with the momentum he'd already created, and faced Mel. 'I've never done anything *other* than set an example for Lily. Who was it that sat down with her and helped her do her homework? Who took her to gymnastics class and the cinema and cooked her dinner while you were "working late"?' He held up his fingers in crooked air quotes. 'Me, that's who, so it's fucking rich of you now to accuse *me* of not being a good parent. While you let that weasel' – he flung an arm out in the direction of the car where Neil was now leaning forward and squinting through the windscreen, monitoring their every move – 'swoop in and act like a goddamned hero, for stealing *my fucking family!*'

'Oh, are you two arguing again?' A small voice came from the roundabout behind him, which had slowed to a stop without his attention.

Scott swung round to face his daughter with a falsely bright expression. 'No, no sweetheart, we weren't fighting. Just deciding what you want to do next!' He added. 'We could see if that cafe has milkshakes?'

He thought he'd just about rescued the situation; Lily looked ready to be placated with milkshakes, even though she wasn't stupid enough to believe that they hadn't been arguing. Mel had stayed tensely quiet and, he hoped, eaten up with guilt for what she'd done. But then the fucking weasel had ruined it all.

'Mel!' Neil's voice had broken on the word so it had come out in almost a squeal. He hadn't quite got out of the car, he was leaning out of the driver's door, shouting over at them. 'Come on, let's go! I saw that, you can't let him treat you like that. Not with Lilypad there!'

Lilypad?

LILYPAD!

He'd dared give Scott's daughter a nickname? He'd dared suggest, loudly, to the whole park, *in front* of Lily, that Scott was treating them poorly. After everything that man had fucking done?

That had been the moment Scott had lost it. Blind with rage, couldn't see or think straight, just knew that something had to happen to that man standing, half-hidden like a coward out of his Honda. Scott had cleared the ground between the playground and the Honda before he even knew what was happening. Mel's calls of protest, Lily's wail, had been drowned out by the rush of blood to his head. Neil had immediately dived back inside the car when he saw Scott coming, locking the doors and cowering behind the steering wheel.

'You fucking COWARD!' Scott had roared, pounding on the bonnet. 'Come out here and face me like a man!' He'd cast wildly around for something, anything he could use, and settled on a nearby broken branch. He pounded the wood into the bonnet the way his own face had once been pounded into the bins behind the school, and wished that Neil's face was on the receiving end of his blows. When the bonnet was suitably cratered with silver-scratched dents, Scott moved round to the windscreen, sending a concentric crack rippling through it.

He felt hands on his shoulders as Mel, joined by a couple of strangers, tried to get him to stop. But it was Lily's voice that had broken through the rushing noise in his ears, through all the other shouts and wails around him.

'Dad!'

He'd stopped at once and stared at her over the smashed-up car. She was hovering at the edge of the park, afraid to come closer, tears pouring down her small, beautiful face. He'd looked down at the branch in his hand, almost surprised to find it there, and let it fall to the ground, revealing red, flushed palms where the wood had grazed his skin.

'You will *never* see your daughter again!' Mel spat at him, yanking Lily by the arm and shoving her roughly into the back seat of the Honda, before jumping into the passenger seat a moment before Neil put the car into drive and pulled off the kerb, forcing Scott to jump clear or risk his toes being run over.

He'd watched the car disappear down the street, Lily's face turned toward him in the rear windscreen until they turned a corner and were gone. An arc of onlookers had gathered around the scene, but Scott ignored them. He'd turned on his heel and headed for his old local, knowing there was only one thing to do now. Get as drunk as possible to black out what had just happened.

He was sure Mel would have called the police as soon as they made it home. No doubt they'd already showed up at his mum's, hoping to pick him up. Maybe he should have taken the opportunity to run tonight. Run out into the black night and make a go of it elsewhere. But Lily had stopped him. Even if he was in prison, even if he was never allowed to see her again, he wanted her to know, in some way, that he hadn't abandoned her.

Thirty-Nine

Jess gazed down at the horribly sad sight of Scott trying to hide his tears. Her body sagging with exhaustion, she leant against the pole and tipped her head back to think. She cast her mind back over every detail, every suspicion, every clue – if she could even call any of them that. Two things snagged at her. If Scott had recognized the driver as a rival football supporter and gone into the cab hell-bent on revenge, why had he bothered to cut all the wires? And then there was the murder weapon. In her mind's eye she saw the knife sticking out of Jenna's neck. There was something about that knife, something significant . . . Jess frowned to herself and lowered the phone from where it had been providing a cascade of weak light to hold it at chest-height, the torch now pointed uselessly at the floor, casting the passengers into black once again.

She swiped the home screen left to bring up the camera, and clicked on the image in the bottom left corner so the photos she'd taken of Jenna's body filled the screen. She gave an involuntary shudder as she remembered the way poor Jenna had gone, rats swarming her body, on the filthy floor of a dank tunnel. She swiped through them until she'd landed on the close-up of the knife buried into Jenna's neck.

She placed two fingers on the screen and spread them apart to zoom in on the handle. What had looked like a manufacturer's logo was in fact Japanese lettering. She stared at it for a moment longer before she understood. It took another moment, a frown toward Scott, for her to realize how wrong they'd all been.

The knife was a key, suddenly the mystery felt unlocked and everything slotted neatly into place. There had never been two killers, no grand conspiracy. It seemed so simple now, obvious really, as if she should have seen it all from the start. But, of course, that would have been impossible – when she'd found the driver dead in his cab, half the mystery had yet to unravel.

The night's events played out in her mind in sharp detail, no question left unanswered. Jess knew who'd done it – she understood how and she understood why.

All that remained was final confirmation.

She hurried forward, falling to her knees in front of the bank of seats.

'Jess?' Chloe asked. 'Are you OK?'

But Jess ignored her, she was too busy examining the bloody mess on Amelia's knee, holding Jenna's torch up to illuminate every detail.

'What are you doing?' Amelia asked, shifting her leg out of Jess's line of scrutiny. 'It's feeling better now,' she added, as if Jess had asked her how she was doing. 'My husband's a doctor, I'll get him to look at it in the morning, see if I need stitches.'

Jess ignored the babble. She shifted her weight onto her heels and looked up at Amelia with a slow shake of her head.

'You've put on such a good show, Amelia. All night.' She gestured vaguely around. 'You had everybody fooled. Even me.

I never really had you in my sights – and why would I? Nicely dressed lady, worried about getting home for her IVF medication after a day of shopping and a hard year. No connection to the driver, no violent tendencies. Why on earth should anyone look at you?'

Amelia's eyes widened, but it was a stiff movement, forced, not natural surprise.

'But it was never about the driver, was it?' Jess continued, glancing sadly toward the cab door. 'He was collateral damage in a plan formed frantically and desperately, taking quick advantage of the hand the universe dealt you. My God, you must have been so surprised when it seemed to have all worked out. Did you ever really think you'd get this far?'

Amelia didn't answer, but she held Jess's gaze, her eyes hardening ever so slightly in the torchlight.

'Hey,' Scott said gruffly, 'what are you talking about?'

'Someone release Scott, please,' Jess said. And when nobody moved, she snapped her head toward Saul. 'NOW!'

Saul, visibly confused but shocked into compliance, got to his feet and fiddled with the buckle on Scott's makeshift restraints, pulling the belt free.

'I don't know what you're talking about,' Amelia said with an incredulous shake of her head.

'Yes you do,' Jess answered, and held the phone up to her face, still displaying the close-up image of the knife. 'This was the knife buried in Jenna's neck. The size of the blade matches the wounds that killed the driver too. And' – she looked pointedly down at Amelia's knee – 'that wound on your leg. Your tights are very neatly cut for a fall, that scratch is too clean to have been caused by grazing it on the tracks.'

'So?' Amelia seemed to be getting her confidence back now. 'If anything, that just proves I was attacked with the same knife!'

Jess looked at her pityingly, hoping Amelia would have the sense to give it up. She was caught.

'The thing is, I know this brand of knife.' Jess pointed to the Japanese lettering on the elegant handle. 'I bought a set for my friend's leaving present. She's a keen cook,' she added with a half-smile of explanation before turning to Amelia's abandoned bags. 'And do you know where I had to go to buy it? The only UK stockist for this particular brand?' Her eyes settled on the distinctive yellow bags. Amelia followed her gaze, her face stilling, her expression unmoving, unreadable. Jess reached for the bags. 'If you only bought a wedding present for your friend, why do you have two bags?'

Her hands connected with the bags, one clearly weighed down by its contents, the other sliding toward her, its solo contents rattling lightly around inside. Jess held the bag by its base and tipped it upside down. A glossy cardboard presentation box, with the same Japanese lettering printed on the side, tumbled to the ground too easily to be weighed down by the steel knife pictured as its contents. Jess picked up the empty box and held it out in front of Amelia. Eyebrows raised, she waited to see if Amelia would offer an explanation. When she didn't speak, Jess continued.

'It was never about the driver,' she repeated, more confident than ever now that the words were true. 'It was always about Jenna. You followed her onto this tube. Why else would you be on a northern-bound Bakerloo line train when, you told me yourself, you live in Islington? I don't think you had a plan about when you wanted to kill her, but you saw her in Selfridges' – the photos Jenna had tried to upload of the designer bag department flared to life in Jess's brain – 'and you knew you had to act. You'd already been in the cookshop, so you went back, bought a knife. And then you followed her, waiting for the right moment. But London on a Friday night is busy, so you never got your chance. You followed her onto the tube.' Jess remembered Amelia boarding at the same time, glancing quickly at Jenna before choosing her seat. 'When the power went out, you saw your opportunity. Perhaps you considered using the knife to kill Jenna right then, but she was all the way at the other end of the carriage, and you'd have to pass through the rest of us. But you were sat nearest the driver. You didn't know how long the power cut would go on for, so you decided to attack him and cut all the wires, so we'd be stuck down here longer. Eventually, you hoped, if you kicked up enough of a fuss about getting home, we'd all go out into the unlit tunnel to walk to safety. You'd hidden the knife in your boot.' She nodded down to Amelia's cut knee. 'In the dark, with everyone focused on making their way along the tunnel, you would have the chance to kill your true victim. It might have taken a little longer than you'd hoped,' Jess held her arms out in a shrug, 'but you got there in the end.'

Amelia seemed to consider Jess's words for a moment before rolling her eyes with a desperate little laugh. 'How very neat for you,' she said in what she clearly hoped was a light, mocking tone. 'But why on earth would I want to kill Jenna?'

Jess could see from the expressions on their faces that this was the question everyone had been asking themselves. The motive had been the last niggling doubt Jess had needed to unravel before setting out the interconnected parts of Amelia's actions that night. But the motive had been there all along; Amelia herself had announced it to them all, unable to keep it in. So Jess had her answer ready to go.

'As revenge for your sister.'

Amelia

Well, hadn't Jess just thought of everything.

Amelia would have rolled her eyes if she wasn't so thoroughly caught out. All she could do was lean back in her seat and give a light shrug. Her eyes flitted to Scott, and when she spoke it was with an exhausted groan.

'Don't tie me up,' she said. 'I've not been violent toward anyone else.'

'Except me,' Jess pointed out, raising her injured arm, still wrapped in Isa's bulky scarf.

'Yes, well, needs must sometimes.' Amelia hadn't regretted what she'd done to Jess in the second blackout – not that she'd known it was Jess at the time. She had seen an opportunity to scare everybody into getting off the train and into the tunnel, and she'd acted on it. Slipped the knife carefully from her boot and just lunged. And it had worked. In fact, it had worked better than she'd anticipated, seeing as she'd ended up in the tunnel with exactly the person she needed. 'But,' she continued with a sigh, 'that was only a means to an end. And end which, as you've so *cleverly*' – she dripped scorn into the word – 'pointed out, I've already achieved. I have nothing to gain by attacking any of you now, except more years added to my prison sentence.'

Jess paused as if considering it, and Amelia glanced around the other passengers, all of whom were staring at her with confused, incredulous looks. The remaining phone torches had been re-illuminated in the wake of this new development and were all pointed directly at Amelia.

'I don't understand.' Isa was the first to verbalize the expression on everyone's face. 'You're admitting it? You *did* do all of this?' Her arm flailed upwards, gesturing to the dark carriage.

'I didn't cause the power cut,' Amelia clarified, this time allowing a roll of her eyes. 'That's a bit excessive. People don't cause citywide power failures just to settle one score.' She felt surprisingly playful, as if a strange freedom had come with being caught. Glancing in Isa's direction, she added, 'And you can take that from a bona fide murderer.'

Isa recoiled, a look of disgust contorting her features, but Amelia was numb to it. The tight knot of tension that had constrained her all night had finally loosened. She'd done the deed and now, she knew, she was going to pay for it. She no longer had to worry about living a life in constant strain, wondering if the next knock at the door would be the police. At some point that night, she'd thought about trying to persuade Lawrence to make the move to Australia. After all, that had been her chosen place of refuge back when his shit had hit the fan. And God knew he needed a fresh start too. But now that would be unnecessary; Amelia would confess her crime and accept her punishment. The realities of that punishment, visions gleamed from prison dramas and true crime documentaries, sent a shiver down her limbs. But, she pushed that aside for now and dwelled instead in the satisfaction of what she'd achieved. Because Jess was only half right, Amelia *had* wanted to avenge Libby. But she had also cut the head off a beast that had been feeding off innocent and vulnerable women for too long. Without Jenna Pace, she was sure, the Burned empire would crumble, and its prisoners would be freed before it was too late. Even though it had been too late for Libby.

When Libby had first started selling the Burned candles Amelia had not thought much of it. Libby had never returned to her executive assistant job after Ruby was born, the cost of childcare for two kids under two in London outstripping her previous wage. Rob was a middle sales manager at some garden supply company, a decent living from what Amelia understood but not quite enough to sustain a family of four in London on one salary. She knew money was tight, even with help from their generous parents, which Libby and Rob never asked for, and never once complained about their circumstances. So, if Libby was making a bit of extra pocket money to take the pressure off, Amelia had not considered it anything to worry about. Their mum had sold make-up in the nineties and that had always seemed to go OK.

In the lead-up to Libby's death though, when Amelia thought back with sharply focused hindsight, her sister *had* seemed more frantic, more removed from the family, drained and sallow-faced. But it was also the lead-up to Amelia's wedding, and now she regretted how wrapped up she'd got in details of guests' accommodation and arrival times, welcome nibbles and finding an Italian hairdresser who understood English. She knew she must have missed countless more warning signs – Libby's despair fading into the background of Amelia's special day. They'd even argued about it on Amelia's hen do, Libby badgering Amelia's friends to not only buy the damned candles but to sign up to sell them too. Libby had been so generous to them that weekend, shown off wealth she didn't have, all to impress them, to prove the lifestyle you could have if only you joined her. But despite Libby's lavish displays, Amelia's friends had seen through her falsely bright pitch, noticing her strained, desperate tinge instead.

It was too late by the time they learnt that Libby owed over twenty thousand pounds. It had been taken out over the previous two years in an assortment of credit cards, bank loans and pay-day loans, beginning with a starter pack of candles running to five thousand pounds, followed by constant top-ups of unsellable stock. A quick look through Libby's phone and emails had revealed the intolerable pressure she'd been put under.

You've got to invest if you want to take this seriously, the woman above her in the chain would message regularly.

> Look at Jenna's Instagram for inspiration if you ever feel down. Do it for the kiddos! You said you wanted to take them to Disneyland, you've got to work for that if you're serious!

Then they'd turned nastier, as Libby complained about the declining quality of the candles, her struggle to sell them.

> No one else is struggling. I've sold £10k worth of stock this month alone.

> If you want to quit you can, no one is stopping you. But think of what you've already invested. You'll throw all that down the drain.

It was like a dossier documenting her poor sister's decline, feeling like she wasn't contributing to the house enough, spiralling and lost as she realized the secret debt that was mounting and mounting with no way out – except by asking for help. And Amelia knew she herself had removed that option when she'd drunkenly mocked Libby on the beachfront in Brighton, a paper bag of chips in one hand, the other trying to keep the tacky plastic veil from blowing into her face.

'Oh my *God*, Lib stop harassing my friends about your fucking scam,' she'd laughed cruelly, stuffing a chip in her mouth. 'It's nice for you to have a little project' – she'd wiggled her fingers in Libby's direction over the words – 'but these girls have real jobs, they don't have time to fuck about with some candle pyramid scheme.'

She'd been too drunk and too wrapped up in herself to truly know the damage she was causing, and afterwards Amelia had blamed herself, too ashamed to tell her parents or Lawrence what she'd said to her poor, vulnerable sister.

And then Lawrence had gone and fucked everything up even more, sending their first year of marriage into a spiral of hellish stress and grief so potent Amelia could feel her actual brain chemistry changing. He'd done something stupid, *so* stupid, claiming he'd been driven by the pressure of the family circumstances. Lawrence had been a surgeon. His undoing had been a private hip replacement for a seventy-eight-year-old who'd never have made the top of the NHS list. Lawrence, in some warped sense of humour or simply losing his mind, had carved at the bottom of the access scar a small 'L' followed by an accompanying 'K'. It was almost explainable as a botched scar – *almost*. If Lawrence hadn't laughed and called the nurses' attention to it while he'd worked.

Amelia had been furious, but she'd stuck by him through the inevitable hearings and press coverage, the headlines making it sound far worse than it even was: *Sicko doc carves name into patient.* Lawrence had, unsurprisingly, been struck off. But he'd soon found a new job selling pharmaceuticals, bringing in even more money than he had before. Life had settled down in the last few months, and they really had decided to try for a baby. They were not quite at the IVF stage yet though, that had just been an early ruse to get them all off the train. The titbit about having to take the drugs at the same time every day cemented in her brain from one housewife's journey on her favourite reality show.

Amelia hadn't quite realized how fractured she still was inside until today. When she'd seen Jenna Pace, not a care in the world, casually shopping for handbags to the tune pretty much of poor Libby's debt. In the past year Amelia had become obsessed with the woman who had engineered her sister's downfall, scrolling sneakily through her Instagram late at night, as if she was illicitly stalking an ex-boyfriend she knew would only cause her more pain – every happy, smiling post ripping apart Amelia's nearly healed wounds. So, seeing Jenna in real life, as glossy and successful as if she'd just stepped out of a phone screen, Amelia had been unable to tear herself away. She was lugging the heavy wrought-iron pan set she'd bought as a wedding present and had been heading out the door when she'd first seen her. Amelia felt like she blacked out, not thinking straight, as she began to trail Jenna around the store, a magnetic force between them that, every time Amelia told herself she needed to get home, pulled her back in. And with every purchase, every designer dress tried on, every piece of expensive jewellery seriously considered, a dark fog had entered Amelia. Jenna Pace was a parasite, stealing and bullying poor women in the guise of inspiring them, and then using their money to buy herself shiny trinkets. It was not *Amelia* who had killed her sister, it was *Jenna*. And she needed to be stopped before she killed anyone else.

It was the black fog that had taken control of her limbs as she followed Jenna back through the cookshop toward the food hall, her brain not really registering as she'd walked past the expensive rack of knives, picking one at random and throwing it down on the counter, keeping one eye on where Jenna had stopped at a luxury chocolate stand. She'd accepted her second purchase and watched as Jenna sat herself down at the champagne bar, snapping photos of her well-plated raw fish. Amelia sat down at the next bar over and ordered a martini without thinking. When they'd decided to try for a baby, for a fresh start, both she and Lawrence had agreed to give up the booze. But today was a different occasion. Amelia needed to calm herself. Or she needed Dutch courage for what she really wanted to do. She hadn't yet decided.

The magnetic pull had dragged her around London with Jenna, eventually onto the tube. Only once she'd sat down had her senses somewhat come back to her, and she'd realized she was on completely the wrong line, going completely the wrong way. She'd sent Lawrence a voice note, promised him she'd be home soon, and, as the martinis cleared, worked out her route home, needing to get off at Baker Street to change lines to get back to Islington.

But then the tube had stopped, the lights had gone out.

And the black fog returned, whispering promises and plans in Amelia's ear. *This is how you do it.* And without really thinking about it, she'd fetched her newly bought knife and used it for the first time for its intended purpose. Then she'd cut the wires, thinking that no one would be able to call for help, and so they'd all have to file out into the tunnel to safety.

Survival instinct had driven the rest of the night. Lies and protestations of innocence that didn't *feel* untrue because she could detach herself from what she'd done, almost forget that it *was* indeed her who'd taken an innocent man's life without knowing anything about him. She blocked it all out and set her sights only on Jenna. She would make up for the driver's death by doing what she'd set out to do in the first place – that would make his sacrifice worth it.

And then they'd been in the tunnel. And Isa had been easy enough to manipulate to leave them be. All Amelia needed was to strike.

She'd lowered her phone as they'd walked, so the light shifted from where it had been pointing ahead, lighting the way, to uselessly illuminating a circular patch of ground instead.

'What's happened?' Jenna's voice had been urgent, on the verge of panic as she stared into the black abyss ahead.

'I stumbled,' Amelia said, and bent low to retrieve the knife from her boot. But her hands had been shaking, the adrenaline coursing through her with the knowledge of what she was about to do, and the blade had caught, slashing her knee. 'Ahh!' she hissed as pain stung through her.

'Are you OK?' Jenna asked. 'Have you hurt yourself?'

Amelia didn't answer, she'd just straightened herself up, let her phone fall to the ground and lunged in the direction of Jenna's voice, one hand grabbing at her hair so she knew she was aiming in the right place. The other plunged the knife into Jenna's neck – her strength driven by guilt and anger, and in that moment the target of the knife was not only Jenna – it was Lawrence, it was herself. Amelia flung Jenna from her and staggered back as she heard the American stumble toward the brick wall and then fall to the ground, a horrible gurgling sound coming from where she landed.

In that moment Amelia's senses really did come back to her.

She had a choice to make. Her knee was hurting from the slash of the knife, and she still didn't know how far away Baker

Street was. They would all know Amelia and Jenna had been alone together in the tunnel; if Amelia were to try and disappear into the night, how long would it take for someone to find Jenna's body and put two and two together? Not long enough for Amelia and Lawrence to hotfoot it to Australia, especially not if there was a power cut shutting down the airports.

No, her best bet would be to feign innocence, posing as another victim.

Using her good leg, she had stamped her heeled boot directly into her fallen phone screen. Multicoloured lines appeared for a moment before, finally, it turned to black.

And then she'd returned, the walking wounded, to the train, fading into the background while the others tore each other apart.

But now it was done. It was all over. And she didn't regret it. Her only regret was not fleeing while she might have had a chance to get away. But if Amelia was going to spend the rest of her life in prison paying for her crimes, then at least she could be soothed by knowing, in some wider way, she'd restored justice to the universe.

Amelia put her head back to the window behind her and closed her eyes, waiting patiently for the others' judgement of whether she was worth restraining or not.

Forty

In the end they didn't bother restraining Amelia. The shock of her confession rippled around the group, leaving them in a state of complete inertia. Even Scott didn't have anything to say about having been unceremoniously shackled despite being completely innocent. He was wrapped up in his own thoughts, head tipped back, eyes closed, cheeks still wet. Jess hovered uncertainly in the standing section, gripping Jenna's phone at waist-height, its light aimed toward Amelia, just in case.

But Jess didn't have to hover uncertainly for too long.

Voices came echoing down the tunnel, spilling in through the still-open tube doors. An urgent shout, then a hurrying of pace, strong torch beams bouncing off the windows as the rescuers slipped down the side of the train and the tunnel.

The first person to appear at the open doors was a flushed young uniformed officer, gripping an industrial torch in one hand, his florescent vest glancing in the light of Jess's pathetic phone torch offering as she turned toward him.

He panted, looking visibly shocked as he said. 'Is everyone all right on here?'

Jess assumed they'd seen Jenna's body. The poor officer just expecting to be coordinating another evacuation, not stumbling across bloody corpses. Another officer joined him by the doors, her own industrial torch shoved under her armpit as she finished speaking into the radio on her shoulder. She looked older and calmer, clearly the more experienced of this particular partnership.

'We're as OK as we can be,' Jess answered honestly, as the two transport police officers climbed up onto the train. 'As you've probably seen' – she gestured outside – 'we've had an incident.' She glanced toward the driver's cab. 'Or rather, two.'

More police officers holding powerful torches passed by the open doors to their carriage, pausing for a moment to liaise with the two who had boarded, before moving on to check the other carriages and evacuate whatever remaining passengers they contained.

'Two?' The more experienced officer turned back to face Jess, surprised lines appearing on her forehead.

Jess gave a deep sigh and looked down for a moment before answering. 'Unfortunately, the driver has also been attacked.'

The officer turned toward the rest of the passengers, passing her light across them. They all sat up straighter, hope that they were finally going to get home settling visibly on their features. Except Amelia, of course, who kept her head down, hands clasped in her lap.

'What on earth has been going on down here?' The officer swung back to Jess, recognizing her as de facto leader and noticing for the first time Jess's bandaged arm. She nodded toward it. 'And are you injured too?'

'I'm fine.' Jess waved the concern away. 'Really, it's superficial only. DI Jessica Hirsch,' she introduced herself with a nod, and then, thinking it best to be honest this time round, she corrected herself. '*Ex*-DI Jessica Hirsch.' She heard a couple of the other passengers shift and murmur at that revelation. 'But I've done my best to secure the crime scene and protect whatever evidence I can. The situation is the driver was attacked, stabbed three times in the neck, during the first blackout. Then, when a group of us decided to go into the tunnel to see how far away the next station was, one of the other passengers was stabbed, this time with a single knife wound, also to the neck. I dare say you saw her as you passed by?'

'Hard to miss,' the younger officer muttered under his breath.

The female officer shot him a look before shaking her head incredulously. 'But why?'

Jess gestured over to Amelia. 'I believe Amelia here can answer all those questions for you,' she said, feeling the palpable relief of officially handing over the events of tonight to somebody still paid to deal with them. 'She's made a confession with all of us present to witness it, and I have some additional evidence gathered that I can hand over too.'

The officer looked toward Amelia, and Jess recognized the slight brace to her stance, waiting to see if she was going to make trouble. But Amelia merely looked up, dejected, and shook her head.

'I'll come willingly,' she said in a weak voice.

After that, it was a flurry of activity. More officers were summoned from the other carriages, and the passengers finally evacuated, escorted to the front of the train led by the powerful industrial torches which illuminated the whole tunnel in a relieving white glow. As she was disembarking, Jess saw two officers head into the driver's cab. Amelia was handcuffed, but she hadn't yet been arrested or read her rights. There was still too much the officers didn't know before they could legally do any of that – they didn't even know who they were arresting her for killing. That would all come, Jess knew. There would be a long night of statements before the passengers would be allowed to go home. Backup had arrived by the time the group passed the site of Jenna's body, the perplexed officers beginning the process of protecting the crime scene, waiting for the SOCOs. The passengers were walking in a line, almost single file, down the centre of the tracks, officers at the head and back of them lighting the way. Amelia trailed behind with her own personal escort.

Jess heard Chloe and Isa gasp as they passed by Jenna, Liam making an uncomfortable groan and turning his head demonstrably away. Jess turned away too, she wanted to spare Jenna any last indignities she could.

There were more police on the platform at Baker Street, hovering in front of the black tiled silhouette of the address's most famous fictional resident, Sherlock Holmes. Jess allowed herself to be hoisted up onto the platform by a strong arm and guided up the clanging emergency staircase. Her thighs were burning long before she expected them to be, grateful for the escalators and lifts that usually did this job for her, but it was the early hours of the morning, and she was nearing twenty-four hours of being awake. No one spoke as they climbed the stairs, everyone's focus only on getting back to the surface. It wasn't until they filed out of the narrow door that usually covered the emergency access stairs into the station's entrance hall, that Saul broke the silence.

'What's been going on?' he asked the officer at the head of their group.

'Sorry it took so long for us to get to you,' the officer said, correctly reading the meaning of Saul's question. 'But the power's gone out across the city.' He shook his head and Jess saw the same signs of exhaustion in the deep, dark bags drawn on his cheeks as she imagined were displayed on her own face. 'It's been chaos. Everyone's been called in, but still, it's been . . .' he trailed off with another shake of his head. 'And obviously, if we'd known the situation down there . . .' He gestured vaguely with a guilty slash across his tired features. 'But we've been getting to the trains as quickly as we could, and with the electrics out, we had no way of knowing where anyone was stuck. It's been quite the task.'

'Can,' Chloe asked in a small voice, 'can we go home now?'

The officer looked at her with a regretful expression. 'I'm afraid not quite yet. With the situation we need to get everyone's statements before we can let you go.'

'But I need to call my dad.'

He nodded understandingly. 'We can arrange that,' he said, his voice soft and kind. 'We've set up an emergency command not far from here, around the corner. We'll take you there, get you all some water and food if you need it, take your statements and then we can arrange to contact anyone you need us to, and get you home.'

Jess fell into silent step with everyone else as they were guided out of the station and toward the emergency command. London felt like a different beast in the total blackness. She'd never before realized quite how much of a glow the city normally had, even in the depths of night. She tipped her head up to the sky and saw the stars prick a brighter white than she'd ever seen them over London before.

'Crazy, isn't it?' Isa said softly, following Jess's lead and also staring into the night sky as they walked.

Jess nodded and adjusted her trench coat where she had it resting over her good arm, relishing the night breeze that sent a shiver across her sweat-sheened skin. She took a deep breath, feeling like she was breathing clean oxygen again for the first time in hours – not something she usually felt about the air quality of central London. But there was no taste of blood or anxious sweat on her tongue, and that alone felt like she could have been on top of the highest alp.

As she walked next to Isa she realized there was still one lie that had been told to her that night. She supposed she didn't deserve an answer – Isa was as entitled to her secrets as anyone else – but Jess's curiosity was still wound tight around her. And it was without really thinking that she asked, 'Isa, where *were* you headed tonight when your friends got off the tube?'

Isa blinked, obviously surprised by the question.

'Oh,' she said, considering for a moment. But she obviously decided there was nothing more to lose at this point, because she did finally answer. 'I was going to continue the protest, but my friends thought it was a step too far.' Jess frowned questioningly and Isa continued. 'Have you heard of this *Hookd & Fookd* trend?'

'That was on your stickers.' Jess nodded down to Isa's tote, clasped tightly to her shoulder.

'Yeah, well it's sprung up around campus and the whole city – guys sending each other naked pictures of girls they've met on the app. Anyway, the founder has said it's nothing to do with him, he did a big old statement saying what people get up to on his app was none of his business. But he was *sorry* if any women had been hurt by the men they'd met.' She rolled her eyes demonstrably.

'So what were you going to do tonight?'

Isa paused for another moment and then answered. 'I found out his address,' she admitted. 'I was going to go and put these stickers up all over his house, maybe spray paint it too. But my friends said we'd get kicked out of uni if we did anything illegal, maybe even end up in prison.' Isa pressed her lips together in a determined line. 'But I reckon some things are worth risking your own skin for, so I told them I had to go home for a family day tomorrow.'

'I see.' Jess accepted the answer, too tired to scrutinize how much truth it contained. She considered telling Isa that her friends were right. There was no point in throwing her future away over a bit of vandalism that would barely make a dent. But she didn't. Isa was an adult, she'd make her own mistakes, learn her own lessons.

They arrived at the emergency command and were immediately handed bottles of water and offered cups of tea or coffee. Jess drank greedily, feeling it spill down her chin as she gulped the precious water down her desert-dry throat. She accepted a cup of tea too, burning the roof of her mouth as she drank that too quickly as well, and ravaged a chocolate biscuit from the tin that was held out.

One by one they were taken off to collect their statements, Jess's taking the longest as she detailed everything she had discovered over the course of the night, and handing over both victims' phones and Amelia's cracked one. They insisted on having someone look at her arm, and as a paramedic wiped it down with stinging disinfectant and considered whether stitches were needed or not, she saw Chloe, Liam and Isa being guided toward a police car. She held up her good arm in farewell, and all three waved back toward her. Chloe mouthing, *Thank you*, before she ducked into the car.

Scott and Saul were given their own rides home, Saul stopping to wish her well and adding that he hoped she wasn't in too much pain with her arm. Scott did not speak to her, but gave a single nod, and he climbed sombrely into the back of a police car, his expression one of waiting for the worst, but not knowing when it would come.

Eventually, she was all tidied up and given the go-ahead to finally return home.

Dawn was tickling the horizon of her tree-lined street when she climbed out of the police car and said thank you to the knackered officer who'd driven her back. There was a new tinge of pink to the fading navy blue over her roof, and as she stuck her key in the lock and turned, she heard Honey give a bark of alarm.

The dog was the first one to greet her as she stepped into the doorway, those clacking feet on the wooden floorboards stopping at Jess's legs to place her front two paws on her thighs and accept the ruffled greeting she wanted.

'Oh Jesus, thank God you're home!' Alex was breathless as he followed in Honey's wake and pulled Jess into a tight, desperate hug. 'I've been so worried, are you OK?' He held her cheeks between his hands, his face crumpled in frantic worry.

'I'm fine,' Jess said with a breathy exhale. And for the first time that night, she really did feel fine. 'I got stuck on the tube, down in the tunnel, with the power cut. I thought you'd be in bed.'

Alex released her at last, and they walked side by side into the living room.

'I woke up and you still weren't home, so I went to check my phone and there was no message from you, and it hadn't been charging. But I checked the news alert which said about the citywide power cut, and so I knew you must be stuck somewhere in it. I couldn't sleep after that, so I've been down here keeping an eye on the news on my laptop. There's been riots and everything.' He rolled his eyes, despairing at the people who took such horrible advantage of situations like this. 'I worried you'd been caught up in one.' As Jess sank down into their comfortable sofa, he seemed to notice her bandaged arm and bloody dress for the first time. 'Oh my God!' He rushed to her side. 'You *are* hurt!'

She gazed into his familiar face that she loved so much and let out a deep sigh as she leant back on the sofa and closed her eyes.

'Have I got a story for you,' she said, before pausing to decide whether she wanted to sleep, shower or talk first. To her surprise, the latter won out and she tipped her head forward and pulled her knees into her chest as Alex settled on the footrest in front of her. And then she began to speak, and as she talked, she felt the night release its hold over her.

Epilogue

Three months later

How did the interview go?

The first message that popped up within minutes of Jess leaving the great white building was from Liv. A small smile tugged at the corner of Jess's lips as she made her way past the iconic grey block sign reading *New Scotland Yard*.

The sun was bright on the early summer morning, the sky blue with streaks of wispy clouds. She typed as she walked, heading along the embankment beside the Thames before turning toward Westminster tube, hurrying quickly past the wrought-iron fenced steps that led into the bowels of London. Jess wouldn't call it a phobia she'd developed exactly, but she had avoided the tube in the last few months, opting instead for the bus or walking. She was sure she'd get back on a tube eventually, but when the weather was so nice it wasn't too much of a hardship to stick to above-ground methods of transportation. She was heading for

St James's Park, a paperback in her bag and a couple of hours to kill with a coffee in the sun before she met Alex for a celebratory lunch. Not that they were celebrating the outcome just yet, but he had insisted that her being ready to go back to work was worth a celebration in and of itself.

> Well, I think! The Superintendent seemed to like me, DSU Williams. She'd heard about my work on the Bryson case, which I think put me in good stead. So fingers crossed!

Three dots appeared to show Liv was immediately typing a response.

> Good! She'd be an idiot not to hire you, you're the best DI I ever worked with.

Jess felt a warm glow on her skin that had nothing to do with the sunshine. The conversation continued on a little longer, until Liv said she had to get back to work, but she was excited to see her at the weekend. They were going on a proper night out, first to dinner at a restaurant Jess had always wanted to try, then cocktails at a bar that had recently won an award. It had been a long time coming, but in the aftermath of the night of the blackout, Jess had realized that it wasn't solely Liv's fault that the only drinks invitation Jess had been stuck with had been from Nicole.

As much as Jess had thought Liv was too wrapped up in work, Jess had also retreated from their friendship. Embarrassed about how she'd left, still too stung to spend time with her friend talking about the work she was doing every day, knowing that she, herself, had run away like a failure. The afternoon after the blackout, after a shower and a good long sleep, Liv had been the first person Jess had called. They'd talked for hours, dissecting what Jess had been through on the tube and what had been happening above ground. At the end of the call, Liv had surprised Jess with a small sigh.

'I've missed you,' she'd said. 'I've missed us. But it sounds like you're coming back to yourself maybe a bit?'

It was that moment that had reframed the last year in Jess's mind, how her own sense of failure had tainted everything. But now she felt different. She'd worked out the holes in Amelia's story, slotted it all into place eventually, and she'd made sure justice had been delivered for both Matt and Jenna. It had been the first step in a long three months of Jess regaining her confidence enough to finally apply for a job at a new command, under a new CO.

She made it to St James's Park and settled herself into a deckchair with her takeaway coffee and pulled the book out of her bag. Before she opened it up to the folded-down page she'd finished on last night, she placed her phone on top and messaged Alex with an update on how the interview had gone, and where she was sitting so he could easily find her later. Then she tapped on her news app, not having had a chance to read the headlines that morning with her stressed preparation for her interview.

Down at the bottom, in the Local News section, was a headline with a familiar thumbnail next to it. She frowned, surprised, and clicked on the article.

Student hit with revenge porn charges over tech magnate

As she scanned down the text that filled her screen, Jess's stomach sank. It seemed there had been one last lie she had never got to the bottom of that night. Isa's plans for the founder of Hookd turned out to be far more sinister than simple vandalism. She'd broken into his home late at night using a lock-snapper bar and taken photos of him sleeping, naked, in bed, her *Hookd THEN Fookd* stickers displayed on the wall behind him. Then she'd posted them, what she'd obviously hoped was anonymously, online. Jess had seen the story break a few weeks ago, and had hoped it had nothing to do with Isa. But, of course, nothing is ever really anonymous online, and Isa it seemed had done little in the way of trying to cover her tracks. She'd bought her housebreaking equipment from Amazon, using her own personal account, and a video had emerged of her at the protest on the night of the blackout. She was furiously telling a news crew that Hookd needed more attention, more scrutiny on them, that the founder should be charged with hundreds of counts of sexual harassment for every woman who'd had her privacy violated thanks to his app. And so Isa had been easily caught, and now named and pictured in the press. Jess shook her head sadly, reading down to the bottom of the article, where there was a photo of Isa, presumably taken from a social media page, face scrunched up and shouting as she held a placard that read *Yes, All Men*.

That would bring the grand total of the passengers on the tube that night charged with crimes to three. Jess had asked the DI in charge of Amelia's case to keep her in the loop, a courtesy the DI had extended, telling her that Amelia had confessed and was pleading guilty to all charges. She was currently in Holloway prison, awaiting sentencing. The second update had come a few weeks later, through the grapevine of old contacts who had heard that she'd been on what the press were delighting in calling the *Murder Tube*. Scott had also been arrested, for assault with a deadly weapon on his ex-wife's new partner. He was out on bail and Jess thought he stood a good chance for a light sentencing, considering he hadn't physically attacked the partner, more his car. A better lawyer, if Scott could have afforded one, Jess knew, would argue for a reduced sentencing to vandalism. But his public defender didn't seem to have considered that possibility. Jess hoped Scott didn't get the book thrown at him. Maybe a short sentence, community service and mandated anger-management classes. If anyone could benefit from those, Jess thought, it was Scott.

She had had updates from Saul and Chloe too. Saul had found her on her relatively defunct Facebook account a week or so later and sent her a message to let her know that he'd appreciated all she'd done the night of the blackout, and that he'd decided to move up to Manchester to be nearer to his son, who was based up there for university. Jess had thanked him in return for his expertise on the night and wished him luck up north.

Chloe had messaged her the very next day on Instagram; Jess had found the message soon after she'd hung up with Liv.

> Hi Jess, I just wanted to say thank you for everything last night. It was a scary situation, but you made us feel much safer, and you saw through Amelia when none of the rest of us did. I hope your arm heals OK. We both got home all right in the end, and Dad's just about started breathing again. Liam's mum had been up and worried too, and has called off work today so he's at home with her now.
>
> Also, I've decided I'm gonna go to the Greenwich uni open day and ask about that criminology course I was telling you about. If I learnt one thing last night, it's that I'm not quite ready yet for investigations. But I'll get there.
>
> Anyway, hope you got home to your family OK, and thanks again.
>
> Chlo

Jess had read the message with a fond smile. She was confident that Chloe would indeed get there and vowed to keep an eye out for Liam on movie posters in the future.

She put her phone down and turned to the page in her book, taking a sip of coffee as she settled back into the deckchair. It was a couple of hours later when Alex found her, two celebratory tins of G&T in each hand. As he approached, she got to her feet, ready to greet him, when her phone rang.

Holding up one finger to Alex, she answered the call.

'Jessica,' the voice on the other end said, 'it's DSU Williams here.'

Jess met Alex's eye as a grin spread across her face.

Acknowledgements

Thank you so much to my editor Amy for all your support in writing this book. You've championed every draft and every idea I had for it as I got lost in the world of the Underground and these eight characters. Thank you to the many blogs and Flickr accounts delving into the world of the London tube that allowed me to put together as close to realistic technical reasonings for everything that happens (and all errors are entirely my own!), and giving me albums of photos of old Bakerloo line stock trains so I could fully picture everyone's movements around the narrow carriage. Thanks to Anne O'Brien for your eagle-eyed copyedits, and the whole Avon team for bringing this book to life. To Steph and Shaz, my always first and most enthusiastic beta-readers, and to Sarah, Dani and Meera for all your support in the trenches of publishing as we navigate it together. My family, as ever, for your endless encouragement and cheerleading – Mum, Dad, Hannah, Theo, Ruby, Steve, Tim and Sarah – and my own little family, Dave and Butter, which is about to grow by one. I love you all and know how lucky I am.

HF DX Basics

Steve Telenius-Lowe, PJ4DX

Radio Society of Great Britain

Published by the Radio Society of Great Britain, 3 Abbey Court, Fraser Road, Priory Business Park, Bedford MK44 3WH. Tel: 01234 832700.
Web: www.rsgb.org

Published 2022.

© Radio Society of Great Britain, 2022. All rights reserved. No part of this publication may be reproduced, stored in a retrieval system, or transmitted, in any form or by any means, electronic, mechanical, photocopying, recording or otherwise, without the prior written permission of the Radio Society of Great Britain.

ISBN: 9781 9139 9522 5

Design and layout: Steve Telenius-Lowe, PJ4DX
Cover design: Kevin Williams, M6CYB
Production: Mark Allgar, M1MPA

Printed in Great Britain by Hobbs the Printer Ltd. of Totton, Hampshire

Acknowledgements

This book is based on *HF SSB DX Basics*, written by Steve Telenius-Lowe, PJ4DX, and published by the RSGB in 2015. The text has been revised and brought fully up to date with much new material added. Some material is adapted and re-edited from passages in *The Amateur Radio Operating Manual* (8th edition) edited by Mike Dennison, G3XDV, and Steve Telenius-Lowe, PJ4DX, which was also published in 2015. The original authors of that material were Don Field, G3XTT; Roger Balister, G3KMA, and Steve Telenius-Lowe, 9M6DXX (now PJ4DX). All material is copyright RSGB.

Contents

	Preface 5
1	Introduction 6
2	What is DX? 13
3	What is SSB? 26
4	The DXer's Transceiver 36
5	Planning Your Antenna 51
6	DX Propagation 72
7	Finding the DX 86
8	Working HF DX – on SSB 94
9	FT8 and DXing on FT8 115
10	Being DX 138
	Index 143

Preface

I wrote *HF SSB DX Basics* in 2015 as an introduction for newcomers to DX working on the HF bands. As the title suggests, the book was written purely with the SSB operator in mind. The reason for that was simple: back in 2015 there were, in effect, just two main modes of transmission used for DX working on HF: CW (Morse code) and SSB. Most newcomers to HF DXing operated only on SSB because they had little or no knowledge of Morse code, for reasons discussed here in Chapter 1.

Furthermore, there was little or no SSB DX operation in the 1.8, 5, 10 and 50MHz bands, so operating on these bands was not covered in *HF SSB DX Basics*.

Little did I know in 2015 that a major upheaval in amateur radio operating – and especially DXing – was about to take place! In mid-2017 Joe Taylor, K1JT, and Steve Franke, K9AN, released FT8 upon the unsuspecting world of radio amateurs and it is no exaggeration to say that, even more than the post-war development of single side-band, FT8 has revolutionised DXing on the HF bands.

Time moves on, and seven years after its publication, it was time to update and publish a second edition of *HF SSB DX Basics*. We therefore took the opportunity to completely revise the text, bring it fully up to date and add much new material about FT8 operating as well as incorporating details of operating in the 1.8, 5, 10 and 50MHz bands.

Now, in 2022, we are at the beginning of a new solar cycle which will bring much improved propagation, especially on the higher-frequency HF bands, making DXing that much more pleasurable than has sometimes been the case during the past several lean years. This is therefore a great time to start DXing on HF and I hope that this book will encourage many more people to take up this fascinating and rewarding aspect of amateur radio.

So give HF DXing a try and and allow the DX 'bug' to bite! It is my hope that, if the DX bug *does* bite, those amateurs 'infected' will go on to improve their stations: once they do so they will find that the DX becomes easier to work. Once the DX bug has bitten it can lead to a lifetime's interest in this fascinating aspect of the hobby.

Steve Telenius-Lowe, PJ4DX
Bonaire, April 2022

Chapter 1

Introduction

In *HF SSB DX Basics* I wrote "The main purpose of this book is to encourage 'newcomers' to dip their toes into the wonderful world of DXing on the HF bands... I use the term "newcomers" in the widest sense. In the UK it includes Foundation and Intermediate licensees but, less obviously maybe, even the recently-licensed Full licensee. In the USA the term would include Technicians and newly-licensed General class licensees. But in this context it also encompasses those licensed for many years who so far have operated either exclusively on the VHF / UHF bands or those who might have operated on HF but who have had little or no interest in working DX."

WHY NOT MORSE CODE?

That *HF SSB DX Basics* was written with the purely SSB operator in mind came about as a result of a resolution adopted at an ITU World Radio Conference. The ITU's requirement for the world's radio regulatory authorities to set a Morse code test as a prerequisite for amateurs to obtain an HF licence was dropped in 2003 and since then nearly all regulatory authorities around the world have abandoned the Morse test. Unless the individual licensee has had a specialist occupation that requires knowledge of Morse code (and such occupations are becoming fewer and fewer) the chances are that the newly-licensed amateur will not know Morse code. Tens or even hundreds of thousands of amateurs around the world who have become licensed in the last two decades have little or no knowledge of Morse code and, since the Morse 'barrier' to HF operation no longer exists, that number is growing all the time.

The use of Morse will not die out, as some had gloomily predicted after the 2003 ITU decision, simply because there is no doubt that it is still a very useful mode of communication. Morse code is still popular with many radio amateurs and some never venture on to any other mode. The bands are full of CW (Morse code) stations during major contests such as the *CQ* World Wide DX contest, the CW leg of which is held at the end of November each year. Some contests, such as the RSGB's Commonwealth Contest in March, are *only* for CW operators. Major DXpeditions operating on Morse code continue to attract huge numbers of callers. So Morse code is very definitely not dead and nor is it likely to die out any time soon.

However, I think it is fair to say that SSB and FT8 will become more and more dominant as time goes by and as more

CHAPTER 1 – INTRODUCTION

and more amateurs who do not have any knowledge of Morse become licensed.

It is for that reason that this new book is an introduction to HF DXing for SSB and FT8 operators. I make no apology for this: if the newcomer does not know Morse code there is little point in discussing the finer points of CW operating techniques.

Having said that, many operators *do* go on to learn Morse and become proficient CW operators and for them there is an excellent book, *The Complete DX'er*, by Bob Locher, W9KNI [1] (although the third edition, published in 2003, does not seem to have been updated since). There is, however, little for SSB or FT8 DXers and even less for newcomers to this field, so I hope that this book will help to fill that gap.

WHY DXING?

DXing – the art and science of making radio contact with the farthest reaches of the planet – is a hugely satisfying and addictive aspect of our hobby. It is practised by hundreds of thousands of radio amateurs around the world and these days more and more are joining in the fun on SSB – and especially now on FT8.

Yet many amateurs, even those who have been licensed for years, have never tried their hand at DXing. Why should that be? Why should someone 'jump through the hoops' of the licensing system, but then be content only to talk to their local amateur neighbours on VHF or perhaps on 3.5MHz? For some, that is all they *want* to do, and that is fine. No amount of encouragement by me or anyone else is going to make someone want to work DX if they have no interest in doing so in the first place. But others, and I suspect the majority, would *like* to work DX but have a feeling that, with a typical station of 100 watts and wire antennas, they cannot compete with those running linear amplifiers and large beam antennas. This book sets out to correct that misconception.

The introduction of FT8 by Joe Taylor, K1JT (**Fig 1.1**), and Steve Franke, K9AN, as part of the WSJT ('Weak Signal Joe Taylor') suite of digital mode programs has to a large extent 'levelled the playing field', as we shall discuss in more detail later in the book. This probably goes a

Fig 1.1: The co-inventor of FT8, Joe Taylor, K1JT, pictured here at the International DX Convention in Visalia, California.

HF DX BASICS

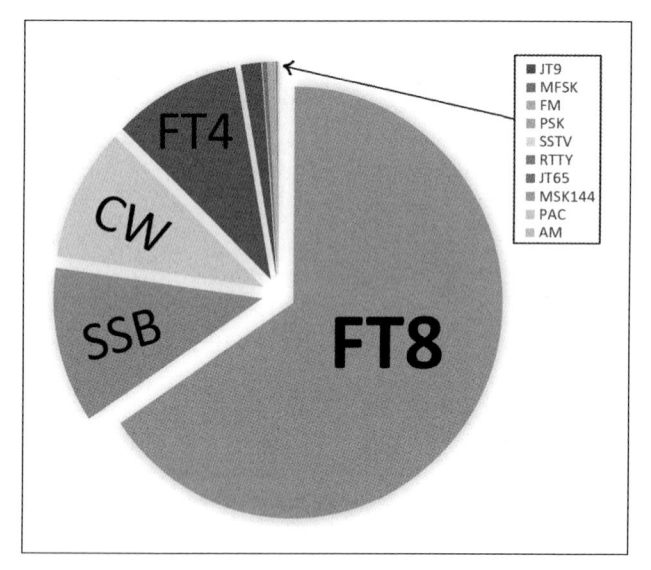

Fig 1.2: Among HF operators FT8 is now more popular than all the other modes combined (source: ZL2IFB's FT8 Operating Guide).

long way to explain the incredible popularity of this new mode, particularly among newcomer DXers. For many years the operating mode of choice for recently-licensed amateurs was SSB but, for the DX chaser in particular, that all changed when FT8 came along. These days FT8 is the most popular operating mode of all; indeed on HF it is more popular than all the other modes combined, as shown in **Fig 1.2**.

The following sections are intended for those new operators who might have had little knowledge of radio before gaining their licence. I hope it may also be useful as a 'refresher course' even for those who have been licensed a while.

WHAT IS HF?

HF stands for High Frequency, which is the part of the radio spectrum that mainly concerns us in this book. HF is also known as 'short wave' and, to all intents and purposes, the two terms are interchangeable: high frequencies equate to short wavelengths.

Thanks to the reflecting properties of the ionosphere, signals transmitted in this part of the radio spectrum have the remarkable property of travelling great distances, potentially all around the world, in a way that signals transmitted in other parts of the radio spectrum simply do not. We will discuss this in more detail later in the book.

The simplest form of radio transmission is called a *carrier wave*. It is in the form of a sine wave and is shown in **Fig 1.3**. By itself a carrier wave contains no information, although it could be pulsed on and off at specific intervals to produce Morse code, for example. Alternatively, modulation (e.g. voice, music or other audio sounds) could be added on to the carrier in different ways to produce an AM or FM transmission – of which more later. But for the moment, let's consider a simple carrier wave containing no other information.

If you imagine a wave, it is easy to understand what is meant by *wavelength* – see **Fig 1.4**. The wave's *frequency* is no more difficult to grasp: it is simply the number of times the wave makes a complete cycle in one second of time – see

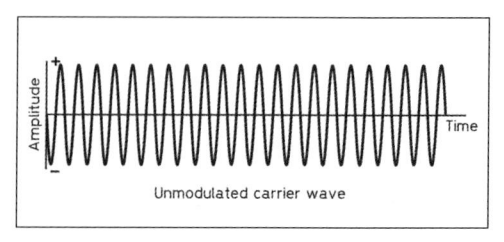

Fig 1.3: A radio carrier wave with no modulation.

CHAPTER 1 – INTRODUCTION

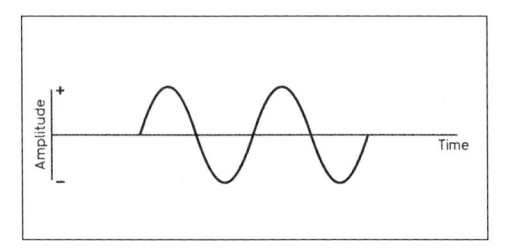

Fig 1.4: The wavelength is the distance from any one point on the graph to the place where that point in repeated. This could be from one peak to the next, or from one trough to the next: the distance will be the same.

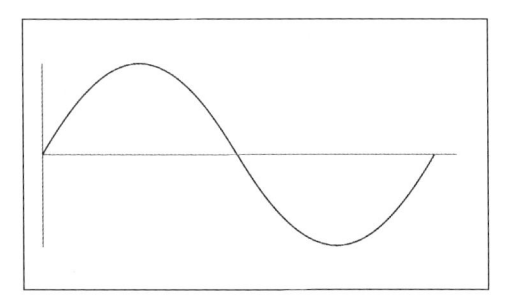

Fig 1.5: One complete cycle of a radio wave.

Fig 1.5. One cycle per second is called one Hertz (Hz), named after the 19th century German physicist Heinrich Hertz, **Fig. 1.6**. In practice, radio waves make many thousands or millions of cycles in one second, so they are generally measured in thousands of Hertz (kilohertz) or millions of Hertz (Megahertz) and we therefore almost always talk about radio frequencies in kHz or MHz rather than in single Hertz:

1MHz = 1000kHz = 1,000,000Hz

Note that the abbreviation for kilohertz, kHz, always has a lower case 'k', whereas the abbreviation for Megahertz, MHz, always has an upper case 'M'.

FREQUENCY AND WAVELENGTH

We have already used both the terms 'frequency' and 'wavelength'. The two are related: the higher the frequency, the shorter the wavelength, and *vice versa*. For example, a radio signal transmitted at a frequency of 5MHz (5000kHz) has a wavelength of 60 metres, while a signal transmitted at a frequency of 20MHz has a wavelength of 15 metres.

There will be almost no mathematics or formulas in this book but, in this case, a very simple formula really does help to explain the relationship between frequency and wavelength:

$$f = 300 / \lambda \quad \text{or} \quad \lambda = 300 / f$$

where f is the frequency in Megahertz (MHz) and λ (the Greek letter lambda) is the wavelength in metres.

Fig 1.6: Heinrich Hertz (1857 – 1894), after whom the unit of frequency is named.

HF DX BASICS

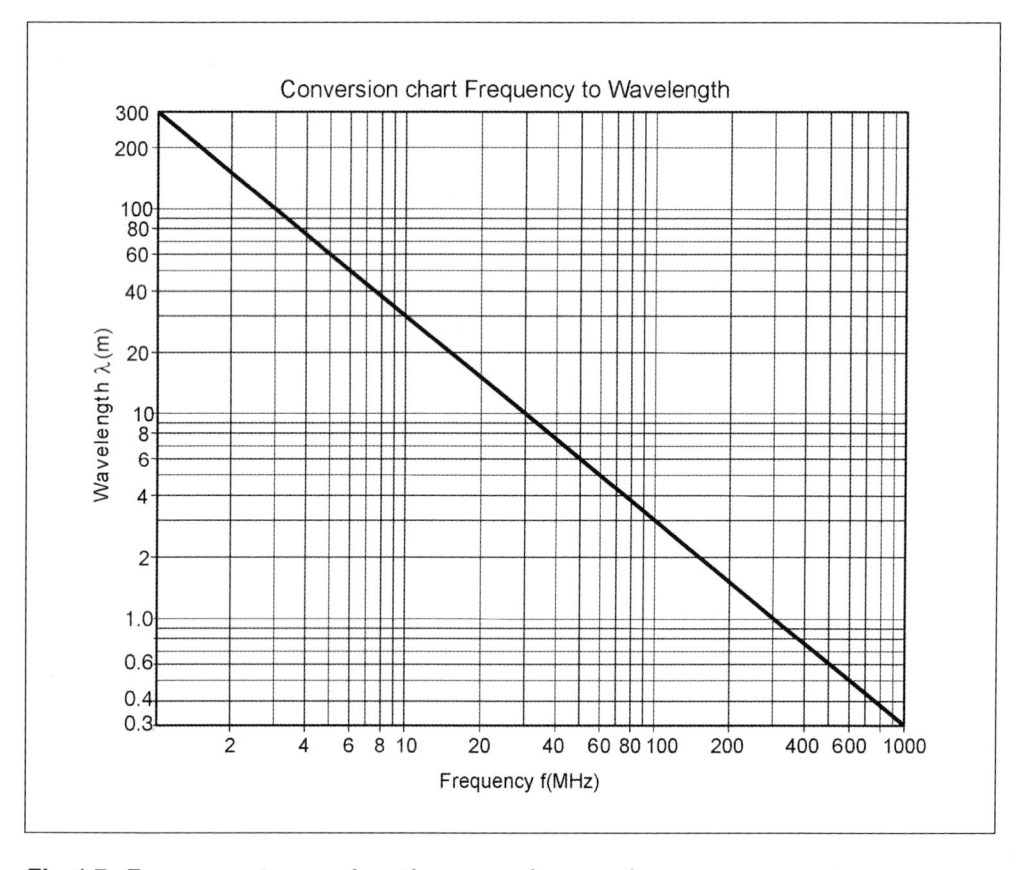

Fig 1.7: Frequency to wavelength conversion graph.

Where does this 'magic number' of 300 come from? Well, radio waves are just a type of light wave and the velocity of light is close enough to 300,000 kilometres per second to use this figure in most calculations.

We could equally well have written the formula as:

$$f = 300{,}000 / \lambda \quad \text{or} \quad \lambda = 300{,}000 / f$$

where *f* is still the frequency, but this time in kilohertz (kHz).

Note that wavelengths in metres are often abbreviated with a lower case 'm' (not to be confused with the upper case 'M' in MHz). So 5MHz = 60m, or 20,000kHz = 15m.

Fig 1.7 shows this relationship between frequency and wavelength in graphical form. The graph can be used to make approximate calculations from frequency to wavelength and vice versa.

If greater accuracy is required, even the most basic of electronic calculators will be up to the job: 300,000 divided by 3800 (kHz) = 78.95 metres.

THE HF AMATEUR BANDS

We started this section with the question "what is HF?" We have explained that the 'H' in HF refers to 'High' Frequencies, and we have explained the relationship between frequency and wavelength. Naturally if there are 'High' Frequencies, there

CHAPTER 1 – INTRODUCTION

Spectrum	Abbreviated	Frequency range in kHz	Frequency range in MHz	Wavelengths in metres
Very Low Frequency	VLF	3 – 30kHz	0.003 – 0.03MHz	100,000 – 10,000m
Low Frequency	LF*	30 – 300kHz	0.03 – 0.3MHz	10,000 – 1000m
Medium Frequency	MF**	300 – 3000kHz	0.3 – 3MHz	1000 – 100m
High Frequency	**HF***	**3000 – 30,000kHz**	**3 – 30MHz**	**100 – 10m**
Very High Frequency	VHF	30,000 – 300,000kHz	30 – 300MHz	10 – 1m
Ultra High Frequency	UHF	300,000 – 3,000,000kHz	3000 – 3000MHz	1 – 0.1m

* Also known as 'long wave'. ** Also known as 'medium wave'. *** Also known as 'short wave'.

Table 1.1: Where HF falls in the radio spectrum.

UK freq. limits (kHz)	Band known as	Notes
1810 – 2000	1.8MHz or 160m	MF, not HF band: also known as 'topband'
3500 – 3800	3.5MHz or 80m	
7000 – 7200	7MHz or 40m	
10,100 – 10,150	10MHz or 30m	
14,000 – 14,350	14MHz or 20m	
18,068 – 18,168	18MHz or 17m	
21,000 – 21,450	21MHz or 15m	
24,890 – 24,990	24MHz or 12m	
28,000 – 29,700	28MHz or 10m	
50,000 – 52,000	50MHz or 6m	VHF, not HF band: known as 'The Magic Band'

Table 1.2: The amateur radio bands available to all three classes of UK amateur licensee that are covered in this book. In addition, in the UK Full licensees (only) may also use 11 separate bands of frequencies between 5258.5kHz and 5406.5kHz.

must also be 'Low' Frequencies (LF). Then there are also 'Medium' Frequencies (MF) and 'Very High' Frequencies – even 'Ultra High' Frequencies. The latter two are better known as 'VHF' and 'UHF' and most people will be familiar with these terms from radio and TV broadcasting. **Table 1.1** shows where HF falls in the radio spectrum.

Below, and especially above (in terms of frequency), the radio spectrum are other types of electromagnetic waves. These include light, X-rays and so on.

For the purposes of this book we are also including the 1.8MHz band (160 metres), which is strictly speaking not an HF band at all, but rather an MF band. We also include the 50MHz band (6 metres), which is also not an HF band but in this case it is in the VHF part of the spectrum. The reason for this is that these days almost all so-called 'HF' transceivers also include the 1.8 and 50MHz bands and, although the propagation characteristics vary enormously between MF and VHF, the techniques used for DX working is much the same across the whole spectrum from 1.8 to 50MHz.

Table 1.2 shows the frequency limits of the bands covered by this book and also the various ways of referring to each band.

A few modern transceivers also include the 70MHz (4m) band which is of course also a VHF band and in some ways similar to 50MHz (6m). For those wanting to explore these two bands in more detail the RSGB has published an excellent guide **[2]**.

When referring to HF frequencies a useful convention, and one used throughout this book, is to use Megahertz when one is referring to either an approximate frequency or a band of frequencies, and to use kilohertz when referring to a specific frequency or a range of frequencies. For example the term '14MHz' is taken to mean the 14MHz band, whereas 14200kHz refers to that specific frequency within the 14MHz band.

REFERENCES
[1] *The Complete DX'er*, Bob Locher, W9KNI, 3rd edition, Idiom Press, 2003.
[2] *The Magic Bands ('A Guide to 6m & 4m Amateur Radio')*, Don Field, G3XTT, RSGB 2020, available from: www.rsgbshop.org

Chapter 2

What is DX?

This book is called *HF DX Basics* but although we have defined HF we have not yet defined precisely what is meant by the term 'DX'. That is not as easy as it may sound, as we shall see. Perhaps the best definition was coined by the late Californian amateur, writer and humorist Hugh 'Cass' Cassidy, WA6AUD, who simply stated "DX IS". In other words, and to paraphrase Lewis Carroll, DX can mean whatever you want it to mean. Some sort of definition would be helpful, though, so here goes...

On the VHF and UHF bands DX equates to distance. The farther the contact, the greater the DX. To some extent the same is true on 1.8MHz, where it can be difficult to make any QSOs outside your own continent, but that's not really the case on the 'true' HF bands from 3.5MHz to 28MHz.

When a station puts out a "CQ DX" call on any of the HF bands it is generally understood to mean that the station is looking for contacts outside their own continent. It would therefore be considered legitimate for a US station to reply to a "CQ DX" call from someone in the UK, for example. Nevertheless, this definition does not really work either: most experienced amateurs would not really consider a contact with the Canary Islands (considered to be in Africa) or New York to be 'real DX'.

On HF, distance isn't really the issue, it's more to do with the 'rarity value' of the station. From the UK, although any contact with North America is outside one's own continent, there are so many amateurs in the US, many of whom have large stations and antenna systems, that the east coast of the US is not considered to be DX by most HF operators. So a contact with Florida wouldn't be DX, yet contacts with the Bahamas (C6A), the Turks and Caicos Islands (VP5) or Cuba (CO) – none far from the coast of Florida – *would* be, even though the distances involved are similar.

DXCC – THE DX CENTURY CLUB

DXCC is the most popular HF amateur radio operating award and it has become the *de facto* measure of one's DX operating success. DXCC is issued by the American Radio Relay League (ARRL) to any radio amateur who can prove that they have made contacts with amateur radio stations in a minimum of 100 'entities' that appear on the 'DXCC List' [1].

The word *entity* is used deliberately: entities include sovereign states, non-independent territories, remote islands or

HF DX BASICS

Fig 2.1: Clinton DeSoto, W1CBD, author of the 1935 article 'How to Count Countries Worked, A New DX Scoring System'.

island groups and even a few anomalies such as the United Nations headquarters building in New York.

The first DXCC List was issued by the ARRL in 1937 following the publication of an article written by Clinton B DeSoto, W1CBD (**Fig 2.1**). In 'How to Count Countries Worked, A New DX Scoring System' published in the ARRL members' journal *QST* in October 1935 **[2]**, DeSoto wrote that *"The basic rule is simple and direct: Each discrete geographical or political entity is considered to be a country."* It was therefore never the case that all DXCC 'countries' would be countries in the literal meaning of the word. The criteria for inclusion on the DXCC List have been changed a number of times over the years but DeSoto's basic definition remains.

Radio amateurs have always been DXers. Indeed, a case can be made that Guglielmo Marconi was the world's first DXer, as he was always striving to make transmissions over greater and greater distances.

The 100th anniversary of the reception, in Scotland, of the first amateur signals from across the Atlantic was celebrated in December 2021. Two-way communications across the Atlantic were achieved by radio amateurs in 1923.

Then, on 18 October 1924, a two-way contact was made by Cecil Goyder, 2SZ, a pupil at Mill Hill School in North London, and Frank Bell, 4AA, a sheep farmer on the South Island of New Zealand. World-wide DX had arrived and radio amateurs started to compare not only how *far* their signals had travelled, but also the *number of countries* they had contacted, which is where Clinton DeSoto and the ARRL DXCC List came into the picture.

Originally, amateurs were striving to work each country just once, regardless of the band or mode. However, as amateur radio activity increased after WWII with many more countries becoming active, higher DXCC totals became easier to achieve and amateurs started to look for new challenges.

In 1969 the DXCC program was extended with the introduction of the 5-band (3.5, 7, 14, 21 and 28MHz) DXCC award. In those days there were no 10, 18 or 24MHz bands, and 1.8MHz was excluded as many countries still had no allocation there. As a result, amateurs who had high country totals on, say, 14 and 21MHz also started to 'chase' countries on 3.5 and 7MHz.

Awards programmes, based on the numbers of entities or islands contacted, are a way of measuring one's DXing success. DXCC is the most popular, followed by the Islands On The Air programme, so let's take a look at both in more detail.

CHAPTER 2 – WHAT IS DX?

DXCC TODAY

In addition to the basic 'all-band' DXCC, the ARRL offers separate DXCC awards for 11 bands, from 1.8 to 144MHz. There is also a 'DX Challenge' programme which includes the 10 bands from 1.8 to 50MHz (excluding 5MHz) and – the ultimate challenge – DXCC Honor Roll, which requires confirmed contacts with all but any 10 entities on the current DXCC List. As it can be decades between activations of some of the rarer entities, achieving DXCC Honor Roll status is often a lifetime's endeavour.

There are also DXCC awards available for those chasing DXCC entities on 'Phone' only (basically SSB these days although FM and AM contacts also count), CW only, and Data modes only, in addition to 'Mixed' where all modes count. The definition of 'Data' includes FT8, FT4 and all the other 'new' digital modes, in additional to the more traditional RTTY and PSK.

Many DXers now look for contacts with any DXCC entity on all 10 bands, and some also on SSB, CW and data modes. The thought of trying to contact every DXCC entity on 10 bands and three modes (which would require over 10,000 contacts) might be enough to put anyone off before they even start but fortunately you don't have to start that way. Set yourself a reasonable goal, such as working DXCC entities on your favourite mode such as SSB or FT8 and on any band or combination of bands.

Today's DXCC List is comprised of 340 entities, the most recent addition being that of the Republic of Kosovo, Z6, **Fig 2.2**, which was added to the list in 2018.

The basic DXCC certificate is awarded to those who can show confirmations, either through the receipt of QSL cards or through electronic verifications made by QSO matches on the ARRL's Logbook of The World (LoTW) system (of which more later), from a minimum of 100 entities on the current DXCC List.

All contacts must be made using callsigns issued to the same licensee although you can 'feed' a single DXCC award from several different callsigns. For example if you start DXCC as a Foundation licensee in England, progress through the Intermediate licence and eventually upgrade to a Full licence, all the contacts made with the M3, M6 or M7 and 2E0 callsigns can be counted towards your M0 DXCC award. Likewise in the USA if you change from the issued '2 x 3' callsign to a shorter 'vanity' call contacts made with the original callsign still count. However, you must make all the contacts *from within the same DXCC entity* so, if you start your DXCC in England but then move to Scotland, you must start DXCC all over again.

Fig 2.2: The world's newest DXCC entity is the Republic of Kosovo, added to the DXCC list in 2018.

HF DX BASICS

Once an entity has been added to the DXCC List, the List remains unchanged until that entity no longer satisfies the criteria under which it was originally added, at which time it is moved to a 'Deleted List'.

Many entities have come and gone over the years. For example, the former German Democratic Republic (East Germany, Y2) ceased to be a separate entity upon the reunification of Germany and so it was moved to the Deleted List. Czechoslovakia, on the other hand, is also now on the Deleted List but was replaced by two *new* entities, the Czech Republic (Czechia, OK / OL), and Slovakia (the Slovak Republic, OM), **Fig 2.3**.

Deleted entities count towards your overall DXCC total (but only if your worked them before the 'deletion date', of course) although only current entities count towards the DXCC Challenge and Honor Roll.

WHAT CONSTITUTES 'RARE' DX?

Earlier we defined 'DX' (sort of). But it is clear that there is what might be called 'ordinary DX' and 'rare DX'. The massive database of *Club Log* **[3]** allows a 'Most Wanted' list to be generated from the three-quarters of a *billion* QSOs uploaded to Club Log (more about Club Log later in this chapter).

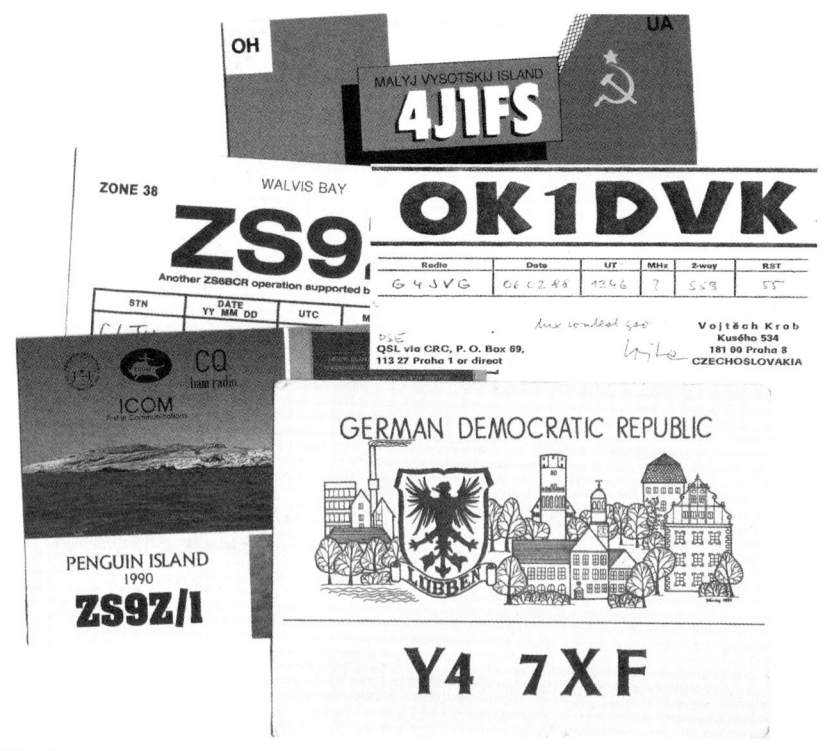

Fig 2.3: Montage of QSLs from some deleted DXCC entities: 4J1FS (Malyj Vysotskij Island, 1988), ZS9Z (Walvis Bay, 1990), OK1DVK (Czechoslovakia, 1988), ZS9Z/1 (Penguin Island, 1990), Y47XF (German Democratic Republic – East Germany, 1981).

CHAPTER 2 – WHAT IS DX?

Rank	Prefix	Entity Name
1	P5	DPRK (North Korea)
2	3Y/B	Bouvet Island
3	FT5W	Crozet Island
4	BS7H	Scarborough Reef
5	BV9P	Pratas Island
6	CE0X	San Felix Islands
7	VK0M	Macquarie Island
8	KH7K	Kure Island
9	3Y/P	Peter 1 Island
10	FT5X	Kerguelen Island
11	KH3	Johnston Island
12	FT5G	Glorioso Island
13	YV0	Aves Island
14	KH4	Midway Island
15	VP8S	South Sandwich Islands
16	JD1/M	Minami Torishima
17	VK0H	Heard Island
18	PY0S	St Peter & St Paul Rocks
19	SV/A	Mount Athos
20	KH5	Palmyra & Jarvis Islands

Table 2.1: The 'top 20' of rarest DXCC entities on Phone (mainly SSB) modes only, based on Club Log's 'Most Wanted' list, April 2022.

Rank	Prefix	Entity Name
1	3Y/B	Bouvet Island
2	FT5W	Crozet Island
3	BS7H	Scarborough Reef
4	KH3	Johnston Island
5	ZS8	Prince Edward & Marion Is
6	KH7K	Kure Island
7	FT5X	Kerguelen Island
8	BV9P	Pratas Island
9	CE0X	San Felix Islands
10	P5	DPRK (North Korea)
11	3Y/P	Peter 1 Island
12	EZ	Turkmenistan
13	ZL9	New Zealand Subantarctic Is
14	YV0	Aves Island
15	KH4	Midway Island
16	PY0T	Trindade & Martim Vaz Is
17	CY0	Sable Island
18	FT5G	Glorioso Island
19	YK	Syria
20	KP5	Desecheo Island

Table 2.2: The 'top 20' of rarest DXCC entities on Data modes (mainly FT8) only, based on Club Log's 'Most Wanted' list, April 2022.

Rank	Prefix	Entity Name	Rank	Prefix	Entity Name
1	P5	DPRK (North Korea)	11	FT5G	Glorioso Island
2	3Y/B	Bouvet Island	12	VK0M	Macquarie Island
3	FT5W	Crozet Island	13	YV0	Aves Island
4	BS7H	Scarborough Reef	14	KH4	Midway Island
5	CE0X	San Felix Islands	15	ZS8	Prince Edward & Marion Is
6	BV9P	Pratas Island	16	PY0S	St Peter & St Paul Rocks
7	KH7K	Kure Island	17	PY0T	Trindade & Martim Vaz Is
8	KH3	Johnston Island	18	KP5	Desecheo Island
9	3Y/P	Peter 1 Island	19	VP8S	South Sandwich Islands
10	FT5X	Kerguelen Island	20	KH5	Palmyra & Jarvis Islands

Table 2.3: The 'top 20' of rarest DXCC entities on all modes (including CW), based on Club Log's 'Most Wanted' list, April 2022.

HF DX BASICS

Fig 2.4: A montage of old QSLs from some 'top 20' rare DXCC entities: ZS8MI (Prince Edward & Marion Islands, 1990); in the days of the Soviet Union Turkmenistan was on the air daily but it is now rare due to licensing restrictions; BQ9P (Pratas Islands, 2002); AH3C/KH5J (Palmyra & Jarvis Islands, 1990); ZL9CI (New Zealand Subantarctic Islands, 1999); and W6LAS/SVA (Mount Athos, 1983).

Tables 2.1, 2.2 and 2.3 on page 17 show the results of interrogations of the Club Log database in April 2022. The data shown in the tables are from QSOs made in all (i.e. world-wide) logs, using all bands, on SSB only, Data modes only, and all modes (including CW), respectively.

It is also possible to determine which are the 'Most Wanted' entities in any particular continent or part of a continent and on any particular band.

Although the Club Log Most Wanted list will change from time to time (for example as a result of an activation by a major DXpedition) some factors remain constant.

DXCC entities are rare for one of two reasons. Bouvet Island and Crozet Island (ranked 2nd and 3rd respectively on both the 'all mode' and SSB Most Wanted lists) are rare because they lie deep in the Southern Ocean, and any expedition is hugely expensive to mount. North Korea (ranked 1st) is relatively easy to reach, has an international airport and modern hotels, but licensing is virtually impossible for political reasons.

Some old QSLs representing 'top 20' rare DXCC entities can be seen in **Fig 2.4.**

LOGBOOK OF THE WORLD

Logbook of The World (LoTW) is an online service provided by the ARRL that allows all amateurs to upload electronic logs to

CHAPTER 2 – WHAT IS DX?

a massive central database. Having done so, DXers can then view their submitted QSOs and check which of their contacts 'match' those of the more than 1.5 billion other QSOs uploaded to LoTW.

If the information in an uploaded QSO matches the information submitted to LoTW by your QSO partner, the LoTW accounts of both you and your QSO partner will show the QSO as 'confirmed'. With your LoTW account, you can then submit a confirmed QSO for credit to your DXCC award. LoTW also allows users to submit credits for the ARRL's Worked All States (WAS) award as well as CQ magazine's Worked All Prefixes (WPX) and Worked All Zones (WAZ) awards.

Having achieved DXCC (**Fig 2.5**) in five different countries where I have been resident, using only traditional paper QSL cards, when I moved to Bonaire in November 2013 and started DXCC all over again – for the sixth time! – I took the decision not to request any further QSLs (though my QSL man-

Fig 2.5: The most recent of five DXCCs awarded to the author and achieved using only paper QSL cards. The QSOs were made while I was living in East Malaysia from 2005.

DXCC Entity	Mixed
1A0KM - SOVEREIGN MILITARY ORDER OF MALTA	1A0KM
3A - MONACO	3A/IW1RBI
3B7 - AGALEGA & SAINT BRANDON ISLANDS	3B7A
3B8 - MAURITIUS ISLAND	3B8CW
3B9 - RODRIGUEZ ISLAND	3B9FR
3C - EQUATORIAL GUINEA	3C7A
3C0 - ANNOBON	3C0BYP
3D2 - FIJI ISLANDS	3D2YJ
3D2 - ROTUMA	3D2EU
3DA - KINGDOM OF ESWATINI	3DA0CC
3V - TUNISIA	3V8SS
3W, XV - VIET NAM	3W3B
3XA - GUINEA	3XY1T
4J - AZERBAIJAN	4K6FO

Award Credits: Selected: 307 Applied for: 0 Awarded: 0 Total: 307
Key: Selected · *Applied*

Fig 2.6: Building a DXCC total using LoTW (307 entities confirmed).

ager will send my card to those who request one from me). Instead I am working towards DXCC entirely through LoTW. To give an indication of how popular LoTW has become in recent years, in my first two years of activity as PJ4DX I worked

280 DXCC entities and 239 of them were confirmed on LoTW. By April 2022 I had worked 312 entities and 307 of them were confirmed using LoTW only (see **Fig 2.6**).

Full information about LoTW and how to register with it can be found on the ARRL website **[4]**. Membership of ARRL is not a requirement and use of LoTW is free of charge (although a charge is made if and when you submit confirmed QSOs to credit an award application). Although LoTW is free and the vast majority of amateurs using it do so without asking for any payment, a small number of amateurs now ask for a "donation" before they will upload their contact with you to LoTW. This is controversial and frowned on by most amateurs.

ISLANDS ON THE AIR (IOTA)

So far we have only discussed the ARRL DXCC award. While that is certainly the most popular DX-orientated on-air activity programme, it is by no means the only one. The other major player on the world DX stage is the Islands On The Air (IOTA) programme. IOTA is now second only to DXCC in terms of on-air activity associated with the programme.

IOTA will be celebrating its Diamond Jubilee (60th anniversary) in July 2024 and during the last six decades the programme has grown to involve around 15,000 'island chasers' around the world. In 2017 management of the IOTA programme was taken over by a newly-formed limited company, IOTA Ltd, and a new website **[5]**, **Fig 2.7**, was created.

The basic building block for IOTA contacts is the IOTA Group, of which there are about 1200, with varying numbers of qualifying islands in each. Each group that is activated is issued with an IOTA reference number, for example EU-005 for Great Britain. The *IOTA Directory* **[6]**, **Fig 2.8**, provides a full listing of all the IOTA groups, together with the names of some 15,000 qualifying islands.

Fig 2.7: The new IOTA website.

CHAPTER 2 – WHAT IS DX?

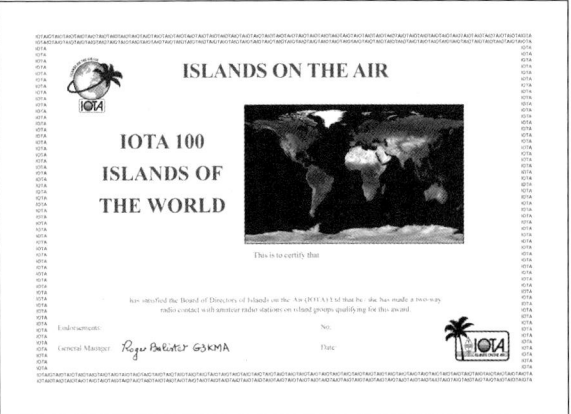

Fig 2.9: The basic IOTA-100 certificate.

Fig 2.8: The 2018 IOTA Directory.

There is a wide range of separate certificates and awards available for island chasers. IOTA also has an Annual Listing and an Honour Roll. The Annual Listing is a list of the callsigns of stations with a checked score of 100 or more IOTA groups but less than the qualifying threshold for entry into the Honour Roll. The Honour Roll is a list of the callsigns of stations with a checked score equalling or exceeding 50% of the total of numbered IOTA groups, excluding those with provisional numbers, at the time of preparation. The Annual Listing and Honour Roll are published on the IOTA website. All you need to enable you to participate in the Annual Listing is the basic IOTA 100 certificate, **Fig 2.9**.

Until 2016 QSL cards were necessary in order to apply for IOTA awards. That all changed with the implementation of 'QSO matching' using Club Log. Full details are in the *IOTA Directory* and on the IOTA website **[5, 6]**.

CLUB LOG

Club Log **[3]**, **Fig 2.10**, is a great tool for all amateurs and is of particular interest to DXers. Established by Michael Wells, G7VJR, and maintained by him and a small team of volunteer helpers, Club Log is a web-based application that analyses logs submitted by amateurs all over the world.

Without actually using Club Log it is almost impossible to envisage just how

HF DX BASICS

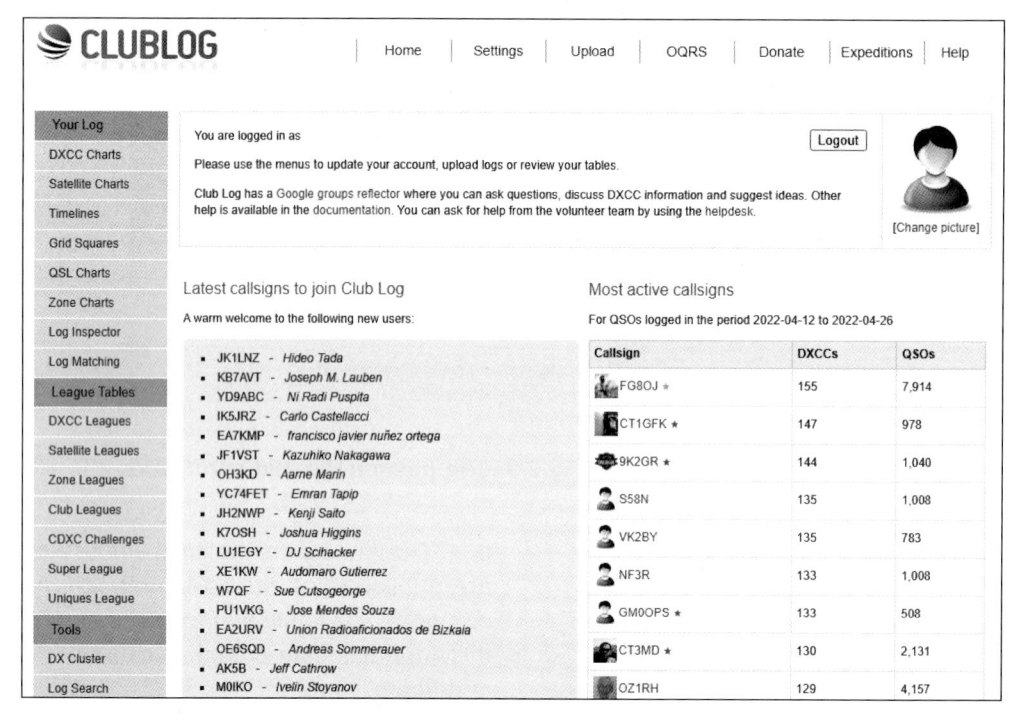

Fig 2.10: The Club Log home page.

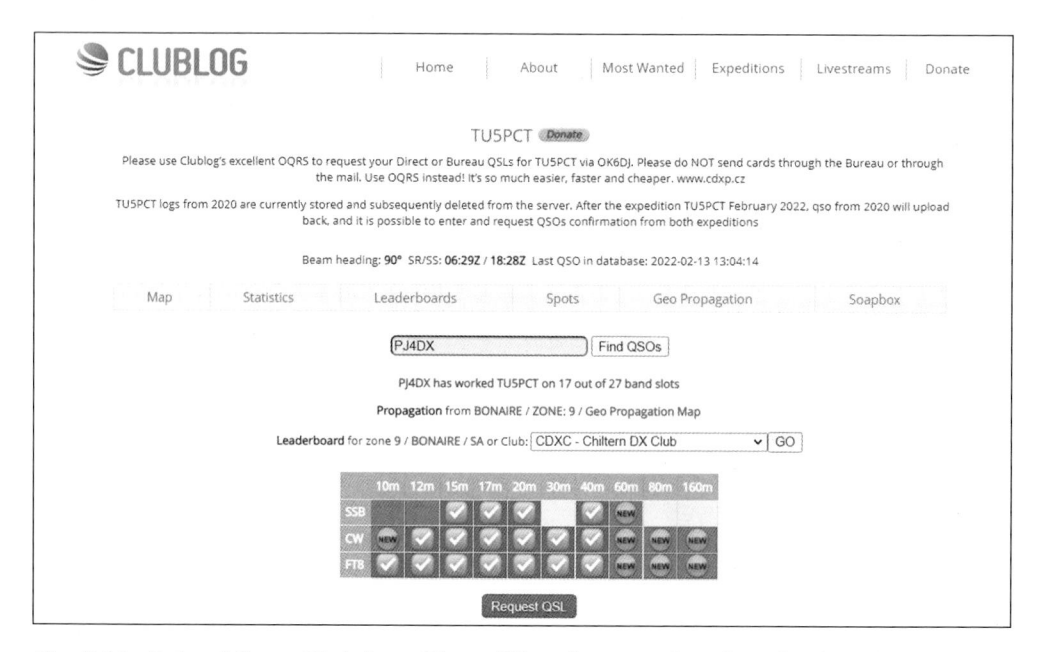

Fig 2.11: Extract from Club Log 'Expeditions' page, showing the band and mode contacts made by the author with the TU5PCT Côte d'Ivoire DXpedition.

CHAPTER 2 – WHAT IS DX?

much useful data it can provide for you. Among the numerous features are personal DXCC reports and analysis of your log, a timeline of your activity with DXCC entities worked each year and band and mode information, access to propagation predictions using everyone's logs, and OQRS (see next section) to make direct and bureau QSLing faster, easier and cheaper – and much more besides.

At the time of writing (early 2022) around 750,000,000 QSOs had been uploaded to Club Log, with some six to seven million more QSOs being added to the database every month.

Everyone is requested to upload their log, no matter how big or small. Many DXpeditions now upload their logs to Club Log during the DXpedition itself (assuming they are in a location that has Internet access), and this allows DXers to check that they are in the DXpedition log, and on which bands and modes. In **Fig 2.11** it can be seen that I worked the February 2022 TU5PCT (Côte d'Ivoire / Ivory Coast) DXpedition on seven of the ten possible bands on data modes (actually all on FT8), on six of the bands on CW and on four of the possible seven bands on SSB.

It also shows that TU5PCT was also active on 60, 80 and 160 metres, but I made no contacts with the station on those bands. Much more analysis can be made from this page alone by clicking on the 'Propagation' and 'Leaderboard' buttons on the screen.

QSLs AND QSLing

QSLs have been around almost since the beginning of amateur radio itself and, even if many DXers (myself included) now mainly use LoTW to provide credits for DXCC, most radio amateurs still collect cards, particularly if they actively participate in the DXCC or IOTA programmes.

Most RSGB members will use the RSGB QSL Bureau **[7]** but, while this is fine for collecting cards from countries with large populations of radio amateurs such as Germany, Italy, USA, Japan etc, **Fig 2.12**, it is actually not a very efficient means of collecting cards from DX stations. Certainly use the QSL bureau in order to receive cards from those 'easy'

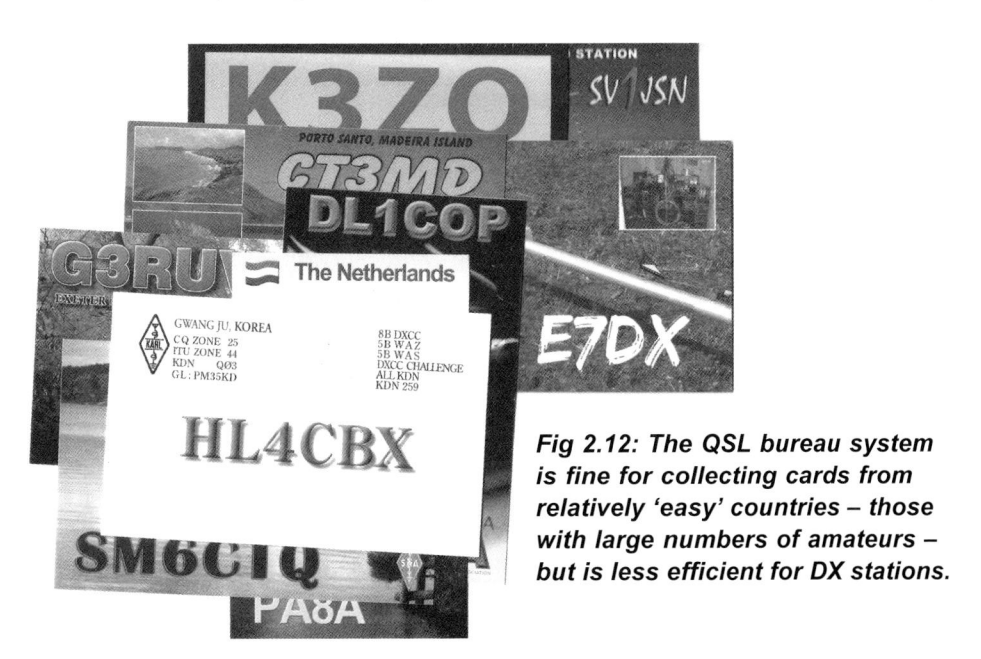

Fig 2.12: The QSL bureau system is fine for collecting cards from relatively 'easy' countries – those with large numbers of amateurs – but is less efficient for DX stations.

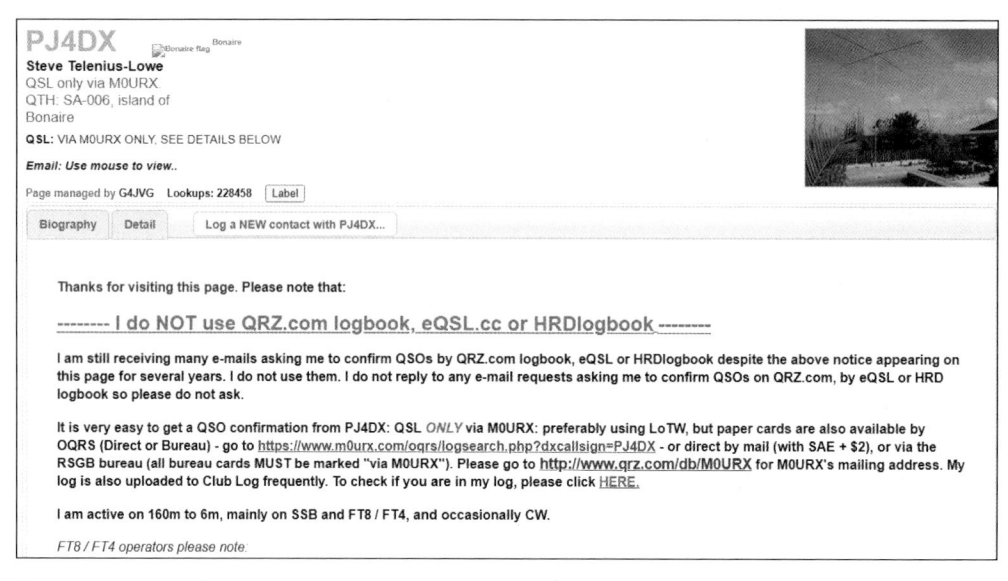

Fig 2.13: Part of the PJ4DX page on the QRZ.com website.

countries, but do bear in mind that very many DXCC entities are in countries that simply do not have a functioning QSL bureau system at all. If you send a card to the RSGB QSL Bureau after you work any of the resident operators in Vietnam, Papua New Guinea, Egypt, St Kitts and Nevis, Azerbaijan or any one of many other 'semi-rare' DXCC entities you are going to be disappointed, because those countries do not have a QSL bureau so I'm afraid you won't get a reply.

Even if the country concerned *does* have a QSL bureau, if the station you work is not a long-term resident in that country there is no point in sending the card through the bureau as he is unlikely to receive it. Some resident amateurs who are not members of the national amateur radio society also cannot receive cards via their QSL bureau.

The trick is always to find out the 'QSL information' of the station you work before sending off your card to the QSL bureau. Fortunately these days that is easy with the introduction of websites specifically for this purpose, the best known of which is QRZ.com [8], **Fig 2.13**. A typical entry on QRZ.com will tell you (a) whether the station QSLs at all (some do not), (b) their postal and email addresses, (c) whether they have a QSL manager, (d) whether they accept QSLs via the bureau or only direct, (e) if direct, whether they accept IRCs (International Reply Coupons, now being phased out in many countries including the UK) or US dollars (so-called 'Green Stamps'), and (f) whether they upload their logs to LoTW [4]. Often there are also photographs and a lot more information besides.

If you are going to QSL direct you must always enclose sufficient return postage for the DX station to reply. This used to always be considered to be US $1 but over the last decade or so postal fees all over the world have increased dramatically. These days $2 is often insufficient to cover the cost of a stamp for air mail postage and in many countries amateurs now ask for a minimum of $3 for a direct QSL. You must also enclose a self-ad-

CHAPTER 2 – WHAT IS DX?

dressed envelope for the DX station to return his QSL card to you.

With a 20 gram letter costing £1.70 (early 2022) and adding $3 for return postage, plus the cost of two envelopes, you can see that getting direct QSLs from 100 DXCC entities would cost around £400, not to mention the cost of having your QSL cards printed in the first place.

Fortunately, there are alternatives. The first is LoTW, as described earlier in this chapter. LoTW will never replace traditional paper QSL cards entirely, because many DXers will still want to collect cards as 'souvenirs' of their most memorable contacts, but for those mainly interested in increasing their DXCC score, LoTW is a boon and I see its use only increasing in the future.

A second alternative is OQRS, standing for Online QSL Request Service, which involves filling in the QSL request and QSO details on an online form. Most DXpeditions that upload their logs to Club Log [3] offer OQRS, as do several individual QSL managers.

Either bureau or direct cards can be requested by OQRS. Because DXpeditions rarely want their incoming QSL cards, requesting a bureau card by OQRS makes a lot of sense, firstly because you do not have to send your card, saving the cost of printing and postage to the QSL bureau and, secondly, halving the turnaround time because the DXpedition's QSL manager has your QSL request immediately, rather than having to wait months or even years for your card to arrive through the bureau system.

OQRS bureau cards are usually (though not always) sent free of charge but you will still have to lodge stamped self-addressed envelopes at the RSGB QSL bureau to receive them and it can still take months – sometimes many months – for the card to arrive.

OQRS can also be used to request a QSL card by direct mail, usually at a cost of $3 – $5, to be paid by PayPal. This saves you the cost of printing your card, posting it to the bureau and buying envelopes, but at $3 per DXCC entity, 100 confirmations would still cost over £200, a considerable saving but still a lot of money for many people.

The Perseverance DX Group, led by Istvan 'Pista' Gaspar, HA5AO, together with UK QSL managers Tim Beaumont, M0URX, and Charles Wilmott, M0OXO, have developed the 'Bespoke OQRS' system which greatly reduces the need for emails to the QSL managers, thus allowing for quicker handling of confirmations.

OQRS also allows those DXers who wish to make a contribution towards the cost of the DXpedition to do so, without having to send dollar bills through the post.

REFERENCES

[1] The DXCC List: www.arrl.org/dxcc (click on 'Country Lists & Prefixes' then 'Go Now' under 'DXCC Entities List').
[2] 'How to Count Countries Worked: A New DX Scoring System', Clinton B DeSoto, W1CBD: www.arrl.org/desoto
[3] Club Log: www.clublog.org
[4] LoTW on the ARRL website: www.arrl.org/logbook-of-the-world
[5] IOTA website: www.iota-world.org
[6] *IOTA Directory* (18th edition), edited by Roger Balister, G3KMA, and Steve Telenius-Lowe, PJ4DX, published by Islands On The Air (IOTA) Ltd 2018, available from iota-world.org/iota-shop.html
[7] RSGB QSL Bureau: http://rsgb.org/main/operating/qsl-bureau
[8] QRZ.com website: www.qrz.com

Chapter 3

What is SSB?

What, exactly, is 'SSB'? SSB stands for 'single side-band'. So, in order to answer the question we first really need to know what a 'side-band' (more usually written simply as 'sideband') is, and then we can find out why we might only need a single one of them.

Even the layman, with no knowledge of amateur radio, is familiar with the names of two different types of radio modulation – AM and FM – even if they do not really know what these terms mean.

Many people confuse AM and FM with the *frequencies* of operation, a state of affairs not helped by the BBC, which insists on announcing that BBC Radio 2, for example, is broadcast on "88 to 91 FM".

In fact, Radio 2 is broadcast from many different transmitter sites around the UK on a number of different discrete frequencies between 88MHz and 91MHz, which are in the very high frequency (VHF) part of the spectrum (see **Table 1.1**). FM stands for 'frequency modulation', which describes the way in which the programme is transmitted or *modulated* on to the carrier wave, but it has nothing to do with the frequency of that carrier signal *per se*.

Radio 4 UK on 198kHz, a long-wave frequency, on the other hand, is transmitted using a different modulation technique called AM, amplitude modulation, as indeed are all the radio stations that broadcast in the long-wave and medium-wave bands.

In fact, AM signals *could* be transmitted on VHF frequencies, and FM signals *could* be transmitted on the medium-wave band: 'AM' and 'FM' refer only to the method (or *mode*) of transmission and not the frequencies on which they are transmitted.

FM is capable of providing very high-quality transmissions, but at a price: an FM transmission takes up a lot more of the spectrum (space on the radio dial) than does an AM one, and it is for this reason that, generally, FM transmissions are restricted to very high frequencies, where there is a lot more spectrum available than on the long, medium and short-wave bands. Furthermore, VHF signals generally travel shorter distances than medium or short-wave signals. This means that Radio 2 on 88 – 91MHz can transmit at exactly the same time and on the same frequencies as, for example, German and Finnish VHF broadcasting stations, without listeners in Germany or Finland receiving interference from Radio 2, or *vice versa*.

CHAPTER 3 – WHAT IS SSB?

Fig 3.1: An AM broadcast station, Trans World Radio Bonaire. This station broadcasts on 800kHz medium wave, using a four-tower directional antenna system.

So, FM is an excellent mode of transmission for high-quality broadcasting purposes over the relatively short distances capable on VHF. FM is also used by radio amateurs, again mainly on VHF, e.g. on the 145MHz (2m) band, as well as on UHF, e.g. on the 430MHz (70cm or 70-centimetre) band, for relatively short-distance communications.

AM TRANSMISSIONS

Let's go back to AM, the mode of transmission used by Radio 4 on long wave, and by BBC Radio 5 Live, as well as all radio stations broadcasting on medium wave, **Fig 3.1**. AM is also used by numerous broadcast stations on the short-wave bands, such as BBC World Service or the Voice of America.

Take a look at **Fig 3.2**. We have already discussed the carrier in Chapter 1. Its frequency of transmission can be anywhere in the radio spectrum (let's say for example it is on 7100kHz) and it takes up only a tiny

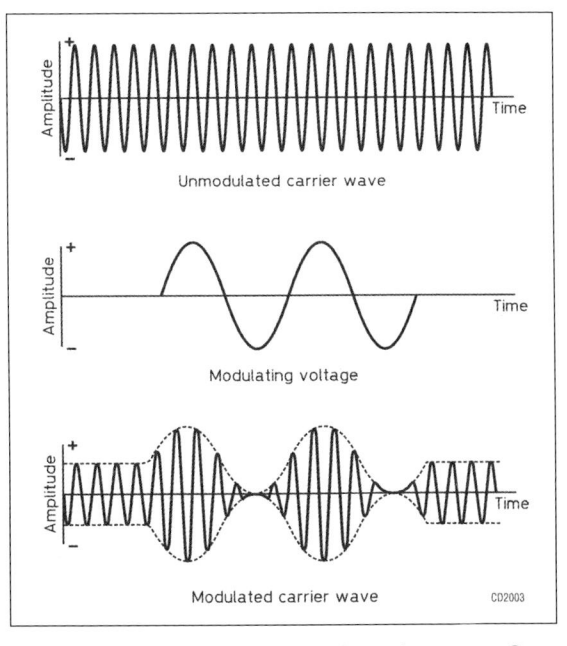

Fig 3.2: Top, an unmodulated carrier wave. Centre, a single audio tone. Bottom, the carrier wave is being modulated by the audio tone.

27

amount of that spectrum. By itself the carrier conveys no information, unless it is pulsed on and off to form Morse code characters.

However, in a process known as *modulating* the carrier, audio information can be added to it. That audio information could be a single-frequency tone at any audio frequency (such as 1000Hz or, for example, a piano's note A above middle C, which is at a frequency of 440Hz), or it could be speech or in fact any sound at all. **Fig 3.3** shows a carrier being modulated by a 1kHz (1000Hz) audio tone.

The process of modulating the carrier produces two sidebands, one below and one above the carrier frequency. If the audio tone is 1kHz, the two sidebands will be 1kHz below and 1kHz above the carrier frequency.

Now instead of a single audio tone, consider human speech. The human voice is capable of producing a wide range of audio frequencies (imagine both basso profundo and soprano opera soloists) but the normal everyday speech of men and women falls mainly in the range of 300Hz to 3kHz. Above 3kHz are harmonics and fricatives such as the sibilant 'S' sound, which add 'presence' to the speech, but do not markedly improve its intelligibility. Most AM transmitters are engineered to transmit audio frequencies of up to approximately 3kHz.

If instead of transmitting a single audio tone, an AM transmitter with a carrier frequency of, say, 6000kHz, were to transmit human speech in the range of 300Hz to 3kHz, the lower sideband would extend from just below the carrier frequency of 6000kHz down to 5997kHz, while the upper sideband would extend from just above 6000kHz up to 6003kHz. The transmission would therefore take up 6kHz of spectrum (5997 to 6003kHz). This is shown in **Fig 3.4**.

Fig 3.5 opposite shows a spectrogram, or 'waterfall display', of an AM transmission. Frequency runs across the image from left to right, while time runs up and down it. The heavy vertical line in the centre is the carrier and the two sidebands are to the

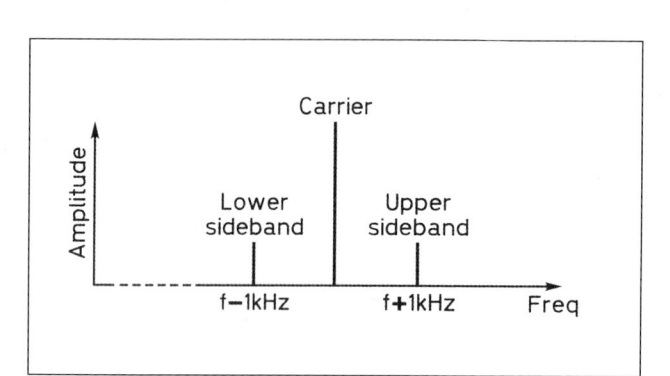

Fig 3.3: A simple AM transmission: a carrier being modulated by a single tone.

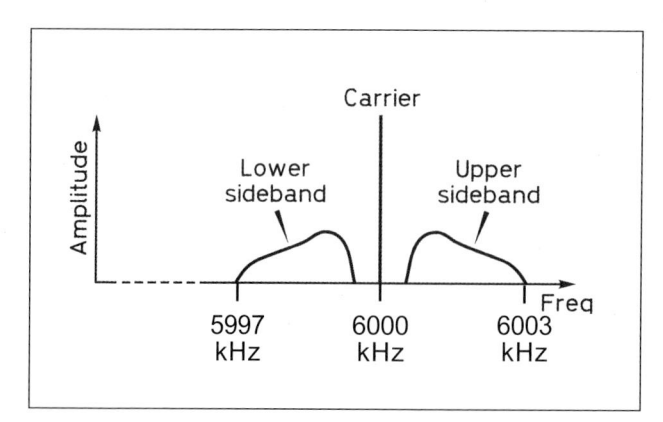

Fig 3.4: An AM transmission being modulated by speech.

CHAPTER 3 – WHAT IS SSB?

left and right. The three black bands running horizontally across the display, roughly one-quarter, one half and three-quarters of the way down the display, are when the transmission is silent, for example during pauses in speech.

Music has a wider audio frequency response than the human voice, from a few Hertz (for the lowest pedal notes on a concert organ) up to around 20kHz, if harmonics are included. An AM transmitter could, theoretically at least, transmit audio frequencies up to 20kHz, but the transmission would then take up 40kHz of spectrum and the limited amount of space available in the long-, medium- and short-wave bands makes this unacceptable: there are simply too many stations trying to fit into the limited amount of spectrum available to make this possible. Being restricted to a bandwidth of 6kHz (that is, audio frequencies of up to 3kHz may be transmitted) means that AM transmissions are fine for speech, but they can sound a little 'muffled' when transmitting music. It is for this reason that music sounds better on an FM transmitter (which is limited to audio frequencies of up to 15kHz).

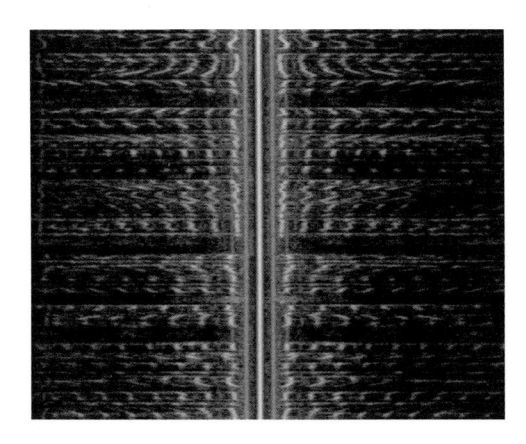

Fig 3.5: 'Waterfall' display of an AM transmission.

FROM AM TO SSB

We have already seen that a single audio tone modulated on to a carrier produces an AM transmission with two sidebands. The tone transmitted by the AM transmitter is the same tone, whether it is on the lower sideband or the upper sideband. Likewise, speech (or music, or any sound) transmitted by an AM transmitter is transmitted both on the lower sideband and, as a 'mirror image', on the upper sideband.

This is not only unnecessary, but it is also wasteful: wasteful both of the amount of spectrum required for the transmission, and of the power that is necessary to transmit it.

Imagine you have a total of 100 watts of power available for your transmitter. In an AM transmitter some of that power is required for the carrier, some for the lower sideband and some for the upper sideband. But only one of those sidebands is necessary, because identical audio is being transmitted on both of them. If one of the sidebands can be suppressed, more of the available power can be put into the carrier and the remaining sideband, thus making the signal stronger at the receiver.

If the upper sideband is suppressed you are left with a lower sideband or LSB transmission; if the lower sideband is suppressed naturally enough you then have an upper sideband or USB transmission. (Those more familiar with computer terminology than that of amateur radio should get used to the term USB meaning upper side-band. It has been around a lot longer than the Universal Serial Bus, which was only invented in 1996!)

As far as the transmission is concerned, it does not matter *which* sideband is suppressed, as the audio information

29

they contain is identical.

Not only is a significant percentage of power saved by suppressing one of the sidebands, but the bandwidth of the signal – the amount of spectrum or space on the radio dial that it takes up – is halved, typically from about 6kHz to about 3kHz. This means that, for a given number of stations operating in a particular band, there is less likely to be interference caused by other stations.

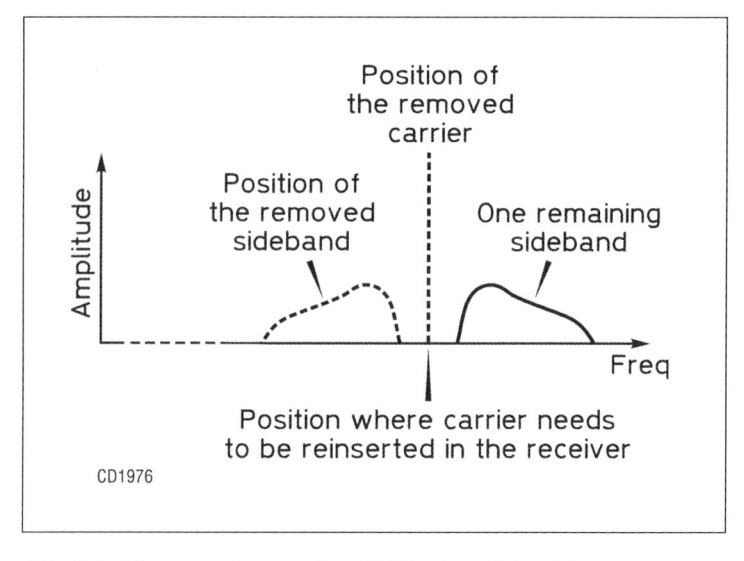

Fig 3.6: The spectrum of an SSB signal, in this case a USB transmission.

We have said that the carrier, by itself, conveys no information. It does, however, have an important function and that is to provide the receiver with a reference point with which to demodulate the audio signal. In other words, the very existence of the carrier tells the receiver the precise frequency of the transmission.

But what if the carrier were also to be suppressed, like the one unnecessary sideband? Two things would happen – and it's good news and bad news. First, the good news: another significant amount of the transmitter's power could be saved or, alternatively, put instead into the one remaining sideband, thus making the signal at the receiver stronger still. Now the bad news: it does make the reception of the signal more complex. Just how to tune in an SSB signal on a receiver is covered later.

Fig 3.6 shows a single sideband transmission with both the lower sideband and the carrier having been suppressed, leaving just the upper sideband remaining.

HOW SSB IS GENERATED

There are two main ways of generating a single sideband signal; the filter method and the phasing method. (There is also a third method, logically but unimaginatively called 'The Third Method', but that is beyond the scope of this brief introduction to SSB.)

Until IF DSP transceivers came along, almost all commercially-made SSB transceivers used the filter method of generating SSB because it was possible to suppress the unwanted sideband to a greater degree than was possible with the phasing method when using analogue techniques. In the filter method, the microphone audio is mixed with the output of the carrier oscillator in a balanced modulator, the output of which is a double sideband signal. This is fed to a crystal or mechanical filter to remove the unwanted sideband, as shown in **Fig 3.7**.

CHAPTER 3 – WHAT IS SSB?

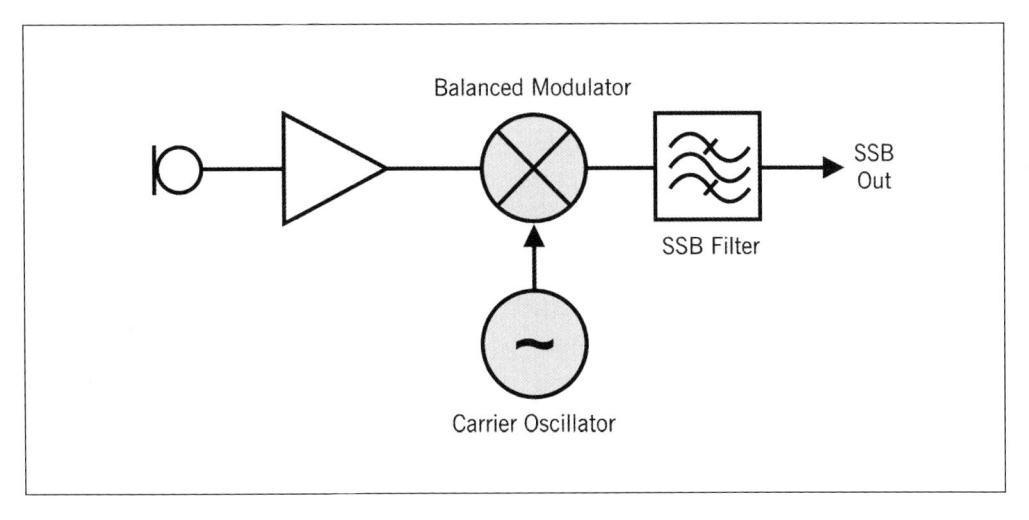

Fig 3.7: Simplified diagram showing the filter method of generating an SSB signal.

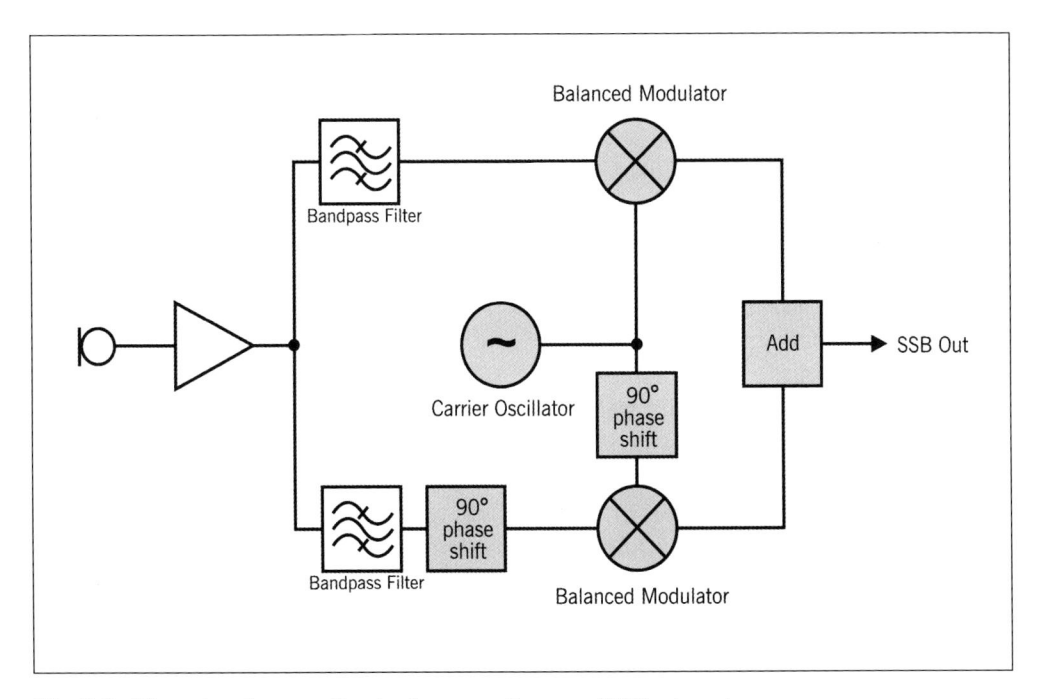

Fig 3.8: The phasing method of generating an SSB signal.

The phasing method has tended to be more popular with home-construction enthusiasts because, although it may look more complicated in **Fig 3.8**, it is actually easier to implement than the filter method. Here, the audio from the microphone is first fed to two filters, both of which filter the audio to the final bandwidth that is to be transmitted, such as 300Hz to 2.7kHz. The output of one of

31

the filters is phase shifted by 90° and the outputs of both are passed to two balanced modulators. Both the balanced modulators are also fed with the output of the single carrier oscillator, but the balanced modulator with the phase-shifted audio receives the carrier oscillator's output also phase shifted by 90°. The outputs of the two balanced modulators are then combined: by adding or subtracting the two outputs either an upper sideband or lower sideband signal can be produced.

Unfortunately, the level of unwanted sideband suppression can often leave something to be desired in home-made phasing method SSB transmitters.

With the advent of IF DSP transceivers the phasing method has had something of a renaissance, as modern digital techniques make it easier to implement the phasing method in software and allow both the unwanted sideband and the carrier to be suppressed by 60dB or more: at least as good as analogue filtering techniques.

Although the term 'suppressed' is used, it is never possible to suppress the unwanted parts of the signal entirely. A level of suppression of 60dB for both the carrier and the unwanted sideband is considered good. This means, though, that in practice if you are receiving an SSB signal at a signal level of S9+60dB (perfectly possible for a powerful local signal) and the carrier is suppressed by 60dB it will still be S9 at your receiver. It is often possible to hear the carrier of strong SSB signals by tuning slightly lower in frequency for a USB signal, or higher in frequency for an LSB signal. This does not by itself indicate a problem with the transmitter; it is the difference between the strength of the wanted sideband and that of the carrier that is the issue.

TUNING IN SSB

Earlier we talked about how an SSB signal is derived from an AM signal and said that the reception of an SSB signal is somewhat more complex than that of an ordinary double sideband (DSB) AM signal.

In fact, the receiver circuitry and the actual process of tuning in the signal are both somewhat more complex than that required for AM. We have already seen that an SSB transmitter is also more complex than an AM one.

When tuning in an ordinary AM signal on a receiver, you do not need to tune the receiver to exactly the same frequency as the carrier; you can be up to a couple of kilohertz higher or lower in frequency than the carrier and it does not matter – the signal sounds more or less the same wherever you are listening, provided the signal falls within the *passband* of the receiver. The same is not true, however, when tuning in a single sideband transmission.

Before the audio can be recovered, the receiver must re-insert the carrier that was suppressed at the transmitter, as was shown in **Fig 3.6**. This is usually done with a circuit called a product detector. A simpler, though somewhat less effective, way of doing it is to add a beat frequency oscillator – or BFO – circuit to a standard AM receiver. Not only must the level (the strength) of the re-inserted carrier be correct in order to demodulate the SSB signal, but also it must be on exactly the correct frequency.

Fortunately for us amateurs the tolerance required when tuning in speech, especially speech of 'communications quality', is much less than that required for music. For ordinary speech to sound 'natural' it needs to be tuned in to within

CHAPTER 3 – WHAT IS SSB?

about 50Hz (0.05kHz) of the suppressed carrier frequency and, with today's modern and stable receivers and transceivers, that is not too difficult to achieve (although it may take a little practice).

Beginners to amateur radio, who may well be used to tuning in AM and FM radio broadcasts, often find it difficult to tune in an SSB transmission at first. But the knack soon comes. How is it done?

All transceivers, and almost all receivers – at least 'communications receivers', those intended for reception of transmissions other than standard AM or FM broadcasts – have a series of push buttons on the front panel to select the appropriate mode. Among the modes available (including CW, AM, probably FM and perhaps RTTY or Data) there will be buttons marked 'LSB' and 'USB', **Fig 3.9**, or simply 'SSB', **Fig 3.10**. Older transceivers will have a mode *switch* rather than buttons.

Virtually all properly-licensed non-amateur SSB transmissions are on USB (no doubt there are a few exceptions, but I am not aware of any). In the case of amateur SSB transmissions, though, there is a convention that dates back to the early days of SSB communications that has LSB being used on the 1.8, 3.5 and 7MHz bands and USB elsewhere. There is nothing sacrosanct about this: amateurs may, if they wish, transmit USB on 1.8, 3.5 and 7MHz and LSB on the other bands (although they might not make too many contacts if they did!)

It is impossible to receive a USB transmission if the receiver is switched to LSB and *vice versa* or, to be pedantic, it is possible to *receive* the signal but it will be impossible to *understand* it, because it will sound completely 'scrambled'. So, before tuning in the SSB signal it is im-

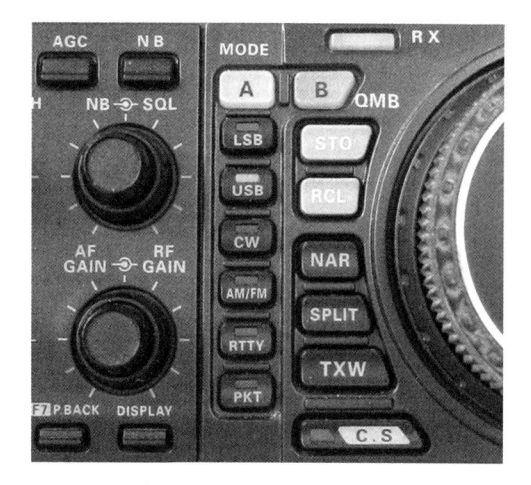

Fig 3.9: The mode buttons on a Yaesu FT-2000 transceiver dating from 2005. Be sure to select the correct sideband before attempting to tune in an SSB signal (LSB on 1.8, 3.5 and 7MHz, USB elsewhere).

Fig 3.10: Some modern transceivers, such as the Icom IC-7300, now use a touch screen rather than physical buttons for mode selection.

portant to know whether the transmission is on lower sideband or upper sideband.

You can assume that nearly 100% of radio amateurs will stick to the LSB / USB convention described. Select the appropriate sideband and tune across the band. You will note that as you tune across an SSB signal, the voice will sound distorted and either unnaturally high-pitched or unnaturally low-pitched. Tune across the signal slowly – very slowly if necessary – and as you do so you will notice that the pitch of the voice changes. At first, it is easy to 'overshoot' and tune beyond the correct point, in which case obviously you must make an adjustment by turning the tuning knob in the opposite direction by a small amount. At one point between too high-pitched and too low-pitched it will be 'spot on'.

At first the process of tuning in an SSB signal may seem quite random, but it will soon be realised that all the signals on the band tune 'the same way'. Which way is dependent on which sideband is being transmitted. On USB if you start tuning from the bottom of the band towards the top end, i.e. if you are tuning higher in frequency, as a signal comes into the passband of the receiver it will first sound too high-pitched and, if you have gone 'too far', it will sound too low-pitched. On LSB it is the other way round.

Although tuning in SSB signals very soon becomes second nature, when starting out many people find it easiest always to tune across a band in the same direction. In that way when a signal is not quite correctly tuned in, the operator instinctively knows which way to turn the tuning knob to make the correct adjustment. This is not a bad habit to get into and even now, more than 50 years after listening to my first SSB signals, I usually find myself tuning 'from high to low' on the 1.8, 3.5 and 7MHz bands, and 'from low to high' on the other bands. For example, on 80 metres I start at 3800kHz and tune lower in frequency, while on 20 metres I start at about 14,110kHz and tune higher in frequency. In both cases SSB signals coming into the receiver's passband start by sounding too high-pitched and go lower in pitch as the signal is tuned in.

This may sound complex but it is one of those things that is much more difficult and long-winded to describe in words than actually to do in practice. After a bit of practice using a particular receiver or transceiver you will find that not only do you know instinctively which way to turn the tuning knob to tune in a signal correctly, but also you will know how much to turn it – even to the extent of being able to judge how far to turn the tuning knob between short transmissions, when the signal is not actually on the air, in order for the signal to sound natural when the transmission recommences.

TUNING RATE

One final tip for tuning in SSB signals. With many transceivers and receivers it is possible to adjust the tuning rate – the amount the equipment changes in frequency as the tuning knob is turned. It is important to ensure that the best rate is selected before attempting to tune in any signals. Too fast and it is all too easy to 'overshoot' and so it becomes very difficult to tune in the signal to exactly the correct spot. Too slow and tuning in the signal becomes laborious and, in 'quick-fire' operating conditions such as during a DXpedition or a contest, the wanted station is likely to have ended its transmission before you have had a chance to tune it in correctly, no matter how fast you try to turn the tuning knob.

So what is the 'best' tuning rate? To some extent this is a matter of personal choice. For example, I like a tuning rate of about 10kHz per 360° rotation of the tuning knob, while some operators may prefer as little as 1kHz per full rotation.

On the other hand, 100kHz per revolution is *way* too fast for SSB (though it might be suitable for tuning in AM shortwave broadcast stations or for rapidly moving from one end of the band to the other).

For Morse code reception a slower tuning rate such as 1kHz per full rotation of the tuning control is preferred and CW (Morse) operators often leave their transceiver set at a slow tuning rate when they do venture on to SSB. Some transceivers, such as the Icom IC-7300, allow the operator to set the tuning rate for each mode separately.

Anywhere between about 5 and 15kHz per 360° rotation is probably about right for SSB reception.

SSB DIGITAL VOICE

A quick word about Digital Voice on SSB. Here we do not mean conventional SSB generated by digital techniques, such as those described earlier in the chapter, but rather a mode in which the voice is first digitised and then transmitted over an SSB signal and bandwidth. It is therefore better described as Digital Voice, or 'DV', than as digital SSB.

The Japanese company AOR manufactures the AR9000 MK2 Digital Voice Modem, **Fig 3.11**, which is a development of their earlier AR9800 'Fast Radio Modem', the first commercially-available SSB digital voice equipment, originally released in 2004.

DV has actually been around for longer than that: pioneering work carried out in 1999 by Charles Brain, G4GUO, and Andy Talbot, G4JNT, led to G4GUO developing an open protocol which is still in use today in the AOR DV equipment.

The AR9000 MK2 is a stand-alone unit, which simply connects to the microphone input and speaker output connections of an SSB transceiver and a suitable 12V DC supply.

The IARU Region 1 HF band plans list Digital Voice centres of activity at 3630, 7070, 14130, 18150, 21180, 24960 and 28330kHz. However, HF Digital Voice has yet to become a 'mainstream' or popular mode, in marked contrast to D-Star and other forms of digital voice used on VHF.

DV provides improved speech quality compared with conventional analogue SSB, equivalent to VHF narrow-band FM quality, but at the price of requiring a signal-to-noise ratio of about 25dB in order to work effectively. It is therefore not a weak-signal mode and so, unlike conventional SSB, DV is quite unsuitable for DX working.

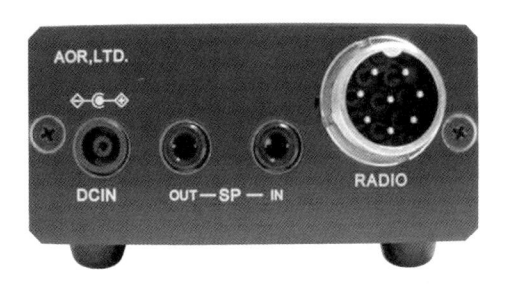

Fig 3.11: Front and rear panels of the AOR AR9000 MK2 Digital Voice Modem for DV SSB.

Chapter 4

The DXer's Transceiver

In this chapter we look at those criteria that are of interest to all DXers, regardless of their mode or modes of operation.

If you were starting from scratch, which transceiver would you buy? There is no 'best' transceiver but, while ostensibly similar – almost all cover all the bands from 1.8 to 50MHz – many of them do have differing features or individual characteristics. Some of these features may be of no importance at all to you, but they may well be to a different type of operator. A good example of this is the built-in second receiver that some high-end transceivers have included as standard. A DXer might consider this a very useful or even an essential feature, whereas an operator who never chases DXpeditions and only ever has 'ragchews' or calls in to 'natter nets' might find this an expensive and completely unnecessary distraction.

Some transceivers also include 144 and 430MHz and a few cover 70MHz too, but those three bands are outside the scope of this book. Other than a few specialist and usually QRP (low power) transceivers, all are multi-mode, in other words they will transmit and receive SSB, CW, FM and AM, and many have a specific provision for data modes too.

Your choice of transceiver will partly be dependent on whether the VHF and UHF bands are important to you or not, and to some extent whether you plan to use CW as well as SSB and FT8. It's a balancing act: a rig that is good on SSB may only offer mediocre performance on CW, for example.

While some criteria (such as receive performance) are equally important for most operators, others (such as whether or not a transceiver has full break-in – 'QSK' – on CW) are of no interest at all to the SSB / FT8 operator. Likewise, while it might be important to an operator who also wanted VHF / UHF capabilities, for the purely HF operator it is not really relevant whether or not a particular transceiver also covers 144 or 430MHz.

SOFTWARE DEFINED RADIO – SDR

Before we look at some of the criteria to be considered when choosing a transceiver for HF DX work on SSB and FT8, a word or two about Software Defined Radio, SDR. The term can be used of both receivers and transceivers and it refers to the basic design of the equipment. In SDR equipment computer software, rather than discrete components, is used to provide the filtering, modulation, demodulation etc.

CHAPTER 4 – THE DXER'S TRANSCEIVER

Fig 4.1: The FLEX-6400 direct sampling SDR transceiver (Photo: FlexRadio website).

Fig 4.3: The Elecraft K4D transceiver.

These days most new transceiver designs employ SDR technology.

The first SDR transceivers on the amateur market were 'black boxes' that also required a separate high-end computer to provide the processing power. They had no external controls, simply a connection to the computer and sockets for a microphone, Morse key, headphones and antenna. There was no front panel; instead the computer screen became a 'virtual front panel' and the transceiver was controlled by software, using the PC's mouse and keyboard.

FlexRadio [1] was one of the pioneers of SDR amateur transceivers and today they have a range of high-end direct sampling SDR transceivers such as the FLEX-6400 (**Fig 4.1**) and the FLEX-6400M (**Fig 4.2**) which includes an integrated 'traditional' radio interface with front panel display and controls.

Most apparently 'conventional' new transceivers do *also* employ SDR technology using an 'embedded system' with the processor built in, so they do not require a separate stand-alone computer in order to be able to function. Such equipment has a conventional-looking front panel, with a frequency display, tuning knob, AF and RF gain controls etc but, inside, the technology is SDR.

At the time of writing one of the newest transceivers on the market that employs direct sampling SDR technology is the Elecraft K4D, **Fig 4.3**.

One of the great advantages of SDR technology is that it allows a panoramic adapter (or 'panadapter'), **Fig 4.4**, to display on a screen spectrum either side of the frequency to which the equipment is tuned, as a waterfall display and / or a 'bandscope'. While these displays un-

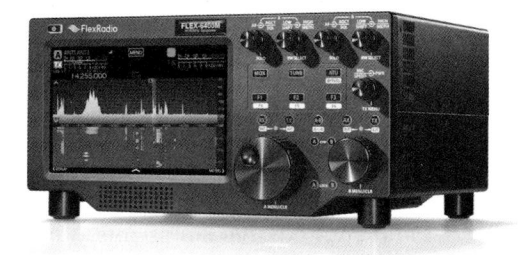

Fig 4.2: The FLEX-6400M SDR transceiver, with front panel controls (Photo: FlexRadio website).

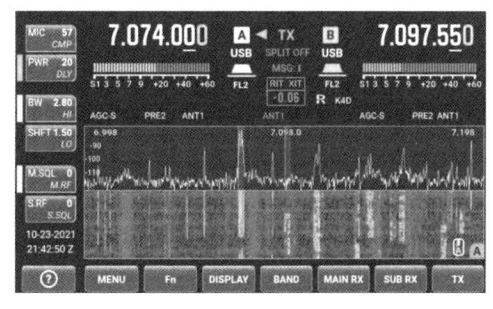

Fig 4.4: The panadapter in the Elecraft K4D.

doubtedly look best on an external computer monitor, all the major manufacturers are now producing equipment in which a panadapter display is incorporated as part of the front panel of the transceiver.

EQUIPMENT CRITERIA

There are quite a few other criteria to look at when considering the purchase of any transceiver. In no particular order these include:

- Front panel display
- Receive performance
- Base, mobile, or portable?
- Power output
- Price (new or used?)
- Internal ATU
- Twin / dual receivers
- Noise blanker
- Monitor facility
- Digital voice keyer
- DSP / Digital noise reduction (DNR)

Since this is *HF DX Basics*, the comments in this chapter are made from the perspective of a DX operator.

FRONT PANEL DISPLAY

We have already shown that new transceiver designs often now incorporate a panadapter display as part of the front panel. At one time, the front panel display on a transceiver was an analogue dial from which you could read the operating frequency to within 1 or 2kHz if you were lucky. (My first HF transceiver was a second-hand KW-2000B, which made 80m SSB DX operating around the band-edge awkward as it was difficult to tell whether I was operating in the band or just above 3800kHz!)

In the 1970s along came digital frequency readout. Frequency synthesisers came in at about the same time and their implementation meant that you could be reasonably certain that the digital frequency readout was accurate to within about 0.1kHz or so.

Transceivers' front panels continued to develop over the years and today there may be several dozen operating parameters displayed, including VFO A operating frequency, VFO B operating frequency, mode, pre-amplifier 1 on / off, pre-amplifier 2 on / off, amount of RF attenuation, power output, AGC setting, RIT offset, S-meter, noise blanker on / off, digital noise reduction on / off, filter selection and bandwidth, roofing filter selection and much more besides.

The 'big three' Japanese manufacturers (Icom, Yaesu and Kenwood) now all use colour thin film transistor (TFT) display screens on most of their transceivers. The respected US manufacturer Elecraft continued to use a monochrome LCD screen on the front panels of all their transceivers until the introduction of the K4 / K4D in 2019 / 2020 which features a 7-inch colour screen as shown in **Fig 4.4**. This incorporates a panadapter to display a bandscope and waterfall display.

Surprisingly, perhaps, this technology is no longer new: it was pioneered by Icom with the introduction of their IC-756Pro transceiver as long ago as 2000.

RECEIVE PERFORMANCE

For many serious HF DXers and contesters a transceiver's receive performance is the single most important consideration when deciding which piece of equipment to buy. Within this single category, there are numerous parameters to consider, including sensitivity, selectivity, dynamic range, image rejection, etc. This is not the place to go into any great de-

CHAPTER 4 – THE DXER'S TRANSCEIVER

tail on the meaning of these terms but, for the moment, suffice to say that what they are measuring is the ability of a receiver to single out a particular wanted weak signal among numerous stronger unwanted signals and to make it readable.

In brief, sensitivity can largely be ignored, because at HF it is not really an issue: just about all commercially-made transceivers have adequate sensitivity these days.

Selectivity, the ability of a receiver to home in on the signal required and reject other nearby signals, is determined by the receiver's filters, which with older equipment would be crystal or mechanical but these days it is more likely to be implemented digitally using DSP (digital signal processing). If the transceiver has IF DSP filtering there is likely to be a wide range of IF selectivity bandwidths available to the operator.

Dynamic range is the difference between the weakest and the strongest signal that the receiver can cope with and is measured in decibels (dB). The higher the figure, the better: anything above 100dB is excellent.

Image rejection is the ability of the receiver to reject the image signals that are generated within the receiver during the mixing process. If image signals are not suppressed they will appear as interference on the wanted signal. Once again, this parameter is measured in dB and the higher the figure the better.

However, even if you have a good knowledge of the meaning of these measurements and – just as importantly – how to interpret them, the best way to determine how well a receiver performs is to compare two pieces of equipment side-by-side on the operating desk and using the same antenna. They may well *sound* different, but the question really is whether one can receive readable signals that the other one cannot, and probably 98% of the time you will notice little or no difference in this respect between two different models of transceiver. The remaining 2% of the time is when the one with the better receiver will be able to winkle out the weakest of signals buried in interference. Such top performance often comes at a price though, and, even if you have aspirations to be a top DXer you will need to ask yourself whether paying, say, twice the price is worth it for that 2% of the time.

The fact is that these days all commercial transceivers have pretty good receiver performance, although it is true that some are better than others. If you know how to interpret them correctly, you can get a good idea of how well a receiver will perform by looking at measurements of the various parameters, preferably those made by an independent reviewer such as Peter Hart, G3SJX, whose excellent and detailed reviews of rigs have been published regularly in *RadCom* for over 40 years now, or the equally authoritative reviews published in the ARRL's *QST* magazine.

BASE, MOBILE OR PORTABLE?

These days, HF transceivers tend to come in three flavours: 'Base station', 'Mobile' and 'Portable'.

What are the differences between these three types of transceiver? Firstly and most obviously, base station transceivers are bigger and heavier than their mobile siblings. The trend in recent years is for the top-performing (and most expensive) base station transceivers to be

HF DX BASICS

Fig 4.5: The Kenwood TS-990S, one of the current (2022) range of big base station transceivers.

large, table-top affairs weighing in from at least 15kg and sometimes a lot more. A good example is Kenwood's TS-990S, **Fig 4.5**, that company's 'elite' top-of-the range base station transceiver.

Most base station transceivers also have a built-in mains power supply unit (which can contribute a lot to the rig's overall size and weight) and therefore they are 'plug-in and go': they operate from 220 – 240V AC mains. (The North American versions work from 110–130V AC, or they may have a dual voltage power supply with a switch so that they can be operated in countries where either mains voltage is the standard.)

'Mobile' sets are just that: they are intended to be operated from cars, so they are designed to work from a car battery of 12V – 15V DC (the standard operating voltage is 13.8V). There's nothing to stop you using a mobile rig from home, but you will need an external mains power supply unit capable of providing 13.8V DC and with a current rating of up to about 22 or 25A on peaks.

In stark contrast to the base station rigs, the trend for mobile transceivers is for each generation to be smaller and lighter than the last. As a result of this, base stations are usually far superior ergonomically to mobile sets. The latter may have front panels so small that only a limited number of controls can be fitted on them. The manufacturers' way round this dilemma is to have all but the most frequently used controls available only via a 'menu' system. What this means in practice is that a function such as, say, reducing the power from 100W to 5W in order to make a QRP contact requires one or two button presses to select the transceiver's menus, then turning a knob to get to the correct menu number, then turning another knob in order to reduce the power level, then pressing a button to confirm the change that has been made and to return to the operating mode, as is the case with the Yaesu FT-857D, **Fig 4.6**. In contrast, on the base station transceiver there will almost certainly be a dedicated 'Power' knob which can be adjusted up and down while the contact is taking place.

Fig 4.6: The diminutive Yaesu FT-857D mobile transceiver. Its size can be estimated from the relative size of its fist microphone.

CHAPTER 4 – THE DXER'S TRANSCEIVER

Many other functions, such as changing the receiver's AGC setting, adjusting the transmitter's speech processor, or operating 'split' on the two VFOs, may require a similar number of button presses and knob adjustments in mobile sets. It is not unusual to find that operators simply cannot remember what is required to achieve some of the lesser-used functions and therefore they need if not the full operating manual then at least an *aide mémoire* available by the rig at all times.

Many base station transceivers have a built-in automatic ATU, most mobile transceivers do not. An internal ATU can be a useful feature but the lack of one is perhaps less important than it might at first appear, as we shall discuss later.

Mobile transceivers are designed to be operated with mobile antennas, such as electrically-short vertical 'whips'. To compensate for the relative inefficiency of the antenna, the rig is designed with high sensitivity. This may sound all very well in theory, but if used at home on a high-gain antenna (such as a quad or Yagi beam on the higher-frequency bands, or a full-size dipole up high and in the clear on 3.5 or 7MHz) some transceivers may be subject to overloading, with spurious ('phantom') signals appearing in the receiver and causing interference to the real signals that you want to hear.

This not necessarily as bad as it sounds, because almost all transceivers these days have a built-in front-end attenuator which can be switched in when required. This decreases the level of the signal going into the transceiver from the antenna and thus eliminates, or at least reduces, the overloading.

Generally speaking the overall receive performance of base stations is superior to that of mobile sets.

Like mobile units, 'portable' transceivers do not usually have a built-in power supply unit but they are generally physically larger than mobile transceivers and have more dedicated controls available on the front panel, without having to delve too deeply into the menus.

These days, their performance can be as good, or nearly as good, as the big desk-top 'base station' transceivers. However, they will still be lacking some features, such as twin receivers, that some DXers find essential.

One of the most popular transceivers in recent years that falls into this portable category is the Icom IC-7300 as shown in **Fig 4.7**.

Because they are smaller and lighter than base station transceivers they are more suitable for operating on field days, from caravans or on DXpeditions.

Fig 4.7: Icom's IC-7300, one of the most popular transceivers, fits into the 'portable' category.

HF DX BASICS

POWER OUTPUT

Most HF transceivers, whether they be base station, portable or mobile models, have a power output of 100W. There are a few exceptions, though. There are low-power transceivers about, such as the Yaesu FT-818ND (6W out), Icom IC-705 (10W) and Elecraft's KX2 (10W) and KX3 (15W).

Fig 4.8: The Yaesu FTdx9000MP, one of the few 400-watt output transceivers available.

Some operators get a kick out of operating with low power ('QRP' operation, usually defined as up to 5 watts output) and the GQRP Club **[2]** has a great following. Most QRP operators tend to stick to CW and data modes such as FT8, as these are much more effective than SSB at the low signal levels often associated with low- power operation. Rigs such as the FT-818ND, IC-705 and KX2 / KX3 are ideal for the dedicated QRP operator, but unless you *never* wish to operate with higher power than this, it is not really worth considering purchasing a transceiver with such a low output power. Even if you are at present a Foundation licensee and limited to a maximum of 10W output, you should have aspirations to upgrade your licence, first to Intermediate level and then to a Full licence. If you are a DXer, once you upgrade you will almost certainly want to use higher power than 10W, so do take this into consideration when choosing your transceiver.

This is particularly the case for SSB DXers: using only 5 or 10W, DXing on SSB is *hard* work, far more so than on FT8 or even CW, unless you are lucky enough to have some spectacularly good antennas.

At the other end of the scale, there are a few transceivers that provide 200W output and there is at least one that can provide 400 watts output (the Yaesu FTdx9000MP, **Fig 4.8**).

Is this sort of power level necessary? The answer will depend on your style of operating. For those who are never going to be DXers, the answer is probably "no": 100W would be sufficient. But for the DXer or contester there will certainly be times when it would be nice to have more than 100W available (depending on your licence class, of course).

Going from 100W to 200W, i.e. doubling the power output, equates to an increase in signal level of 3dB. An increase of 2dB is only just noticeable at the far end, so on the face of it there seems little point in going for a 200W transceiver over a 100W transceiver, all other things being equal. Going from 100W to 400W, on the other hand – quadrupling the power output – provides an increase in signal level of 6dB. This is equivalent to 1 or 2 S-units, depending on how the receiver's S-meter is calibrated (traditionally an S-unit was taken to be 6dB, but most modern transceivers have only 3dB per S-unit). This sort of increase *is* worth having. It may not appear to be important if signal levels are around S9 at the 100W level, but if the signal is only about S3, an increase to S5 might make all the dif-

CHAPTER 4 – THE DXER'S TRANSCEIVER

ference between being heard and being buried in interference.

The most common way of increasing one's power output above 100W is to use a separate linear amplifier after the transceiver. Most commercial linear amplifiers are capable of power outputs of between 500W and 1500W, depending on the model and the design. In order to achieve that power output, generally they need to be 'driven' (by the transceiver) with an input power of anywhere between about 60W and 100W (again, depending on the design). A 200W output transceiver, therefore, is unnecessary if you have a linear amplifier: 100W is ample power to drive the linear amplifier to its full power output. A 400W transceiver would be even more 'overkill' – if you have a linear amplifier, that is.

In the UK the maximum power limit is 400W, so does it not make sense to cut out the linear amplifier altogether and instead buy a transceiver with 400W output? There are a few reasons why this may not be the best option, logical though it sounds. Firstly, a 400W-output transceiver might only provide a maximum of 400W output when there is a perfect 1:1 match between the transceiver and the antenna system. If the SWR is above 1.5:1 or 2:1 the power output might well be reduced. This can be counteracted by using the transceiver's internal ATU, but this also introduces a loss, sometimes of 10% or even 20%.

Secondly, the Full UK licence allows 400W input *at the antenna*, i.e. you can use more than 400W out of the transmitter if there is loss between the transmitter and the antenna itself. Obviously there will always be *some* loss: the question is 'how much?'

While it is always good practice to ensure that feeder losses are kept to a minimum, with a long feeder run it is possible that on 28MHz or 50MHz there may be a loss of, say, 3dB between the final amplifier and the antenna, when insertion loss of an ATU and a low-pass or band-pass filter (see **Fig 4.9**) are included. With 3dB loss it would be permissible to run 800W out of the amplifier so as to provide 400W at the input of the antenna. It is therefore important to be able to measure the power at the antenna, or know precisely how much loss there is, so as not to exceed the power limit.

Thirdly, choice: there is a very limited choice of transceivers available that give 400W out. Finally, cost: a 400W-output transceiver is very much a top-of-the-range rig and will cost more than a modest, though perfectly acceptable, 100W transceiver and medium-sized linear amplifier capable of the 500 to 800W necessary if you really do wish to run 400W at the input of the antenna.

All the above suggests that the best option is a 100W transceiver: many operators do not require more power than this, and those who do are usually best served by using a separate linear amplifier, which only needs 100W (or less) of drive power.

However, there are a couple of reasons for buying a higher-power transceiver. If you intend to do portable operation or go on DXpeditions, for several reasons it may not be possible to take a linear amplifier with you – for a start they are generally large and very heavy. Under those circumstances, a 200W-output transceiver will give your signal just that little extra edge over a 100W station.

Unfortunately for the lightweight traveller, most of the 200W radios are also pretty large and quite heavy.

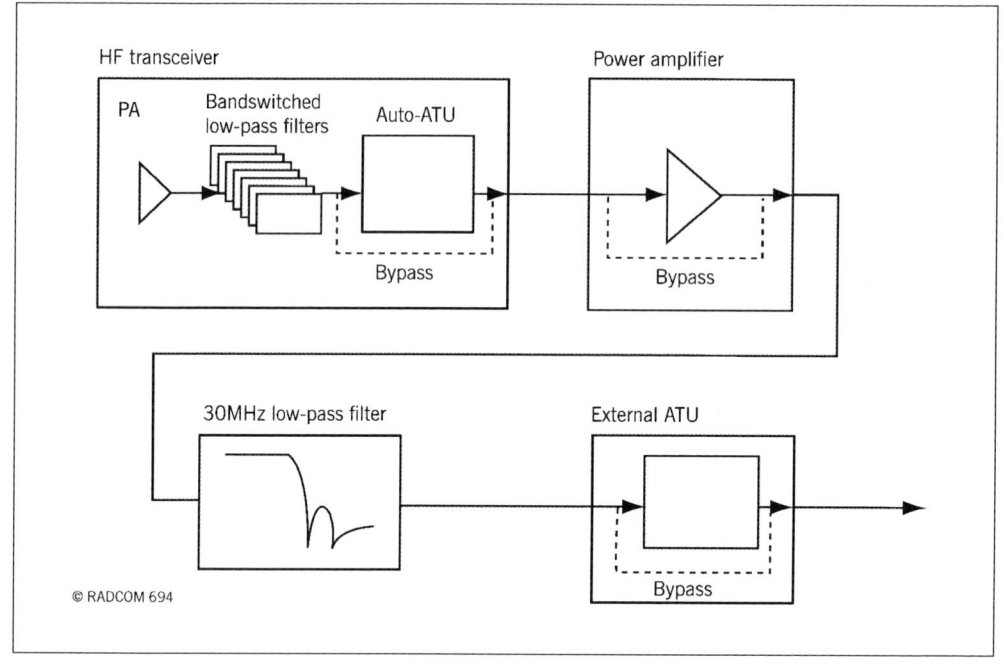

Fig 4.9: Typical HF station consisting of transceiver with internal ATU, external power (linear) amplifier, low-pass filter and external ATU.

There is one exception, though: the Kenwood TS-480HX, **Fig 4.10**, weighs only 3.7kg, although it should be noted that due to the higher power output it requires a 40 – 45A 13.8V power supply (or two identical 20 – 23A PSUs).

The other reason, once again, comes down to cost. If you want all the power that you can muster yet have decided that you cannot justify the expense of a separate linear amplifier, a 200W transceiver might be the answer: certainly some 200W transceivers are cheaper than some 100W rigs that have a higher specification in aspects other than power output.

PRICE (NEW OR USED?)

A Rolls-Royce or Ferrari costs many times the price of a basic Mini or Hyundai, yet all will get you perfectly well from A to B. Some simply do it faster, more comfortably or in more style than others. It is much the same with HF transceivers: the top

Fig 4.10: The Kenwood TS-480HX, the smallest and, at 3.7kg, the lightest 200-watt output HF transceiver currently available.

CHAPTER 4 – THE DXER'S TRANSCEIVER

Fig 4.11: The Yaesu FT-891, at the time of writing the cheapest 100W output HF + 50MHz transceiver.

of the range transceivers cost several times the amount of the most basic.

It could well be that price is the most important factor to you. If so, at the time of writing the cheapest new 100-watt HF + 50MHz transceiver you can buy is the Yaesu FT-891, **Fig 4.11**, at £680. I have not used one but I am sure it would perform perfectly well for SSB and FT8 DXing. If money is no object, you could spend £12,250 on a new Hilberling PT-8000A.

Most of us will probably be somewhere in between: we will want several features that the more basic transceivers do not include, and so we will be prepared to pay for them, but we may feel that we cannot justify the expense of buying any of the absolute top-of-the-range models.

If you're really hard up, a second-hand transceiver may be the only realistic option. I have already mentioned that my first HF transceiver, back in the 1970s, was a used KW-2000B. A decade later I owned a used Kenwood TS-930S, a superb piece of equipment in its day. Now no longer in production, the Yaesu FT-450D, **Fig 4.12**, was a good-value transceiver that can now often be found in good used condition on the second-hand market. Although older second-hand equipment may not always have the wide variety of features (the so-called 'bells and whistles') that a present-day transceiver possesses, its basic performance may be at least as good as some modern-day equipment.

'Bells and whistles' is the rather derogatory term for the features that come with your transceiver that you may not really need. However, one man's bells and whistles are another man's essential requirements and I regard several of them as being very important for the DXer, and especially the SSB DXer. On the other hand, I have never used the memories that all modern HF transceivers have, finding the band-stacking registers perfectly adequate. To me memories are merely bells and whistles, but no doubt some operators would find them essential.

INTERNAL ATU

ATU stands for antenna (or aerial) tuning unit or, more correctly perhaps, 'antenna-system tuning unit'. It is also sometimes known as an 'antenna matching unit'. Some

Fig 4.12: The Yaesu FT-450D is a popular transceiver that can often be found on the second-hand market.

transceivers have a built-in automatic ATU, while others do not. In some, it is an option available at extra cost. While it can only really be an advantage for a rig to have an internal ATU, in my opinion it is not a great advantage and should not be seen as a necessity, nor even a particularly important feature.

There are several reasons for this. Firstly, many amateurs only use antennas with an impedance of close to 50Ω, in which case an ATU is unnecessary.

Secondly, transceivers' internal automatic ATUs can generally only match SWRs of up to about 3:1, i.e. impedances of approximately 16Ω to 150Ω. A few can do somewhat better than this, but rarely can they cope with the very wide range of impedances that might be provided when trying to match, for example, a long-wire antenna or multi-band doublet. For that you will need an external wide-range ATU (either manual or automatic).

Thirdly, putting an internal ATU into circuit can introduce a power loss of up to 10 or 20%.

Finally, if you ever intend to use a linear amplifier, the linear goes between the transceiver and the antenna, so the transceiver's internal ATU will be of no use in matching to the antenna system: what the ATU will 'see' is the input of the linear amplifier, which should itself always be close to 50Ω.

If a linear amplifier is in use what is needed then is an automatic ATU at the output of the linear amplifier, or an outboard ATU between the linear amplifier and the antenna system, as shown in **Fig 4.9** (however, once again, if the antenna has an impedance close to 50Ω the ATU is unnecessary anyway).

Where an internal ATU *is* of use is as a 'line-flattener'. Transceivers need an SWR of better than 2:1 (or sometimes as little as 1.5:1) in order to deliver their full power to the antenna. If you are using an antenna with a high 'Q' (one with a sharp or steep SWR curve), the SWR may rise to above 1.5:1 or 2:1 in part of the band, even if it is an ideal 1.0:1 at another part of the band. Where the SWR rises, it is likely the transceiver will automatically reduce its power output. The internal ATU can be useful to 'flatten' the SWR curve and provide a 1:1 SWR match, thus enabling the transceiver to put out its maximum power on a wider range of frequencies than would otherwise be the case. In practice, these circumstances are most likely in the 1.8 or 3.5MHz bands. If the antenna has minimum SWR at 3800kHz for working DX on SSB, the SWR may well be above 2:1 at 3573kHz, the main FT8 frequency in this band. Here, the internal ATU could be brought into service to reduce the SWR seen at the transceiver to 1.0:1 at 3573kHz.

Note again, though, that an internal ATU in the transceiver is of no use at all if you are using a linear amplifier.

TWIN / DUAL RECEIVERS

All transceivers by definition have one receiver, but a growing number have two, and these transceivers are of particular interest to DXers. (Here we are not talking about twin VFOs – all modern HF transceivers have two VFOs these days – but two quite separate, independent, receivers.)

Having twin receivers allows the operator to monitor two different frequencies simultaneously, with the audio from one receiver going to the left side of a pair of stereo headphones and the audio from the other going to the right side.

The top-of-the-range transceivers from

CHAPTER 4 – THE DXER'S TRANSCEIVER

Fig 4.13: The Icom IC-7610 has two independent receivers.

all the major manufacturers now feature twin receivers: the Icom IC-7610 is one such and is shown in **Fig 4.13**.

What is the purpose of the second receiver? How is it used? Many operators may never find they need to use the second receiver and will quite happily make all their contacts with just the standard first receiver that all transceivers have. But for the DXer, dual receivers give them a distinct advantage.

When a DX station has many callers, they often use a technique called 'split' operation, in which they transmit and receive on slightly different frequencies. Without twin receivers, you can listen either to the DX station *or* the stations calling him (the pile-up), but you cannot listen to both at the same time. With twin receivers you can, and this gives the operator with twin receivers quite an advantage over those who do not have this facility when chasing DX stations. There is more about split frequency operation in Chapter 8.

Ask DXers who have upgraded from a transceiver with a single receiver to one with two receivers and invariably they will say that they would not want to go back to a single receiver. As a DXer, it is therefore definitely worth considering buying a transceiver with two receivers.

NOISE BLANKER

This important feature is, surprisingly, often completely overlooked when considering the purchase of a new transceiver. (Note that here we are discussing the Noise Blanker, abbreviated NB and not Digital Noise Reduction, DNR, which is covered later.)

If you happen to live in an area with a high local noise level the best receiver in the world can be rendered almost useless if its noise blanker is ineffective. If you do live in a noisy area – and sadly this is becoming more and more common wherever you live in the world – it is essential that your transceiver's noise blanker can eliminate, or at least reduce, this noise level.

Unfortunately, while most are good at eliminating the noise generated by car ignition systems, not all noise blankers work well on other types of noise, such as that often radiated by overhead power lines, LED lights, plasma TVs etc. If at all possible, therefore, try to check out a couple of different transceivers' noise blankers at your own location before buying if you do suffer from local noise.

It should be noted that when the noise blanker is switched in, the receive performance can deteriorate, often quite markedly. The effect of this is that strong signals close to the frequency being received – even those outside the receiver's passband – will appear to be 'wider' and sound as if they are splattering badly. This can cause a level of interference to the wanted signal that is simply not there with the noise blanker out of circuit.

Many an operator has been accused of overdriving his amplifier and causing splatter when the real reason is that the use of a noise blanker has compromised the receiving station's performance. At the same time there will be noticeable distortion on the audio of the signal being received, particularly if that is itself a strong signal.

All this may be a small price to pay, though, if using the noise blanker can reduce your noise from S9 to a much more manageable S4 or S5.

MONITOR FACILITY

Like the noise blanker discussed above, the Monitor facility is an often overlooked facility that can be very important, especially for the SSB DXer. It allows you to hear your own voice as you are transmitting so as to get an indication of your outgoing transmitted audio quality. In my opinion the Monitor facility is, if not essential, then at least a very important feature for the SSB operator.

Because the Monitor facility allows you to hear your own voice when you are transmitting this necessarily means that you must be wearing headphones, so as to avoid audio feedback or 'howl-round' caused by the microphone picking up sound from the loudspeaker and retransmitting it. It is anyway highly recommended always to wear headphones for all but 'armchair copy' local contacts.

Being able to monitor your own voice has three advantages. Firstly, you will immediately be able to tell if something is amiss with your transmitted audio, such as a loose microphone connection causing intermittent loss of transmission, or maybe RF feedback caused perhaps by a poorly-soldered PL-259 antenna plug or a poor or non-existent earth connection.

Secondly, if you are wearing headphones but have no 'sidetone' provided by the monitor facility you are inclined to shout. This is bad news: it makes your transmitted audio difficult to understand at the far end, you are more inclined to overdrive the transceiver if you are shouting, causing further distortion and probably splatter, and if you are transmitting for long periods of time, e.g. during a 24-hour or even 48-hour contest, your voice will eventually give out and you will end up with a sore throat or possibly even lose your voice altogether.

Finally, to a limited extent anyway, you will be able to make adjustments to your own transmitted audio, such as adjusting the speech processor settings or your transmitted audio bandwidth, and judge the results yourself in your headphones. I say "to a limited extent" because the monitor facility rarely gives a true reflection of the real transmitted audio quality and, besides, it is very difficult to make a fair assessment of your own voice when you can also hear yourself speaking, through bone conduction in your head. You really need someone else to give critical comments. Nevertheless, the monitor facility is a good start and allows you, for example, to rule out extreme settings that you can immediately tell sound unacceptable.

DIGITAL VOICE KEYER

The digital voice keyer (DVK), also known as a digital voice recorder, is generally thought of as a requirement for serious contest operators – but not so for DXers. Nevertheless, they can be a very useful feature for SSB DXers, as we shall see. (Note that the DVK has nothing at all to do with the DV digital voice mode that was discussed in Chapter 3.)

DVKs allow the operator to record several messages that are repeated fre-

CHAPTER 4 – THE DXER'S TRANSCEIVER

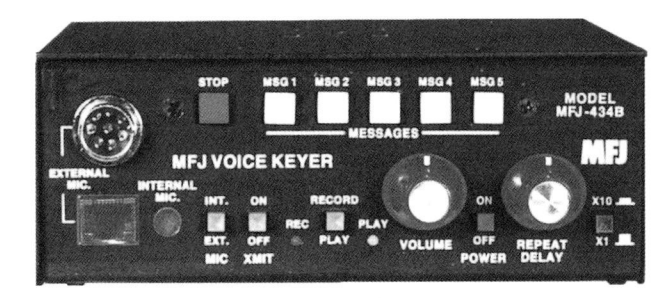

Fig 4.14: The MFJ-434B digital voice keyer.

quently, such as a CQ call, thus saving the voice. For many operators the DVK will fall into the 'bells and whistles' category, but a top contest operator can make several thousand QSOs in a weekend and so will have to call CQ, and give his callsign and the contest exchange thousands of times. Having this automated is, in these circumstances, a real boon.

DVKs are found in many top-end and mid-range transceivers. A few add-on units are also available, such as the MFJ-434B **[3]**, **Fig 4.14**.

So how is a DVK used by the SSB DXer? When attempting to make contact with a rare DXpedition station it is not uncommon to have to call for a long period of time – many minutes or hours (or sometimes off and on even for days!) – before the desired contact is made.

Instead of having to say your callsign over and over again it is easier just to push a button on the front of your transceiver and have the DVK call the DXpedition instead. Beware of overusing this facility, though: 'continuous calling' is the bane of many a DXpedition operator's life and if you do this it will make you very unpopular. Since it is easier just to push a button than deliberately to transmit your callsign by using your voice, many would-be DXers become over-enthusiastic and get 'carried away' and so call using the DVK when they should not be transmitting at all. (Naturally you should only call when the DXpedition station is specifically listening for callers and never when he is in contact with another station, or trying to receive the callsign of a station that is clearly not you!)

Most DVKs will also record the transceiver's received audio, usually on a continuous 'loop' system, for a period of, say, 30 seconds. When the operator wishes to hear something again he can stop the recording and play it back as many times as he wishes. This facility is also useful for DXers, especially when conditions are marginal, as it allows the DXer to confirm to themselves that the DX station did indeed respond to them and that it was a 'good QSO'.

Some DXers keep their best contacts or the rarest DX QSOs in the form of digital audio files stored on their computer or smartphone. These can be fascinating to listen to years later and provide a much more vivid historical record than just a logbook entry or even a QSL card.

Finally, DX stations sometimes use DVKs to 'broadcast' frequently-sent pieces of information, such as QSL information, listening frequencies, or perhaps name and QTH. One Far Eastern operator I knew (sadly now a Silent Key) sometimes conducted virtually the whole of his SSB QSOs using the various memory buttons of his digital voice recorder, with a CQ call on memory 1, name and QTH spelled phonetically on memory 2, QSL information on memory 3, and "QRZ?" plus his callsign on memory 4. The only time he actually used his voice was to give the callsign of the station he was working. It may be argued that this is taking station automation a step too far, but of course this use of a DVK is perfect for those operators who have speech difficulties (or perhaps have simply 'lost their voice') but who still wish to operate on SSB.

DSP & DIGITAL NOISE REDUCTION (DNR)

DSP stands for digital signal processing and was originally used at audio frequencies (AF DSP) to provide noise reduction facilities, a notch filter and bandwidth filtering on receive only. Before DSP was offered in transceivers, outboard AF DSP units were available from the late 1980s onwards. Placed at the end of the audio chain, between the transceiver and loudspeaker (or, more likely, the headphones) these could be used to filter the received audio. The intermediate frequency (IF) filters in the transceiver were still conventional crystal or mechanical filters.

More recently, DSP has been employed at the intermediate frequency of transceivers (IF DSP) and these days it is used in most current transceivers to carry out the IF filtering, both on transmit and receive, and several of the receiver's functions including noise reduction and notch filtering.

DSP notch filters can be useful by removing a single frequency heterodyne, or tone, that is causing interference to the wanted signal. In some transceivers, DSP is also used to put a variable-frequency peak or dip in the received audio (the so-called 'contour' control).

In 2015, writing in *HF SSB DX Basics*, I said that although I felt I might be in the minority, I thought that digital noise reduction (as opposed to DSP notch filters, which can be very effective) had something of the 'Emperor's new clothes' syndrome about it. Well, technology moves on all the time and the Icom IC-7300, among other rigs, does now offer very effective digital noise reduction facilities. I am still not sure that it could make a completely unreadable signal completely readable, but it can definitely improve the intelligibility of signals, particularly on SSB, and make them more pleasant to listen to, without that annoying 'frying eggs' sound of electrical interference.

Where IF DSP really comes into its own is in the flexibility it provides for the transceiver's IF filtering, on both transmit and receive. On receive, a wide variety of bandwidths can be made available, allowing the operator great flexibility when combatting interference.

On transmit, DSP can be used to tailor the transmitted audio by emphasising different parts of the audio spectrum, and to vary the overall width of the transmitted signal. This facility warrants a section all to itself and it is covered in more detail in Chapter 8. So too is the subject of speech processing, because it is no longer a factor to consider when choosing to buy a transceiver as just about all current HF transceivers have a speech processor built-in.

Further details of the features provided by various transceivers can be found in *The Rig Guide* [4], published by the RSGB.

REFERENCES

[1] FlexRadio: www.flexradio.com
[2] GQRP Club: www.gqrp.com
[3] MFJ Enterprises, Inc: www.mfjenterprises.com
[4] *The Rig Guide*, edited by Steve White, G3ZVW, available from www.rsgbshop.org

Chapter 5

Planning Your Antenna

There is a tendency for newcomers to buy a commercially-made HF antenna at the same time as they buy an HF transceiver. After all, you need both a transceiver and an antenna in order to start making some contacts. However, I would urge you not to do this. Even those of us who might best be described as 'non-technical' hams, and for whom building an HF transceiver from scratch would be about as likely as building our own jet aircraft in our garage, can nevertheless still easily build very effective HF antennas.

Those who do buy a commercial HF antenna invariably buy something that they think they can 'get away with' in their garden, in other words something low profile such as a small vertical or the ubiquitous G5RV. But these antennas are not necessarily the most suitable for many people's circumstances. Sometimes something that can easily be made at home will not only cost a fraction of the amount of a commercially-made antenna but also actually be far more effective.

We HF operators have a distinct advantage over VHF / UHF enthusiasts when it comes to building antennas. Because the wavelengths we are dealing with are much longer, the permissible tolerances when making antennas are much greater. When building an antenna for the 1.8MHz band, it is quite normal to have to trim it by a metre of more (3 or 4 feet). Someone building a 70cm beam has to be accurate to within a few millimetres or a tiny fraction of an inch.

This chapter is entitled *planning your antenna*, though, and not 'building your antenna', because the intention is to give you enough information to enable you to make a decision about what sort of antenna would be suitable for your particular set of circumstances. There are many excellent antenna books available, some of which are listed as references at the end of this chapter (e.g. **[1], [2], [3]**) which will provide you with far more information about the theory and practice of HF antennas. Nevertheless, a few antenna designs are given, if only to illustrate how simple many of these are to make.

HORIZONTAL OR VERTICAL?

First, though, a few words about the differences between horizontal and vertical antennas. Generally, an antenna that is erected in the horizontal plane will have horizontal polarisation and one in the vertical plane vertical polarisation. Actually, at HF, whether it is horizontally or vertically polarised is not important as the polarisation will be mixed up in the ionosphere and the signal returning to earth will have components of both. Either horizontal or vertical antennas can be used: each have their own distinct properties.

A *vertically-polarised* antenna will tend to have a low vertical angle of radiation (this is the angle between the major lobe of the antenna, where the maximum radiation occurs, and the horizon) and, for the long-distance working that is of most interest to DXers, the lower the angle of radiation the better. There are exceptions: a three-quarter wavelength long vertical antenna has a high angle of radiation, for example. However, almost all practical vertical antennas are less than 5/8-wave long and have a low angle of radiation.

A *horizontally-polarised* antenna's angle of radiation is generally determined by its height above ground. The higher the antenna, the lower the angle of radiation. And herein lies a problem for horizontally-polarised antennas, particularly on the lower-frequency bands. In order for a horizontal dipole (for example) to have a good low angle of radiation, it must be mounted *at least* a half-wavelength above ground. In the case of 3.5MHz this means around 42 metres (137ft) high, or in the case of 1.8MHz it means 82 metres or 269ft high. Clearly these are heights that are not realisable unless you have access to some big towers or perhaps can put up an antenna between two high-rise blocks!

This does not mean that a dipole for 3.5MHz that is less than 42m high won't work at all, though. On the contrary, it will actually work very well for some purposes at more or less any height. What is does mean, though, is that the main lobe of the dipole's radiation will be at a relatively high angle. This is actually *good* for short and medium-distance communications, e.g. for working around the UK and most of Europe, but it will be lacking for long-distance communications, such as into South America, Southern Africa, East and South-East Asia and particularly the Pacific.

To work into these parts of the world a low angle of radiation is necessary, and on the lower-frequency bands this means either a very high horizontal antenna or a vertically-polarised one (even if the latter is ground mounted). On 14MHz and above there is less of a problem: a half-wave at 14MHz is only 10m (33ft), so it is feasible to raise a simple horizontal antenna such as a dipole to this height or greater.

Many DXers, whose main interest is in working as many countries as possible around the world, tend to use horizontally-polarised antennas (such as a Yagi beam) around 12m (40ft) or more high for the bands between 14 and 50MHz, and vertically-polarised antennas for the lower-frequency bands.

WHICH ANTENNA?

The whole point of this chapter is to give some pointers as to which antenna or antennas might be best for DXing on the bands between 1.8 and 50MHz. First, though, we need to make some assumptions. It is assumed that most people will not start out with monoband Yagi beams on each of the higher-frequency bands, with perhaps a 4-Square array of four quarter-wave verticals on 3.5MHz and a full-size 40m / 130ft high vertical for 1.8MHz. If you have that sort of wherewithal, you need read no further in this chapter! But for the average person, how to start – bearing in mind that the intention is to work DX?

Holders of Foundation or Intermediate licences are restricted to using 10W or 50W power output respectively, and so their signal will already be several deci-

CHAPTER 5 – PLANNING YOUR ANTENNA

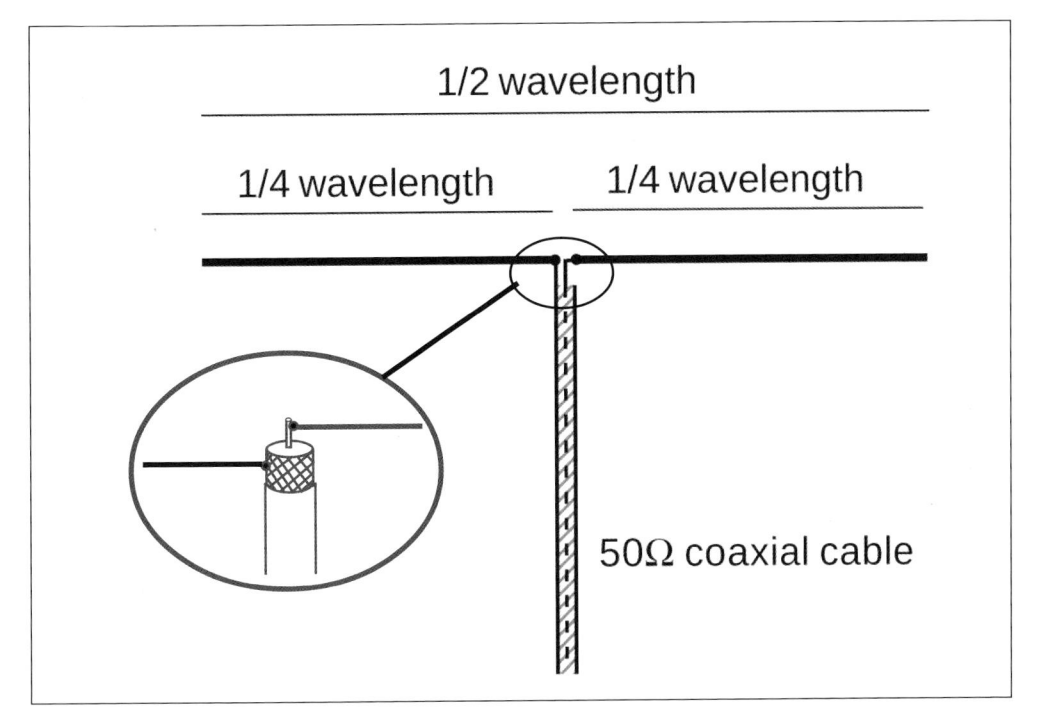

Fig 5.1: The half-wave dipole antenna.

bels down on someone using 100W or more. The important thing, therefore, is to use the most efficient antenna possible in your own particular circumstances.

If you live on a farm out in the country you will have few restrictions in this respect. For the average amateur living in suburbia, though, it is a matter of using compromise antennas that the neighbours will allow them to 'get away with' – that phrase again. What you should definitely *not* do, though, is put up the smallest or least conspicuous antenna you can, as it probably would not be very effective, especially for DX working.

DIPOLES

The humble dipole should not be ignored as a practical DX antenna on the HF bands. It is a half-wavelength long and consists of two wires of identical length 'fed' in the centre, usually with coaxial cable (see **Fig 5.1**). A dipole is very simple to make, it is light in weight, by using thin wire it can be made almost invisible (so is suitable for those who may have intolerant neighbours), by using the house and a suitable tree as supports no mast is required and therefore there is unlikely to be a requirement for planning permission and, last but certainly not least, the dipole is actually a very efficient antenna.

The only two downsides are that (with one or two exceptions) it is a single-band antenna, so if you wanted to operate on, say, seven HF bands you would ideally need seven separate dipoles, and that it needs to be mounted up high and 'in the clear' if it is to be really effective as a DX antenna.

Table 5.1 shows the approximate 'real life' lengths of half-wave dipoles for various frequencies in each of the bands covered in this book. Note that on the lower-

HF DX BASICS

Metre band	Frequency kHz	Length Metric	Length Imperial	Notes
160m	1843	77.32m	253ft 8in	160m FT8 frequency
160m	1905	74.80m	245ft 5in	160m mid-band frequency
80m	3573	39.88m	130ft 10in	Main 80m FT8 frequency
80m	3800	37.50m	123ft 0in	80m SSB 'DX Window'
60m	5357	26.60m	87ft 3in	Main 60m FT8 frequency
40m	7100	20.07m	65ft 10in	40m mid-band frequency
30m	10136	14.06m	46ft 2in	Main 30m FT8 frequency
20m	14175	10.05m	33ft 0in	20m mid-band frequency
17m	18118	7.86m	25ft 10in	17m mid-band frequency
15m	21225	6.71m	22ft 0in	15m mid-band frequency
12m	24940	5.71m	18ft 9in	12m mid-band frequency
10m	28074	5.07m	16ft 8in	Main 10m FT8 frequency
10m	28850	4.94m	16ft 2in	10m mid-band frequency
6m	50313	2.83m	9ft 4in	Main 6m FT8 frequency

Table 5.1: Approximate 'real life' lengths of half-wave dipoles for various frequencies for each of the bands covered in this book.

frequency bands (1.8 and 3.5MHz) a relatively small change of frequency makes a big difference in the lengths of the antennas. Conversely on the higher-frequency bands although the antennas are smaller, the required tolerance is greater.

All home-made dipoles will probably need to be 'pruned' to size: no matter how carefully measured, 'real life' gets in the way and unless you are really lucky no antenna is resonant precisely where you expect it to be. Usually they are somewhat too long, which is fortunate, for it is always easier to shorten a wire antenna rather than to have to make it longer by adding bits of wire on.

Theoretically the impedance of a half-wave dipole at its centre is around 73Ω but in practice it is normally a little lower than this and therefore a good match can be achieved using 50Ω coaxial cable. As the impedance of all transceivers is also 50Ω, it is usually possible to achieve an SWR of close to 1:1, thus ensuring maximum transfer of power from the transceiver to the antenna.

The dipole theoretically has a so-called 'figure-of-eight' horizontal radiation pattern, **Fig 5.2**, with maximum radiation

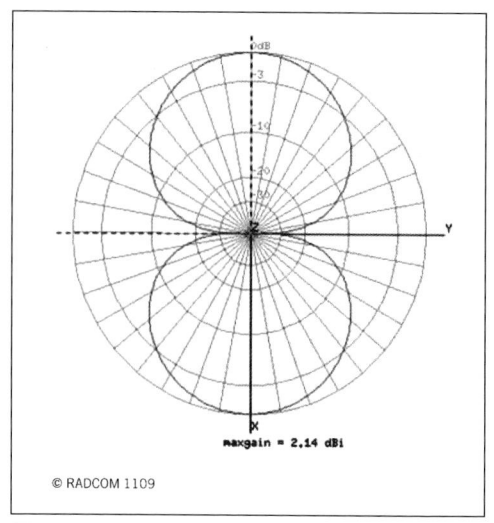

Fig 5.2: The dipole's theoretical 'figure-of-eight' radiation pattern.

CHAPTER 5 – PLANNING YOUR ANTENNA

broadside to the direction of the wires and little radiation off the ends of the wires. Most antenna books will tell you to ensure that you orientate it so that the maximum radiation is in the directions you want. However, this is in 'an ideal world' situation which in practice rarely exists and most practical dipoles in the real world, while having something of a null off the ends of the wires, have a radiation pattern that is far less well defined than that shown in **Fig 5.2**. In practice this means that it does not really matter too much in which direction the dipole is erected and its orientation can be dictated by the presence of existing suitable supports without worrying too much about the radiation pattern.

Variations on a Theme

The classic dipole is horizontal, but there is nothing to prevent you from mounting a dipole in an inverted-V, **Fig 5.3(a)**, or sloping, **Fig 5.3(b)**, configuration if that is more convenient in your particular circumstances. A dipole can also be mounted vertically, for example by dropping it from the branch of a high tree. Whatever the configuration, the antenna will work although the radiation pattern will be different, tending away even more from the horizontal dipole's 'figure-of-eight' pattern and becoming omnidirectional when the dipole is mounted vertically.

There are some practical and theoretical advantages to these 'variations on a theme': they only require one high support rather than two for the horizontal dipole and, as the antenna becomes more vertically polarised, so the angle of radiation is lowered.

However, vertical antennas are inclined to pick up more unwanted local noise when receiving than horizontal ones, so this advantage may be negated by an increased noise level.

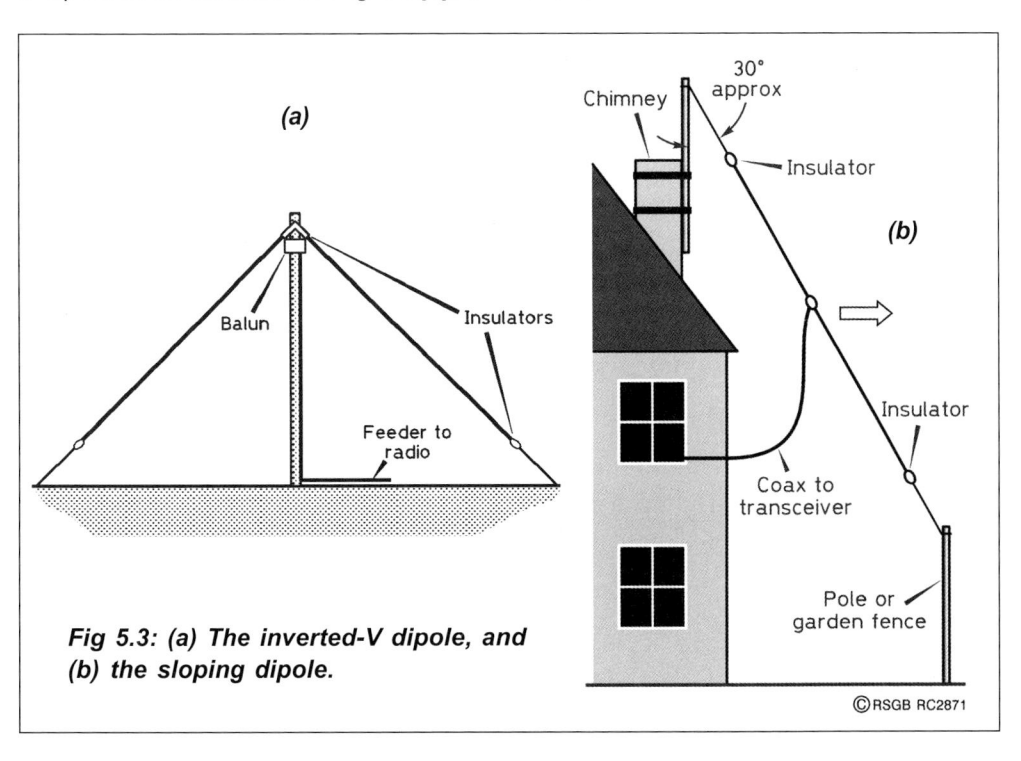

Fig 5.3: (a) The inverted-V dipole, and (b) the sloping dipole.

The sloping dipole exhibits a small amount of directivity in the direction of the slope, i.e. off the end of the wire, looking from the top towards the low end of the dipole, as shown by the arrow in **Fig 5.3 (b)** – but only a little (it is not a beam antenna!)

Due to the height requirement of the support for a sloping or vertical dipole these antennas can only really be considered for the bands from 14MHz and higher in frequency, unless you happen to live in a high-rise building.

We said earlier that a dipole is basically a single-band antenna. While this is true, there are a couple of ways that a dipole can work, or be made to work, on more than one band. The first, and simplest, way is to take advantage of the fact that the low impedance at the centre feedpoint of the antenna occurs not only when it is one half-wavelength long, but also when it is three half-waves long (and five half-waves etc). We can take advantage of this where amateur bands have such a harmonic relationship, i.e. where one band is three times the frequency of another, e.g. with the 7 and 21MHz bands.

What this means is that a 7MHz half-wave dipole will also work on 21MHz. Well, sort of. Unfortunately, life isn't quite that simple. The so-called 'end effect' means that a half-wave dipole is actually physically about 5% shorter than the theoretical half-wave length. However, when operating on its third harmonic, the antenna becomes 15% shorter than the physical length of a three half-waves antenna, so it is resonant higher in frequency than you might expect.

In practice, the way around this problem is to resonate the 7MHz dipole at the very bottom of the band, 7000kHz, or even make it somewhat longer still, so that the minimum SWR point is actually a little below the bottom of the band on, say, 6980kHz. On 21MHz you will find the minimum SWR point is at the top of the band, around 21450kHz. An external ATU or the internal automatic ATU in your rig should be able to reduce the SWR to 1:1 at your operating frequency of choice in both the 7 and 21MHz bands.

Another way of getting a dipole to work on more than one band is simply by connecting two or three dipoles for different frequency bands to the same feeder (see **Fig 5.4**). This arrangement is sometimes called a 'fan-dipole'. In theory any number of dipoles can be connected together in this way, but in practice each one interacts with each of the others in one way or another. I have had a lot of success using two dipoles on the same feeder but have found it difficult to get three or more different bands all working together.

It is important to separate the dipoles for the different bands physically. For example, if two dipoles are on the same feeder and if you have sufficient space you could have the two dipoles at 90° to each other, or one dipole supported horizontally and the other hanging as an inverted-V beneath it.

The final variation on the theme of a dipole is the doublet (**Fig 5.5**). This is simply a dipole fed in the centre with twin feeder (slotted twin, open-wire feeder, ladder line or ribbon) instead of coaxial cable, and matched with an ATU. The wire can be any convenient length but should preferably be around a half-wave long at the lowest intended frequency of operation. While the theoretical impedance of a half-wave dipole is 73Ω and therefore it matches well to 50Ω coax, the same length of wire will present completely different impedances on other bands, per-

CHAPTER 5 – PLANNING YOUR ANTENNA

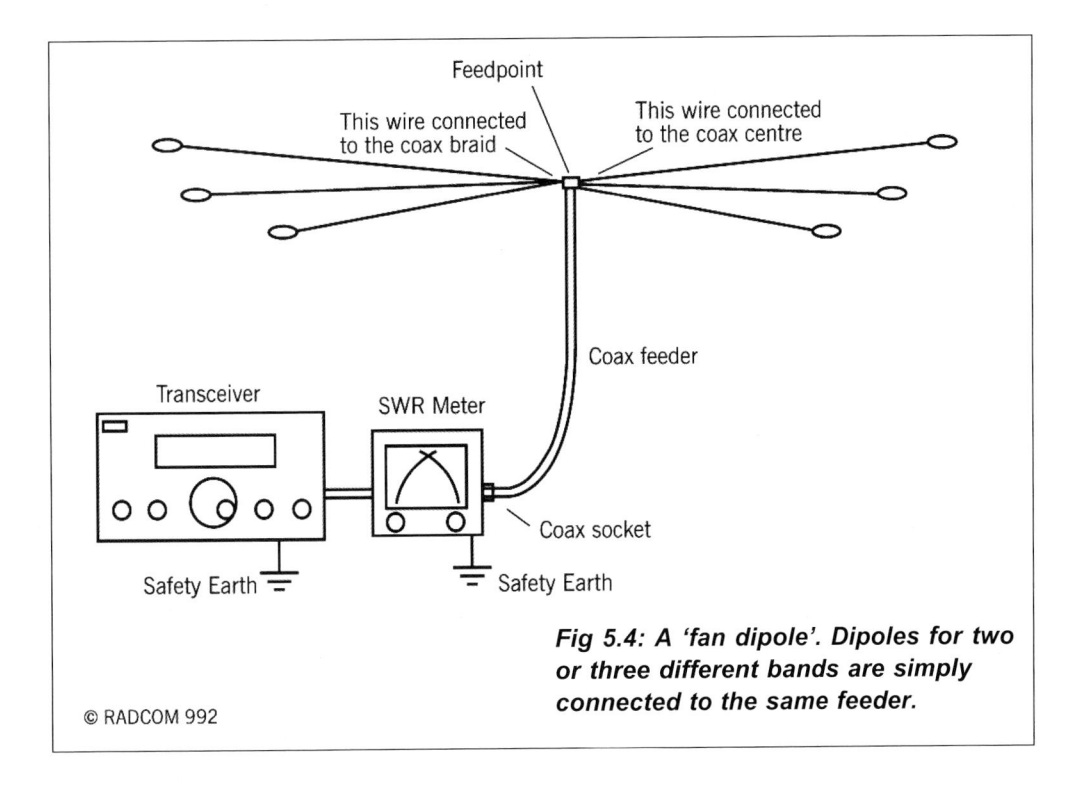

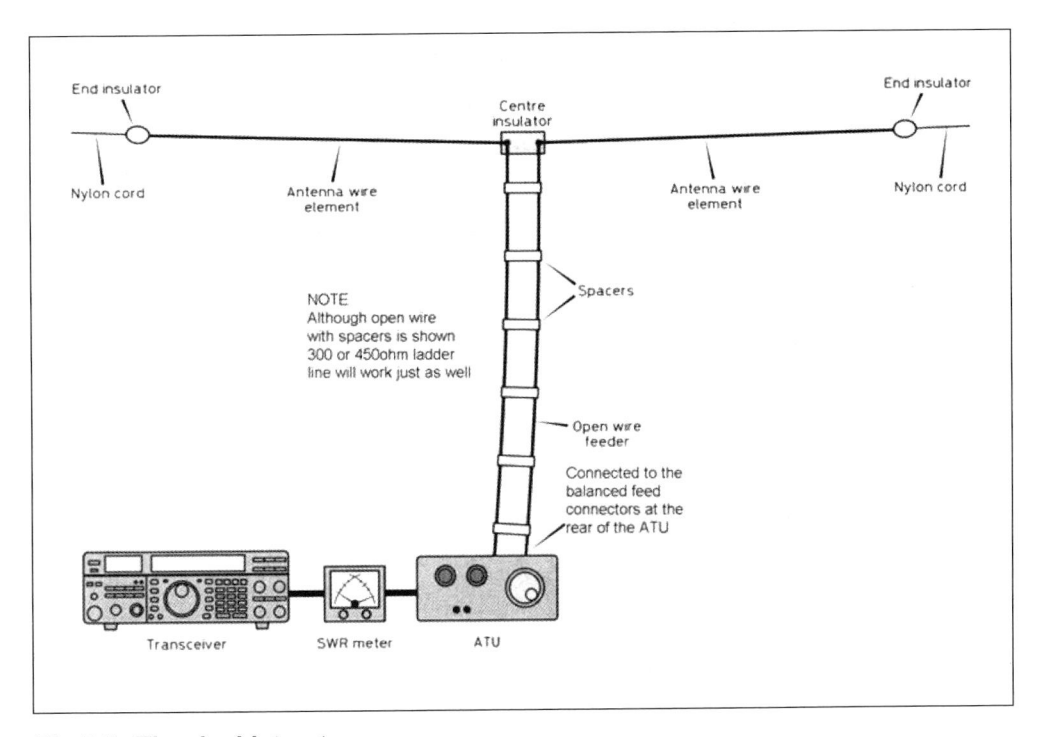

Fig 5.4: A 'fan dipole'. Dipoles for two or three different bands are simply connected to the same feeder.

Fig 5.5: The doublet antenna.

57

haps in the region of thousands of ohms. There is therefore a large mismatch with the 50Ω coax and this is why the dipole is generally considered to be a single band antenna.

The doublet has two advantages over a coax-fed dipole. Firstly, when used with a wide-range ATU, it becomes a multi-band antenna. Secondly, twin feeder has less loss than coaxial cable, especially at a high level of SWR, so more of the transmitter's power is delivered to the antenna, particularly on the higher-frequency bands such as 28 or 50MHz. However, there is also the disadvantage that a wide-range ATU is necessary; the transceiver's internal ATU is unlikely to work on any band.

Baluns

All dipoles that are fed by coaxial cable (whether horizontal, vertical, sloping or inverted-V) should have a 1:1 *balun* at the feedpoint. 'Balun' is short for BALanced-to-UNbalanced' and a balun may be needed when *unbalanced* feeder cable, such as coaxial cable, is connected to a *balanced* antenna such as a dipole. **Fig 9.6** shows two types of balun.

Not using a balun at the feedpoint can result in unwanted currents flowing down the outer of the coax, which can lead to EMC (electro-magnetic compatibility) problems such as interference to televisions, loudspeakers, computer monitors or keyboards, alarm systems etc.

The radiation pattern of the dipole is also likely to be affected: instead of the clean pattern shown in **Fig 5.2** the dipole may radiate in unpredictable directions. This is not necessarily a bad thing: it is possible that *not* using a balun may help to 'fill in' the nulls off the end of the dipole and, depending on how your dipole is ori-

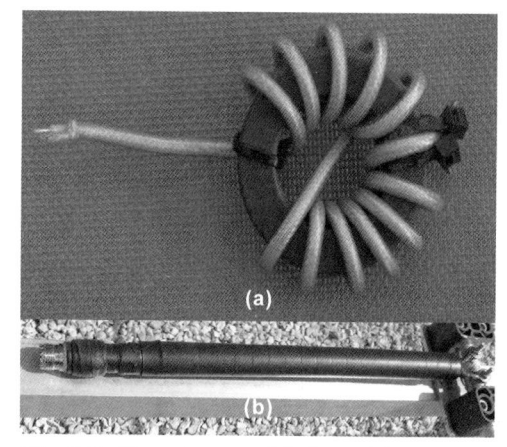

Fig 5.6: Two types of balun: (a) toroidal balun, (b) choke balun made of ferrite beads slipped over the coax.

entated, allow you more easily to make contacts that are in those directions. A dipole will work, with *or without* a balun.

It is probably worth trying a dipole without a balun first but, should you find you have EMC problems, fit one later to see if that fixes the problem.

G5RV / ZS6BKW ANTENNAS

The famous G5RV antenna, designed in 1946 by the late Louis Varney, G5RV, is still very popular today, particularly with some beginners who perhaps see it as a convenient way of getting on all bands from 3.5 to 28MHz with a single, relatively inconspicuous, wire antenna. It is easy enough to make one, but numerous commercial versions are available from the usual retailers and its wide availability has probably added to its popularity.

The antenna is a type of doublet but of specific length, with a 31m (102ft) horizontal 'flat top' and a vertical matching section preferably 10.36m (34ft) long if made from open wire feeder, or 8.99m (29ft 6in) long if made from 300Ω ribbon feeder. From the end of the matching section, G5RV said that 75Ω twin lead or 80Ω

CHAPTER 5 – PLANNING YOUR ANTENNA

coax can be used to the ATU (these days, 50Ω coax is used instead). Note that a wide-range ATU is required.

G5RV designed the antenna for optimum performance on the 14MHz band, where it is a three half-wavelengths long dipole. Its multi-band capabilities are something of a bonus, although it should be pointed out that any random length of antenna fed with open wire feeder will work on any band with the use of a wide-range ATU, provided it is close to a half-wave (say 0.4λ) in length or longer.

In 2007 Brian Austin, ZS6BKW (now G0GSF), used technology unavailable to G5RV – computer modelling – to re-compute the design, while also taking into account the three additional bands at 10, 18 and 24MHz that were allocated to amateurs at the World Administrative Radio Conference in 1979. He came up with the lengths shown in **Fig 5.7** for an antenna that presents a better than 2:1 SWR *without the use of an ATU* in the 7, 14, 18, 24 and 28MHz bands. It can also be used *with* an ATU in the 3.5, 10 and 21MHz bands.

The antenna is 28.5m (93ft 6in) long, and the matching section (or 'series section impedance matching transformer' as G0CSF calls it **[4]**) of 400Ω twin feeder should be 13.3m (43ft 6in) multiplied by the velocity factor of the feeder (so if the velocity factor is 0.95 the length should be 12.6m or 41ft 4in). The dimensions are not overly critical but the antenna should always be horizontal and not used in the inverted-V configuration.

If a simple single-band wire antenna is required, it is hard to beat a dipole (whether horizontal, as an inverted-V, or sloping) as high and in the clear as possible. For multi-band use try a fan dipole; alternatively the ZS6BKW design should be a better bet than the G5RV, as an ATU is not required for operation on five bands.

VERTICALS

If a dipole is the easiest HF antenna to make yourself, the single-band quarter-wave vertical must run it a close second. It is a little more difficult to get a vertical to work really well, though...

In order to work properly, a quarter-wave vertical must be tuned against some form of ground system. The earth or ground plane forms the 'missing' other half of the antenna if compared with a half-wave vertical dipole.

The earth can be thought of as a mirror: if a quarter-wave vertical is placed on top of a mirror the reflection in the mirror is the 'missing' half of a vertical dipole.

A vertical antenna tuned against ground in this way is sometimes called a Marconi antenna, after Guglielmo Marconi, **Fig 5.8**, the first to utilise such an antenna.

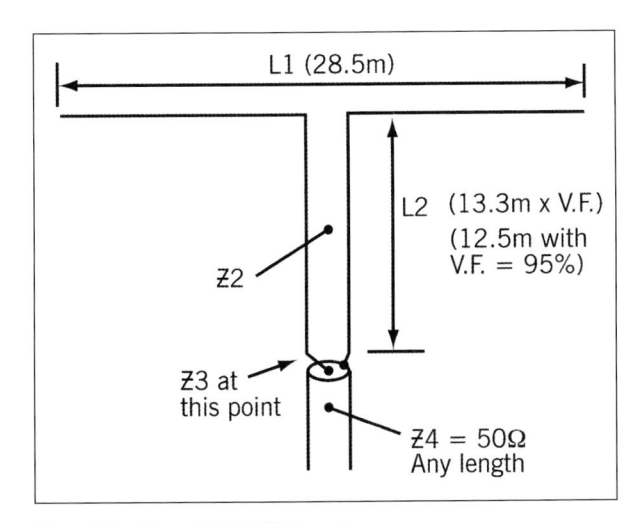

Fig 5.7: The ZS6BKW antenna.

HF DX BASICS

Fig 5.8: Guglielmo Marconi.

The quarter-wave vertical can be ground mounted, or elevated, e.g. mounted on a pole or chimney. Let's look at the ground-mounted version first (**Fig 5.9**). The antenna is a quarter-wave long and is fed by 50Ω coaxial cable at the base. The vertical radiating element is connected to the inner of the coaxial cable and the braid to the earth system.

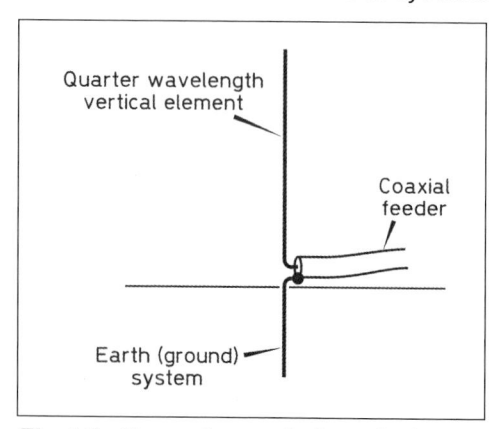

Fig 5.9: Ground-mounted vertical.

This should preferably be a system of radial wires extending from the base of the vertical radiating element like the spokes of a bicycle wheel, rather than the single ground connection shown in **Fig 5.9**.

The radials are wires which may or may not be insulated and which can be either buried a few centimetres (an inch or two) under the ground, laid on top of the ground, or elevated above the ground. If the radials are on the ground or buried there should be as many radials as possible and preferably they should be as long as possible, though for a particular total length of wire it is better to have many shorter radials than fewer longer ones. The golden rule, though, is 'the more, the merrier' and many amateurs spend a great deal of time and effort laying down more and more of them. There is a law of diminishing returns, though, and many settle for around 16 to 32 radial wires. The generally accepted maximum is 120 half-wavelength long radials – beyond that there is little or no improvement and the extra work is certainly not worth the effort.

If the radials are *elevated* it is usual for them to be resonant, i.e. they should also be a quarter-wave long. They should be elevated at least a few feet above the ground. If the radials are elevated, you can get away with using fewer of them: as few as two at 180° to each other, although it is more common to use four, one every 90°. It is even possible to use just one elevated radial (a quarter-wave vertical with a single elevated radial is in fact just an inverted-V dipole rotated on to its side).

If the quarter-wave vertical is itself elevated, e.g. by being mounted on top of a pole, there is no choice *but* to have elevated radials. This is the classic ground-

CHAPTER 5 – PLANNING YOUR ANTENNA

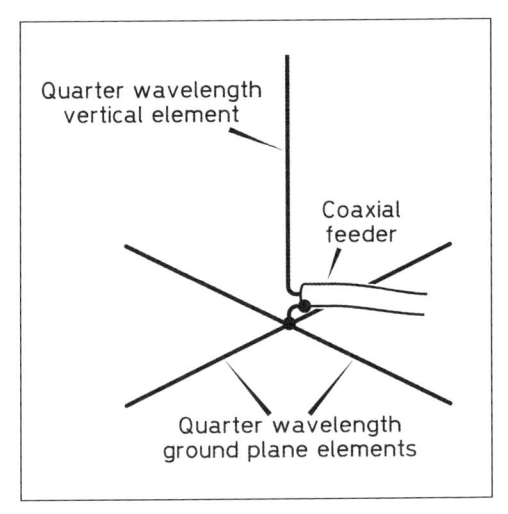

Fig 5.10: The classic ground-plane vertical antenna: a quarter-wave radiating element and four quarter-wave long radials.

plane antenna (**Fig 5.10**): a quarter-wave vertical radiating element with four quarter-wave long radials that form the ground plane. It is more often used on VHF / UHF (where the radials are short enough to be made rigid and therefore self-supporting) than on HF. On HF the radials can be made of light wire terminated in an insulator and then tied off with string to any four convenient points. They do not have to be perpendicular to the vertical element, they can slope down towards the ground and doing this can actually improve the match to 50Ω cable.

We have already said that, for a simple wire antenna, it is hard to beat a resonant half-wave dipole, whether mounted horizontally, or in an inverted-V or sloping configuration. Why then might one want to use a quarter-wave vertical? The answer is that, for DX working, what is required is a low angle of radiation. As discussed earlier in this chapter, a horizontal dipole needs to be mounted high up for this to occur. A vertical antenna, on the other hand, provides low-angle radiation even when ground mounted.

However, while a horizontal dipole is inherently an efficient radiator, the conductivity of the earth is of prime importance when it comes to the efficiency of vertical antennas. If the vertical is erected over dry, stony ground it will be inefficient and therefore the size of the ground plane underneath it – the number of radials – assumes great importance. If, on the other hand, the natural earth is of good conductivity, the antenna will work more efficiently. The best natural earth is salt water, and verticals situated very close to the sea therefore perform exceptionally well.

As the ground conductivity increases, so the angle of radiation decreases. What is happening is that instead of the power being applied to the antenna radiating from it in all directions and at all angles from straight up into the sky and down to the horizon, all the power is concentrated into a narrow beam a few degrees above the

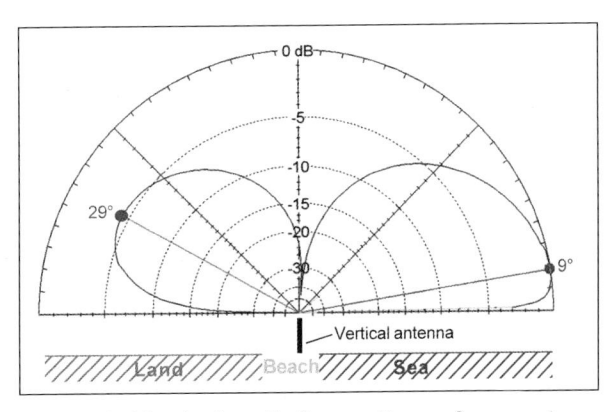

Fig 5.11: Vertical radiation pattern of a quarter-wave vertical mounted on the edge of the ocean.

horizon. This provides a considerable amount of gain at that angle.

Fig 5.11 shows the vertical radiation pattern of a quarter-wave vertical located at the edge of the ocean. In this diagram the land is to the left and the sea to the right. The vertical's maximum angle of radiation over the land is at 29° above the horizon but over the sea this angle has decreased to just 9°. That's not all: at 9° above the horizon the radiation is 10dB greater over the sea than over the land.

This makes the vertical antenna mounted close to the sea the perfect DX antenna, **Fig 5.12**. If, however, you don't happen to live in a beach house, the vertical can still be a good DX antenna, but then you will need to put a lot of effort into the radial system.

Fig 5.12: The perfect DX antenna: a quarter-wave vertical for 7MHz within a few metres of the sea (9M6DXX/P, Labuan Island, IOTA OC-133).

INVERTED-L ANTENNA

The inverted-L antenna can be thought of as being the 'poor man's vertical'. It is used when it is not possible to put up a full-length quarter-wave vertical, either because the height required is too great for a self-supporting aluminium or fibreglass vertical or because there is no high enough support available from which to suspend a wire. Since it is relatively simple to make or support full-size quarter-wave verticals for all the bands from 7MHz upwards, the inverted-L is usually only used on 1.8, 3.5 and 5MHz.

The inverted-L is simply a quarter-wave vertical with the top part bent over horizontally, as shown in **Fig 5.13**. Like the quarter-wave vertical, the inverted-L requires a good ground system of radials to work properly, unless you are lucky enough to be able to use one next to the sea, as in **Fig 5.14**. The vertical section should always be as long (high) as possible.

The horizontal section introduces some horizontal polarisation so, for DX working, the inverted-L is not quite as effective as a full-size quarter-wave vertical. However, for those without the possibility of erecting a full-size vertical it can come a close second.

I once made a dual-band 3.5 / 7MHz antenna that worked well on both bands. It started out life as a full-size quarter-wave vertical for 7MHz, made of lightweight but strong telescoping aluminium tubing which was guyed about half-way up. The antenna stood in the middle of the back garden, about 12 metres from the back of the house. It was fed at ground level against four buried quarter-wave radials (more would certainly have been better!) The antenna was resonant in the middle of the SSB part of the 7MHz band.

CHAPTER 5 – PLANNING YOUR ANTENNA

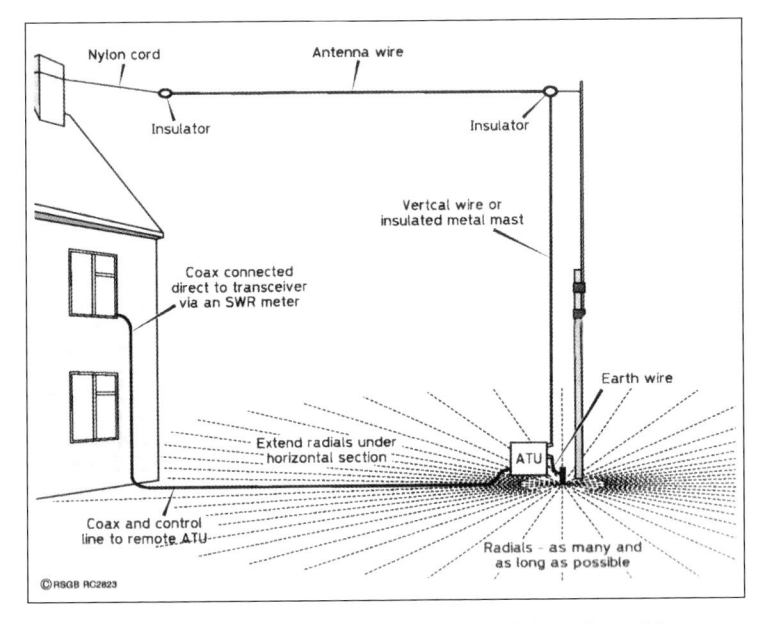

Fig 5.13: The inverted-L antenna. The ATU makes this a multi-band antenna. Without the ATU the antenna should be a quarter-wave long.

To convert it to operation on 80m I connected a very light wire about 8.80m (29ft) long using a small hose clamp at the top of the antenna. At the other end of the wire was a light-weight plastic insulator and then some garden twine to make up the length required to take it to an upstairs bedroom window at the back of the house. The wire, insulator and twine all had to be light in weight as

Fig 5.14: A 3.5MHz inverted-L antenna at sunset (the horizontal part of the antenna has been drawn in for clarity: 9M6DXX/P, Labuan Island, IOTA OC-133).

VERTICAL / INVERTED-L ANTENNA NOTES

Whether commercial or home-made, there are some important points to note about the performance of all vertical antennas, including the inverted-L:
- The vertical only comes into its own on long-haul DX contacts. If you want to have a big signal around the UK and Europe on 1.8 or 3.5MHz, a horizontal antenna such as a dipole or doublet will outperform pretty much any vertical, and sometimes by a large margin...
- Quarter-wave verticals only work well if they have a good earth connection in the form of radial wires or a ground plane. An earth spike is not sufficient...
- Verticals mounted very close to the sea have a very low angle of radiation and gain at those low angles, so they are great for DX working. Inland, on the other hand, you really need to put the effort into the ground system...
- Don't be fooled into thinking that a vertical does not require much horizontal space. Ideally, you need quarter-wave long radials in all directions, i.e. a square 20m x 20m for a 7MHz vertical, with the vertical in the centre of the square...
- The performance of a vertical is affected by close objects such as buildings, trees, masts etc (another reason for suggesting that they need at least as much space as a horizontal antenna for the same band)...
- Verticals tend to pick up more local noise than horizontal antennas (yet another reason for putting them in their own space). If you live in an electrically noisy neighbourhood, a horizontal antenna may be better – at least for receiving...
- Shortened verticals don't work as well as full-size quarter-wave verticals...
- If you really have very little or no horizontal space for antennas, consider a half-wave design vertical, but ensure you mount it as high and in the clear as possible.

the top of the 7MHz vertical was quite spindly and would not support heavier materials without bending dramatically.

Pulling the wire out horizontally converted the antenna into an 80m inverted-L which resonated around 3790kHz. From my station in south-east England I regularly worked ZL (New Zealand) stations on 80m SSB in the mornings, usually receiving genuine reports of between 55 and 57. This was on the long-path – the long way round the world – a distance well in excess of 20,000km. To convert the antenna back to 7MHz use was simply a matter of releasing the twine from the upstairs window and allowing the wire to drop down vertically from the top of the 40m vertical, where it was secured loosely near the base of the vertical.

Undoubtedly a full-size (18.8m / 62ft) vertical would have worked better on 80m SSB, and having more than four 10m (33ft) radials would have worked better too, but for the horizontal space it took up (only 20m or 66ft, including the radials), and its height above ground (a maximum of only 10m or 33ft), I doubt it would be possible to make a better-performing 80m DX antenna.

COMMERCIAL MULTI-BAND VERTICALS

I started this chapter by urging new licensees not to buy a commercial HF antenna at the same time that they buy a transceiver, and instead to try to build an antenna themselves. However, there is no doubt that commercially-made

CHAPTER 5 – PLANNING YOUR ANTENNA

multi-band HF verticals are very popular, and for good reason too. That's because, while it is easy to construct an efficient single-band quarter-wave vertical, to make a successful vertical that operates on multiple HF bands yourself is rather more difficult. If you want to have the flexibility of operating on several, or all, of the HF bands but do not have the space for many different antennas, then a commercial vertical may well be the answer.

While there are numerous manufacturers of commercial HF multi-band verticals, in fact there are only two main types: the *quarter-wave design* and the *half-wave design*. Both have their advantages and disadvantages.

The quarter-wave type, manufactured by such companies as Butternut, MFJ, Hustler, Hy-Gain, etc, requires ground radials and is therefore more suitable for ground mounting than for an elevated location such as on a pole or chimney.

Quarter-wave verticals *can* be elevated, but the difficulty then is in accommodating the radials. Elevated radials should be a quarter-wave long and, even if there are only two per band, that still means 12 wires of various different lengths for a six-band vertical. In most locations it would be difficult to find suitable places to tie off the ends of 12 different wires around the antenna, an exception being if you have access to a large flat roof.

Another issue is that most verticals require some sort of adjustment, either of coils or lengths of tubing, in order to place the frequency of resonance precisely where you want it. This adjustment can be fiddly and require several iterations so if the antenna is mounted on the chimney it could become quite tedious, to say the least, to get it 'spot on'. The quarter-wave design of multi-band vertical is there-

Fig 5.15: The Butternut HF6V commercial multi-band vertical.

fore best suited for ground mounting.

I have used the Butternut HF6V vertical, **Fig 5.15**, on DXpeditions for decades. It is a loaded quarter-wave vertical on 3.5 and 7MHz, a full-size quarter-wave on 10 and 21MHz, but its clever design utilising an impedance matching stub makes it a 3/8-wave vertical on 14MHz, while on 28MHz it works as a 3/4-wave vertical.

A relative newcomer on the scene is the 'DX Commander', **Fig 5.16**, made in the UK by Callum McCormick, M0MCX [5]. Callum now offers several different verticals but the Classic (the original DX Commander) is based on a 9m fibreglass vertical with spacers around which several quarter-wave wires are mounted. It comes as a kit, complete with radial wires, allowing the user to choose the precise configuration required. The most usual setup is for an antenna that works on the 7, 10, 14, 18, 21, 24 and 28MHz

Fig 5.16: The DX Commander 'Classic', showing six vertical wires and one of the spacers.

bands, with a 'bonus' resonance within the 50MHz band too. An alternative arrangement is to swap the 10MHz quarter-wave wire for a 3.5MHz quarter-wave, which is then configured as an inverted-L.

The alternative to the quarter-wave design of commercial multi-band vertical is the half-wave type, which does not require radials. If you do wish to mount a multi-band HF vertical well above ground, the half-wave design is certainly simpler to erect.

The best-known manufacturers of the half-wave design of multi-band verticals are Cushcraft and Hy-Gain (Hy-Gain makes both quarter and half-wave designs). In fact these verticals do incorporate short spoke-like 'radials' as part of the antenna design, although they are not radials in the usually accepted meaning of a ground plane, but rather a form of capacitance to help in providing a suitable match. Being an electrical half-wave long, and end-fed, the impedance at the base of the antenna is very high and it therefore needs a matching circuit to match the antenna to 50Ω coax. This is provided by the spokes, together with a transformer in the small 'black box' at the base of the antenna.

It should be noted that although these antennas are electrically a half-wave long, on some bands they are physically much less than this and all shortened antennas are lossy to some extent.

The efficiency of a quarter-wave vertical is dependent on its physical length as a proportion of a full-size quarter-wavelength. A full-size quarter-wave vertical will always outperform one that is physically only, say, one-eighth of a wavelength long. Generally on the higher frequency bands this is not an issue, as a quarter-wave vertical on 14MHz is only 5m (16ft) high. It becomes slightly more of an issue at 7MHz, where a full-size quarter-wave vertical is 10m (32ft) high but the length of a vertical is most important on 3.5 and 1.8MHz, where full-size quarter-wave verticals would be 19.5m (64ft) and 38.5m (126ft 4in) long respectively. Most multi-band verticals covering 3.8MHz are much shorter than this and therefore all are something of a compromise on this band, but one 10m (32ft) long is going to be more efficient than one of only, say, 5m (16ft).

Which work better – commercial quarter-wave or half-wave antennas? I don't know. Probably ground-mounted, side-by-side, the quarter-wave design would be superior if it had a good radial system. If a half-wave design vertical is mounted high up and in the clear and a multi-band

CHAPTER 5 – PLANNING YOUR ANTENNA

quarter-wave design vertical is ground mounted I would imagine it might be a more close-run race.

FULL-WAVE LOOPS

Having discussed half-wave dipoles and quarter-wave verticals it is time to look at full-wave loops. Loops can be constructed in the horizontal plane but for DX work they are more usually made in the vertical plane as this can (depending on how the loop is fed) give a low angle of radiation. The full-wave loop also has a small amount of gain over a dipole.

The loop can be more or less any shape: the ideal shape would be a circle but as this is mechanically difficult to con-

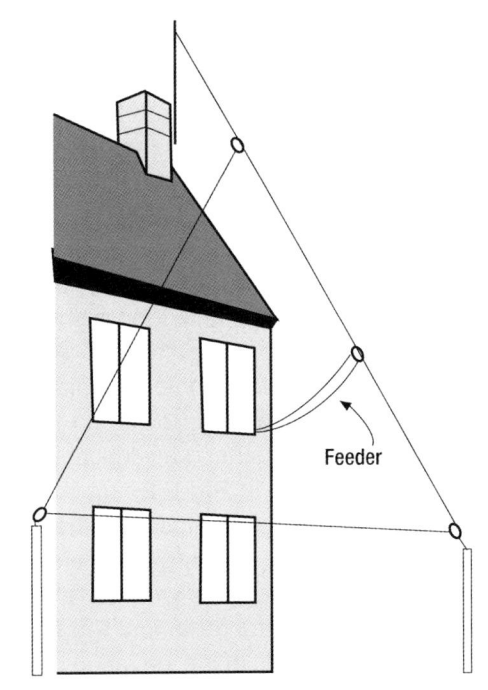

Fig 5.19: Installation of a delta loop antenna.

struct most loops are either rectangular (preferably square or nearly square), **Fig 5.17**, or triangular, **Fig 5.18**, in shape. A square (or a diamond-shaped) loop is

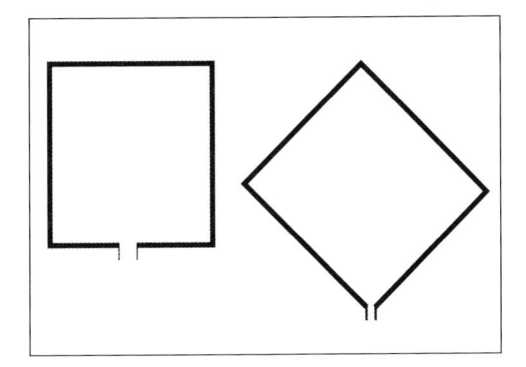

Fig 5.17: Square and diamond-shaped quad loops.

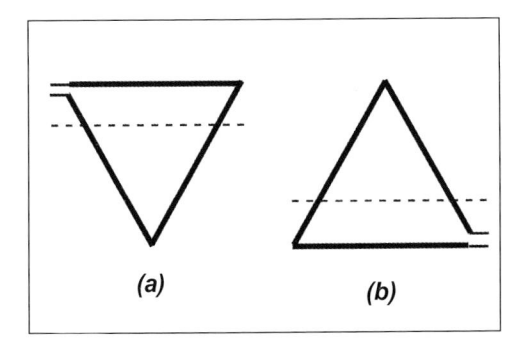

Fig 5.18: Delta loops: (a) 'apex down' and (b) 'apex up'. The dotted lines indicate the effective average height above ground for each antenna.

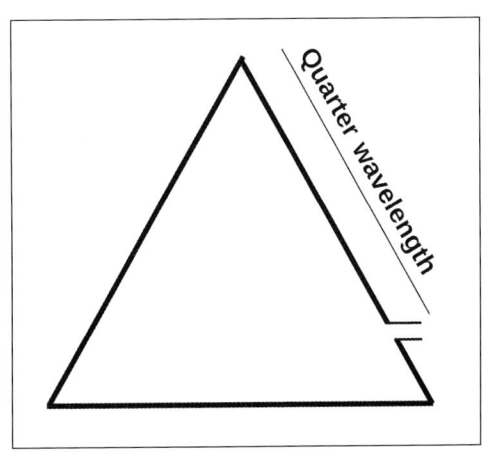

Fig 5.20: Ideally, for the low angle of radiation required for DX working, the delta loop should be fed a quarter-wavelength from the top.

usually called a quad loop whereas a triangular one is a delta loop.

For home-made wire antennas, the delta loop is probably more popular than the square or diamond-shaped quad loop. One reason for this is that only one high support is required for the 'apex up' configuration as shown in **Fig 5.18(b)**. One method of installing a delta loop is shown in **Fig 5.19**.

To provide the low angle of radiation suitable for DX working, the delta loop should to be fed a quarter-wavelength from the top, as shown in **Fig 5.20** or, if this cannot easily be accommodated, then at one of the corners. Feeding it in the centre of the horizontal wire would provide high-angle horizontal radiation. **Fig 5.21** shows a comparison of the elevation plots of a delta loop fed at one corner and at the base.

The formula for calculating the length of the loop is $306/f$ (MHz) in metres, or $1005/f$ (MHz) in feet, for example $306/7.1 = 43.10$m (or 141ft 7in) for a delta loop resonant in the middle of the 40m band at 7100kHz. These formulas normally produce a loop that is somewhat too long but, as with the dipole, it is always easier to shorten the antenna than to have to add more wire later.

BEAM ANTENNAS

So far we have looked only at single-element wire antennas and verticals made of wire or thin tubing. But, if you have the possibility to put up some sort of beam antenna, there is no doubt that, for DX working in particular, it will give you a great advantage over a single-element antenna.

A beam antenna is one with both directivity and gain. See **Fig 5.22**, which compares the theoretical horizontal radiation pattern of a dipole with that of a beam antenna, in this case a 4-element Yagi. It can be seen that the major lobe of the Yagi is much greater than that of the bi-directional dipole, with little radiation off the back and the sides of the antenna.

A Yagi beam consists of at least two elements: a driven element which is usually a half-wave dipole, and at least one parasitic element. In a 2-element Yagi the parasitic element is usually a reflector. A 3-element Yagi will also have a direc-

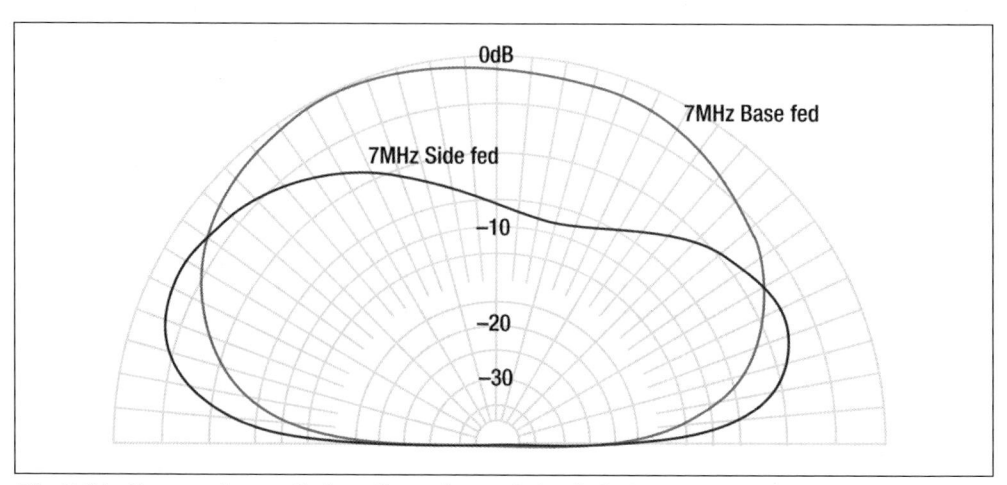

Fig 5.21: Comparison of elevation plots of the full-wave delta loop, fed at the base and at the side.

CHAPTER 5 – PLANNING YOUR ANTENNA

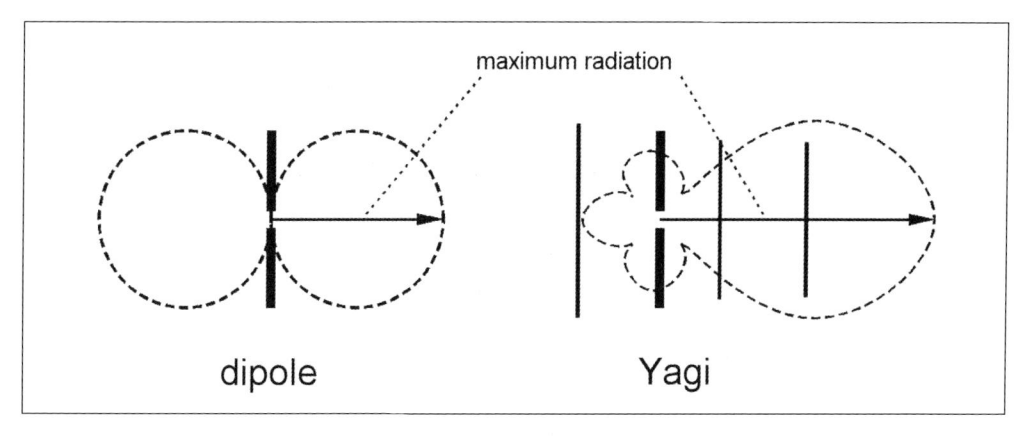

Fig 5.22: Comparison between the horizontal radiation patterns of a dipole and a Yagi beam antenna.

tor. If a Yagi has more than three elements there will usually be multiple directors: it is normal for there to be just one driven element and one reflector, no matter how many elements there are in total.

The gain of a Yagi is not primarily dependent on the number of elements but rather on the boom length of the antenna, i.e. the physical spacing between the elements.

A *cubical quad* is a beam antenna made from a full-wavelength long quad loop in either a square or diamond-shaped configuration plus a parasitic reflector element, also a loop of the same shape and physically or electrically approximately 5% larger. This is a 2-element quad: additional director elements may be added to make 3-element or greater quads.

Since a single-element quad loop has a small amount of gain over a dipole, a 2-element cubical quad has about the same gain as a 3-element Yagi. In other words, roughly the same amount of gain is achieved in a quad with a boom only about half as long as a Yagi's; but the disadvantage is that a quad has height as well as length and breadth. It can therefore be a far more unwieldy structure than a Yagi. Because a quad increases in size in all three dimensions as you go lower in frequency, a 14MHz quad – even a 2-element one – is a big antenna. The reverse is also true, though, making quads for 28MHz and especially 50MHz quite compact antennas.

While it is perfectly possible to build both Yagis and quads, the size and physical construction make home construction of any HF beam a fairly major project. Designs for traditional aluminium tube Yagis can be found in *The ARRL Antenna Book* [1] and also in a new RSGB book, *Yagi Antennas Explained* [6].

In recent years there have been several interesting designs published for wire beams, including the Spiderbeam [7], the Moxon Rectangle [8] and the Hexbeam [9]. All three designs use a frame made of fibreglass poles which act as spreaders to keep the wire elements at the correct spacing with respect to each other. The fibreglass and wire construction makes these designs much lighter than traditional all-metal Yagis and all three would be good projects for those who wish to take up the challenge of making their own HF beam antenna.

GAIN FIGURES – WHAT DO THEY MEAN?

The gain of a beam antenna is expressed in decibels (dB), but it must always be given with reference to something, otherwise the figure is quite meaningless.

Often the gain is quoted with reference to a dipole in free space, e.g. a particular antenna might be said to have 5.0dBd gain. But it can also be given with reference to an *isotropic radiator*, a theoretical point source that radiates at the same intensity in all directions. That same antenna might be said to have 7.15dBi gain. A (theoretically lossless) dipole in free space has 2.15dBi gain, so it is easy to convert between gain figures quoted in dBd and dBi simply by adding or subtracting 2.15dB from the quoted figure.

Real life is a little more complicated though, because any antenna, when placed over the real earth, actually exhibits *more* than the theoretical amount of gain, due to so-called 'ground gain'. The amount of this extra ground gain varies depending on the characteristics of the ground and the height of the antenna above it, so it is not easy to quantify, but it *can* be as high as 8dBi for a dipole, i.e. an additional 5.85dB.

Antenna gain figures should therefore be quoted in units of either dBd or dBi, but if a gain figure is quoted as, say, '9dBd over typical ground' you have no idea what this really means *unless* the amount of additional ground gain is also given. '9dBd gain including typical ground gain of 4dB', simply means the true gain is 5dBd (or 7.15dBi). Clear?!

COMMERCIAL BEAMS

Most amateurs, if they plan to use a beam antenna at all – and whether they be newcomers or the very experienced – opt to purchase a commercial beam.

Many British radio amateurs though, living in typical suburban houses with small gardens, do not even consider the possibility of putting up an HF beam antenna due to its size and the perceived objections they will face from their neighbours or the difficulty they will encounter when applying for planning permission. However, when considering an HF beam almost everyone has either a 3-element triband aluminium Yagi or a 14 to 28MHz 2-element cubical quad in mind. It is true that these are big antennas, but there are smaller commercial beams available that should definitely be considered.

The first worth considering is a monoband 3-element Yagi for 24 or 28MHz. With typical dimensions of only 5.5m wide by 2.45m long (and weighing only 4 or 5kg) a 28MHz beam is not really a big antenna at all (and, if mounted at roof height or above, it will appear even smaller!) A 24MHz Yagi is not much larger. It is also possible to buy cheap Yagis intended for 27MHz (11m) CB and modify them for use on 10m (e.g. **[10]**).

Now, in 2022, solar cycle 25 is progressing nicely and propagation on the higher HF bands such as 21, 24 and 28MHz is improving all the time. There have already been some good openings to Japan, Australia and New Zealand on 28MHz. If the predictions are correct, there should be world-wide DX available on all these bands in 2024 and / or 2025

CHAPTER 5 – PLANNING YOUR ANTENNA

Fig 5.22: The lightweight DXpedition version of the Hexbeam for 14 to 50MHz, on a 5.5m (18ft) pole, just above the house roof.

and probably for a year or two after that, making a 24 or 28MHz monoband Yagi a good choice.

That said, most DXers will want a beam antenna that also covers 14, 18 and / or 21MHz and yet is still not too big. The Moxon Rectangle [8] is a good design, but there are few commercial versions available for HF and the design does not lend itself well to multi-banding.

One design that *does* is the Hexbeam [9] and a number of commercial manufacturers around the world (e.g. [11]) offer either 5-band (14 – 28MHz) or 6-band (14 – 50MHz) versions. The Hexbeam is a 2-element wire Yagi on each band, the unusual design of which, like the ribs of an upturned umbrella – see **Fig 5.22** – allows for optimum spacing between the elements on each of the bands. The origi-nal design was improved upon by Steve Hunt, G3TXQ (SK), who came up with a broadband version of the beam. The two elements are bent into 'C' and 'W' shapes, making an antenna that is only 6.5m across and with a turning radius of 3.25m.

The fibreglass spreaders and wire construction allow for a very lightweight antenna. The version shown in **Fig 5.22** weighs in at only 6kg, making it possible to install the Hexbeam on a lightweight push-up mast and rotate it with a cheap 'TV-type' rotator.

REFERENCES

[1] *The ARRL Antenna Book*, 24th edition, ARRL, available from www.rsgbshop.org

[2] *RSGB Antenna File*, available from www.rsgbshop.org

[3] *Successful Wire Antennas*, edited by Ian Poole, G3YWX, and Steve Telenius-Lowe, 9M6DXX (now PJ4DX), available from www.rsgbshop.org

[4] 'Technical Topics', *RadCom*, May 2007.

[5] DX Commander: www.m0mcx.co.uk

[6] *Yagi Antennas Explained*, Mike Parkin, G0JMI, RSGB 2021, available from www.rsgbshop.org

[7] DF4SA's Spiderbeam site: www.spiderbeam.com

[8] KD6WD's Moxon Rectangle site: www.moxonantennaproject.com

[9] G3TXQ's Hexbeam site: www.karinya.net/g3txq/hexbeam

[10] Sirio SY 27-3 / SY 27-4 27-29MHz antennas: www.nevadaradio.co.uk/product/sirio-sy-27-3 (or ...sy-27-4)

[11] Hexbeam UK (G3TXQ-designed Hexbeams manufactured by MW0JZE): www.g3txq-hexbeam.com

Chapter 6
DX Propagation

There are many books written about propagation and a short book such as this cannot even scratch the surface of what is a very wide-ranging subject in itself. So rather than go into any great detail, I will try to give an indication of what DX can be worked on each band and when, touching on how the solar cycle affects each of the bands and briefly mentioning the various modes of propagation involved.

All of the HF bands are affected in one way or another by the 11-year solar cycles (**Fig 6.1**). As this is being written, in April 2022, we are on the upward slope of solar cycle 25, which is expected to peak in 2025. Solar activity is therefore increasing, and will continue to increase for a few more years. Although many experts predicted that cycle 25 will be a very weak one, similar to that of cycle 24, the speed with which cycle 25 activity started to increase has surprised many – see **Fig 6.2**. So it remains to be seen if this will be a great cycle, a weak one, or perhaps something in between. Suffice to say that from now and for the next several years propagation on the HF bands will be better than it has been for quite a while.

Most long-distance propagation on the HF bands is by refraction from the F2-layer of the ionosphere (see **Fig 6.3**). It is F2 propagation that is most affected by the solar cycles. Much simplified, the

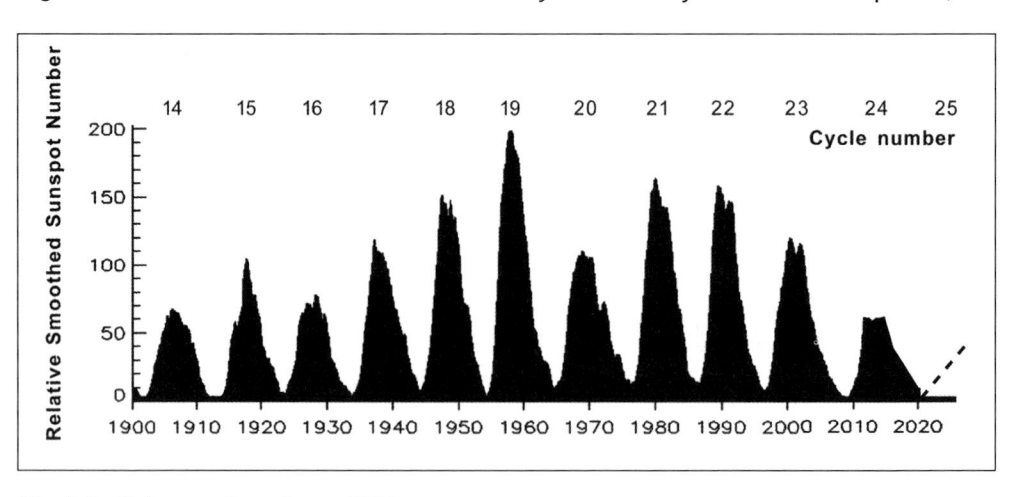

Fig 6.1: Solar cycles since 1900.

CHAPTER 6 – DX PROPAGATION

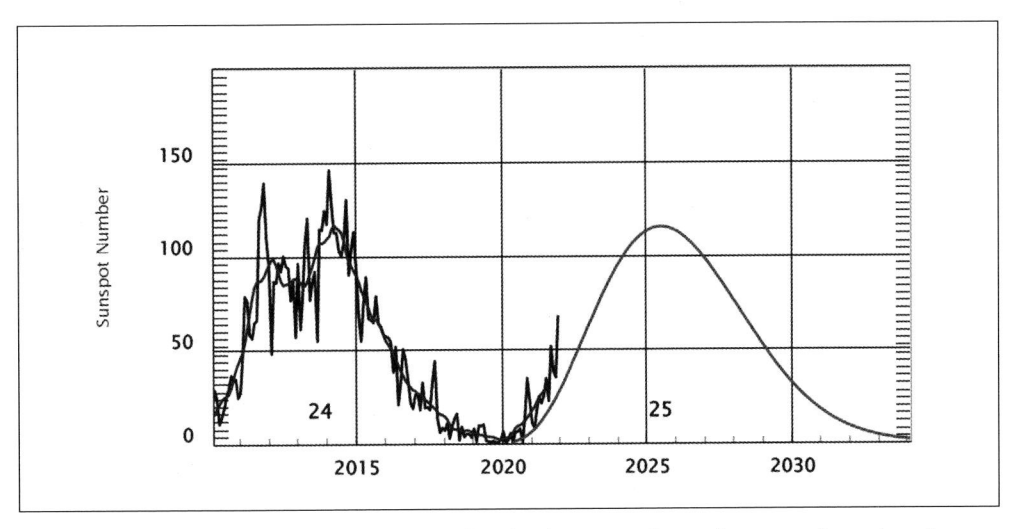

Fig 6.2: Solar cycle 25 prediction and actual sunspot numbers so far, showing that cycle 25 is progressing quicker than predicted (Source: Space Weather Prediction Center, National Oceanic and Atmospheric Administration.)

higher the frequency band, the more it is affected by the stage of the cycle and, generally, the greater the solar activity the better the propagation, particularly on the higher-frequency bands (14MHz and above).

F2 propagation tends to peak in the autumn (in the northern hemisphere mid-September to mid-November) and spring (March to mid-April) periods, with another smaller peak in mid-winter (December), but be at its poorest during the summer

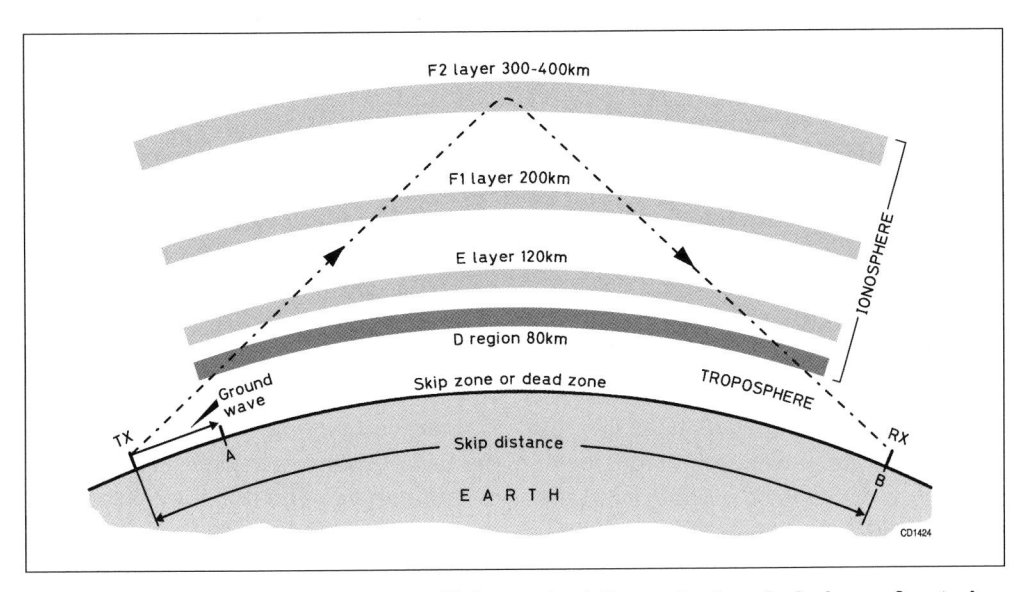

Fig 6.3: Most HF DX (though not all) is worked through signals being refracted from the F2 layer of the atmosphere.

months (May to August). The other layers of the ionosphere shown in **Fig 6.3** have different effects on HF propagation. The D-layer is only present during daylight hours and dissipates shortly after dark, re-forming again soon after dawn. This layer is responsible for the *absorption* of radio waves, particularly below 14MHz, which is why DX contacts are generally only possible on 1.8MHz and 3.5MHz after dark. The E-layer is mainly of interest during Sporadic E events, of which more later.

For further reading on this subject, a good introduction is *Radio Propagation Explained* [1].

Now we'll take a look at each band in turn, from 1.8 to 50MHz.

1.8MHz – 160-METRE BAND

The 1.8MHz band (160 metres, also known as 'topband') is from 1810 to 2000kHz in ITU Region 1, and from 1800 to 2000kHz in Regions 2 and 3.

There is little DX activity on SSB on 1.8MHz, most DXing having traditionally taken place on CW although these days FT8 has taken over as the predominant mode on this band. There is, however, still plenty of CW and SSB activity during contests, particularly the ARRL DX, ARRL 160, CQ World-Wide and CQ 160-Meter events.

The 1.8MHz-band's standard FT8 frequency is 1840kHz, where activity can be heard every evening and night. When there is DX activity on SSB it tends to be around 1850kHz, although in the UK the licence restricts power output to a maximum of 32 watts above 1850kHz. With FT8 signals taking up 1840 – 1843kHz, UK Full licensees wishing to run 400W on SSB should use 1843 – 1850kHz, a rather narrow 'DX window'.

It is fair to say that propagation on 1.8MHz is quite different from that on the other bands; not surprising perhaps when it is considered that 1.8MHz is an MF (medium frequency) band, and not an HF one. More so than on all the other bands, D-layer absorption means that all long-distance contacts take place from dusk (or very shortly before dusk) until just after sunrise. At dusk, therefore, propagation is to the east – where it is already dark – while before sunrise propagation is to the west, where the sun has yet to rise.

It is difficult to predict when good propagation will occur on 1.8MHz. Unlike the higher HF bands, DX propagation on 1.8MHz does not peak with high solar activity and is often better at times of solar *minimum*, because there are less likely to be magnetic storms that cause severe attenuation of signals during periods of low solar activity. The best clue is to check the K-index, which measures the amount of disturbance to the earth's magnetic field. The K-index can range from 0 to 9, with 0 indicating no disturbance and 5 to 9 indicating increasing levels of geomagnetic storms. Look for good DX propagation on 1.8MHz when the K-index has been at 0 or 1 for two or three days in a row. A regularly updated graphic indicating the K-index (as well as the A-index, solar flux, sunspot number and other data) is provided by Paul Herrman, N0NBH [2], and this is carried on a number of websites, including *DX Summit* [3].

Many a DXpedition has operated on the 1.8MHz band each night for two weeks or more only to find that they only make good DX contacts on one or two of those nights.

Many true DX signals on 1.8MHz are very weak and the high levels of static

CHAPTER 6 – DX PROPAGATION

from thunderstorms, particularly in the summer, makes DXing on this band something of a specialist pursuit, with efficient low-angle antennas virtually a necessity. Most DXers who specialise in 1.8MHz use high verticals or inverted-L antennas for transmitting and separate receive antennas in order to reduce the noise level.

3.5MHz – 80-METRE BAND

The 3.5MHz band is from 3500 – 3800kHz in ITU Region 1 and 3500 – 4000kHz in Region 2 and some parts of Region 3. In Region 1, SSB operation takes place between 3600 and 3800kHz although almost all DX activity on SSB is concentrated in the top 15kHz of the band, between 3785 and 3800kHz, the so-called 'DX Window'. In fact, the top 25kHz of the band, 3775 – 3800kHz, is considered to be "Priority for Inter-Continental Telephony (SSB) Operation" in the IARU and RSGB Band Plans **[4]**, (**Fig 6.4**). Despite this, many local and semi-local contacts can be heard taking place in that part of the band. During the major contests DX activity on SSB can be found anywhere in the 3600 to 3800kHz part of the band.

Many North American stations making local and semi-local contacts operate between 3800 and 4000kHz but this part of the band (known as '75 meters' in the USA) is not available for use in the UK or other countries in Region 1.

FT8 and FT4 activity takes places between 3567 and 3588kHz.

During the day, the 3.5MHz band is

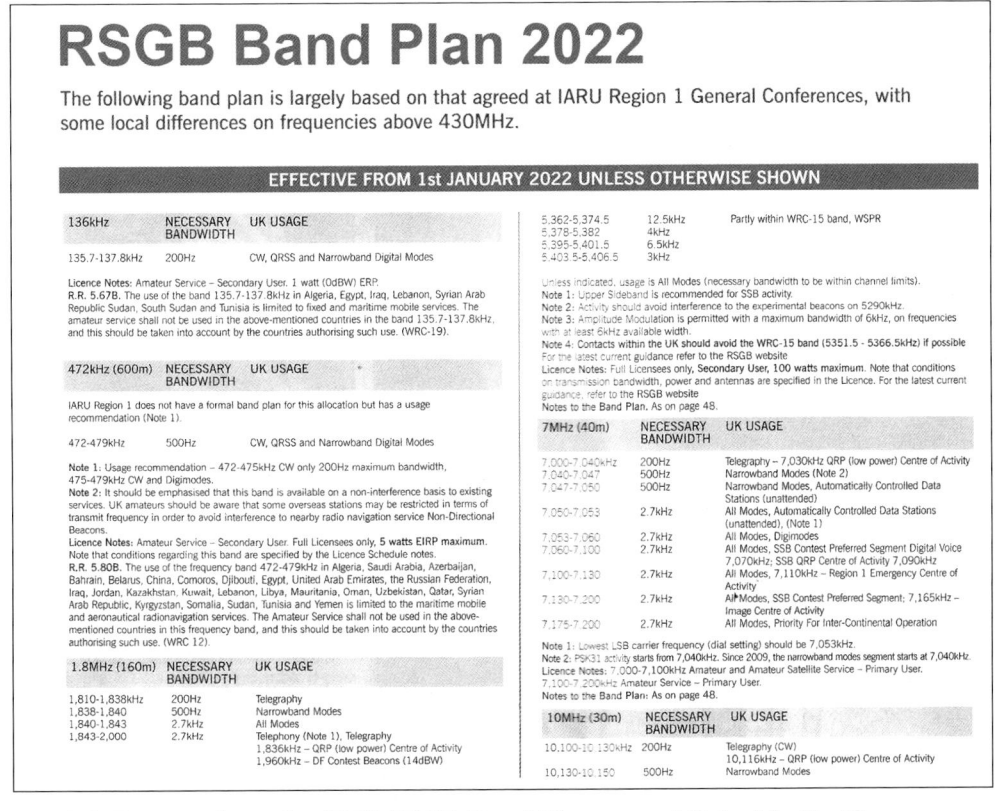

Fig 6.4: Excerpt from the 2022 RSGB Band Plan, as published in RadCom.

only suitable for short-distance contacts (around the UK and perhaps into Belgium and France). Like 1.8MHz, 3.5MHz is very much a night-time DX band. The grey-line, the twilight zone that separates the day and night sides of earth, can provide some excellent DX on 3.5MHz, with long-path New Zealand stations audible around sunrise in the UK when that coincides with sunset in New Zealand.

Like the 1.8MHz band, DX propagation on 3.5MHz tends to be better close to solar minimum. This is due to the lower chance of magnetic storms and because there is less ionisation of the D-layer during periods of low solar activity, leading to less absorption of signals.

Propagation is also noticeably better during the winter months than during the summer. There are two main reasons for this: firstly the greater periods of darkness during the winter months means that propagation can take place to larger areas of the world and for longer periods of time with no D-layer absorption and, secondly, because there tend to be fewer thunderstorms, which cause high levels of static interference, during the winter.

Bear in mind, though, that when it is summer in the northern hemisphere, it is winter in the southern hemisphere and therefore propagation to Australasia, South America and southern Africa can be best in the spring and autumn, when it is not summer in either hemisphere.

5MHz – 60-METRE BAND

In the UK, the 5MHz 'band' is not a band at all, but a series of 11 separate narrow frequency allocations. In this regard, the UK is out of step with most of the rest of the world because, at the World Radio Conference in 2015, 5351.5 – 5366.5kHz was allocated to the Amateur Service on a Secondary basis, although not all countries have yet released the WRC-15 frequencies to their amateurs. Meanwhile, in the USA, the Federal Communications Commission (FCC) has allocated five 3kHz-wide channels to their amateurs. **Table 6.1** summarises all these allocations.

The disparate nature of allocations around 5MHz means that there is little SSB DX activity. In the UK it is *recommended* that SSB transmissions should be on upper sideband (while in the USA upper sideband is *mandatory* on their 5MHz channels).

Most DX activity takes place on FT8, using the frequency 5357kHz, which is one of the few frequencies that can be used (albeit with some restrictions) in the UK, the USA and all the countries that have been allocated the WRC-15 band (see **Table 9.1** on page 119 for further notes about UK FT8 activity on this band).

In the UK, only Full licensees have access to the 11 band segments and with a maximum power of 100 watts. In the USA, General, Advanced and Amateur Extra licensees (though not Technician or Novice licensees) have access to their five channels, also with a power limit of 100W (PEP, relative to a half-wave dipole). In Region 1 the power limit in the WRC-15 5MHz band is 15W, whereas in Region 2 it is 25W EIRP.

Propagation on 5MHz is most similar to that on 7MHz, though the band openings are rather shorter. During daylight hours signals can be expected on FT8 from most of Europe whereas after dark world-wide propagation is possible. As with the other bands from 1.8 to 7MHz, propagation around 5MHz is generally better during the winter months.

CHAPTER 6 – DX PROPAGATION

Frequencies kHz	Allocation	Notes
5258.5 – 5264.0	UK allocation	(1) Avoid interference to beacons operating on 5290kHz.
5276.0 – 5284.0	UK allocation	
5288.5 – 5292.0	UK allocation [1]	(2) FCC, the USA Federal Communications Commission. FCC allocations can be used by amateurs in all US territories including Alaska, Hawaii, Puerto Rico, US Virgin Islands etc.
5298.0 – 5307.0	UK allocation	
5313.0 – 5323.0	UK allocation	
5330.5 – 5333.5	FCC allocation [2]	
5333.0 – 5338.0	UK allocation	
5346.5 – 5349.5	FCC allocation [2]	(3) The main FT8 frequency is 5357.0kHz. UK licensees should use tones of 950Hz or less to avoid transmitting outside the UK allocation.
5351.5 – 5366.5	**WRC-15 band** [3]	
5354.0 – 5358.0	UK allocation [3, 4]	
5357.5 – 5360.5	FCC allocation [2]	
5362.0 – 5374.5	UK allocation [5]	(4) This UK allocation lies within the WRC-15 band. UK-to-UK contacts should avoid using this segment.
5371.5 – 5374.5	FCC allocation [2]	
5378.0 – 5382.0	UK allocation	
5395.5 – 5401.5	UK allocation	(5) This UK allocation lies partly within the WRC-15 band. UK-to-UK contacts should avoid using 5362.0 – 5366.5kHz.
5403.5 – 5406.5	FCC allocation [2]	
5403.5 – 5406.5	UK allocation	

Table 6.1: UK, FCC (USA) and WRC-15 allocations around 5MHz.

7MHz – 40-METRE BAND

In most of the world the 7MHz-band is now 200kHz wide, from 7000 to 7200kHz, or greater. In the UK, the SSB part of the band is considered to be 7050 – 7200kHz although 7047.5 – 7083kHz is used for FT8 and FT4 transmissions world-wide, while in the USA 7000 – 7125kHz is used for Morse and data mode transmissions but not for SSB. The RSGB Band Plan [4] lists 7175 – 7200kHz as "Priority for Inter-Continental Operation" but DX stations generally operate on SSB anywhere between 7100 and 7200kHz and, in contests, as low as 7050kHz.

The main FT8 frequency is 7074kHz and activity can generally be heard here 24 hours a day. FT4 is also used more on 7MHz than on most of the other HF bands, with the exception of 14MHz. The main FT4 frequency is 7047.5kHz.

In ITU Region 2 (North and South America) and in some parts of the Pacific 7000 – 7300kHz is allocated to amateurs, although in the rest of the world high-power AM broadcast stations operate between 7200 and 7450kHz.

During daylight hours, the 7MHz band supports only relatively short-distance working (from the UK, around the British Isles and into north and western Europe). Unlike the higher-frequency bands, 7MHz is a night-time DX band: DX can be worked from an hour or two before sunset to the east, throughout the night, and for up to an hour or two after sunrise towards the west.

Grey-line propagation is also very important on 7MHz, see **Fig 6.5**. In this example (0800UTC on 21 December), it is just after sunrise in the UK and the sun is overhead (i.e. it is midday) in the Indian Ocean. A DXer on 7MHz in the UK might expect to be able to work DX stations towards the dark side of the earth, in this case westwards to the whole of

HF DX BASICS

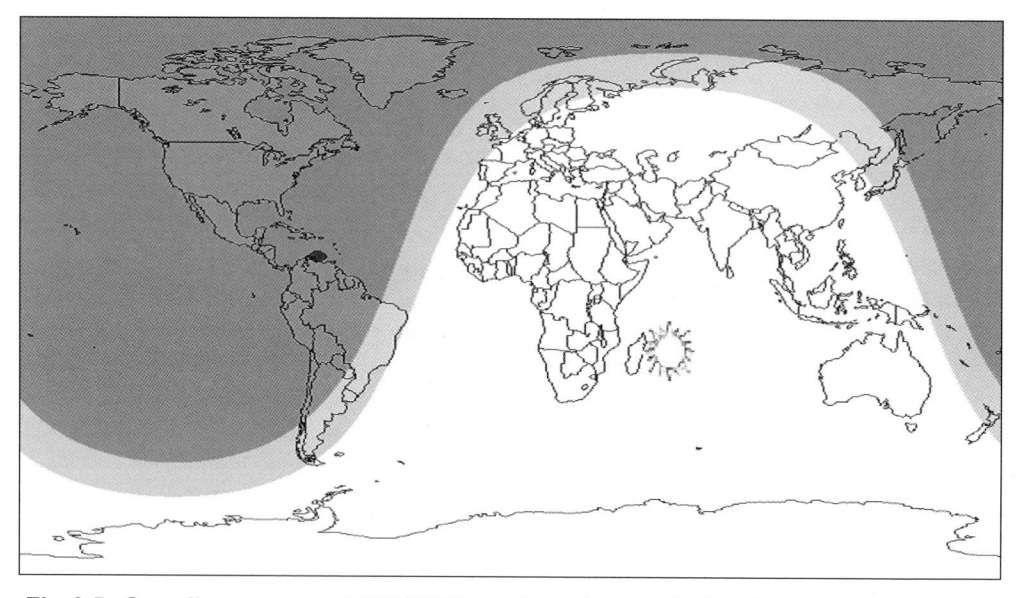

Fig 6.5: Grey-line map as at 0800UTC on the winter solstice, 21 December. The map clearly shows the daylight and darkness parts of the world and also the twilight zone or 'grey-line' along which DX may be worked.

North and Central America, and to most of South America.

However, it can be seen from **Fig 6.5** that the whole of the British Isles is within the grey-line, which crosses the Atlantic and continues down the east part of Brazil, covering Uruguay, the eastern half of Argentina and the south of Chile, before crossing the Pacific Ocean. A DXer might therefore reasonably expect *enhanced* signals from PY, CX, LU and parts of CE during this time. The grey-line continues across the North Island of New Zealand, Vanuatu and the Solomon Islands before crossing Japan, then going across northern Russia and Scandinavia before returning to the British Isles again. So not only can DX in South America be worked at this time, but also New Zealand, the western Pacific islands and Japan.

The grey-line map also shows that countries such as Indonesia, Malaysia, Singapore, the Philippines and Thailand are in broad daylight (at 0800UTC on 21 December), so there is little to zero chance of making contacts with these countries even when Japanese and perhaps Korean stations are being worked.

10MHz – 30-METRE BAND

10MHz is the narrowest HF band, from 10100 to 10150kHz. As it is only 50kHz wide, by international agreement wideband modes such as SSB should not be used on 10MHz. This band is, however, very popular with CW and data mode users, and with good reason. Long-distance propagation can be good on 10MHz when the lower-frequency bands are poor due to high absorption and – especially during periods of low solar activity – 10MHz may well be 'open' to parts of the world when 14MHz and the higher-frequency bands are closed.

For this reason, 10MHz is very popular with DXers using FT8. The main FT8

CHAPTER 6 – DX PROPAGATION

frequency is 10136kHz but a couple of other channels are also used, particularly by DXpeditions wishing to avoid the overcrowded main FT8 channel.

14MHz – 20-METRE BAND

20m is the quintessential DX band. 350kHz wide, from 14000 to 14350kHz world-wide, SSB activity can be found from 14112 to 14350kHz. The US General licence class (roughly equivalent to the UK Intermediate class) is allowed to operate from 14225 to 14350kHz with a power limit of 1.5kW, so this is a good part of the band to work US stations. However, within the USA the General part of the band is mainly used for domestic contacts and numerous US nets, so most (though certainly not all) DX activity takes place below 14225kHz.

14190 – 14200kHz is listed as "Priority for DXpeditions" in the RSGB Band Plan [4] and in the IARU Band Plan, although in practice DXpedition stations also often use other frequencies: 14145 and 14185kHz are particular favourites. IOTA DXpeditions tend to operate on, or close to, 14260kHz. Because no USA stations are allowed to operate on SSB lower than 14150kHz, 14112 – 14150kHz is often used by stations in Canada, the Caribbean and South America when they wish to work DX outside the North America area.

14225 – 14235kHz, within the SSB part of the band, is shared with SSTV (slow scan television) operators, so it is best to avoid those frequencies when operating on SSB.

The 14MHz band is arguably the most popular one for those using FT8. The main FT8 frequency is 14074kHz and activity can be heard here virtually 24 hours a day. As 14074kHz can often get overcrowded there are three other channels used for FT8: 14071, 14090 and 14095kHz. These are mainly used by DXpeditions using the so-called 'Fox and Hounds' (F/H) mode, of which more later. There is also more activity on FT4 on 14MHz than on any other band. Here the main frequency is 14080kHz.

DX signals can be found on 14MHz throughout the solar cycle and at all times of year, although the spring and autumn seasons provide definite peaks in propagation. Conversely, during the summer months, and particularly during periods of low solar activity, 14MHz can be quiet, particularly on SSB, with only semi-local stations around Europe to be found, though it is never too long on 14MHz before some DX signals return.

Long-path propagation is quite reliable on 14MHz when signals arrive from the long way around the world, at 180° to the expected heading. Look for signals from eastern Australia (VK1 – VK4 and VK7), New Zealand (ZL) and, if you are lucky, other parts of the western Pacific, typically for an hour or two after sunrise, coming in from the direction of South America.

18MHz – 17-METRE BAND

This is a narrow band, only 100kHz wide, between 18068 and 18168kHz. SSB activity is to be found between about 18115 and 18168kHz and DX stations operate anywhere in that part of the band. Most FT8 activity is on 18100kHz.

There is no contest activity in the 18MHz band, making it a 'refuge' for those who dislike contests. 18MHz is a popular band, and justifiably so because it is less affected by low solar activity than are 21, 24 and 28MHz. Therefore there is usually some DX to be found on the band, even when the higher frequency bands are apparently dead. However, because of its popularity and because the band is so narrow it can often get crowded, making it difficult to find a clear frequency.

18MHz can stay open till late at night during periods of high solar activity, but it is likely to close not long after sunset during low solar activity years.

21MHz – 15-METRE BAND

The 21MHz band is much wider than 18MHz, at 450kHz (21000 – 21450kHz). SSB stations operate between 21150 and 21450kHz, and there is also some AM and FM activity above 21400kHz. No US stations are allowed to operate on SSB below 21200kHz which means that 21150 – 21200kHz is often used by stations in the western hemisphere (Canada, Central America, Caribbean etc) and sometimes the Pacific, in order to avoid interference to or from USA stations. DXpeditions often use 21295kHz and IOTA DXpeditions 21260kHz.

Most FT8 activity is on 21074kHz.

Being a wide band, 21MHz is rarely overcrowded, except during the major contests at times of solar maximum. During solar maximum, and for a year or two before and after, 21MHz is an excellent DX band. However, at solar minimum and for a couple of years either side of the minimum, 21MHz can often appear to be dead. When there is little activity on 21MHz, most stations tend to operate between about 21210 and 21310kHz.

Like 24 and 28MHz, propagation on 21MHz is mainly during daylight hours but it tends to stay open later in the evenings than both 24 and 28MHz and, during periods of high solar activity, it may remain open until midnight or 1.00am local time, with strong signals from Central and South America, the west coast of North America, and – when conditions are particularly good – Hawaii and elsewhere in the Pacific. However, in contrast at solar minimum 21MHz might appear to be dead for several days at a time.

24.9MHz – 12-METRE BAND

The 24MHz band, 24890 – 24990kHz, is another narrow band which sees rather less activity than the adjacent 21 and 28MHz bands. SSB stations operate between 24930 and 24990kHz and DX can be found anywhere in that 60kHz.

FT8 activity is concentrated on 24915kHz. Along with 10 and 18MHz, by international agreement there is no contest activity in the 24MHz band.

Propagation is very similar to that of 28MHz except that, during periods of marginal openings, 24MHz is more likely to be open than 28MHz. It is therefore worth checking the band and perhaps trying a CQ call even when both 24 and 28MHz appear to be dead.

As with 21 and 28MHz, F2 propagation on 24MHz is mainly during daylight hours. That's not to say that contacts cannot be made after dark – they certainly can – but then they will usually be made in the direction of the sun. For example, after dark in the evening contacts will be made towards the west, where it is still daylight.

During periods of high solar activity, 24MHz may stay open until well after dark, typically with signals from the Americas. However, during periods of low solar activity it may well close quickly after sunset and at solar minimum it might not open at all for days at a time.

As with 28MHz and 50MHz, Sporadic E contacts around Europe and, and often further afield, can often be made on 24MHz during the summer months.

CHAPTER 6 – DX PROPAGATION

28MHz – 10-METRE BAND

The 28MHz band is the widest of the HF bands with no less than 1.7MHz of spectrum available: 28000 – 29700kHz. According to the latest RSGB Band Plan **[4]** which is based on the IARU Region 1 band plans, the 'All Mode' part of the 10m band (which obviously includes SSB) is from 28225 – 29700kHz. However, the SSB part of the band is normally considered to be 28300 – 29000kHz, with beacons operating from 28190kHz to 28300kHz, and AM and FM stations above 29000kHz. Most FT8 activity is on 28074kHz.

During the major contests at times of high solar activity the band may be so crowded that SSB stations will operate as low as 28225kHz and as high as 29200kHz or so. However, at times of low solar activity far fewer stations will be heard and SSB operation then tends to be between 28400 and 28550kHz. When there is very little long-distance propagation on 28MHz almost all SSB activity is within a few tens of kilohertz of 28500kHz.

DXpedition stations tend to use 28495kHz and generally listen 5kHz (or 5 to 10kHz) higher, whereas IOTA DXpeditions often use 28460kHz.

28MHz is the HF band that is most affected by solar activity, with excellent DX propagation available during the peaks of the solar cycle and strong signals from literally all over the world via both the short path and long path – but with long lean years during solar minima.

At the time of writing (April 2022) it is still too early to tell whether solar cycle 25 will be a weak, average or strong cycle. However, early signs have been encouraging, with cycle 25 activity rising more quickly than predicted (see **Fig 6.2** on page 73) and openings from the UK to Australia and New Zealand having already taken place.

Even when the 28MHz band is otherwise dead, north-south propagation can occur. From the UK, stations in southern and central Africa, or Brazil, Uruguay and Argentina can sometimes be worked, often with good signals, when stations to the north of them are quite inaudible.

Although by definition an HF band, in some ways propagation on 28MHz more closely resembles that of a low VHF band than that of the other HF bands. For example, auroral and Sporadic E (Es) propagation, both normally considered to be VHF phenomena, are in fact also present on 28MHz.

Sporadic E propagation takes place during the summer months (typically May to July or early August) throughout the solar cycle. There is also a less pronounced period of Es in winter, usually in December – January. By its very nature, this type of propagation is, well, sporadic and may occur on one day but not the next. From the UK, Es will bring in strong signals from around Europe and perhaps North Africa and the closer parts of the Middle East (Turkey, Cyprus, Israel, Jordan etc). Double or multiple-hop Sporadic E might allow for openings to the North America or the Caribbean.

50MHz – 6-METRE BAND

The 50MHz band, 6 metres, is from 50000 to 52000kHz in the UK and most of Europe, and from 50000 to 54000kHz in the USA and certain other countries. However, almost all DX activity, whether on CW, SSB or FT8, is between 50000 and 50400kHz.

These days, the majority of DX contacts on the 50MHz band are made using FT8. The main FT8 frequency is 50313kHz but during good openings this frequency can get very crowded, so 50323kHz is also used, with the intention that only inter-continental contacts are made on the latter frequency.

The IARU Region 1 and RSGB band plans [4] list 50100 – 50130kHz as being for "Inter-Continental DX Telegraphy & SSB" with 50110kHz the "Inter-Continental DX Centre of Activity": 50110kHz is therefore like a 'calling channel' and once a contact is established you should move to a different frequency in order to leave 50110kHz clear for other users.

50MHz is a VHF band, not HF, and therefore propagation is very different to that on most of the HF bands, though it does bear some similarities to propagation on 28MHz.

F2 Propagation

F2 propagation generally only occurs at the peak of the solar cycle on 50MHz, and some solar cycles are too weak to allow for refraction from the F2 layer of the ionosphere (**Fig 6.3**). While the maximum usable frequency (MUF) will exceed 30MHz at the peak of a solar cycle, it does not always reach as high as the 50MHz band.

If it is a good cycle, world-wide contacts can be made via F2 propagation on 50MHz at the peak of the cycle, and for a year or two either side of the peak.

Sporadic E Propagation (Es)

Even if there is no F2 propagation available, the 50MHz band is still an interesting DX band. Other than F2, when it occurs, the main mode of DX propagation on 50MHz is Sporadic E (abbreviated E_s or more usually Es), see **Fig 6.6**. In the northern hemisphere the Sporadic E 'season' is from late April or May to August each year, irrespective of the state of the solar cycle. The height of the E-layer, where Es 'clouds' form at that time of year, is about 90 to 140km, which permits contacts of approximately 500 to

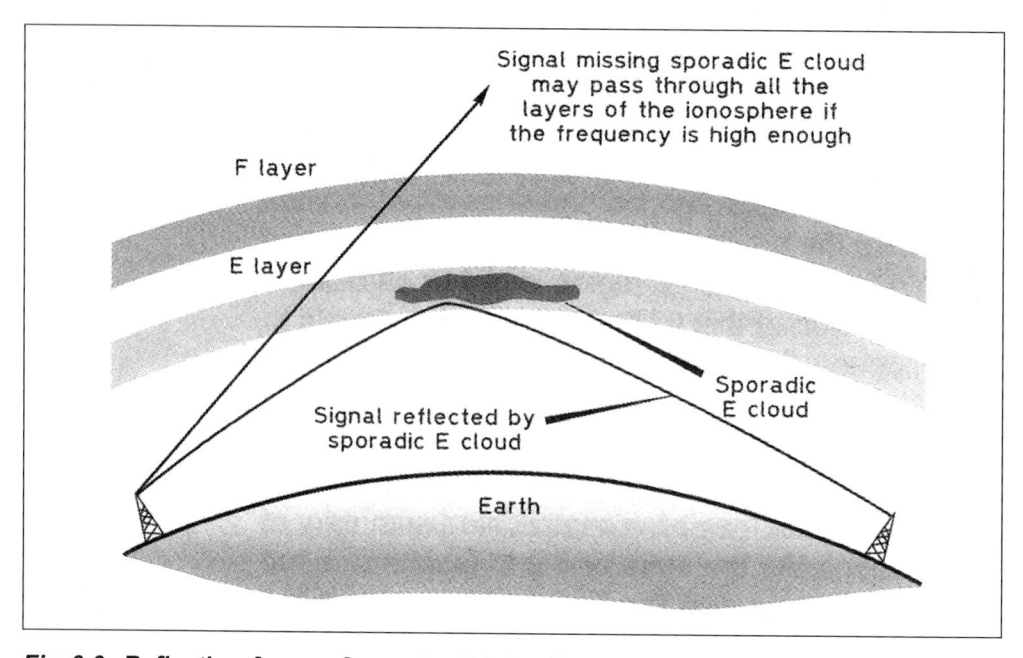

Fig 6.6: Reflection from a Sporadic E 'cloud'.

CHAPTER 6 – DX PROPAGATION

2500km to be made by Es. However, quite frequently double or even multiple-hop Sporadic E takes place, allowing for real DX contacts up to 10,000km or slightly more.

During the 2021 Es season I worked as far as Cyprus on 50MHz, a distance of around 10,200km from Bonaire, using just a home-made wire ground plane antenna on a 10m-high fibreglass pole. I was using FT8, with about 300W output as signals were very weak. The contact took place during an intense Es opening to Europe.

SSSP Propagation

Not all 50MHz QSOs can easily be explained with the usually-accepted theories of propagation. Almost every year, for a few weeks around the northern hemisphere's summer solstice, some contacts are made between Europe (including the UK) and Japan. This has in the past been explained as multiple-hop Es but signals, although not strong, are generally steady and the number of hops that would be required by E-layer reflections have led to speculation that this is in fact a different mode of propagation altogether, which has been named 'Short-Path Summer Solstice Propagation' (SSSP).

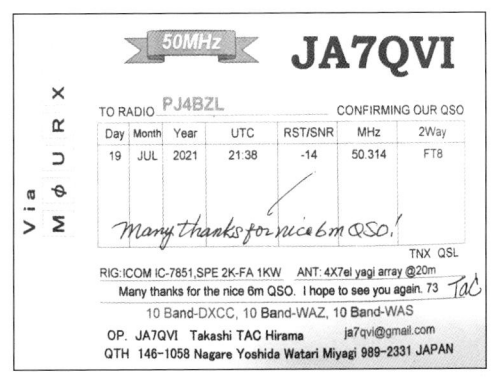

Fig 6.7: At over 13,500km was this QSO by SSSP or multiple-hop Es?

On 19 July 2021, Berry Smulders, PJ4BZL, contacted JA7QVI on 50MHz FT8, **Fig 6.7**. As this was shortly after the solar minimum between cycles 24 and 25 it is very unlikely for this QSO to have taken place by F2 propagation. The distance was over 13,500km, which also makes it unlikely that it would have been by multiple-hop Es; SSSP would seem to be the most likely explanation.

Trans-Equatorial Propagation (TEP)

TEP is a form of F2 propagation and takes place between stations approximately the same distance north and south of the geomagnetic equator, **Fig 6.8**. (Note that the geomagnetic equator does not closely follow the 0° latitude line of the geographic equator.)

From here in Bonaire, contacts are made by TEP quite regularly into central Chile and central Argentina, over distances of 5000 to 6000km.

As can be seen from **Fig 6.8**, the northernmost limit of TEP is southern England but, for those lucky enough to be within the TEP zone, contacts can be made over great distances into South America, southern Africa and the Indian Ocean area.

Auroral Propagation

At high latitudes propagation via the auroral curtain can take place on 50MHz. Auroras tend to happen during periods of high solar activity and particularly in the two or three years after the peak of the solar cycle.

A radio aurora can occur even when there is no visual aurora apparent, but if the 'northern lights', **Fig 6.9**, are being seen – typically in Scandinavia or Scotland – then there is a strong possibility

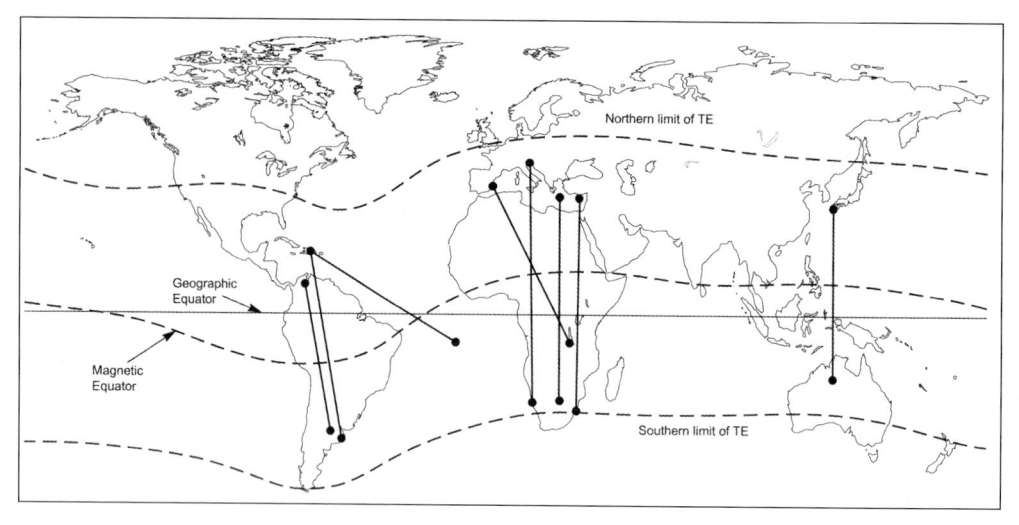

Fig 6.8: Typical TEP contacts made either side of the geomagnetic equator (image courtest of ARRL Handbook).

Fig 6.9: The 'northern lights', a spectacular visual aurora at Tromsø, Norway, on 16 March 2022 (photo credit: Pamela Davies).

CHAPTER 6 – DX PROPAGATION

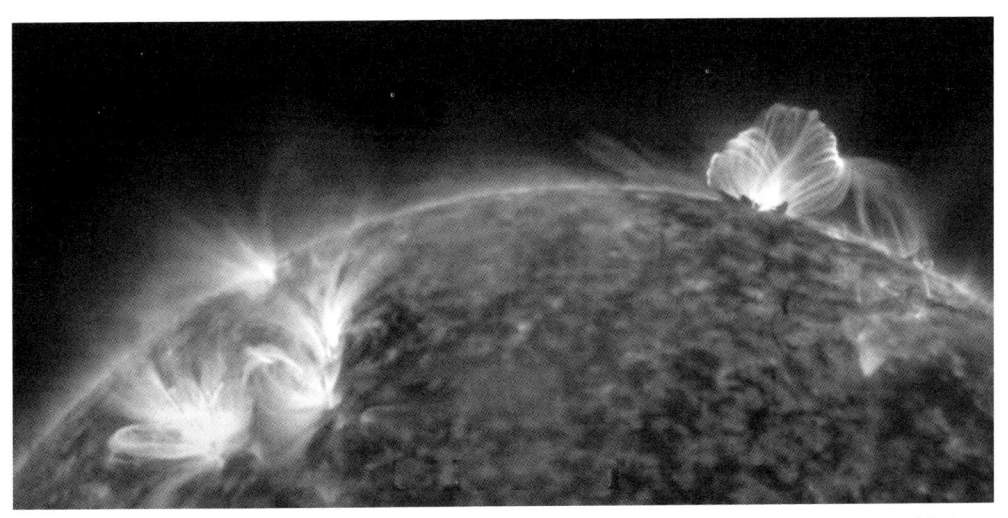

Fig 6.10: Between 25 and 28 October 2021 there were several solar flares which lead to widespread auroras in northern Europe and North America (photo credit: NASA / GSFC / SDO).

of auroral conditions on the radio.

Auroras occur after a solar disturbance such as a solar flare, **Fig 6.10**. Precisely how the aurora is formed is beyond the scope of this book, but this is explained in detail in *Radio Auroras* by the late Charlie Newton, G2FKZ **[5]**. On 50MHz (as well as on 28MHz and the higher VHF bands) contacts from the UK can be made via the aurora with stations in northern parts of Europe such as Scandinavia, Poland and the Baltic States.

The 50MHz modes of propagation are well covered in G3XTT's book *The Magic Bands* **[6]**. 50MHz is known as 'The Magic Band' because of the unusual and unexpected contacts that can occur at almost any time. A good example of this was on 14 March 2022 when, on an otherwise completely 'dead' band, I made an FT8 QSO with VK4MA in Queensland, Australia, over a distance of 15,400km. My 50MHz antenna was on the ground, so I was using a 7MHz inverted-V dipole!

REFERENCES

[1] *Radio Propagation Explained*, Steve Nichols, G0KYA, RSGB 2016, available from www.rsgbshop.org
[2] Paul Herrman, N0NBH: hamqsl.com/solar.html
[3] DX Summit: dxsummit.fi
[4] RSGB Band Plans: www.rsgb.org/bandplans
[5] *Radio Auroras*, Charlie Newton, G2FKZ (revised edition, 2012), RSGB, available from www.rsgbshop.org
[6] *The Magic Bands*, Don Field, G3XTT, RSGB 2020, available from www.rsgbshop.org

Chapter 7

Finding the DX

In this chapter we look at how and where to find the DX: after all, if you don't hear it, you can't work it. Most of the monthly amateur radio magazines carry information about forthcoming DX activity, provided it has been notified to them in time for their publishing deadlines. The 'HF' column in *RadCom* and the 'How's DX?' column in *QST* are good examples.

The good old-fashioned method of simply tuning the bands to find the DX still exists of course but it is always good to be forewarned of upcoming DXpeditions.

These days printed DX newsletters sent by post have all been superseded by websites and email bulletins. A good DX news website, well illustrated with photographs of the DX locations mentioned,

Fig 7.1: The DX-World website is updated daily.

CHAPTER 7 – FINDING THE DX

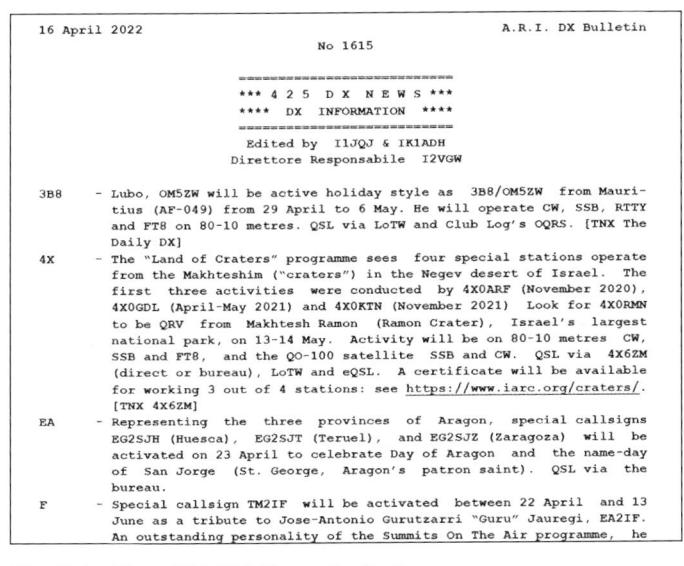

```
16 April 2022                           A.R.I. DX Bulletin
                    No 1615
            ===============================
            *** 4 2 5  D X  N E W S ***
            ****  DX  INFORMATION  ****
            ===============================
               Edited by I1JQJ & IK1ADH
               Direttore Responsabile I2VGW

3B8   - Lubo, OM5ZW will be active holiday style as 3B8/OM5ZW from Mauri-
        tius (AF-049) from 29 April to 6 May. He will operate CW, SSB, RTTY
        and FT8 on 80-10 metres. QSL via LoTW and Club Log's OQRS. [TNX The
        Daily DX]
4X    - The "Land of Craters" programme sees four special stations operate
        from the Makhteshim ("craters") in the Negev desert of Israel. The
        first three activities were conducted by 4X0ARF (November 2020),
        4X0GDL (April-May 2021) and 4X0KTN (November 2021) Look for 4X0RMN
        to be QRV from Makhtesh Ramon (Ramon Crater), Israel's largest
        national park, on 13-14 May. Activity will be on 80-10 metres CW,
        SSB and FT8, and the QO-100 satellite SSB and CW. QSL via 4X6ZM
        (direct or bureau), LoTW and eQSL. A certificate will be available
        for working 3 out of 4 stations: see https://www.iarc.org/craters/.
        [TNX 4X6ZM]
EA    - Representing the three provinces of Aragon, special callsigns
        EG2SJH (Huesca), EG2SJT (Teruel), and EG2SJZ (Zaragoza) will be
        activated on 23 April to celebrate Day of Aragon and the name-day
        of San Jorge (St. George, Aragon's patron saint). QSL via the
        bureau.
F     - Special callsign TM2IF will be activated between 22 April and 13
        June as a tribute to Jose-Antonio Gurutzarri "Guru" Jauregi, EA2IF.
        An outstanding personality of the Summits On The Air programme, he
```

Fig 7.2: The 425 DX News bulletin.

is *DX-World* [1], **Fig 7.1**, run by Col McGowan, MM0NDX. Another is *DXNews.com* [2], run by Al Teimurazov, 4L5A, from Georgia.

The *425 DX News* [3], **Fig 7.2**, edited by Mauro Pregliasco, I1JQJ, and Valeria Gualerzi, IK1ADH, is a weekly newsletter sent by email free of charge every Friday to anyone who signs up for it. *The OPDX Bulletin* [4], edited by Tedd Mirgliotta, KB8NW, is another free DX bulletin available on the internet, or you can also subscribe to the OPDX mailing list. Finally, *The Weekly DX* and *The Daily DX* [5] are bulletins sent out by email, but both of these are available only on (paid) subscription.

All these bulletins contain information about forthcoming and current DX activity, after-the-event information on many operations, QSL information and lots of other information of interest to DXers.

FINDING THE DX

You may know from DX-World or one of the DX news bulletins that a DXpedition is taking place, but how to find it?

Real-time DX information is available from the global Cluster network linked by the Internet. The Clusters carry live 'spots' of DX activity, solar data etc. The popular web-based Cluster 'My DX Summit' (usually just called DX Summit) [6] is run by the OH8X group in Finland. DX Summit collects Cluster spots from around the world and displays them in various ways according to which filters are selected. In **Fig 7.3** the 'HF', '50MHz', 'Phone' and 'Digi' filters have been selected, so spots made of stations using CW, or on bands higher in frequency than 50MHz, are not shown. You can set your own inclusive and exclusive filters if you are interested in, for example, 14 and 18MHz but not (say) 1.8 or 3.5MHz. You can also post your own spots and announcements on to the Cluster network via the DX Summit website.

The next aspect is to think about propagation. In **Fig 7.3**, VP8NO in the Falkland Islands has been spotted on 28074kHz (therefore using FT8) at 2151UTC by 9Z4Y in Trinidad and Tobago, but are you likely to be able to decode VP8NO where *you* are located?

Which band or bands are likely to support propagation to that part of the world, and at what times? Hopefully the information in Chapter 6 will give you a fair idea of what should be possible but it is a good idea to use propagation prediction software or tables.

HF DX BASICS

Fig 7.3: The DX Summit website, showing 'spots' made by DXers from all over the world.

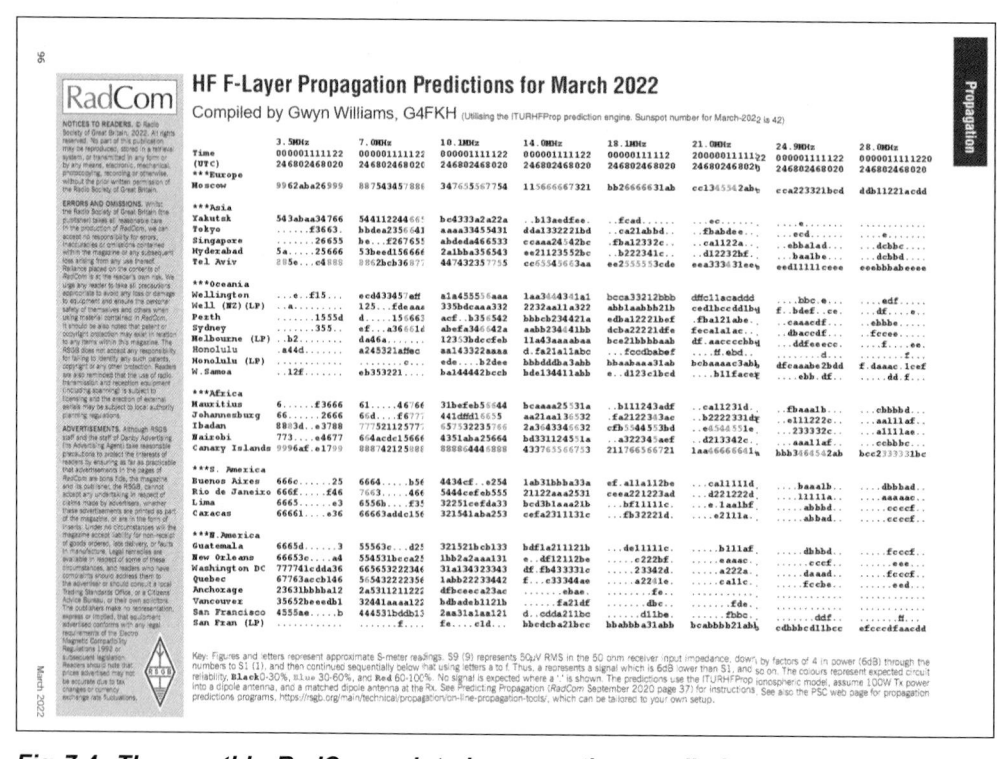

Fig 7.4: The monthly RadCom printed propagation predictions.

CHAPTER 7 – FINDING THE DX

PROPAGATION PREDICTIONS

No matter how good your knowledge of propagation and of what is likely to be heard on each band at any particular time, propagation predictions will be able to provide you with more information and thus increase your chances of working the DX.

For RSGB members, each month a page of propagation predictions is published in *RadCom*, **Fig 7.4**. They provide predictions from the UK for 28 locations around the world via short path (plus a few long-path predictions where appropriate), giving an indication of the probability of a path being open and a predicted signal strength, assuming 100 watts transmitter power and half-wave dipoles at both ends of the path. The *RadCom* predictions are fine as far as they go, but there are a few disadvantages. The first is that due to the time taken for the publication to be printed and then distributed to members, the predictions must necessarily be made several weeks before the calendar month for which they are intended. A predicted smoothed sunspot number is used, but this could be quite inaccurate by the time the propagation predictions are actually being used. The second issue is that they do only cover 28 world locations – what if you are interested in working the Falkland Islands or Barbados, neither of which are covered? Finally, the predictions do not take into account high-gain antennas (at either end of the path) or for modes such as FT8 which require a much lower signal threshold for successful QSOs to be made.

The *RadCom* propagation predictions are compiled by the RSGB's Propagation Studies Committee using the ITUR-HFPROP program. James Watson, M0DNS / HZ1JW, has created a web-based application that uses ITURHFPROP and which he calls 'Proppy' **[7]**, **Fig 7.5**. Using Proppy you can create your own interactive area predictions,

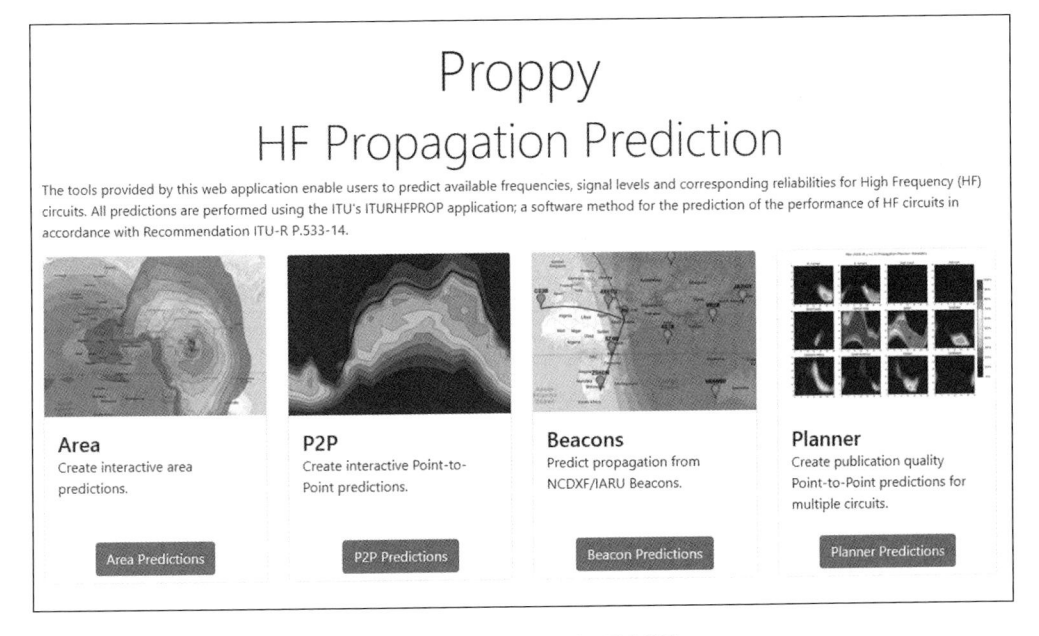

Fig 7.5: 'Proppy' by James Watson, M0DNS / HZ1JW.

HF DX BASICS

point-to-point predictions, predictions for the NCDXF / IARU beacons and point-to-point predictions for multiple circuits.

Steve Nichols, G0KYA, a member of the RSGB Propagation Studies Committee, has also created a web-based application called 'Short-Path Propagation from UK' **[8]**, **Fig 7.6**. This can be used to create prediction maps, **Fig 7.7**, based on the predicted smooth sunspot number for the month selected and 100 watts of CW to a dipole at 11m (35ft) high. The map in **Fig 7.7** shows the predictions for 7MHz during the month of October at 2100 – 2200UTC.

Short-Path Propagation from UK is based on the *HamCAP* program by Alex Shovkoplyas, VE3NEA. If you want to try it for yourself, HamCAP is freeware and it can be downloaded from **[9]**.

VOACAP, standing for Voice Of America Coverage Analysis Program, is a professional program which, as its name suggests, was developed for making coverage predictions for the US Gov-

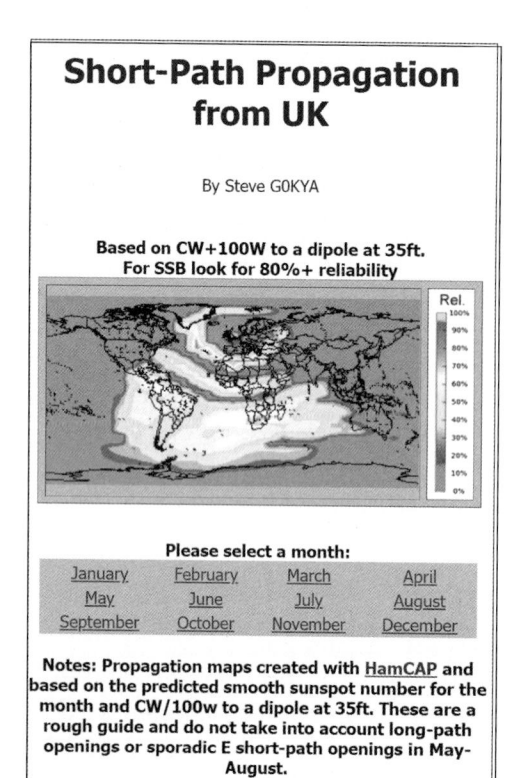

Fig 7.6: 'Short-Path Propagation from UK', by Steve Nichols, G0KYA.

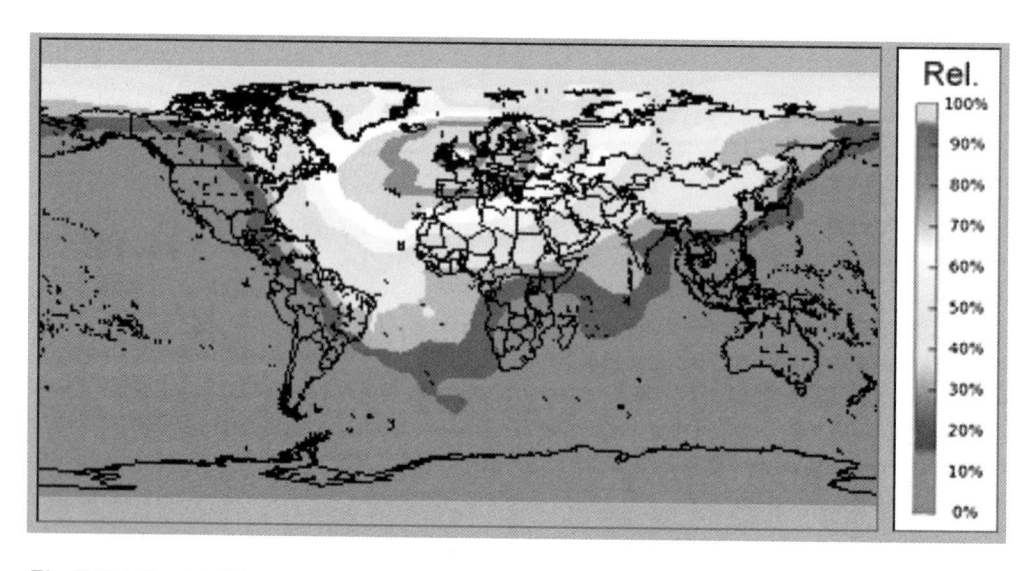

Fig 7.7: World-wide coverage prediction map made using G0KYA's 'Short-Path Propagation from UK' application.

CHAPTER 7 – FINDING THE DX

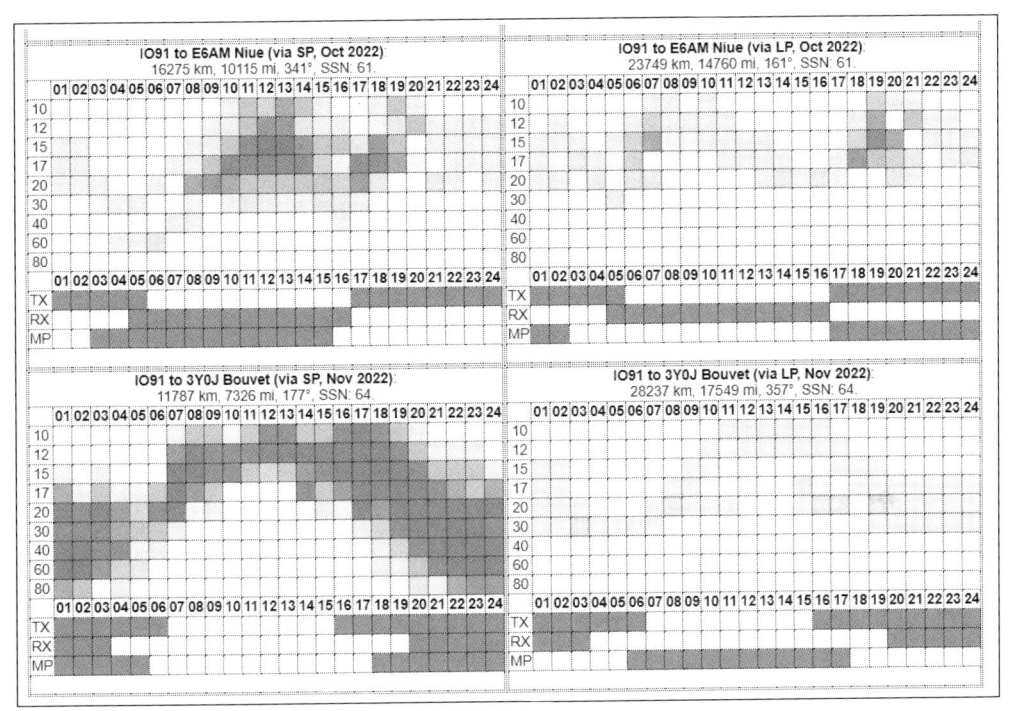

Fig 7.8: VOACAP 'DX Charts' propagation predictions for two of the planned DXpeditions in October and November 2022.

ernment's external radio broadcaster, the Voice of America.

As a professional program, it is quite complex to use, but a team led by Jari Perkiömäki, OH6BG / OG6G, has developed a simple user interface that harnesses the full power of VOACAP **[10]**.

One interesting feature of this development is the VOACAP DX Charts **[11]**, **Fig 7.8**, which provides ready-made predictions from your location to most of the major pre-announced future DXpeditions. By inputting your own grid reference and simply clicking the "Run!" button, short-path and long-path predictions are calculated for your own location to all the DXpeditions.

At the time of writing (early 2022) there are predictions for DXpeditions as far ahead as the W8S Swains Island operation, planned for March 2023 and still more than a year away. **Fig 7.8** shows the predictions from Grid locator IO91 (south-east England) to Niue (the E6AM DXpedition planned for October 2022) and to Bouvet Island (the 3Y0J DXpedition, originally planned for November 2022 but since rescheduled to January 2023).

Note that HF propagation prediction programs are precisely that: *HF* prediction programs, and results on 1.8MHz and 50MHz are not likely to be accurate, except at the peak of the solar cycle if there is F2 propagation on the 50MHz band (and perhaps not even then). For 1.8MHz and, to a lesser extent, also 3.5MHz the best guide to the likelihood of propagation is a set of sunrise and sunset tables, along with a check of the K-index (see '1.8MHz – 160-Metre Band' on page 74). Fortunately, sunrise and sunset times for every DXCC entity in the world,

HF DX BASICS

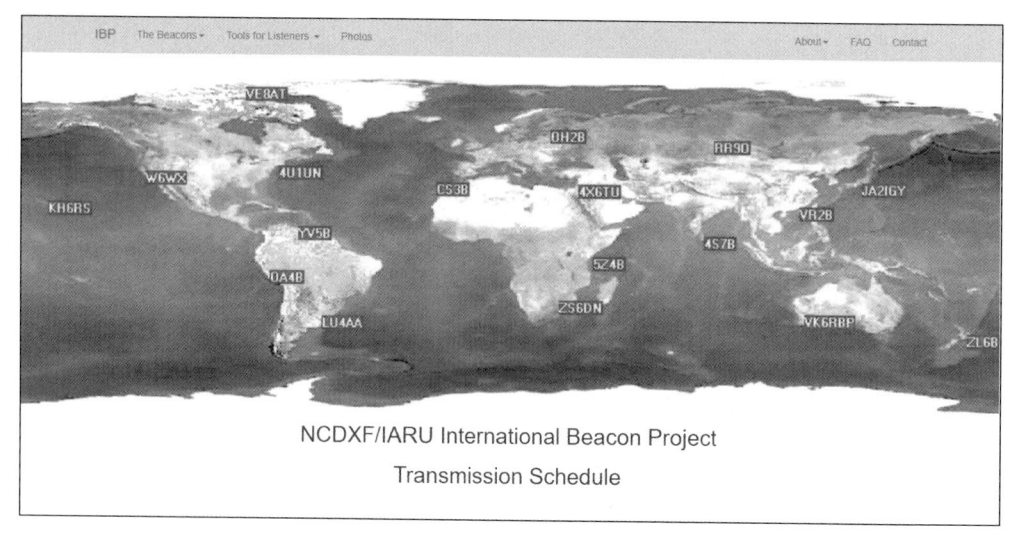

Fig 7.9: The NCDXF / IARU beacons transmit from 18 locations around the world.

updated daily, can also be found on the VOACAP website, at **[12]**.

The VOACAP website is well worth checking out, as there is a vast amount of other information on propagation also available on the site.

For real-time propagation information, the NCDXF / IARU International Beacon Project **[13]**, **Fig 7.9**, can give a good indication of how propagation actually is, compared with what was predicted, although there are only 18 locations around the world with beacons.

SUMMING UP

When you've worked out that propagation is likely to be favourable, it is a good idea to check what that means in terms of local time at the distant end. If it is a major DXpedition that you are chasing, they will probably be around whenever propagation is likely, whatever the time of day or night. But if it is a local amateur, on weekdays they will probably be at work and at night (their time) they will probably be asleep.

DXpeditions often stick close to specific frequencies. On SSB, 3795, 14145, 14185 – 14200, 18145, 21295, 24945, 28495 and 50110kHz are perhaps the most usual DXpedition frequencies while, as mentioned in Chapter 6, IOTA DXpeditions can often be found around 14260, 21260 and 28460kHz, although many expeditions assume that these days almost all DXers will have Cluster access and will therefore find them wherever they choose to operate.

From the UK, Pacific stations operating on SSB are often identifiable by having some 'flutter' on their signals, resulting from signals passing through the auroral zone. A local amateur, trying to avoid major pile-ups, might make a point of operating away from the more popular areas of the band, so may, for example, operate below 14150kHz or above 14300kHz on SSB. He may also take refuge in a DX net.

Operators' accents are important in alerting to you to a possible DX station. An Australian or Japanese accent is usually distinctive, while an American accent does not necessarily mean the station is in the USA: he could be in somewhere

CHAPTER 7 – FINDING THE DX

like Hawaii or Guam, or perhaps he is a missionary working in Africa or Papua New Guinea.

Often an immediate pointer to a rare DX station is the existence of a pile-up. This is bad news in a way, as it means you will be competing with others – and sometimes very many other stations. It is far better to be the first person to find a DX station, when he calls CQ.

There is an alternative, which is to call "CQ DX" yourself, but this tends not to be terribly productive unless you have a big signal. However, some DX stations will prefer to call others, rather than call CQ themselves, so as to avoid getting into a pile-up situation, so it is always worth a try.

REFERENCES

[1] DX-World: www.dx-world.net
[2] DXNews: www.dxnews.com
[3] 425 DX News: www.425dxn.org
[4] OPDX Bulletin: www.papays.com/opdx.html
[5] *The Daily DX* and *The Weekly DX*: www.dailydx.com
[6] DX Summit: www.dxsummit.fi
[7] Proppy by James Watson, M0DNS / HZ1JW: https://soundbytes.asia/proppy
[8] Short-Path Propagation from UK, by Steve Nichols, G0KYA: http://infotechcomms.co.uk/propcharts
[9] HamCAP by Alex Shovkoplyas, VE3NEA: www.dxatlas.com/hamcap
[10] VOACAP: www.voacap.com
[11] VOACAP DX Charts: www.voacap.com/dx
[12] Sunrise / sunset tables (VOACAP Greyline): www.voacap.com/greyline/index.html
[13] NCDXF beacons: www.ncdxf.org/beacon

Chapter 8

Working HF DX on SSB

Before attempting to work any DX stations on SSB it is worthwhile examining the quality of your own transmitted signal. In Chapter 4 several features of interest to be found in modern transceivers were discussed, whether you wish to use SSB, CW or data modes. But for the SSB operator, particularly SSB DXers, there are several parameters that need to be adjusted in order to make your SSB signal sound good. More to the point, these adjustments can also make the signal sound more 'punchy' – which is exactly what is required so as to be copied by DX stations when signal strengths are low.

In this section we will look at the ways in which you can have a superb-sounding SSB signal – and the ways in which you can destroy perfectly good audio and make it sound terrible (or rather avoid doing so).

Not so many years ago, you would buy your transceiver, plug in a microphone and antenna, switch on and start working the DX on SSB. You can still do that of course, but many modern transceivers offer a bewildering variety of features that need to be set up in order to get the best out of the set. Most of these are intended to tailor the transceiver to your particular operating habits, voice characteristics etc, and are 'set and forget' controls, i.e. once adjusted you will only rarely need to touch them again.

If you tune across the SSB part of any band you will hear signals which vary widely in quality, from the outstanding to the frankly dreadful. Why is there such a wide range of SSB sound quality? There could be many reasons: the transceiver itself, the microphone, whether or not the transmitter is being overdriven, speech processing, the width of the transmit filter, the transceiver's internal audio tailoring, the use of an outboard audio equalisation unit and so on.

In the same way that hi-fi audiophiles reckon that valve audio amplifiers always produce a better, more rounded, 'fuller-sounding' quality than newer transistorised amplifiers, so there are those amateurs who believe that old valve transmitters produce better-sounding SSB than their newer solid-state counterparts. There could be something in this, although the reason may have nothing to do with the use of valves but instead perhaps be because older transmitters tended to use wider SSB filters. Anyway, these days – unless you are going to home-build your own transmitter or transceiver using valves – there is no choice in the matter since all current HF SSB transceivers are solid state.

CHAPTER 8 – WORKING HF DX ON SSB

That is not to say that modern transistorised SSB transceivers all sound alike. The basic transmitted audio quality of transceivers does vary from manufacturer to manufacturer and even from model to model. Indeed, the ability to tailor the transmitted audio of many modern transceivers means that it is possible to make their transmission quality very poor if you do not know what you are doing – more on this later in the chapter. Nevertheless, most (though not all) transceivers allow for very good SSB speech quality if they are set up or adjusted sensibly.

Assuming the transceiver itself is capable of providing good quality transmitted audio on SSB, the first stage to look at is the microphone.

MICROPHONES

These days, microphones are generally supplied with new transceivers. Most manufacturers use dynamic microphones; the exception being Icom, which uses electret microphones for their transceivers.

The microphones that come with most transceivers can provide perfectly acceptable (although not usually outstanding) audio quality. In almost all cases, they are hand (or 'fist') microphones, with a press-to-talk (PTT) switch on the side, **Fig 8.1**. These are fine for casual operating, but their use becomes awkward if you are trying to adjust the controls on the transceiver at the same time as speaking, and especially if you use computer logging and are attempting to use a keyboard while talking.

An alternative is the desk microphone, but if anything their use is more awkward still, as it is rarely possible to have them at the correct height for speaking into if they are sitting on a desk as designed. As a result, most operators end up holding their desk mics, and these are always larger and heavier than the equivalent hand mic.

The stock mics supplied with the transceiver are not necessarily made by the equipment manufacturers themselves; in most cases they are OEM devices and simply 'badged' with the familiar names. Even when manufacturers use similar mics, the plugs are wired differently, so an otherwise almost-identical Yaesu mic cannot be used on a Kenwood transceiver, or vice versa.

In some cases these microphones, or the inserts in the mics, are not designed primarily for radio transmission use but instead for karaoke (a vast market, especially in the Far East), public address or paging announcements. Even when they *are* designed for radio, they might be intended for FM communications rather than SSB, where it is desirable to have a peak around 2kHz. Also, the mass production

Fig 8.1 Left: The Icom HM-219, an electret condenser microphone, as used with the popular Icom IC-7300 transceiver. Right: The Yaesu MH-31 dynamic microphone, as supplied with many Yaesu transceivers including the FT-857D.

HF DX BASICS

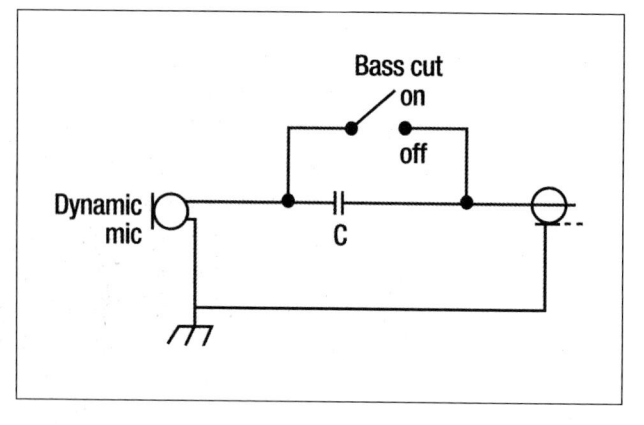

Fig 8.2: Adding a capacitor can decrease the bass response and improve the communications quality of a microphone.

allows the capacitor to be bypassed when necessary – see **Fig 8.2**. Not all mics (or voices) require this: depending on your own voice characteristics, the microphone used and the transceiver, you may well find that a stock microphone works well for you. I used a Kenwood TS-930S for many years and received nothing but positive comments on my transmitted audio when using the Kenwood MC-43S hand microphone.

techniques used to produce hundreds of thousands of microphones at a cheap price simply do not allow for the precision required for high-quality audio.

The result is that, on SSB, many stock mics tend to sound too bassy for the average Caucasian male voice. If your microphone is too bassy, one simple way of cutting its bass response is to put a capacitor between the mic itself and the mic socket on the transceiver. A switch

ALTERNATIVE MICS AND HEADSETS

Bob Heil, K9EID, worked as an audio engineer with many of the big name rock bands of the 1970s. When it came to amateur radio SSB operation he disliked the audio quality provided by many microphones, which he described as "mushy". He developed his own microphone insert, which can be used as a 'drop-in' replacement for many of the

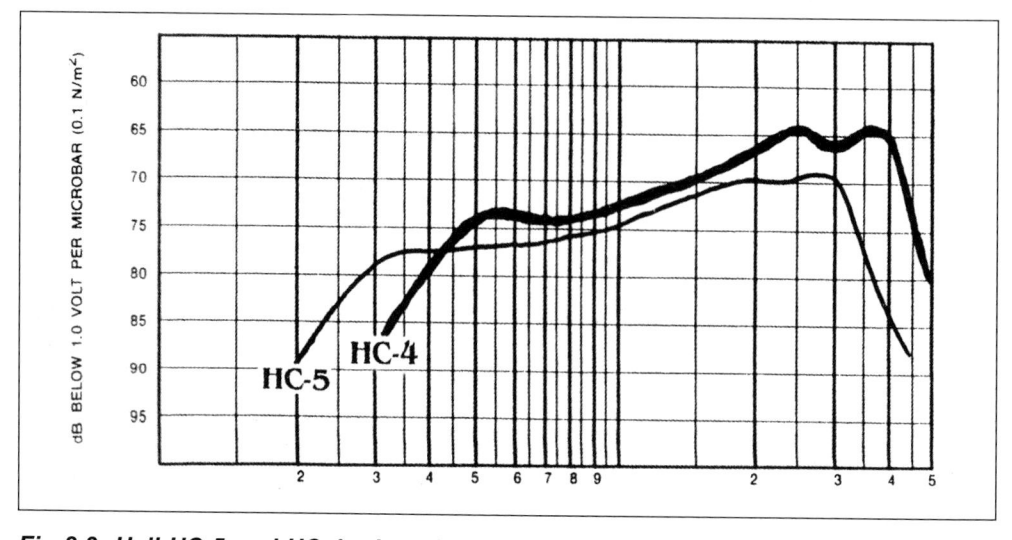

Fig 8.3: Heil HC-5 and HC-4 microphone elements' frequency responses.

CHAPTER 8 – WORKING HF DX ON SSB

stock dynamic microphones. The result was the Heil [1] HC-5, a ceramic microphone insert with an audio peak between 1.5 and 3kHz (+6dB at 2kHz), providing clear and 'pleasant' sounding audio quality with most voices. To cater for the DXer and contester, Heil also developed the HC-4 insert, which has a stronger peak than the HC-5 (+10dB at 2kHz), and at higher frequencies: between 2 and 4kHz. This provides 'toppy' sounding audio that is designed to really cut through the QRM. As Heil himself says, "not pretty sounding – but in your face extreme audio". It may not sound very attractive for local communications, but it is what is required for weak-signal DX working and contest operating. **Fig 8.3** shows the frequency responses of the HC-5 and HC-4 microphone elements.

Heil also developed a series of headsets – headphones with boom microphones attached – using either the HC-5 or HC-4 mic insert, **Fig 8.4**. These proved very popular with SSB operators and particularly among DXers, DXpedition operators and contesters because their use, with a footswitch replacing the PTT switch on the microphone, allowed both hands to remain free to use a computer keyboard for logging and to operate the transceiver (see the box 'Why Use a Headset?' below).

Fig 8.4: Well-known contest operator and YOTA enthusiast, Philipp Springer, DK6SP, using a Heil headset with HC-4 microphone.

WHY USE A HEADSET?

Most (though not all) transceivers come with a hand microphone, and most amateurs already possess at least one pair of headphones, so why buy a headset? Firstly, some stock microphones sold with transceivers tend to produce rather muffled, 'boxy' sounding audio and a headset microphone may well improve your transmitted audio quality. But even if you are perfectly satisfied with the audio from your hand microphone the added convenience of using a headset cannot be overemphasised. Using a headset frees up both hands for tuning or otherwise adjusting the transceiver and for logging, whether by computer keyboard or pen and paper. For those who have only ever used a loudspeaker to listen to signals, using the headphones in a headset will be a revelation. Whether using CW or SSB, it is so much easier to copy weak signals, or those suffering from interference, when using headphones compared with listening on a loudspeaker. I would go so far as to say that I know no-one using a headset who would voluntarily go back to using either a hand microphone or a loudspeaker when operating.

Fig 8.5: The W1 headset from US manufacturer INRAD.

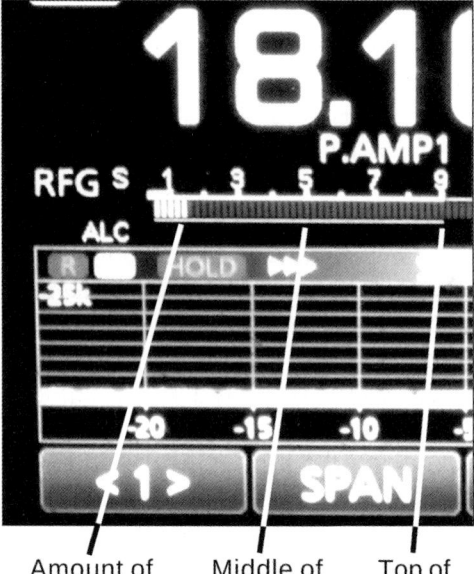

Fig 8.6: Close-up of Icom IC-7300 front panel display, showing the ALC meter.

There are, of course, many other manufacturers of headsets incorporating microphones. In addition to the Heil headsets I have also used a Yamaha CM500 headset with excellent results, although this particular model seems now to have been discontinued.

INRAD is a welcome new manufacturer from USA. I reviewed their W1 headset, **Fig 8.5**, in *RadCom* **[3]**.

ALC

No matter how good the microphone – or the transceiver for that matter – an SSB transmission can be rendered almost unintelligible simply by the transmitter being overdriven.

A good way to prevent this from happening is by always keeping one eye on the ALC (automatic level control) meter of the transceiver, **Fig 8.6**. In this example, the Icom IC-7300 meter display is showing ALC with a small amount of ALC deflection when transmitting. A deflection of up to roughly the middle of the ALC scale would be acceptable but if you exceed the top of the range shown on the ALC meter, your signal does not get any stronger, nor your audio any 'louder'. Instead your signal becomes distorted and wider, and so causes unnecessary interference to other stations operating close to your frequency.

TRANSMISSION AUDIO TAILORING

The advent of IF DSP has brought about the possibility of being able to tailor both the transmitted audio quality and the overall width and shape of the transmitted signal. Top-end transceivers and, increasingly now, mid-range ones too, normally

CHAPTER 8 – WORKING HF DX ON SSB

allow the operator to increase or decrease the relative level of the low, middle and upper range of frequencies of the audio chain.

Even some budget transceivers have a simple form of audio tailoring, be it a bass cut and / or top cut filter, which can be used to match more closely the operator's voice to the microphone used with the transceiver. The Yaesu FT-857 for example (a budget mobile transceiver and now a relatively old design), uses DSP to provide high cut (emphasising lower frequencies), low cut (emphasising higher frequencies) or high and low cut (emphasising mid-range frequencies). This provides a limited way of altering the frequency response of the transmitted audio by allowing you to roll off any excessively high or low frequency components in your voice.

Newer and more sophisticated mid to top-end transceivers, on the other hand, often provide a vast range of audio tailoring possibilities. Such equipment often has a 'parametric microphone equaliser' which allows the centre frequency of the low, middle and high range to be adjusted independently in (for example) 100Hz steps between 100Hz and 3200Hz. For each of the low, middle and high range of frequencies, the relative level can be adjusted up or down. The Q-factor (width) of each can also be adjusted. Together with the possibility of changing the actual bandwidth of the transmitted signal (see later), there are hundreds of thousands of possible permutations, all of which will make the transmitted audio sound a little different.

The bad news is that extreme settings will certainly make the audio sound extreme – extremely poor. Many operators adjust these settings only to come to the conclusion, after much time and effort, that the best-sounding audio is produced using the default settings – the ones the rig comes with out of the box!

If your transceiver does not have transmission audio tailoring built in, it is possible to buy outboard units to do the job. W2IHY Technology Inc [3], run by Julius Jones from Staatsburg, New York, produces a range of audio equipment for the SSB operator. The two best-known units are the '8 Band EQ' and the 'EQplus', **Fig 8.7**. The 8 Band EQ is an equaliser with eight slider controls to adjust the low,

Fig 8.7: The '8 Band EQ' and 'EQplus'. both by W2IHY Technology Inc.

mid and high components in the audio. It includes a noise gate to reduce background noise. The EQplus has dual band equalisation, a 'Downward Expander' for noise reduction and it includes a compressor and limiter to increase talk power.

Either can be used as a stand-alone unit or the two can be used together for greater flexibility. Both have a universal interface to allow the use of almost any microphone with any transceiver.

TRANSMISSION BANDWIDTH

Many newer transceivers also allow the operator to select the actual *bandwidth* of the transmitted SSB signal. The bandwidth of an SSB signal is normally around 2.4kHz, with audio frequencies of typically 300 – 2700Hz being transmitted.

Taking the Yaesu FT-2000 as an example, in addition to the default of 2.4kHz (300 – 2700Hz), a narrower setting of 2.2kHz (400 – 2600Hz) can be selected, or no fewer than four wider settings. These are 2.6kHz (200 – 2800Hz), 2.8kHz (100 – 2900Hz) and 2.95kHz (50 – 3000Hz), plus a special so-called 'hi-fidelity' setting whereby the transmitted bandwidth is in excess of 3kHz.

What is the effect of changing the transmitted bandwidth – what does the SSB signal actually sound like after these changes have been made?

The narrower setting of 2.2kHz limits the lowest audio frequency being transmitted to 400Hz and the highest to 2600Hz. This restricted bandwidth has been described as sounding like a tinny telephone line and most people tend to dislike the sound of the audio thus produced. For DXing, however, this may give a slight advantage in as much as none of the power is being 'wasted' in the audio frequencies below 400Hz, which do not contribute much to the intelligibility of the signal if the signal path is marginal. Arguably, another small advantage is that because all the available power (e.g. 100 watts) is concentrated into just 2.2kHz, instead of being spread out over 2.4kHz or more, the signal strength of the narrower signal will be slightly greater.

However, those operators who are able to adjust their transmitted bandwidth generally opt not for the narrower setting but for one of the wider ones. The change from the default 2.4kHz to a slightly wider 2.6kHz bandwidth provides a subtle change in the audio quality which many operators might prefer. It's true that it does provide 'smoother', more 'rounded', sounding audio, but it is less effective at cutting through interference than the 2.4kHz setting, so it is less use for DXers or contest operators. However, this might be considered a small price to pay for those operators who normally enjoy chatting with local or semi-local stations at good signal strength levels, and only occasionally chase DX stations or go in for contest operation. Besides, it is not a difficult operation to return the transceiver to its default setting when required.

Wide-band SSB is sometimes referred to as 'Extended SSB' ('eSSB'), but when does 'standard SSB' ('sSSB' perhaps?) become eSSB? John Anning, NU9N [4] is an enthusiastic advocate of eSSB transmission and by his definition it is any SSB transmission with a bandwidth of 3kHz or more. He explains, "The reason for this is that high-frequency audio from 3kHz and above starts to support a significant difference in clarity, 'openness' and fidelity of the audio signal that better reproduces natural energy found in the human voice. Even though vocal chord energy diminishes rapidly above 3kHz, the all-important high-frequency consonants of human speech such as the 'S', 'T', 'SH', 'CH', 'K' and 'Z' sounds that are formed with various combinations of the tongue, roof of the mouth and teeth are well above 3kHz. The accurate reproduction of these sounds is essential for high-definition speech with less listener fatigue." By NU9N's definition, the FT-2000's wider bandwidth settings of 2.6, 2.8 and 2.95kHz are not eSSB but simply wider than normal – though still standard – SSB transmissions.

It should be noted, though, that if the station receiving a wide-band 'hi-fi' SSB transmission is receiving it in a standard 2.4kHz bandwidth, any advantage will be lost; the receiver's bandwidth needs to be set to match the width of the transmitted signal. In practice this is easy to do with transceivers that use IF DSP for their filtering as there is likely to be a wide range of IF filter bandwidth settings available to the operator.

One problem, though, is that under crowded or noisy band conditions, opening up a receiver's bandwidth to 3kHz or greater is likely to let in adjacent-frequency interference as well as more local noise such as the pops and crackles that are, sadly, normal in most urban and suburban locations. So a wide-band 'hi-fi' SSB signal can really only be received under quiet band conditions and, preferably, with strong local signals (which begs the question "why not use FM on VHF or UHF instead?") It is certainly not a suitable method of transmission for SSB DXers (although using a wider bandwidth filter is actually useful for FT8 operating because many FT8 transmissions are up to 3000Hz above the standard suppressed-carrier 'dial' frequencies).

An audiophile's definition of 'hi-fi' would be accurately-reproduced audio over a bandwidth ranging from about 20Hz to 20kHz, so clearly no amateur SSB transmission can even approach true hi-fi quality. However, in relative terms, an SSB transmission which is 3kHz wide or greater is capable of reproducing the human voice more accurately than one restricted to just 2.4kHz, so there is some justification in using the term.

However, those who use eSSB should be aware that they may be accused of 'splattering' because their signal will indeed be somewhat wider than the majority of well-adjusted SSB transmissions on the band.

Those operators who wish to transmit eSSB usually do not stop at adjusting the transceiver, but also use wide-range broadcast-quality microphones and outboard audio processing equipment too, Behringer [5] being a particular favourite brand. The results can, no doubt, be astounding, but they can also be abysmal if the transceiver and peripheral equipment are not set up well. Unfortunately, some amateur radio operators appear to aspire to be 'broadcast announcers' with booming bass voices. Since they do not have a natural booming bass voice, they set their transceivers to the widest possible setting (as this increases the low frequencies transmitted as well as the high frequencies), then adjust the audio tailoring to emphasise the lowest frequencies possible. The result can be virtually unintelligible: on one evening I was called by a station whose signal strength was S9+20dB yet I could hardly understand a word being said. There was no 'top' or even middle element to his transmission, just a bass rumble each time he spoke. This is not what eSSB should be all about.

SPEECH PROCESSING

Those operators who only ever take part in local 'natter nets', where signals are S9 or more, may not want or need to use speech processing, but for all SSB DXers some form of speech processing or clipping is virtually essential. A *correctly set up* speech processor can increase the readability of the signal and increase your signal strength at the far end.

Almost all modern transceivers have a speech processor built in. It is a pity that speech processing has become something of a rude word among many operators, who therefore refuse to use this important and useful facility. The reason for this is that so many operators *abuse*, rather than use, speech processing, and overdrive their transceivers, causing distorted signals and splatter, which in turn causes unnecessary interference to other band users.

The trick is to learn how to use the speech processor properly – how to set the levels correctly, and then leave them alone.

In its simplest form, speech processing works by both *compression* and *limiting*, decreasing the dynamic range of the voice: the quieter sounds are made louder (decreasing or compressing the audio dynamic range) and the louder sounds are limited, so that they do not exceed a certain level.

Without a speech processor in circuit, the transceiver's microphone gain control would have to be set so that the loudest of speech peaks did not overdrive the transceiver, thus causing distortion and splatter. In an ideal world, the loudest speech peaks would equate to the transceiver putting out its maximum power, say, 100W PEP (100 watts peak envelope power). However, most of the speech

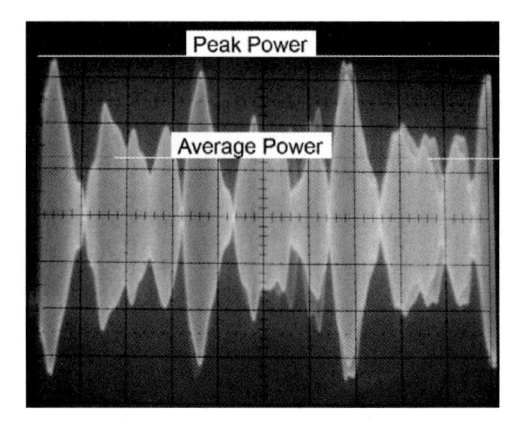

Fig 8.8: An SSB signal with a moderate amount of speech processing.

would be at a much lower level than this and therefore most of the time the transceiver would be radiating a *much* lower amount of power than 100 watts PEP. With the processor in circuit, the maximum speech peaks are limited so they do not overdrive the transceiver, but the quieter sounds are brought up much closer to this level.

Fig 8.8 shows an oscilloscope display of an SSB signal, with the average and peak power levels marked. When the speech processor is in circuit, the average power level of the transceiver is much closer to the maximum peak power output of the transceiver (i.e. 100W PEP in this example) than it is when the speech processor is not being used.

There are two main types of speech processing: AF and RF.

In AF speech processing, as the name suggests, the processing takes place at audio (voice) frequencies. One effective way to increase the average level of speech is by 'clipping', i.e. limiting the speech peaks to a certain level. Increasing the level of the signal going into the speech clipper has no effect on the output level but the *average* level increases,

CHAPTER 8 – WORKING HF DX ON SSB

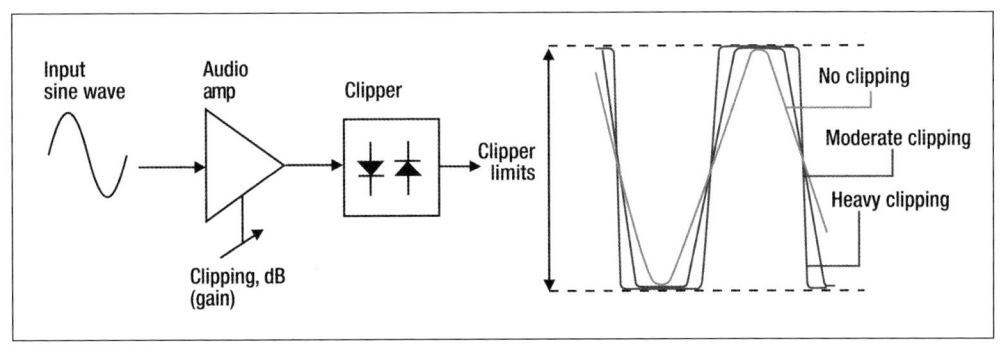

Fig 8.9: An audio speech clipper. The clipper stage limits its peak-to-peak output signal. The higher the gain ahead of the clipper, the more heavily clipped the output waveform will be.

as shown in **Fig 8.9**. The problem with this technique is that the clipping creates harmonics and mixing products which cause distortion to the audio. It is impossible to remove all of these harmonics by filtering them out, because some fall within the normal SSB bandwidth of about 300 – 2800Hz. For example, an important part of the human voice spectrum is around 500 – 1500Hz. There will be harmonics of the 500Hz part of the spectrum at 1000, 1500, 2000 and 2500Hz, while the harmonics of the 750Hz part of the voice will fall at 1500 and 2250Hz and so on. The 2250Hz harmonic will mix with the one at 1000 to produce a mixing product at 1250Hz. Meanwhile, the second harmonic of the 1000Hz part of the voice spectrum will be at 2000Hz and this will mix with the other harmonics. The net result of all the harmonics mixing is that the signal may sound 'loud', but it will also sound distorted – horribly so if the level of clipping or compression is set too high.

A simplified block diagram of an *RF speech clipper* is shown in **Fig 8.10**. With RF speech processing the audio is translated to much higher radio frequencies where the processing is done, and then translated back to audio. In this case, any harmonics generated by the clipping are at multiples of the RF frequency at which the clipping takes place and so can be removed with an SSB filter. It is these unwanted harmonics that cause the distor-

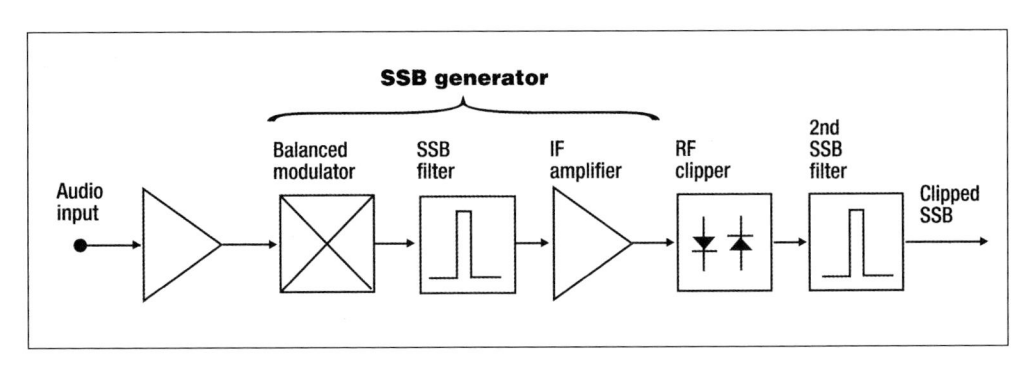

Fig 8.10: Block diagram of an RF speech clipper.

103

tion: remove them and the resulting signal sounds much 'louder' but without appreciable distortion.

For the reasons discussed, RF processing is superior to AF, although it has to be said that very satisfactory results can also be obtained by AF speech processors provided the amount of clipping is not too great. For a more detailed description of how speech clipping works, a very good article by Ian White, G(M)3SEK was published in *RadCom* **[6]**.

WORKING THE DX

So you're happy with the quality of headset or microphone, you've adjusted the ALC so as not to overdrive the transceiver, you've set the transmit bandwidth and adjusted the equalisation and speech processing so that you have a clear but 'punchy' signal.

Now, as you tune across the band, you hear a DX station on what appears to be a clear frequency, working stations that you can't hear. The temptation is to call him as soon as he ends a contact. Wrong, on several counts! The first thing is to determine what is going on. Spend a minute or two listening. It will pay dividends.

The chances are that the reason you can't hear the stations he is working is because he is operating split-frequency, in other words listening on a frequency other than the one on which he is transmitting. Assuming he is a competent operator, he will announce his listening frequency often. If he is operating split, this will dictate how and where you call him (see the section later, on split frequency operation).

Keep any call short: give your callsign just once, using recognised phonetics. If he is working quickly through a pile-up, don't give his callsign: he knows it already! By giving your callsign just once, you are helping everybody.

Let's say the DX station is E6ZZ on the small Pacific island of Niue. If you are the first station he hears, he will come back to you immediately and give you a report. For example:

Him: "Two Echo Zero Alpha Alpha Alpha, 59".
You: "Thanks, also 59"
Him: "QSL, Echo Six Zulu Zulu QRZ?"

. . . and away he goes with the next contact. If 2E0AAA had called twice his second call would just have slowed things down. Or if E6ZZ had responded to someone else's first call, 2E0AAA would just have been causing unnecessary interference. If E6ZZ had only heard *part* of 2E0AAA's callsign, no problem, the gaps can be filled on the next transmission:

Him: "Two Echo Zero Alpha, 59"
You: "Roger, Two Echo Zero Alpha Alpha Alpha, 2E0 Alpha Alpha Alpha, also 59"
Him: "QSL, Two Echo Zero Alpha Alpha Alpha. Echo Six Zulu Zulu QRZ?"

In this example 2E0AAA *did* give his callsign twice, because it was clear that the DX station was calling him and also clear that the DX station was having problems picking out full callsigns (probably due to the number of stations calling him). Also, if other stations were still calling, by giving their callsigns more than once, it is likely that 2E0AAA would have faced interference if he had only given his callsign once and so would have had to repeat again.

Some amateurs call with only a part

of their callsign, typically the last two letters, such as "Alpha Alpha". This is bad operating and seems to have originated because DX stations often respond with a partial call. That's not actually because they *want* partial calls, it's simply that that is all they have been able to hear through the pile-up. By coming back with at least a partial call, rather than calling "QRZ?" again, they can press on with the contact rather than wasting time, assuming there was only one station in the pile-up with "Alpha Alpha" in the call. Assuming, also, that everyone else takes the hint and stands by which, sadly, isn't always the case. But if you were only to send a partial callsign rather than your full call (quite apart from the licensing issues, whereby you are required to identify yourself when making "calls to establish contact with another amateur") you are wasting time. If you only send a partial call and the DX station only hears part of that, he may end up with just a single letter, which is of no use at all. And, if he hears you clearly, he will still require you to give your full callsign on the next transmission, so you may as well give it in full the first time round!

Don't slow things down with unnecessary requests of questions: if you want to know when the DX will be on another band, wait for him to announce that, or leave him on the loudspeaker while you do something else in the shack, and wait for him to close on that band and move to another.

It used to be the case that DX stations would announce their QSL information frequently but these days the QRZ.com website **[7]** has comprehensively taken over that role. Virtually every DX station, whether a resident operator or on a DXpedition, now has a QRZ.com entry and so it should no longer ever be necessary to ask a DX station for their QSL information.

If you are used to exchanging pleasantries with other amateurs, these brief exchanges with DX stations may seem rather impersonal, but because DXing is immensely popular and most DX stations want to give as many people as possible the chance to make a contact, it would be rude to keep the DX station chatting if there are many more people wanting to make a contact and are waiting for you to complete yours. That said, it can be the case that some resident DX operators get tired of the constant pile-ups and often *want* to have a chat, so the main piece of advice is always to take your cue from the DX station.

WORKING BY NUMBERS AND OTHER TECHNIQUES

If the pile-up gets very large, some DX operators may start 'working by numbers'. For example, he might call for "Only stations with Number One in the callsign". If he starts with One and you are an M0, it can be pretty frustrating to sit while he works his way through all the other numbers, but if callers step out of line all it does is slow things down and, in the extreme, the DX operator will give up and switch off.

I do not recommend the working by numbers technique, for several reasons. Firstly, as suggested, it does cause frustration among amateurs with the 'wrong' number in their callsign. It is particularly frustrating if, when you first tune in to him, he has just passed 'your' number. Secondly, it is unfair because some amateurs with two digits in their callsign get two bites of the cherry – a 2E0 could legitimately call when the DX station is asking for Number Zero and Number Two, whereas an M7 station does not have that luxury. Finally, and most importantly, propagation windows – especially to very distant stations – are often short and while you may have good propagation and be able to work the DX when you first hear him, if you have to wait 20 or 30 minutes before you can even make your first call, conditions could well have changed for the worse and you may have no chance of making the contact.

Nevertheless, if the DX station chooses to use this technique there is nothing you can do about it other than to wait your turn. Calling out of turn only causes even more frustration by other stations and potentially leads to an ill-disciplined free-for-all. If you call out of turn the DX station will probably not log you anyway.

If you only have a modest station you may find you're getting nowhere in calling the DX – despite doing all the right things. If that's the case you could try to be first on frequency the following day by looking for the DX station around the same frequency, but earlier. A look at the spots reported on DX Summit [8] will give a good indication of when the DX station is likely to be active.

If it is a big expedition, on the air for a week or two, you might just have to sit things out for a few days. As the number of callers diminishes towards the end of the operation there is always far less competition. Often DXpeditions, even to rare locations, have to call CQ and are said to be "begging" for callers towards the end of an operation.

But it is always worth hanging in there, as propagation may suddenly change and favour you, or the DX station himself, recognising that southern European stations (Italy, Spain, Portugal etc) have a clear propagation advantage over northern Europe, might switch the odds to your favour by announcing: "Please stand by everybody, UK only now" (or whatever).

However, decades of experience has shown that the best technique for handling pile-ups is *split frequency operation*, and so that deserves a section all to itself.

SPLIT FREQUENCY

If you hear a DX operator making plenty of contacts, but you can't hear the callers, the chances are that you are listening to a split-frequency operation.

Before calling any DX station on his own frequency, it's always worth listening for a while to determine whether he is working split: if you call him co-channel, you risk the wrath of others who have been waiting and who will almost certainly inform you of the error of your ways!

Most DXpeditions and many resident DX operators choose to operate split frequency. The concept is simple: by transmitting on one frequency and listening on another, callers can hear the DX station clearly, rather than through a mass of other callers, and therefore know when to go ahead with their contact and, more importantly, when to remain silent while another contact is taking place.

The DX station may choose to listen on a single spot frequency, or perhaps over a narrow band of frequencies in order to make it easier for the DX station to pick out an individual caller. If he chooses to listen on a single discrete frequency it is normally 5kHz higher than his transmitting frequency, although it could be as close as 3kHz (it should not be any closer than 3kHz, because stations calling less than 3kHz away would cause interference to the DX station and prevent others from

CHAPTER 8 – WORKING HF DX ON SSB

Fig 8.11: Jamie, M0SDV, operating split on a DXpedition.

hearing the DX well, which would defeat one of the purposes of the split frequency operation). In **Fig 8.11**, Jamie Williams, M0SDV, is listening 5 to 10kHz up while operating split on SSB as PJ4/M0SDV from Bonaire in 2018.

However, it could be that there are already other stations operating between 3kHz and 8kHz higher than the DX station's transmit frequency and if that is the case the DX obviously cannot listen 5kHz above his transmit frequency, because the stations calling would cause interference to the already-existing QSO. Instead, the DX station might nominate a frequency perhaps 10kHz higher than his transmit frequency if that is clear, or maybe 5kHz *lower* in frequency. As always, listen to the instructions from the DX station and follow his lead.

If there are very many stations calling the DX station, instead of listening on a single discrete frequency, he might choose to listen over a narrow band of frequencies, say 5 to 10kHz higher or, with a very large pile-up, 5 to 15kHz higher. Spreading out the pile-up over 5 or 10kHz makes it easier for the DX station to pick out individual callers.

Some operators, particularly those who are relatively inexperienced at DXpedition operating, find it very difficult to pick out an individual callsign when there are many calling, so instead of spreading the pile-up over 5 or 10kHz, they listen over a much wider range of frequencies. This is poor operating practice as it will certainly cause interference to other band users, causing resentment and in some cases even deliberate interference to the DX station (though this is never to be condoned).

Another poor operating technique on SSB is for the DXpedition operator simply to announce they are listening "up", but without specifying where up. This seems to be prevalent among those who are primarily CW operators but who are making an occasional foray on to SSB. On CW it is normal to operate split by listening just 1kHz up, but by sending "up" (as opposed to "up 1") on CW the DX station expects the pile-up to spread out over, say, 1 to 3kHz.

This technique does not work on SSB, though, as the pile-up is likely to be already calling 5 to 10kHz higher. By just saying "up" on SSB, in an attempt to call on a clearer frequency, stations will start calling first 11 or 12kHz higher, then if that fails, 14 or 15kHz higher and before long the DX station has an unnecessarily wide pile-up causing interference to other band users.

The DXpedition station should always announce their QSX (listening frequencies) if they are operating split, preferably after every QSO but certainly after every two or three QSOs. Unfortunately, not all do so as frequently as would be ideal. Failure to announce a separate listening frequency or frequencies causes stations to call the DX station on his transmit frequency, defeating one of the main objects of operating split in the first place.

Suppose a DX station is transmitting on 14195kHz and operating split. Typically he might say "listening on 14200" or "listening 5 to 10kHz up". Sometimes he might just say "five to ten", meaning 5 to 10kHz higher in frequency, or "two hundred to two-oh-five" meaning 14200 to 14205kHz.

A few moments listening before transmitting yourself should allow you to find the callers a DX station is working. Listen a little longer and you may also determine a listening pattern: does the DX station always respond to callers on the same frequency or does he listen a little higher up the band after each contact, finally dropping back down the band and starting the whole process anew?

Many DX operators only respond to callers sending their complete callsign so ensure you always send the complete call and *not* just the last two letters.

Unless the DX station is specifically taking 'tail enders', i.e. stations who call as the previous contact is coming to an end, never call over the top of a contact in progress but wait until the DX station signs and calls "QRZ?" or similar. Listening pays dividends, compared with simply calling at random. This is how experienced operators running low power can often get through more quickly than less experienced operators running high power.

Some DX stations deliberately try to favour more attentive callers, for example by suddenly announcing a spot listening frequency elsewhere in the band. If you're on the ball you can move there, call and work him, while others are still calling on the original frequency. DXpedition operators from continental Europe sometimes make a brief announcement in their own language, which is often an invitation for their compatriots to call on a specific frequency. If you can understand enough of that language to work out what frequency the DX station is listening on, you may find yourself only competing with, say, Dutch or Norwegian stations and not the whole of Europe!

HOW TO OPERATE SPLIT

If a DX station is working split, what should you do? If your transceiver only has a single receiver you would need to utilise the transceiver's two VFOs, one to receive (on the DX station's frequency – let's call this one VFO A) and the other to transmit (on what you *hope* will be the DX station's receive frequency – VFO B). Just about every transceiver available today has twin VFOs, so this technique can be used with any transceiver.

The difficulty is that when the DX station is listening not on one discrete frequency, but over a range of frequencies, you will not know on which frequency you should be transmitting in order for the DX station to hear you. You can of course listen on VFO B to hear who is calling the DX station, but when you are listening to VFO B you cannot hear what is happening on VFO A, i.e. the DX station himself.

What is required is for A and B not to be two VFOs, but rather completely separate and independent receivers. Using stereo headphones, you can then listen either to RX A or RX B, or you can listen to RX A (the DX station) in your left ear, and RX B (the pile-up) in your right ear. When you hear the DX respond to a particular station, if you can use the second receiver to find that station, you know that

CHAPTER 8 – WORKING HF DX ON SSB

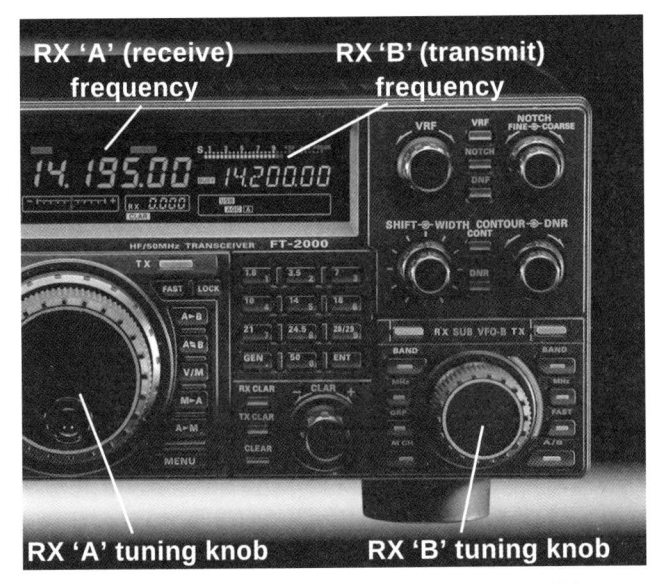

Fig 8.12: With RX 'A' on 14195kHz and RX 'B' on 14200kHz, this transceiver is ready to go on split frequency operation.

that is the frequency the DX station is listening on. When the QSO is completed (and only then, not before) you can call with the knowledge that, for that moment at least, the DX station is listening on that frequency. The technique is illustrated in **Fig 8.12**. It gives those operators with dual receivers a distinct advantage over those who only have twin VFOs. Unfortunately, very many operators now have transceivers with dual receivers and the advantage is not as great as it once was, as the majority of stations calling the DX may well be using the same technique!

The second receiver can still help, though. If you can hear that almost everyone is calling on the same frequency, the chances are the DX station will find it difficult to pick out a callsign from the *mêlée*. Using your second receiver, you might be able to find a frequency that is relatively clear of others calling, though still within the range of receive frequencies announced by the DX station. If you call on this frequency, it is likely that the DX station will hear you more clearly than if you were to try to battle it out with everyone else.

An alternative to twin receivers is a facility known as 'dual watch'. Here the audio from the transceiver's two receivers is combined, with separate AF gains or a balance control adjusting the relative volume of audio from each frequency, although there is no facility to hear the two receivers simultaneously but separately. There is a danger in a DXpedition station using dual watch to monitor his own frequency when working split, though. Because the audio from the two receivers is combined, the DX station cannot tell which of the two frequencies a station is calling on. If the DX should respond to someone who has called on his transmit frequency, it will soon lead to chaos as other callers will take this as their cue also to call on that frequency.

NETS AND LIST OPERATIONS

Many nets are associated with a particular organisation such as a local radio club or the Royal Signals Amateur Radio Society, but in this section we look at nets and lists specifically run for the purpose of enabling participants to work DX.

It should be noted that some DXers consider nets and lists to be a form of cheating, in that you are enlisting the help of a third party (the Master of Ceremonies, or MC) to run the operation and keep other stations at bay while you make your call to the DX station.

DX nets meet on (or near: a DX net has no more right to the use of a particular frequency than any other amateur) frequencies that are usually well-publicised, and at regular times. Usually, at the beginning of the net, the MC will ask for DX check-ins, then other check-ins will be called. The MC will then go round each of the participants in turn, asking them if they wish to call any of the DX stations. When your turn comes, make the call and complete the contact as efficiently as possible, and hand back to the MC. There may well be a lot of sitting around waiting your turn, but when things work well it means you don't have to compete with other amateurs (potentially running higher power) all calling at the same time.

The participants in the DX net will know the callsign of the DX stations who have checked in (although this is no different than being alerted to the presence of a DX station by monitoring the Cluster), but under no circumstances should the MC or any other participant 'help' a contact to take place by giving the full callsign of the participant to the DX station, or by

---

PITFALLS – WORKING DX ON SSB
Beware of the following pitfalls when chasing DX

1. *Always* use phonetics when calling a DX station. Try alternatives (such as "Mexico" instead of "Mike") if there is difficulty in understanding the standard phonetics, but *don't* use 'funny' phonetics.

2. *Never* call a DX station using only the last two letters of your callsign. *Always* send your complete call.

3. Only send your callsign *once* when making an initial call to a DX station. Should he *clearly* be responding to you, but has only received part of your callsign, you could then send your callsign twice if interference etc makes this necessary, perhaps using different phonetics the second time.

4. *Don't* repeat your callsign if the DX station already has it correctly. This only makes him doubt that he had it correctly the first time, especially if copy is marginal.

5. If the DX station responds to someone other than you, do *not* call again until he has completed that contact.

6. Beware of 'continuous calling': *only* call a DX station when he is listening for new callers (e.g. after saying "QRZ?")

7. If a DX station is operating split, *never* transmit on the DX frequency.

8. *Don't* ask a DX station for QSL information or similar information. Such details will invariably be on QRZ.com

9. *Never* append /QRP ("stroke QRP") to your callsign: the DX station does not need to know your power level, only your callsign.

10. In a DX net or list operation *never* 'help' a participant by relaying information such as callsigns or signal reports.

11. Jargon such as "The personal is..." or (even worse) "The personal would be..." (instead of "My name is...") is considered poor operating. Use standard English wherever possible. The use of widely-recognised Q-codes such as QSL, QTH, QSO, QRX etc is of course acceptable and even encouraged in contacts with those whose first language is not English.

CHAPTER 8 – WORKING HF DX ON SSB

relaying a signal report in either direction.

Lists are similar to nets, but tend to happen more spontaneously. Let's suppose a station appears from a rare entity, but using low power and a simple antenna. The demand for the station is such that, whenever he goes on the air, he is swamped by callers. He tries the obvious solution and operates split frequency (see previous section), but his signal isn't strong enough to compete with those causing interference on his own frequency and his rate of making contacts falls almost to zero. What he may do is to ask one of the stronger, better-equipped, stations to "make a list". He will take maybe 10 callers at a time, then indicate when each should call.

One problem with list operations and DX nets is that, due to propagation characteristics, the MC will pick up stations that have a strong signal with *him*, but which may have marginal or no propagation to the DX station they are trying to contact. At the same time, there may be many amateurs in a different part of the world that can copy the DX station well, but which are too weak with the MC to get on the list. Thus a lot of time is wasted by stations giving RS 33 reports to the DX station and struggling to receive the sent signal report while many stations who can copy the DX station well are not given an opportunity to make a contact at all.

LOW-POWER / QRP DXING ON SSB

Having a modest station should not preclude anyone from chasing DX and QRP DXing has been a growth activity recently. The GQRP Club [9] has a loyal following and the club has published many designs for home-built QRP transmitters and transceivers, several of which are also featured in the *QRP Scrapbook* [10].

What, precisely, is meant by the term 'QRP', though? It is generally taken to mean an output power level of 5 watts or less, although many increase this limit to 10 watts PEP output for SSB transmissions. (Note, though, that the definition of QRP for the *CQ* World Wide DX Contests is that the "total output power must not exceed 5 watts" – even on SSB.)

Until fairly recently there were few commercial designs developed specifically for QRP operation (though most transceivers can have their power reduced to QRP levels when required). However, in recent years a number of QRP transceivers have come on the market and have proved popular with QRP enthusiasts who enjoy trying to work DX at low power levels. These include the Icom IC-705 (**Fig 8.13**), the Yaesu FT-818ND, the Elad FDM-Duo and the Elecraft KX3 (**Fig 8.14**). The Chinese manufacturer Xiegu is a new player in the market and, so far, all their products are low-power: the X5105 is a 5-watt HF plus 50MHz SDR transceiver and the X6100 a 10-watt version. Both have built-in automatic ATUs.

QRP DXing is certainly harder than DXing with high power and requires more patience, particularly when using SSB. It

Fig 8.13: The Icom IC-705 has become a popular transceiver for DXers who use QRP.

Fig 8.14: The Elecraft KX3 transceiver has become a firm favourite among QRP DXers.

is perhaps more suited to experienced DXers who want a new challenge but those with limited-power licences should not be discouraged from chasing DX. It's not transmitter power, as such, that is relevant but the combination of that and antenna gain. So a UK (or Australian) Foundation licensee using 10W PEP output to an antenna with a 10dBi gain antenna (by no means impossible on HF when ground gain is also taken into account) will actually be *more* effective than a Full licensee running 100W output to a lossy trapped vertical or similar antenna.

There is plenty that can be done to maximise your chances of QRP DX success. For example, be active in the major DX contests, whether you consider yourself a contester or not. The bands will be full of activity, including plenty of DX stations, so the chasers won't all be after just one DX station. They will be scattered throughout the bands, divided between lots of DX stations to chase. So you shouldn't have so much competition, especially if you wait until well into the contest, for example the second day of a 48-hour event.

Also, the major DXpeditions set out to ensure that they work not only the best-equipped DXers, but also those with more modest stations. They recognise that many amateurs have restrictions on the sort of stations they can put together, but nevertheless want to participate in the DX game. The biggest DXpeditions will have round-the-clock operation on all bands with good antennas and will be on the air long enough to work their way through all the strongest callers and be left with more than enough time to ensure that QRP stations can also be worked.

Although QRP DXing may require more perseverance, remember that it is the QRO (high-power) station being called who is the one that has to have the receiving skills and equipment ("good ears"), as well as the patience, to pick out the weak QRP signal. Bear in mind that if a low-power station, running, say 10W PEP output on SSB, is only hearing a DX station running 1kW (legal in many countries although not the UK) at S8, then the high power station will only receive the QRP station at about S1, which will probably be below his local noise level (there is a 20dB difference between 10W and 1000W and, assuming 3dB per S-unit, S1 to S8 is a difference of 21dB). If a QRP operator is only receiving a high-power station at S6 or so, there is probably little likelihood of being heard at all. On the other hand, if the QRO station is being received at S9+20dB the QRP station might well be heard at S9.

A couple of final comments. Firstly, it isn't considered legitimate to call with high power to attract the attention of the DX station and then to drop to QRP to conduct the exchange of signal reports. Secondly, don't append "/QRP" to your callsign when calling stations. In the UK it is against licence conditions, as the only allowable suffixes are /A, /P, /M and /MM, but it is also counter-productive. Your time is better spent giving your callsign. If you want to chase DX as a QRP enthusiast, you have to be prepared to join in with everyone else and take your chances.

DX CODE OF CONDUCT

The 'DX Code of Conduct' **[14]** was developed as far back as 1997 in an attempt to improve the poor operating standards of some amateurs when calling DXpeditions (see the boxed text below).

It could be argued that after a quarter of a century it has not had very much effect and there are those who consider one or two of its items to be rather patronising. Nevertheless, it makes some important points that cannot be argued against and, if all DXers were to adhere to the

---

THE DX CODE OF CONDUCT

1. I will listen, and listen, and then listen again before calling.
2. I will only call if I can copy the DX station properly.
3. I will not trust the DX cluster and will be sure of the DX station's call sign before calling.
4. I will not interfere with the DX station nor anyone calling and will never tune up on the DX frequency or in the QSX slot.
5. I will wait for the DX station to end a contact before I call.
6. I will always send my full call sign.
7. I will call and then listen for a reasonable interval. I will not call continuously.
8. I will not transmit when the DX operator calls another call sign, not mine.
9. I will not transmit when the DX operator queries a call sign not like mine.
10. I will not transmit when the DX station requests geographic areas other than mine.
11. When the DX operator calls me, I will not repeat my call sign unless I think he has copied it incorrectly.
12. I will be thankful if and when I do make a contact.
13. I will respect my fellow hams and conduct myself so as to earn their respect.

code of conduct, the sometimes poor operating standards witnessed when a major DXpedition is on the air would be a thing of the past.

REFERENCES

[1] Heil Sound: https://heilhamradio.com
[2] 'INRAD W1 Headset' (review), Steve Telenius-Lowe, PJ4DX, *RadCom*, January 2020, pp24 – 25.
[3] W2IHY Technologies: ww.w2ihy.com
[4] Extended SSB (eSSB), John Anning, NU9N: www.nu9n.com
[5] Behringer audio equipment: www.behringer.com
[6] 'Loud and Clear' ('In Practice'), Ian White, G3SEK, *RadCom*, May 2003.
[7] QRZ.com website: www.qrz.com
[8] DX Summit: www.dxsummit.fi
[9] QRP Club: www.gqrp.com
[10] *The QRP Scrapbook*, compiled and edited by Steve Telenius-Lowe, PJ4DX, RSGB 2019, available from: www.rsgbshop.org
[14] DX Code of Conduct: dx-code.com

Chapter 9
FT8 and DXing on FT8

FT8 is the new digital transmission mode that has revolutionised amateur radio operating, and particularly DXing. Developed in 2017 by Joe Taylor, K1JT, and Steve Franke, K9AN, FT8 was released as part of a suite of open-source programs called WSJT ('Weak Signal Joe Taylor'). The latest version is known as *WSJT-X* and it also includes FT4 plus other data mode programs that are aimed at those interested in specialist weak-signal working on the LF, VHF and UHF bands. In this chapter we will also discuss FT4 as that is also becoming a very popular mode for HF DX working.

To operate FT8 / FT4 you will need a normal SSB transceiver, a computer and, unless your transceiver has a built-in sound card, you will also need an interface unit such as those in **Fig 9.1** between your transceiver and computer.

There are several programs which include FT8 (and other weak-signal modes) and all are available as free downloads:

WSJT-X is at **[1]**, *JTDX* by Igor Chernikov, UA3DJY, and Arvo Järve, ES1JA, is at **[2]** and *MSHV* by Christo Hristov, LZ2HV (**Fig 9.2**) is at **[3]**.

The program I use is JTDX but the user interfaces are similar as can be seen in

Fig 9.2: Christo Hristov, LZ2HV, the developer of the MSHV program (source: LZ2HV website).

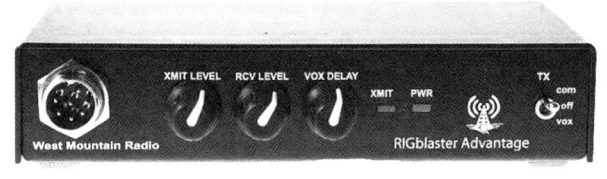

Fig 9.1: Two types of interface suitable for FT8 – left: RIGblaster from West Mountain Radio, right: the Tigertronics SignaLink.

HF DX BASICS

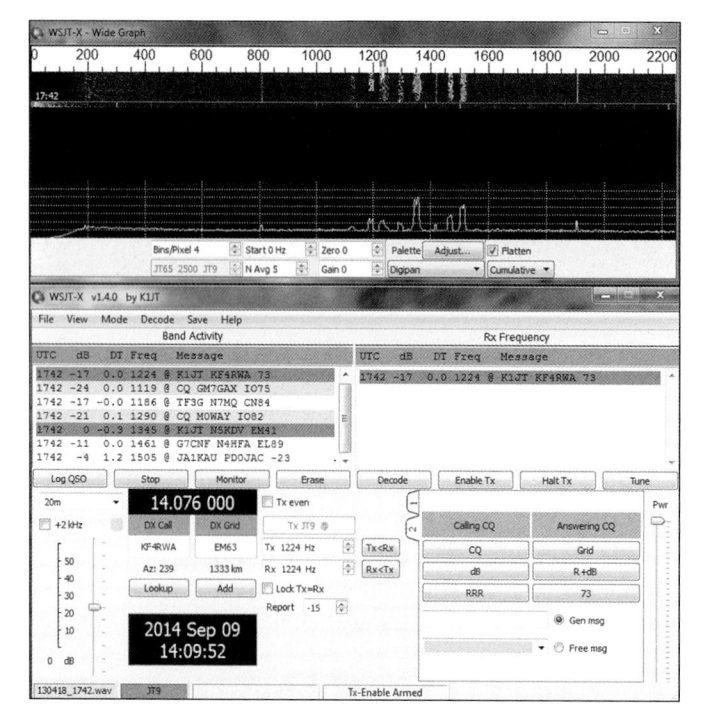

Fig 9.3: FT8 screenshot from WSJT-X program (source: WSJT-X website).

Fig 9.3, Fig 9.4 and **Fig 9.5** and, other than occasional references specific to JTDX, the information in this book is relevant to any FT8 program.

FT8 allows the barest minimum of information in order to complete a contact between two stations – that is, an exchange of callsigns, an exchange of signal reports and confirmations of receipt of the reports. Sometimes, though not always, the stations' four-character Grid locators (e.g. IO91 or FK52) are also exchanged.

WHY USE FT8?

With such a limited exchange of information pos-

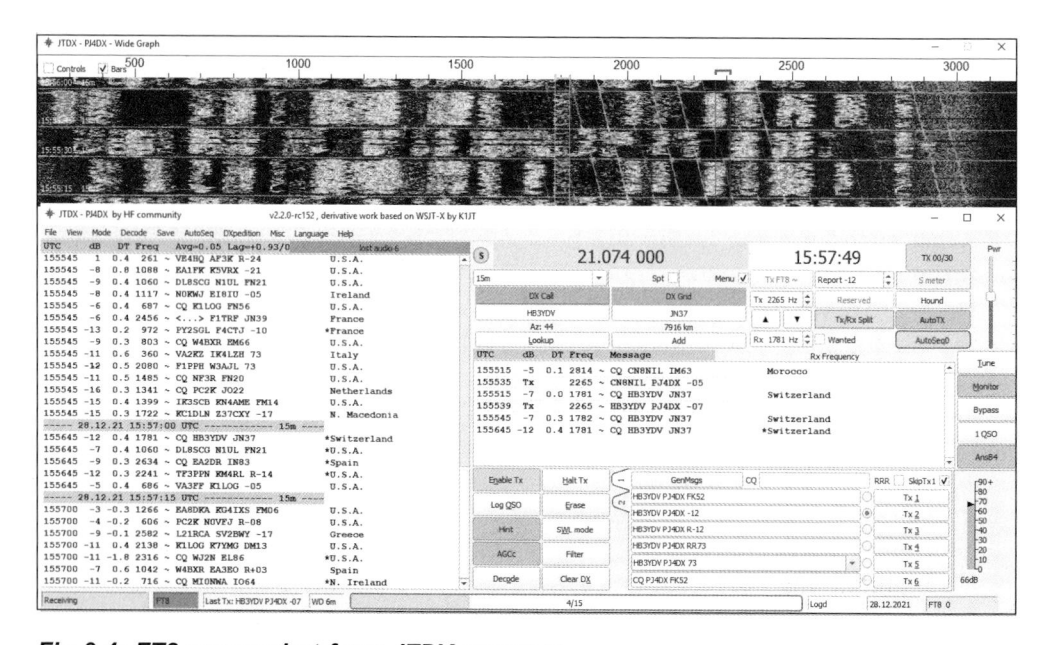

Fig 9.4: FT8 screenshot from JTDX program.

CHAPTER 9 – FT8 AND DXING ON FT8

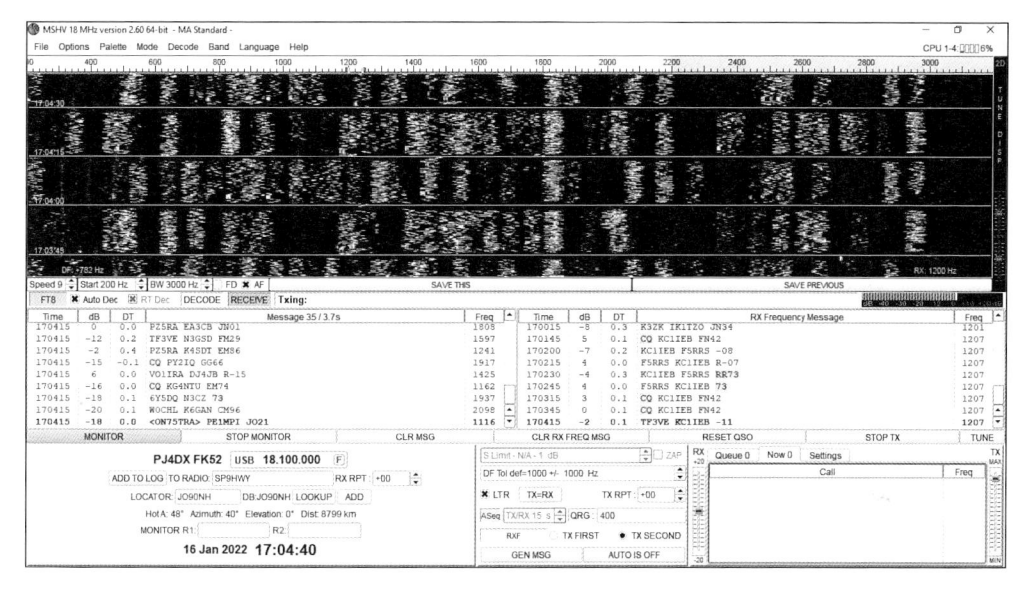

Fig 9.5: FT8 screenshot from MSHV program.

sible it could be asked why anyone would want to use FT8, as opposed to (for example) SSB? There are numerous reasons: here are a few, in no particular order:

● FT8 allows signals to be decoded to a level below one's band noise, making it possible to complete contacts on FT8 that would be quite impossible on SSB or even CW.
● As a result of the above, it allows contacts to be made by those who have limited antenna possibilities, for example those refused planning permission for an external antenna or those living in flats who have to use indoor antennas.
● It makes it possible for amateurs who only use low power (either because they only *wish* to use low power, or due to interference problems or licensing restrictions) to make DX contacts.
● It is therefore an ideal mode of transmission for UK Foundation licensees, restricted to 10 watts.

● Intercontinental contacts are possible throughout the solar cycle – DX contacts can be made on FT8 even at solar minimum when signals would be too weak on SSB or CW.
● FT8 is incredibly popular: many DX stations now use FT8 and no other mode, so FT8 is now "where the DX is". This is particularly the case on both 5MHz and 50MHz and, to a lesser extent, also on 1.8MHz.
● There is no language barrier. Propagation permitting, you can make a contact with a radio amateur in China who speaks no English whatsoever just as easily as one in Australia or New Zealand with English as his mother tongue.
● Even those fluent in languages are sometimes 'mic shy': FT8 allows them to make contacts without having to use a microphone.
● It allows radio amateurs who are profoundly deaf, or who are unable to speak, to make contacts.
● It's strangely addictive!

HF DX BASICS

Those are some of the 'pros'. There are, of course, also a few 'cons':

- There is little human involvement: it is computer-to-computer communications, so some people would argue that "it's not a proper QSO".
- Only a minimum exchange of information is possible (some DXers might consider this a pro rather than a con!)
- The very fact that DX contacts can be made by limited licensees, running low power and with poor antennas, provides no incentive for them to upgrade to higher licence classes or to install better antennas.
- It's slow. This is of no real concern to the average amateur but those on DXpeditions, attempting to make as many contacts as possible, would make far more QSOs on either SSB or CW. (However, there are ways and means to speed up DXpedition contacts as we shall discuss later.)
- It's boring! (This is the counter-argument to "it's strangely addictive": some feel one way, some the other.)

If you think the pros outweigh the cons, it is time to download one of the data mode programs: see [1, 2, or 3].

SET-UP AND CONFIGURATION

Follow the installation instructions provided on the download website of your choice and you should see a screen similar to that in **Fig 9.6**.

JTDX has an online 51-page *User Guide* [4] to help and there is plenty of useful documentation for the other programs on their websites as well as on *YouTube*.

After downloading the program you will need to configure it. The minimum information you need to provide is your callsign, your Grid locator and rig control information. If you do not need an external interface, because your transceiver has a built-in sound card, this is the type of transceiver which can be selected from a drop-down list, or you could select your logging program. Along with numerous others I use an Icom IC-7300 for FT8 work and therefore no interface is necessary: the IC-7300 is connected directly to the computer using a standard USB cable.

FT8 TRANSMISSIONS

The recognised FT8 and FT4 frequencies in the bands from 1.8 to 50MHz are shown in **Table 9.1**.

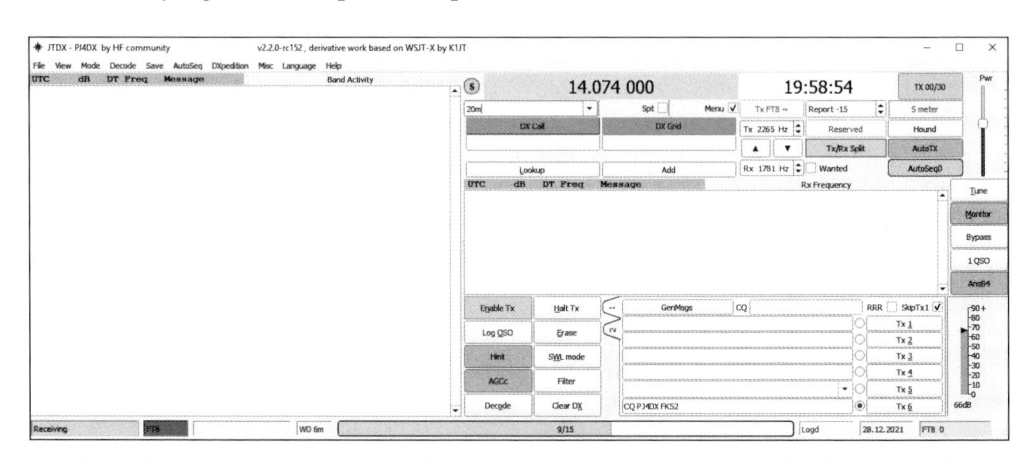

Fig 9.6: FT8 opening screen (in this case JTDX: WSJT-X and MSHV are similar).

CHAPTER 9 – FT8 AND DXING ON FT8

Band	FT8 (MAIN)	FT8 (SECONDARY)	FT4
	---------- Frequencies in kHz ----------		
160m	1840	–[1]	–[2]
80m	3573	3567 3585	3575[3]
60m	5357[4]	5126[5] 5362[6]	–[7]
40m	7074	7056 7071 7080	7047.5
30m	10,136	10,131 10,143	10,140
20m	14,074	14,071 14,090 14,095	14,080
17m	18,100	18,095	18,104
15m	21,074	21,091	21,140
12m	24,915	24,911	24,919
10m	28,074	28,095	28,180
6m	50,313 50,323	50,310	50,318

Notes:

[1] There is no recognised Secondary FT8 frequency on 160m.
[2] There is no recognised FT4 frequency on 160m but 1843kHz is recommended for use in RSGB FT4 contests).
[3] 3576, 3579 and 3582kHz are recommended for use in RSGB FT4 contests.
[4] In the UK, available to Full licensees only. Tone frequencies must be *lower than* 950Hz so that the entire transmission falls within the UK allocation of 5354 – 5358kHz.
[5] Not for use in the UK.
[6] In the UK, Full licensees only.
[7] There is no recognised FT4 frequency on 60m.

Table 9.1: The recognised Main and Secondary FT8 frequencies and recognised FT4 frequencies on each band from 1.8 to 50MHz.

Audio Tones

FT8 transmissions are made using an SSB transmitter. The SSB filter bandwidth is approximately 2.8kHz wide, from about 200Hz to 3000Hz.

An FT8 transmission consists of eight audio tones spaced 6.25Hz apart. An FT8 signal is therefore 50Hz wide and it can be placed anywhere in that 2.8kHz bandwidth. For example "1000Hz tones", means the tones are at 1000 to 1050Hz above the nominal FT8 frequency (because upper sideband is used). Therefore if a station is operating FT8 on 14074kHz but with, say, "2300Hz" tones, his transmission is actually between 14076.3 and 14076.8kHz. That is why you may see stations using FT8 being 'spotted' on the DX Cluster on frequencies which are listed up to 3kHz above the standard FT8 transmitting frequency.

Timing

An FT8 transmission is 15 seconds long, from 00 to 15, 15 to 30, 30 to 45 or 45 to 60 seconds in each minute. Each 15-second transmission alternates with a 15-second receive period. The transmit sessions are known as 00/30 ('Even' or 'First') or 15/45 ('Odd' or 'Second').

It is essential that the computer clock is synchronised with Internet time. Your computer's internal clock is not accurate enough: even as little as a one-second error will cause troubles with FT8 decodes.

To synchronise the computer clock, you should download a program such as *Dimension 4* [5] or the *Network Time Protocol* [6] if not already running in the background on the PC. Both have been downloaded many millions of times and they keep the world's computers synchronised with Internet time.

COMPUTER REQUIREMENTS

Until quite recently I used an old HP laptop with a 1.6GHz processor, 4GB of RAM and a hard disk drive (HDD) for FT8 operating. This worked (I made contacts with 218 DXCC entities on it using FT8 and FT4 during 2021), but experience has since shown that it was rather marginal.

I later changed to a machine with a 2.4GHz i5 processor and 8GB of RAM. This has made a massive difference: previously I could only decode around 25 stations during a 15-second receive period. Now, with the higher-specification PC, I am regularly decoding 50, 60 or occasionally even more stations, and down to a lower signal level too.

That said, for optimum FT8 decoding Kees van Zuilen, PA7TWO / M5TWO (one of the developers of JTDX), recommends a minimum of 16GB RAM (and preferably 32GB) with a 2.4GHz i7 processor and a fast solid state drive (SSD). With this set-up Kees regularly decodes FT8 signals as low as –27dB whereas my weakest decodes were around –21dB on the older laptop. While PA7TWO's setup is top of the range, my experience is that 8GB RAM with a 2.4GHz processor is perfectly adequate, while 4GB RAM and a 1.6GHz processor works, but is rather marginal.

Gary Hinson, ZL2IFB / G4IFB, produced a table for his online *FT8 Operating Guide* [5] which compares the lowest copyable signal-to-noise ratios in a 2.5kHz bandwidth and an extract of this is reproduced in **Table 9.2**. As can be seen, an FT8 signal can be about 31dB weaker than an SSB transmission and still be copied. However, the experience of Kees, PA7TWO, is that with a high-specification computer FT8 signals can be a further 6dB weaker than this and still be decoded, giving around 37dB advan-

CHAPTER 9 – FT8 AND DXING ON FT8

SSB:	approx +10dB
CW:	–15dB
FT4:	–17.5dB
FT8:	–21dB
WSPR:	–31dB

Table 9.2: Extract from 'Lowest copiable signal-to-noise ratios in 2.5kHz bandwidth' (source: ZL2IFB's FT8 Operating Guide).

tage over SSB.

For DXing, which is what this book is all about, this is clearly important as it allows signals at the limits of what is propagationally possible to be decoded and a contact made.

Lag

The term 'lag' refers to the time needed to complete the decoding of signals in each receive period and it is a good indication of whether or not your computer is adequate for the job in hand. In JTDX, the amount of lag at any time is indicated at the top of the decode screen, as shown in **Fig 9.7**.

The higher the band occupancy (i.e. the larger the number of stations that are crammed into the approximately 2.8kHz-wide SSB 'channel'), the greater the lag is likely to be.

A lag figure of over 2.0 (i.e. 2 seconds) means your computer's processor is not fast enough or you don't have enough RAM (or, probably, both). I often had to contend with a lag of over 2.0 when I used the older laptop with a 1.6GHz processor and 4GB of RAM. (I was told that a solid state drive – SSD – to replace the slow HDD might have improved the situation, but I did not try this.) But now, with the faster processor and 8GB of RAM, the lag is almost always below 1.0, even when decoding 50, 60 or more stations during a 15-second receive period.

The effect of a lag time in excess of 2.0 is that decoding of received signals is still taking place after the next transmit period has started. For example, if your lag is 5.5, decoding is still taking place 3.5 seconds after you have started to transmit. The upshot of this is that very often your computer did not have sufficient time to decode the message being

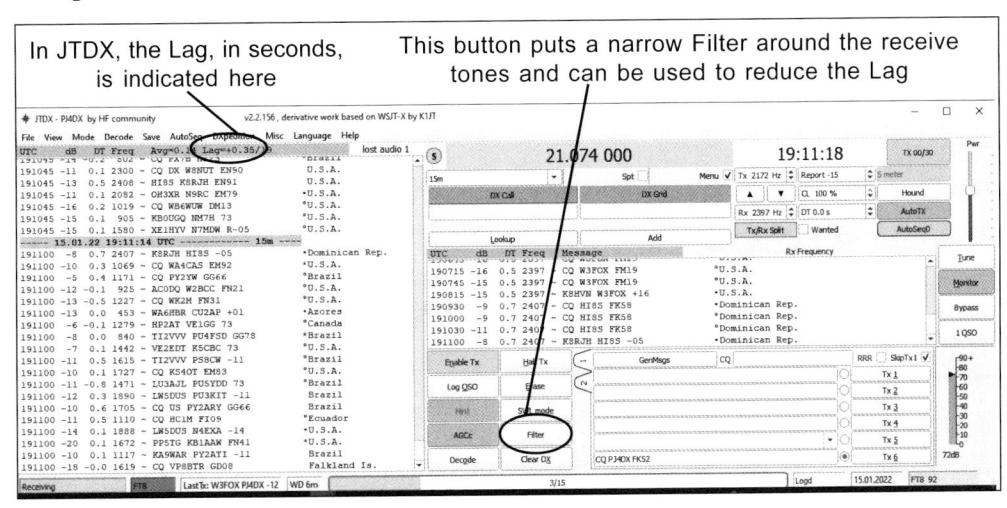

Fig 9.7: The Lag indication and Filter control.

sent to you and, as a result, you are sending the wrong message back to that station – in other words, you get 'out of sync' with the station you are working.

What can be done about this? There is one feature that dramatically decreases the lag – although at a cost. Clicking on the 'Filter' button, as shown in **Fig 9.7**, puts a narrow filter around the receive tone frequencies that you are attempting to decode. In JTDX the Filter is 170Hz wide in standard FT8 mode, 580Hz wide in 'Fox & Hound' mode, and 274Hz wide in FT4 mode. Clicking on the Filter means that, instead of trying to decode maybe 60 or even more stations over a bandwidth of 2.8kHz, your computer will only have to decode the two or three stations in the 170Hz bandwidth of the filter.

The downside is that you will not be able to decode any stations transmitting tones on frequencies outside that very narrow filter bandwidth, so you will not be able to see if there is anyone else calling you, or if there is any other station that you wish to call. Therefore, immediately after you have completed a contact where it has been necessary to use the Filter function, you must remove it. You will then be receiving over the full 2.8kHz again and your lag will probably once again rise to above 2.0.

Inserting and removing the Filter with every contact gets old after a while and you may find it easier just to put up with the fact that you have to wait for one or two additional receive periods in order to complete the contact.

Another potential issue with using the Filter is that if the station you are trying to decode should decide to move frequency, perhaps because he feels his transmit tone frequencies are being QRMd, you will not decode anything.

The reception of noise adds to decoding time and so the lag time can be reduced a little by turning off the receiver pre-amplifier(s), or switching in some attenuation, or simply reducing the RF gain to reduce the received noise level. This won't reduce a lag of over 5.0 to under 2.0 but it may make a small difference and help a little.

Short of going out to buy a higher-specification computer, there's not a lot more you can do. You could try only operating at times when the bands have lower occupancy, but 7 and 14MHz in particular are usually full of stations and, often, this is where and when the DX is.

RECEIVING FT8

Assuming the program has been downloaded and configured correctly and that your computer is talking to your transceiver, you should see the screen starting to fill with received FT8 transmissions.

It is important not to overload the sound card on receive. The receiver level should be set so that it is in the WSJT-X green zone; in JTDX the optimum receive level as shown on the vertical bar meter is around 65dB – 70dB. Set your receiver pre-amp(s) accordingly and adjust the RF gain control so that the levels fall within this range for optimal decoding.

The received signals will be displayed something like this:

```
164315  -15  0.7  1263  CQ W4AAA FN34       U.S.A.
164315  -11  0.3  2612  K1AAA M7ZZZ IO91    England
164315   -3  0.1  1599  DL0AA M6YYY -10     England
164315   -8  0.5  1121  I1ABC M3XXX R-05    England
164315   +1  0.6  1679  MM0AAA F6ZZZ RR73   France
```

What does this all mean? The first group of figures (164315 in this example) is the time: 15 seconds past 1643UTC. Note that all five transmissions received were in the same time period of 15 to 30

CHAPTER 9 – FT8 AND DXING ON FT8

seconds past 1643UTC. In practice, on a busy band 60 or more transmissions may be received simultaneously.

The second column represents the signal-to-noise ratio of the transmission *as received by you* (i.e. you are receiving W4AAA at a level of –15dB).

The next column is the time difference compared with Internet time. This figure *should* always be below 1.0 but it may not be if you or the transmitting station lose time synchronisation for whatever reason.

The fourth column shows the frequency of the station's transmitted audio tones. In the case of W4AAA his tones are from 1263Hz (to 1313Hz, as the transmitted tones are 50Hz wide).

The fifth column is indicating the QSO information, and now we will look at each line in turn. In the first line, clearly, W4AAA is calling CQ and will be looking for any callers in the following time period (i.e. at 30 to 45 seconds past 1643UTC in this example). FN34 is W4AAA's Grid locator.

In the second line, M7ZZZ in Grid IO91 is calling K1AAA. This suggests that M7ZZZ heard a transmission from K1AAA in the previous time period and he has decided to call him.

In the third line, M6YYY is responding to DL0AA and giving DL0AA a signal report of –10dB. This suggests that, in the previous time period, DL0AA had responded to M6YYY (for example if M6YYY had been calling CQ).

In the fourth line, M3XXX is giving an "R" report to I1ABC. The "R" (meaning 'Roger') means that M3XXX has copied the report that I1ABC sent in the previous time period and he is telling I1ABC that he has received that report and that I1ABC's report with him is –5dB.

In the fifth and final line in this example, F6ZZZ is sending "RR73" to MM0AAA. This means that F6ZZZ has received the "R" report sent previously by MM0AAA and so the QSO has been completed and can therefore be logged.

The final column shows the DXCC entity of the station you are receiving (this is an optional setting but is useful unless you are absolutely familiar with all the world's prefixes).

Note that where you see two callsigns in one line, one after the other, the *first* callsign (on the left) is the station being called, and which you may (or may not) be able to receive in the *following* 15-second receive period. The *second* callsign (to the right) is the station calling the one on the left and this is the station that you are *now* receiving.

Some 'special' or long callsigns, including those of stations operating with a reciprocal licence or under CEPT Recommendation T/R 61-01 can sometimes only be displayed as <...> This is due to the limited amount of data that can be transmitted in a single FT8 transmission. Some examples of callsigns that would be truncated in this way are PD2022HNY (who was indeed active on FT8 over the 2022 New Year period) or PJ4/G4JVG. However, the full callsign *is* displayed when the station calls CQ or when they send a "73" message, indicating that their existing QSO has been completed.

The programs can be configured to display new stations (those you have not worked before), new DXCC entities, new zones etc, in different colours. In my opinion this just makes the screen look more confusing and difficult to read. After experimenting a little I have the barest minimum of colours set: all stations appear in black on white except when they are calling me, in which case they appear in red. My own transmissions are also in black but highlighted on a yellow background.

TRANSMITTING FT8

Once you are familiar with the reception of FT8 signals it is time to try transmitting. There are two important transmit parameters to set before you attempt to make any contacts. The first is to reduce your transceiver's power output. FT8 is a 100% duty-cycle mode and each transmission is 15 seconds long. There is then only a 15-second receive period before the next 15-second long transmission. Most amateur transceivers are not rated for this sort of use and even if they will happily transmit at 100 watts output for 48 hours during an SSB or CW contest, they are likely to fail sooner or later if used at 100 watts on FT8 for lengthy periods. I know of at least one case of a transceiver's final PA transistors failing after being used at full power on FT8. I would recommend a maximum of 40 or 50 watts output from a 100-watt transceiver and preferably less. (More on how much power is actually *necessary* later.)

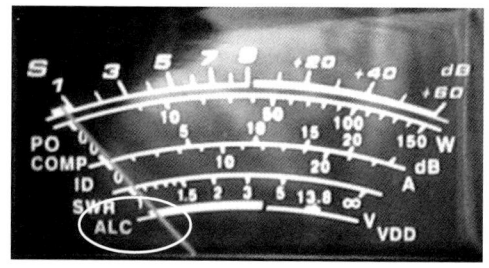

Fig 9.9: Use the absolute minimum of ALC deflection for FT8.

The second parameter to check is to ensure that your transceiver's ALC (automatic level control) is set correctly. Too much ALC deflection and your signal will be unnecessarily wide and thus cause interference to other band users. Select the ALC meter on your transceiver. It should only *just* deflect a little when transmitting, regardless of the power output.

Fig 9.8 shows the ALC meter deflection on the Icom IC-7300 screen and on a moving-needle meter (e.g. on a Yaesu FT-2000) in **Fig 9.9**. The ALC level can be adjusted in the FT8 program (in the case of JTDX this is done using the slider control labelled 'Pwr', **Fig 9.10**).

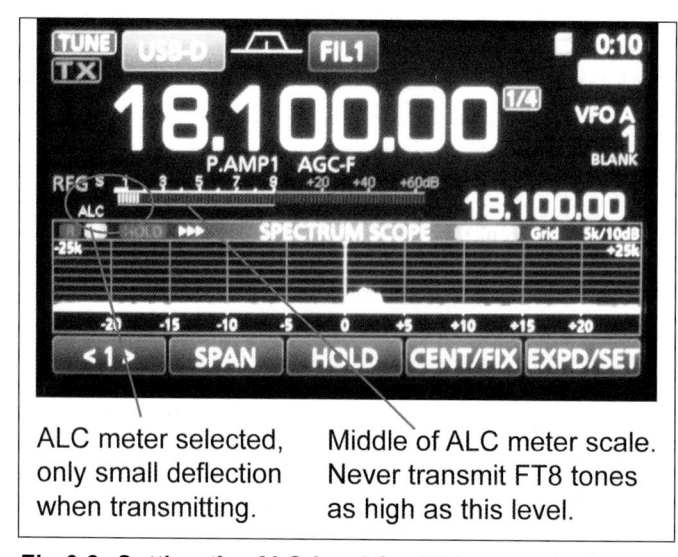

ALC meter selected, only small deflection when transmitting.

Middle of ALC meter scale. Never transmit FT8 tones as high as this level.

Fig 9.8: Setting the ALC level for FT8 transmissions.

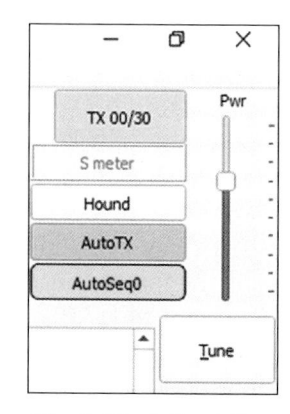

Fig 9.10: Adjust the ALC level with the 'Pwr' slider control.

CHAPTER 9 – FT8 AND DXING ON FT8

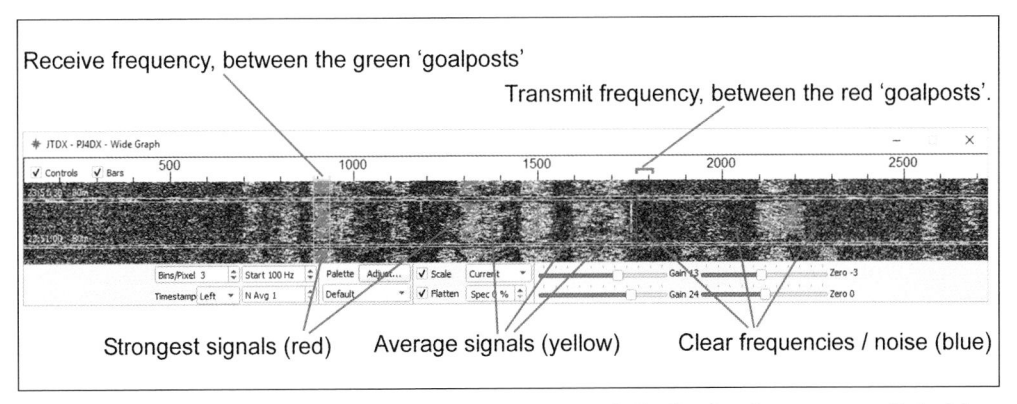

Fig 9.11: Common to all FT8 programs, the waterfall display is an essential aid that indicates band activity and most importantly helps you to select a clear frequency for your transmit tones.

All the FT8 programs incorporate a *waterfall display*. This is an important aid that allows you to monitor band activity and select a clear frequency for your own transmissions. **Fig 9.11** explains what the waterfall display is showing. For JTDX, the suggested waterfall settings are:

GAIN 13, ZERO -3
GAIN 24, ZERO 0
SCALE, FLATTEN, BARS and
Frequency all enabled.

Before initiating a contact you need to find a clear transmit frequency for yourself, using the waterfall display as a guide. Note that because FT8 transmissions alternate between 15-second transmit and receive periods you must view the waterfall display for a minimum of 30 seconds (and preferably a minute or so) before selecting your transmit frequency. Anywhere in the SSB bandwidth of approximately 200Hz to 3000Hz can be used.

Once you have started to transmit, though, there is no way of telling if your frequency *remains* clear, because the waterfall 'freezes' during your transmit periods (obviously it cannot receive what is on the band while you are transmitting). There could be someone with a stronger signal using exactly the same tone frequencies and transmitting at exactly the same time as you and you would never know. It therefore pays dividends to check your transmit frequency from time to time by viewing the waterfall display for a couple of transmit / receive cycles.

MAKING AN FT8 QSO

Once you have set your transmit parameters (reduced RF power to 50% or less, adjusted the ALC level correctly and selected a clear transmit frequency using the waterfall) you have a choice of three ways to initiate an FT8 QSO:

● You could call CQ yourself;

● You could answer someone else's CQ call; or

● You could call a station that is either calling someone else, or who is already in QSO with someone else.

This last suggestion may sound surprising to those who are used to making contacts on SSB or CW, where it is definitely considered to be bad form to call a station before they have completed their existing contact. FT8 is different though because, *always provided you are not using the same tone frequencies as the station being worked,* you will not cause interference either to him or to the station you are calling.

The station you are calling will be decoding the entire 2.8kHz channel and so he will be able to see that you are calling him, even if he is yet to complete his existing contact. He is unlikely to respond to you until he *has* completed that contact, but it is still worth calling because he should be able to see that you are there and waiting. You will be able to see when he completes his existing QSO as he will send:

[OTHER CALL] [HIS CALL] 73 *or*
[OTHER CALL] [HIS CALL] RR73 *or perhaps*
[OTHER CALL] [HIS CALL] RRR

When he has completed the contact he may then reply to you. However, if he has several stations calling him simultaneously he may not respond to you immediately – but he should still at least have noted that you are calling. So it is worth persisting if you want to make a contact with that particular station.

mit tones frequency by keying it directly into the box, but then you would have no idea if the frequency you are inputting is clear or not: it is always preferable to use the waterfall display for this.

The 'Tx/Rx Split' button should *always* be illuminated. This allows you to transmit on different tone frequencies to those of the station being called. If this button is *not* illuminated your transmit frequency will automatically jump on to the station you are calling – and you do not want to do this, for reasons that we will go into later.

The other features highlighted are simply the current UTC time, which should be correct to within better than 1 second, and a button with which you can toggle your transmit periods between 'Even' (or 'First', 00/30) and 'Odd' (or 'Second', 15/45). Note that if you were to call a station that is transmitting in the 'Even' time period the program will automatically switch you to 'Odd' and *vice versa*. The use of the button is to allow you to choose in which time period you want to transmit if you decide to call CQ yourself.

Before starting to make any contacts it is a good idea to set the program to prompt you to log the contact when the

The FT8 Screen

Fig 9.12 is a screenshot of part of the main FT8 operating screen (when using JTDX: other programs have similar control panels) with some of the important parameters highlighted. Here, the current transmit and receive tone frequencies, as set using the waterfall display shown in **Fig 9.11**, are indicated. You *could* also input your trans-

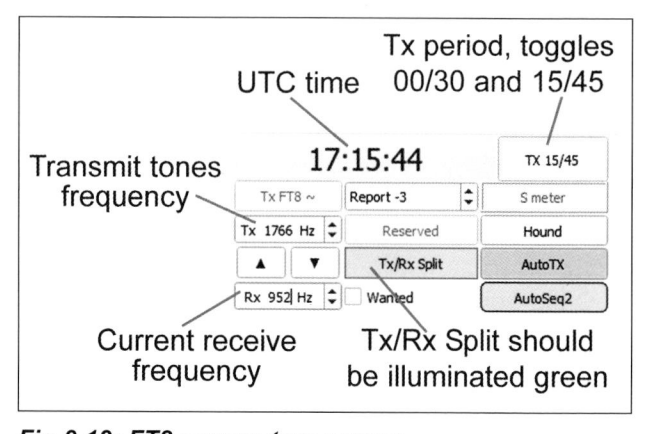

Fig 9.12: FT8 parameters screen.

CHAPTER 9 – FT8 AND DXING ON FT8

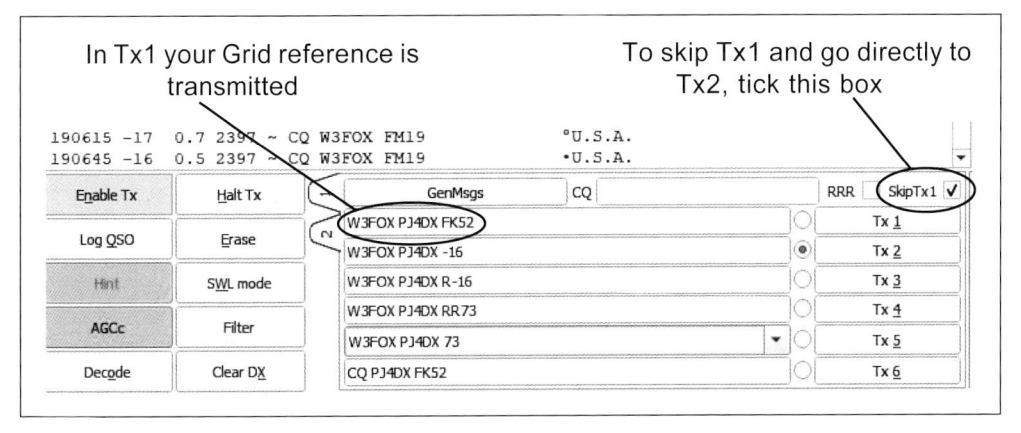

Fig 9.13: FT8 sequence of transmissions.

QSO is completed (if using JTDX this is done by going to File—Settings—Reporting and then ticking the 'Prompt me to log QSO' box: the other programs have a similar setting).

Fig 9.13 shows the sequence of transmissions of an FT8 contact. In this example W3FOX has called CQ twice and I (PJ4DX) have decided to call him. The first transmission (Tx1) would be:

W3FOX PJ4DX FK52

(FK52 is my Grid locator.) However, most of the time it is unnecessary to call with the Grid locator (more about this later) so instead – and as shown in **Fig 9.13** – I clicked on 'Skip Tx1' and made my initial call to W3FOX by going straight to the report (the Tx2 message), which is:

W3FOX PJ4DX –16

...which means I am calling W3FOX and his S/N report with me is –16dB.

Hopefully, W3FOX then replies to me with a 'Roger' and his report, e.g.:

PJ4DX W3FOX R–10 *(or whatever)*

and, if so, my next transmission to him – *assuming that I started with Tx2* – would be Tx4:

W3FOX PJ4DX RR73

At this point the QSO could be logged, although it's often better to wait in order to receive W3FOX's final transmission to me, which would be:

PJ4DX W3FOX 73

Note that if I had *not* skipped Tx1, after the exchange of reports W3FOX would have sent the RR73 message (Tx4) and I would have concluded the QSO by sending the 73 message (Tx5).

Skip Tx1 or Not?

I said earlier in this section that most of the time it is unnecessary to make an initial call to a station with your Grid locator, i.e. Tx1. There is a bit of controversy about this: i.e. whether to initiate a call to a station by sending Tx1, which includes your Grid locator, or to skip Tx1 and go straight to Tx2, which sends the station's S/N report instead of the Grid.

I prefer the latter. After all, if I am called by a VK2 station I know that he is in New South Wales: I don't need to be told he is in QF56 or wherever. Most of the time the Grid is irrelevant on HF and not sending Tx1 saves a minimum of 30 seconds from the duration of a contact (more, if repeats are required).

There are a few occasions where sending the Grid is useful, though. One would be for USA stations that are not in the call district that is suggested by their callsign. I also hold a US Amateur Extra licence with the callsign KH0UN, which was issued to me when I was living in the Far East. I can use KH0UN from anywhere in the USA and, having since moved to Bonaire, I am now far more likely to operate from Florida than I am from Saipan in the Northern Mariana Islands, the place where KH0UN was originally issued. It would therefore be helpful to other amateurs if I sent:

M7XXX KH0UN EL95 (or whatever)
rather than:
M7XXX KH0UN –05 (or whatever)

...if I were ever to operate from Miami, otherwise M7XXX would be likely to think he is being called by someone from the north-west Pacific!

Grids are mainly used on VHF and it is still normal to exchange Grid locators when using FT8 on the 50MHz band. That said, during the 2021 Sporadic E season when I was active on 50MHz FT8 I noticed that even on that band many stations skipped the Grid and went straight to the report on FT8.

There are some contests (on FT4 as well as FT8) where different Grid locators count as multipliers for the competitors, so it is important to send the Grid if participating in any of those events.

Finally, it should be pointed out that a small number of HF operators 'collect' Grids on FT8. I know of one station who actually refuses to respond to any station who does *not* send their Grid locator when they call him. Fortunately this is very much a minority view and most operators are happy to make the contact, whether or not the Grid locator is sent.

HOW MUCH POWER IS NECESSARY?

I said there is "a bit" of controversy about whether or not to 'Skip Tx1', but that is as nothing compared with the question of how much power should be used when on FT8. Now that is a *really* thorny subject!

Some amateurs insist that FT8 is a low-power mode only and so QRP power levels should *always* be used, and they can get very upset if you try to tell them that you need more than 5W to make a particular contact. Others are equally insistent that, while FT8 may be a weak-signal mode, that does not necessarily make it a low-*power* mode.

Certainly it is possible to make far more QRP contacts on FT8 than it would be on SSB or even CW. FT8's ability to decode signals below the received noise level make that a given: after all, you have to be able physically to hear an SSB or CW signal with your ears to make a contact on those modes which you are not able to do if the SSB or CW signal is below your noise.

But FT8 is not magic: clearly there does still have to be propagation between you and the station you are trying to contact, and sometimes that propagation might well be highly marginal. If that's the case, some signals will be below a certain threshold and won't be decoded, but with higher power they would be.

This book is about DXing: you could certainly work plenty of German, Italian or Spanish stations on 7 or 14MHz if running 5 watts or less and you might even work some DX stations, but not very frequently if propagation is marginal (which is when most DX contacts are made).

Earlier in this chapter I cautioned about running a 100-watt transceiver at 100 watts output when operating on FT8. I never run more than 50W from my 100W transceiver and usually considerably less. But if I find I *need* to use more than about 50W output to make a DX contact I turn *down* the transceiver power output and use a linear amplifier to put out, say, 150W.

It is not usually necessary to use high power on FT8 and, if you are receiving S/N reports greater than, say, +02dB or +03dB you are probably running an unnecessarily high amount of power.

There is another reason for *not* running too much power on FT8. If you have a very strong signal, even if it is an absolutely clean signal, it can prevent those FT8 users who are receiving you at a very high level from decoding as many other stations as would otherwise be the case. This is actually nothing to do with your power level *per se* and only to do with the strength of your signal, but clearly the more power you run the stronger your signal will be.

I have an amateur neighbour who lives less than 500m from me and our antennas are literally in line of sight with each other. On some bands when he is operating on FT8 I am unable to decode any other stations on the same band during his transmit periods, and he has the same issue with me. In practice this is not a problem provided we transmit in the same time periods when we are both operating on the same band.

To summarise, while there is definitely no need to run 400W output all the time on FT8, and you will be able to make many contacts with very low power, if you are DXing you will want to make QSOs with stations when propagation is marginal and under those conditions you will find you need to use more than just QRP power levels.

WHY OPERATE SPLIT?

FT8 allows you to put your transmit tones anywhere in the approximately 2.8kHz-wide channel and, as shown in **Fig 9.11**, the waterfall display should be used to select a clear frequency (or *frequencies* plural would be more accurate since there are eight tones over a range of 50Hz) before you start to transmit. I stated before that (in JTDX) the 'Tx/Rx Split' button should *always* be illuminated (in WSJT-X this is 'Hold TX freq') and this allows you to transmit on different tone frequencies to those of the station being called.

Why not call using the same tone frequencies as the station you are calling?

Firstly, and perhaps most obviously, if a rare DX station comes on the air and calls CQ he will undoubtedly soon have a pile-up of stations calling him. If all the stations called on exactly the same frequency clearly they would interfere with each other and the DX station would likely not be able to receive any of them.

But even 'ordinary' stations, not in rare DX locations, can often have several stations calling them simultaneously, so this advice applies in all circumstances and not only when calling a DXpedition or another rare DX station.

FT8 is actually quite good at separating two stations calling on the same frequencies but there is a limit to what can be achieved and if there are three or four stations using the same audio tones and at roughly the same strength it is likely that none of them will be decoded.

Secondly, there is simply no need to call on the same frequency: every station is decoding the whole of the 2.8kHz-wide channel during every receive cycle, so why call on the same frequency as anybody else?

If you decide you really *must* call me on "my" frequency, and if I should then reply to you, after our QSO is completed please do not then call CQ yourself, or answer anyone else calling you on my frequency. To do so would mean you would QRM anyone else calling me on that frequency. It would be even worse if the station calling you *also* decided to use the same frequency! See also the boxed text 'A Poor Operating Practice'.

This is why it is always far better to find a clear frequency in the waterfall display and call there, and not on the same frequency as the station you are calling.

Note that when you call CQ, your tone receive frequency is automatically set to the same frequency as the transmit tones that you have chosen. This is actually bad news, because if several stations were to call you simultaneously and one of them should call on your frequency, that is the station that will be decoded first. If more than one station responds to a CQ call that I make, I therefore always quickly check which station I want to respond to, rather than simply double clicking on the first station to be decoded.

A POOR OPERATING PRACTICE

Both my wife Eva, PJ4EVA, and I have been affected by an operating practice that we feel ought to be strictly outlawed! We have been unable to complete FT8 QSOs with DX stations because we are being called on exactly the same frequency as the DX station.

What happens is that the DX station calls CQ, we call them on a different frequency sending the report (e.g. '–05dB') and, hopefully, the DX station replies to us with a 'Roger' ('R') and their report (e.g. 'R–10dB'). However, sometimes this cannot be received because another station has by then started to call *us, but using the same frequency as the DX station*. If they are local or semi-local stations they could be up to 30 or 40dB stronger than the DX station and so the response from the DX station is completely lost.

This happened to PJ4EVA when a QSO with Johannes, 5T5PA, in Mauritania was not completed because a strong USA station started calling Eva on 5T5PA's frequency. I was unable to complete a QSO with EP2HAM in Tehran on 14MHz when a Dutch station started to call me on EP2HAM's frequency.

It is normal operating practice on FT8 to call a station *before* their existing QSO is completed. While this is perfectly acceptable *provided* different tone frequencies are used, it is definitely *not* if you call on exactly the same frequencies as the station being worked.

It is unacceptable even if you wait until you are sure the contact has been completed because you would still cause interference to others wishing to call the DX station. Needless to say, neither PJ4EVA nor I reply to stations causing QRM in this way.

CHAPTER 9 – FT8 AND DXING ON FT8

DXING ON FT8

DXing on FT8 is much like DXing on SSB or any other mode: you hear (or more accurately on FT8 "see") a 'wanted' station, you call him, hopefully he replies and you then complete the QSO. Or you call CQ yourself and you are rewarded with a response from the one and only resident amateur in, say, the North Cook Islands (unlikely, I know, but it does occasionally happen!)

But there are some subtle differences when DXing on FT8 due to the way the mode works. The most obvious one, perhaps, is that it is *possible* to automate FT8 contacts to a large extent. This is not to be recommended, particularly when DXing. In JTDX if you set the auto sequencer (AutoSeq) at 0 (**Fig 9.14**) *you* will be in charge of the contacts. You will need to decide who *you* want to call, or who you respond to if they call you, and initiate the contact by double clicking on the wanted callsign. After that, the AutoSeq will take you through each step of the contact as previously described.

Bear in mind that many DX stations also like to chase DX themselves. As already stated several times, it is normal to call a station on FT8 before their existing QSO has finished (provided the station is calling on different tone frequencies). Even so, if I am calling a rare DX station, perhaps several times, and you start to call me, I am *very* unlikely to respond to you unless you are in North Korea or somewhere else even rarer than the DX station that I am calling!

On the other hand, do not call a station once or twice and then start to call a different station if the first one does not respond straight away. Don't give up! It often happens that I am called by several stations (e.g. Stations A, B, C and D) simultaneously. I can only work one at a time, so if I don't come back to Station C or D immediately, they should keep calling. I will have noticed that they are calling and are patiently waiting. It often happens that by the time I respond to Station C or D, I find that he is then calling someone else. At that point, I respond to one of the other stations calling me, figuring that Station C or D cannot really

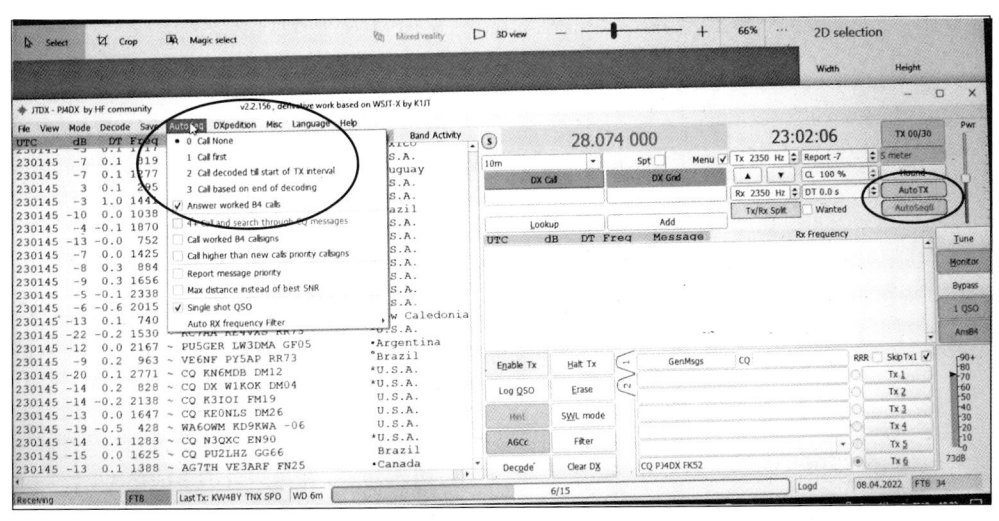

Fig 9.14: For DXing, set the AutoSeq at 0 ('Call None'). The selection is confirmed by the 'button' at the top right of the screen.

131

HF DX BASICS

want to make the QSO if they have given up so quickly! It is annoying for a DX station to respond to someone who has called him, only to find that station has already given up and is now calling someone else.

If I am calling "CQ DX" (as opposed to just calling CQ) please forgive me if I do not respond to you. Unfortunately the definition of DX is not reciprocal: I may be DX to you but, sadly, you may not be DX to me! As a DXer, looking at the FT8 screen can be a bit dispiriting here in Bonaire. It is normally *full* of North American (mainly USA) stations. You know that if you call CQ DX, CQ AS or CQ EU you will nevertheless still be called by many American stations which are not DX to you, even if they perceive that you are DX to them.

The way I look at it is that if I just call CQ I should reply to Americans who call me, but if I call CQ JA or CQ AS (for example) I can legitimately ignore the North Americans while attempting to work the Asians.

Sad to say, but most of the time on FT8 directional CQ calls such as CQ EU or CQ AS are ignored. But this is one of those subtle differences between DXing on FT8 and on SSB. On FT8 if you call CQ AS and you are called only by European stations it is not only legitimate but also perfectly possible to ignore them. On SSB a station that becomes overwhelmed by non-DX stations calling finds it very difficult to ignore them because – even with split frequency operation – the DX and non-DX signals tend to be on the same frequencies. Generally the non-DX stations are much stronger, usually several S-points stronger, than the wanted, distant, stations which can make it almost impossible to make real DX contacts.

On FT8, however, this is simply not an issue because all of the 50Hz-wide signals are spread out over the 2.8kHz-wide 'channel' (once again emphasising the importance of *not* calling on the same frequency as the station you are calling) thus allowing the DX station to concentrate on those signals he wants to work.

If you have a beam antenna, you should always check the left-hand side of the left-hand decode column to see what is being worked in your part of the world – see **Fig 9.15**. Even though you are not decoding the DX station on your present beam heading, it is clear that other stations are and if you were to rotate your beam to the correct heading you may well be able to decode the DX yourself.

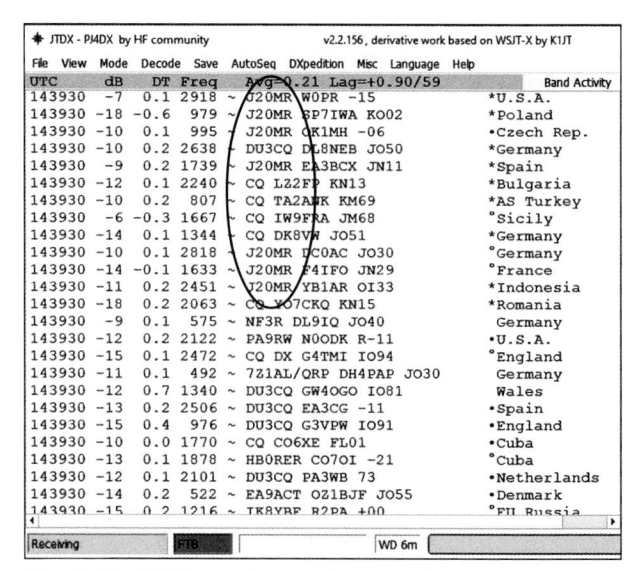

Fig 9.15: With my beam due north to receive both North America and Europe, I was unable to decode J20MR in Djibouti, but turning the beam to the east brought him in.

CHAPTER 9 – FT8 AND DXING ON FT8

Do *not* call a station *unless* you are decoding him. It may not be immediately apparent when you first start to use FT8 but in fact you can call anybody, such as DX stations that you have seen being called on the left side of the screen but have not decoded yourself, by typing their callsign in the 'DX Call' box and then clicking 'GenMsgs' to generate the standard messages – but please do not do this! See **Fig 9.16** – here a Cuban station is calling ET3AA in Ethiopia at the same time that ET3AA is transmitting, so there is no way a QSO will *ever* take place! It is clear that the Cuban did not decode ET3AA but either saw him spotted on the DX Cluster or saw that other stations were calling ET3AA and decided to call himself. Unfortunately he had the wrong time period selected (00/30 instead of 15/45), or it could be that earlier ET3AA had decided to change *his* time period for some reason, leaving the Cuban calling at the wrong time.

You would think it should be obvious never to call a station you have not decoded yourself, because even if the station being called decodes you, you won't see his response and so you will just be wasting everyone's time. Yet on many occasions I have replied to a station calling me who then simply does not respond and just keeps on calling. After three attempts without a reply I normally then go on to another station who has been patiently waiting.

Sometimes, though, 'Station A' eventually *does* reply with his "R" report. Why should this happen? The reason *could* be that he was asleep, but it's probably more likely that he had QRM on my transmit frequency or perhaps his lag time was high and so he had not received my earlier responses.

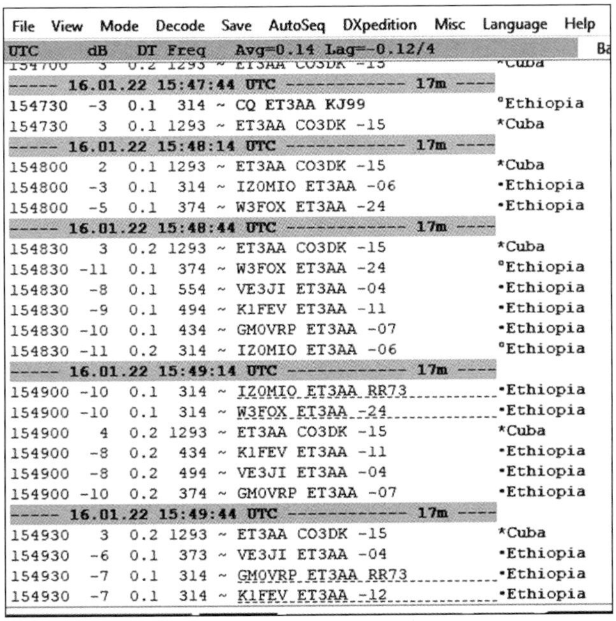

When this happens it is important to return to 'Station A' who sent you the "R" report even if, by that time, you have already initiated a contact with another station. You will find that, as soon as you respond to 'Station A' with your "RR73" transmission, your FT8 program will prompt you to log the QSO.

In fact, if the contact is marginal (such as that being described here) it is wise *not* to log the contact immediately, but rather to wait to ensure you receive the "73" transmission from Station A. If you do *not* receive this, your FT8 program will re-send your "RR73" message (multiple times if necessary). If you *do*

Fig 9.16: Calling in the wrong time period. The Cuban station will never make a contact with ET3AA like this!

receive Station A's "73" transmission your program will stop transmitting "RR73" and you can then log the contact.

If you had logged the contact when initially prompted to do so it could well be that 'Station A' did not receive your "RR" message, in which case he should not have logged the contact. Only when the "RR73" and / or "73" messages have been received by both parties is the QSO considered to have been completed. See the boxed text 'When to Log a Contact'.

SPEEDING THINGS UP...

By now, you will have noticed that FT8 is rather a slow mode. There are ways and means to speed things up, though. If several stations are calling you (as opposed

---

WHEN TO LOG A CONTACT

One of the problems with FT8 is that it is quite possible for one of the QSO partners to log a contact, believing the QSO to be completed, whilst the other side of the contact does not log it, because he has not received the final transmission from the other station. In fact the same situation can arise when using SSB or CW, but it does seem to happen far more frequently when using FT8, leading to far more 'Not In Log' responses when applying for a QSL.

When, then, is it 'safe' to log an FT8 QSO? The question is complicated by the fact that it depends on whether you or the other station initiates the contact *and* whether or not the first transmission is Tx1 (or Tx6) or Tx2. Although the majority of FT8 users initiate a contact by sending their Grid locator (e.g. **[HIS CALL] [YOUR CALL] [GRID]**), a large minority skip that first transmission (Tx1) and instead send **[HIS CALL] [YOUR CALL] [S/N REPORT]** (Tx2).

As the FT8 AutoSeq sends the standard messages depending on what has just been received, this has a knock-on effect on when the QSO can be considered to have been completed.

If you initiate a contact by sending Tx1 (i.e. including your Grid) *or* if you call CQ yourself (Tx6, which also includes your Grid), then after the exchange of "R" reports the *other* station will send "RR73". When you receive it, log the QSO and then send "73".

If, however, you call another station and start by sending Tx2 (i.e. you send the other station's S/N report with your first transmission to him), then *you* will send the "RR73" message and the other station should respond with "73".

Your FT8 logging program will prompt you to log the contact when you send "RR73" but – and it's a big "but" – you do not know that the other station has received this until you receive his "73". If you do *not* receive "73" it could be that your "RR73" message was not received and therefore the QSO was not complete. (It *could* also be the case that your "RR73" *was* received but you simply didn't receive the other station's "73" message.) It therefore makes sense *not* to log the QSO when first prompted to do so but to wait until you receive the other station's "73" message. If you do not log the QSO straight away your FT8 program will continue to send your "RR73" message (multiple times if necessary) until either "73" is received *or* you choose to log the contact.

to you calling stations) it is possible to 'interleave' the QSOs by answering a second station *before* receiving the final "73" from the first one. Nine times out of 10 you will receive the "73" after you have already started the next QSO, thus saving 30 seconds per QSO.

Should the first station *not* receive your "RR73", his program will keep on repeating his "R" report to you, so you will know that you do then have to repeat your "RR73" message to him.

'Fox & Hound' Mode

DXpeditions (and also some resident DX stations) often use the so-called 'Fox and Hound' (F/H) mode. F/H is available to WSJT-X users, though not to those who use JTDX. JTDX users can be a Hound, but not a Fox.

In F/H mode, the DXpedition station may answer several callers simultaneously, thus tripling or quadrupling the rate of making contacts. The downsides are that the DX station's total power is split into two, three or more streams, so the signal strength of each is considerably less; and the fact that instead of taking up only 50Hz of bandwidth he might be occupying four or even five times that.

Because of this, no F/H operation should take place on the main FT8 frequencies. Most F/H operation takes place on the secondary FT8 frequencies (see **Table 9.1**), although some operators choose to use different frequencies again, usually within a few kilohertz of the secondary frequencies.

When operating in F/H mode the 'Fox' (the DX station) will *always* transmit audio tones below 1000Hz, and usually between, say, 250Hz and 600Hz. The 'Hounds' (you, the callers) *must* call above 1000Hz, see **Fig 9.17** (if you don't call above 1000Hz the DX station will not receive your transmission and so a QSO cannot take place).

When you are a Hound you only transmit Tx1 and Tx3. When the Fox responds to you with a S/N report the program automatically moves *your* transmit frequency on to what should be a clear

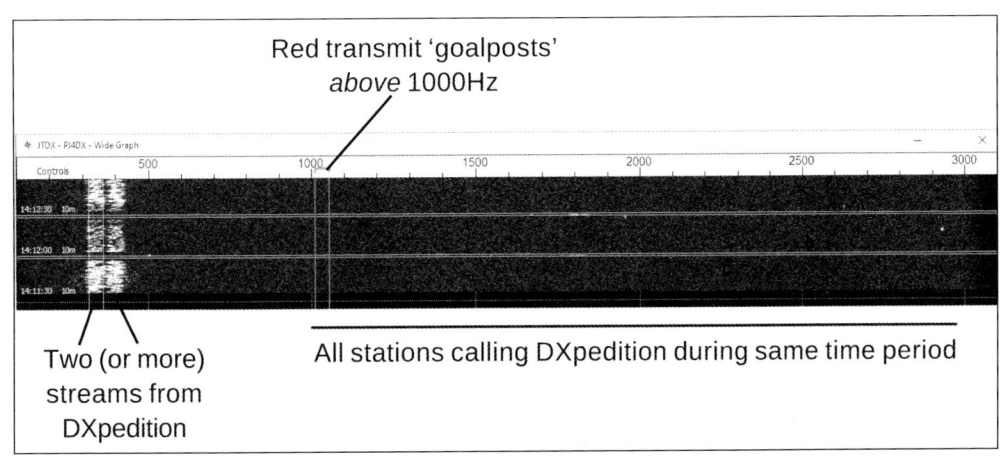

Fig 9.17: This is how the screen should look if you are a 'Hound' calling a 'Fox'. Here there are only two streams from the Fox (at approximately 315 and 375Hz): there could be three or more. You are calling above 1000Hz. All the other callers, between 1000 and 3000Hz are calling at the same time as you (the opposite time period to the DXpedition), so are not visible on the waterfall display.

frequency *below* 1000Hz in order to complete the QSO. The Fox logs the contact when he sends you an "R" report and the program prompts you to log the QSO at the same time – the Fox does not need to get an "RR73" or "73" from you (in fact if you are using JTDX it doesn't allow you to send one).

MSHV 'Multi-Answering Protocol'

In order to speed up the rate of making contacts DXpeditions using MSHV **[3]** can answer up to five stations simultaneously using the program's 'multi-answering protocol'. This is similar to Fox & Hound mode and, to the DX chaser, a DXpedition using MSHV multi-answering protocol looks on the waterfall display like one using F/H. However, the chaser does not need to call as a 'Hound' and the contact is completed in the same way as a standard FT8 contact: the program does not move your audio tones to below 1000Hz when the DX station responds to you.

As with F/H, DXpeditions using MSHV multi-streaming should not use the main FT8 frequencies.

FT4

We have mentioned FT4 several times but not yet described it. That's because its operation is actually identical with that of FT8, except that it is twice as fast: each transmit and receive period is 7.5 seconds compared with FT8's 15 seconds.

The disadvantage is that, compared with FT8, the threshold for signals to be decoded is 3.5dB higher (i.e. signals need to be 3.5dB stronger than they would be on FT8 in order to be decoded), but on HF absolute signal strength is not generally an issue.

FT4 was originally developed for contest operating and indeed the RSGB holds

Fig 9.18: The RSGB organises an FT4 International Activity Day contest.

a series of 90-minute long FT4 'sprint' contests throughout the year as well as an annual 12-hour FT4 'International Activity Day contest' in April, **Fig 9.18**, **[8]**. However, FT4 is increasingly also being used for making general DX contacts, especially in the 7MHz and 14MHz bands, where the main FT8 frequencies are often overcrowded.

I suspect that in future DXpeditions will tend to use FT4 rather than standard FT8 because it's twice as fast, with only a 3.5dB disadvantage. Although F/H and MSHV DXpedition mode can be faster still, they come with the disadvantage of lower signal strengths than FT4 if multiple streams are used.

SOME FINAL POINTS

● The FT8 programs produce an ADIF log file but (depending on how your computer has been configured) it is in a directory normally hidden by Windows and usually it cannot be accessed by using Windows File Manager. To access your ADIF log directly go to File—Open wsjt_log.adi or alternatively you can open the directory by going to File—Open log directory.

The directory also includes a CSV text file and an ALL.txt file. The ALL file is a record of everything transmitted and also *everything that has been decoded* – even if you have left FT8 running on receive when you pop down to the pub for a couple of hours! This file can therefore become quite large, so JTDX starts a new ALL file every calendar month, named 202207_ALL.txt etc. (I don't use WSJT-X but I understand it does not do this, so it would be worthwhile archiving the ALL.txt file every month or so.)

If you get a log query (someone claiming a QSO with you that is not in your log) or if for some reason you forgot to log a contact, you should be able to find the QSO in the ALL file and be able to determine whether or not it was completed satisfactorily and, if so, then add it to your log manually.

- How many stations can be squeezed into a single FT8 'channel'? As each transmission is 50Hz wide and the channel width is 2.8kHz (assuming audio tones of 200 to 3000Hz) there can only be 56 stations without any overlapping of signals. We have already seen that FT8 is quite good at separating transmissions from two stations using the same, or nearly the same, audio tones. However, if you are decoding around 50 or more stations on one FT8 channel the chances are high that some signals will be on the same frequencies as others and so QRM may make some contacts difficult.

This is the reason the busier bands have secondary frequencies in addition to the main FT8 frequency, and these are listed in **Table 9.1**. The difficulty is getting people actually to use the secondary frequencies: it is often the case that 14074kHz is absolutely full and yet the three 14MHz FT8 secondary frequencies are completely devoid of any activity.

If the main FT8 frequency is really busy, give the FT8 secondary frequencies a go, or perhaps try FT4 instead.

- The Tx5 message can also be used to key in free form text, but only up to 13 characters, including spaces. This facility can be used for sending simple greetings messages after the completion of a contact, such as **"HI JOHN 73"** or **"TNX NEW ONE"**.

- Use the FT8 program Filter button with caution. You could be being called by a really rare DX station on audio tone frequencies that are outside the Filter's passband, so you would have no idea he was calling you.

REFERENCES

[1] WSJT-X download:
https://physics.princeton.edu/pulsar/k1jt/
[2] JTDX download: https://jtdx.tech/en/
[3] MSHV download: http://www.lz2hv.org
[4] *JTDX User Guide*: www.jtdx.tech/en
[5] Dimension 4 download:
www.thinkman.com/dimension4/download.htm
[6] Network Time Protocol (NTP) download: www.ntp.org
[7] *FT8 Operating Guide: Weak signal HF DXing for technophiles*, Gary Hinson, ZL2IFB: https://www.g4ifb.com
[8] RSGB HF Contests:
www.rsgbcc.org/hf

Chapter 10
Being DX

Having 'chased' and worked a few DXpeditions, you might want to try your hand at organising your own, either as part of a family holiday (the so-called 'holiday expedition') or with a group of like-minded amateurs.

An IOTA DXpedition, possibly to one of the islands off the coast of the British Isles, is ideal for starters but (despite the rising cost of air fares) the small, light-weight transceivers and antennas available today mean it is also easy to mount DXpeditions to overseas destinations.

Many locations are in demand, even if they do not feature in the 'Most Wanted' surveys such as those described in Chapter 2. A lot of fun can be had by operating from DXCC entities such as Corsica, Madeira, Crete or Malta, not forgetting Jersey, Guernsey or the Isle of Man. The Channel Islands may be considered fairly commonplace within Europe, but they are among the rarest of the European DXCC entities in Japan, for example and, with the improving propagation as solar cycle 25 progresses, you can be sure of big Japanese pile-ups if you were to operate from GU or GJ.

If you would like to give overseas DXpeditioning a go yourself, take a look at the *World Licensing and Operating Directory* [1], which is full of advice on how to get licensed abroad and where to operate from when you get that licence. I compiled and wrote the book in 2008 and although it is now getting rather old, much of the information in it remains relevant today.

IOTA DXPEDITIONS

IOTA DXpeditions are an ideal way to get started in DXpeditioning. Many IOTA islands lie within a few hours' reach and can be put on the air relatively easily. **Table 10.1** lists all 28 IOTA Groups within the British Isles (including the Republic of Ireland) in their order of 'rarity'. Some of these – notably Rockall! – are remote and difficult to reach but others, such as Arran or Bute in the Scottish Coastal Islands Group (EU-123), or even Lindisfarne or the Isle of Wight in the English Coastal Islands (EU-120) are easy to get to. (I find it surprising that only 82.2% of participants have claimed a contact with EU-005, the mainland of Great Britain!) For a list of all the islands included in these groups, refer to the IOTA website [2] or the *IOTA Directory* [3].

Those amateurs who are able to activate a rare or even semi-rare IOTA Group can expect to generate big pile-ups and make many contacts even during a short two- or three-day operation. Not all rare

CHAPTER 10 – BEING DX

BRITISH ISLES IOTA GROUPS

1	EU-189 Rockall	10.8%	15	EU-011 Isles of Scilly	54.6%
2	EU-111 Monach Is	31.8%	16	EU-124 Welsh Coastal Is	54.7%
3	EU-118 Flannan Is	32.9%	17	EU-121 Irish Coastal Is	56.3%
4	EU-112 Shiant Is	33.3%	18	EU-123 Scottish Coastal Is	58.4%
5	EU-106 St Tudwal's Is	35.1%	19	EU-120 English Coastal Is	59.9%
6	EU-108 Treshnish Is	36.9%	20	EU-012 Shetland	63.2%
7	EU-109 Farne Is	37.7%	21	EU-010 Outer Hebrides	65.5%
8	EU-059 St Kilda	38.4%	22	EU-008 Inner Hebrides	66.4%
9	EU-103 Saltee Is	43.0%	23	EU-009 Orkney	71.5%
10	EU-122 Northern Irish Coastal Is	45.3%	24	EU-013 Jersey	78.5%
11	EU-092 Summer Is	46.3%	25	EU-114 Guernsey Group	79.2%
12	EU-007 Blasket Is	48.5%	26	EU-116 Isle of Man	79.8%
13	EU-099 Les Minquiers Is	50.8%	27	EU-115 Ireland	80.4%
14	EU-006 Aran Is	53.4%	28	EU-005 Great Britain	82.2%

Table 10.1: All the IOTA groups of the British Isles, including the Republic of Ireland. They are ranked in order of 'rarity value': the percentage figure refers to the number of all-time IOTA participants that have claimed that IOTA reference (as of April 2022).

groups are remote and difficult to access: there are many even in Europe that are needed by IOTA chasers. A list of the most wanted IOTA Groups in each continent, ranked by rarity, is published in the *IOTA Directory* [3].

DXPEDITION EQUIPMENT

As with most aspects of amateur radio, the sky is the limit. The UK-based Five Star DXers Association filled a 20ft shipping container with transceivers, linear amplifiers, antennas, masts and literally kilometres of coax for their DXpeditions to places such as the Comoros (D68C, 2001) and St Brandon (3B7C, 2007), both in the Indian Ocean. But let's discuss what might be reasonable for a 'holiday expedition' with the family, or a one- or two-man operation.

While living in the Far East between 2005 and 2013, I managed to obtain a licence to operate as XW8XZ from Laos, one of the least-activated countries in South East Asia and in 2013 well within the Top 100 of Most Wanted DXCC entities. This was a fly-in, fly-out, operation with no sponsorship and, so as to pay as little in excess baggage fees as possible, I wanted to keep the equipment as light as possible.

I took a Yaesu FT-857D as the transceiver, with an MFJ-4125 25A switching power supply and a Heil BM-10 lightweight headset. I logged on an old Acer notebook PC using the freeware N1MM logging program: **Fig 10.1** shows the setup. The antenna was a Butternut HF6V fed with Aircell 5, a lightweight coaxial cable and a good compromise between excessive loss and weight. The XW8XZ licence had a 100W power limit, so a linear amplifier was not a consideration.

Now, in 2022, a favourite combination

Fig 10.1: The author operating as XW8XZ from Laos in March 2013.

for a one- or two-man DXpedition where high-power *is* permitted is to use the Juma PA1000 amplifier **[4]**, which weighs only 5.5kg and uses a LDMOS transistor that requires only 5W of drive for the full 1kW output. This means a small and lightweight QRP transceiver such as an Icom IC-705 or Elecraft KX3 can be used as the driver, with an equally small and light power supply.

If the expedition is to a location that is by the sea, the choice of antennas is simple: use ground-mounted quarter-wave verticals which give up to 10dB gain at a very low angle of radiation (see pages 61 – 62) or, for a single-operator DXpedition, a multiband vertical such as the Butternut HF6V or DX Commander – see pages 64 – 66.

With a slightly larger DXpedition group, it is worth considering taking a beam antenna for 14 to 28MHz, especially if the location is inland, away from the ocean. The Hexbeam antenna (see page 71) is ideal: not only does the lightweight DXpedition version weigh only 6kg, but it packs down into a box or bag only 1m long, so it can easily be checked-in on flights. Bear in mind, though, that you will also need a suitable mast or pole on which to mount it.

These days, logging DXpedition contacts on a computer can be considered to be almost obligatory. On an SSB-only DXpedition you do not need the latest-high specification machine for logging – an old laptop or notebook will do just fine. Several suitable logging programs are available: I use N1MM+ (N1MM Logger Plus) **[5]**. Although intended primarily as a contest logging program, N1MM+ allows the logs to be exported as ADIF files and also works well as a DXpedition logging program, **Fig 10.2**. N1MM+ can be downloaded free of charge from **[5]**.

If you intend to operate on FT8 (or FT4) on your DXpedition you will need a moderately high specification computer (see pages 120 – 122), though the same machine can of course then also be used for logging on SSB.

More detail about DXpedition equipment can be found in *Mini DXpeditions for Everyone*, published by the RSGB **[6]**.

DXPEDITION OPERATING

When you have many callers because you are the 'rare' station, it is up to you to take control, or it may quickly get out of hand. There are several methods avail-

CHAPTER 10 – BEING DX

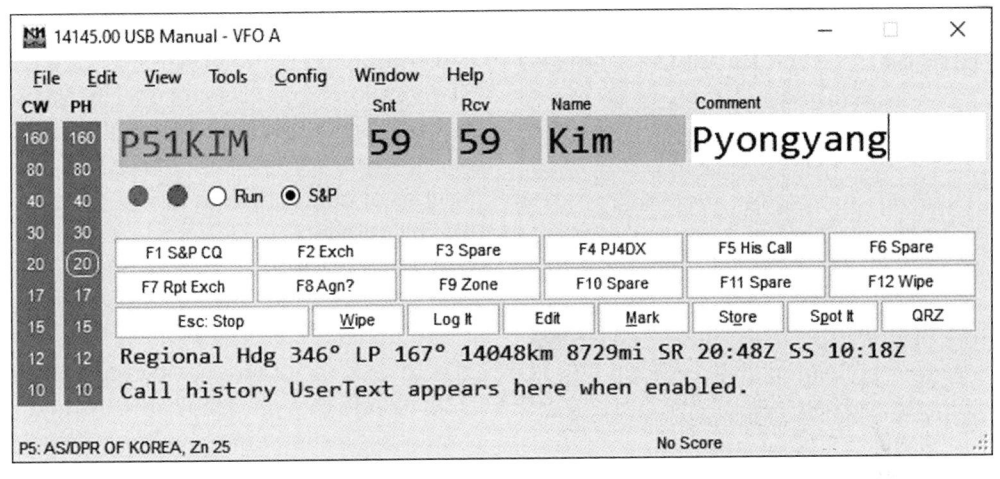

Fig 10.2: The N1MM+ contest logging program can also be used for general logging and DXpedition logging, as in this (fictitious!) example.

able: the first is to start operating split, as described in Chapter 8. This time, though, it is you who stays in the one place and you are asking others to call you away from your transmit frequency.

When it becomes clear that you will need to operate in this manner, ask the pile-up to stand by while you look for a suitable frequency to listen on. It should be close by, usually about 5kHz higher than the frequency you are operating on. But do find a clear frequency first, rather than moving your pile-up on top of an existing contact. Now callers should be able to hear you clearly, so your instructions should be understood and followed.

Try to pick a complete callsign out of the pile-up within the first few seconds or, if not a full one, enough of a call that there is no doubt who you are answering. If you can only copy a partial callsign, never work anyone other than the station you initially answered, e.g. if you go back to "the Alpha Alpha", don't then work Papa Juliet Four Delta X-Ray! If you are heard to do this, other callers will take it as the green light for a free-for-all.

Do ensure you transmit regularly: if you stay silent for long periods the callers will engage in longer and longer calls, just adding to the level of interference.

If it is still too hectic, you can spread out the callers over a range of frequencies, though keep it to no more than 5 or 10kHz or you will start to take over the band. Even a 10kHz split is really only acceptable if you are on a major expedition to a rare spot.

Another technique is to make directional calls, by standing by for a particular continent or a part of a continent. For example, if you are operating from Europe (or close to Europe), the European stations will be workable for many hours at a time, whereas band openings to North America or Asia may be very short. So ask European stations to stand by while you check for calls from other continents.

If you are getting many callers from the East Coast of the USA it is worth taking a listen for the West Coast (or *vice versa* if you're operating from the Far East or Pacific). Many US operators make a point of giving their State with their signal

> **BEING DX – DOS AND DON'TS**
> *Beware of the following pitfalls when operating as DX*
>
> 1. *Don't* operate anonymously: announce your callsign after every QSO, or at least every two or three QSOs.
> 2. *Don't* 'work by numbers', it frustrates people with the 'wrong' number. Instead operate split if the pile-up is too much to handle co-channel.
> 3. *Always* announce *where* you are listening when operating split, *don't* just say "up".
> 4. When operating split keep your split narrow, preferably 5kHz and not more than 10kHz.
> 5. Stick to a rhythm: *don't* remain silent for too long as this encourages continuous calling.
> 6. *Do* stand by frequently for callers from other continents who might otherwise not be heard.

report, for example "Five Nine North Carolina", a useful habit since the numeral in US callsigns now often gives no indication of the location of the station.

With a less rare location, split-frequency operation may not be necessary, but you should still keep your operating crisp and avoid unnecessary exchanges of information. Give your callsign with every contact, or at least every two or three contacts, but there is usually no need to give out a lot of information such as name, equipment (the 'working conditions'), weather, QSL information etc. You can have longer chats when you are operating from home but, when you are the one who is sought after, it is only polite to those waiting to try to accommodate as many callers as possible.

Try to avoid being drawn into nets or list operations if possible as they increase the overall number of exchanges that need to take place and hence reduce the number of contacts that can be made in the time available.

If you have limited battery power and want to keep your transmit time to an absolute minimum it may then be reasonable to ask for someone to maintain a list of callers for you. Ideally the list taker should be in the same part of the world as you are: It does not work when, for example, a European station takes a list of other Europeans on behalf of a weak Pacific station. He will hear those other Europeans who are strong with him on short-skip (quite possibly because they have high-angle antennas) but who may have little or no chance of working into the Pacific. On the other hand, he may well not hear the well-equipped European station in his dead zone who could easily have made the contact.

REFERENCES

[1] *World Licensing and Operating Directory*, Steve Telenius-Lowe, 9M6DXX (PJ4DX), RSGB 2008, available from www.rsgbshop.org
[2] IOTA website: iota-world.org
[3] *IOTA Directory* (18th edition), edited by Roger Balister, G3KMA, and Steve Telenius-Lowe, PJ4DX, published by Islands On The Air (IOTA) Ltd 2018, available from iota-world.org/iota-shop.html
[4] Juma PA1000 linear amplifier: www.jumaradio.com/juma-pa1000/
[5] N1MM+ logging program: https://n1mm.hamdocs.com/mmfiles
[6] *Mini DXpeditions for Everyone*, Billy McFarland, GM6DX, RSGB 2022, available from www.rsgbshop.org

INDEX

425 DX News, 87
5MHz frequency allocations, 76-77
Al Teimurazov, 4L5A, 87
ALC (setting levels), 98, 124
Alex Shovkoplyas, VE3NEA, 90
AM, 27-30
antennas, 51-71
Arvo Järve, ES1JA, 115
ATU / internal ATU, 45-46
audio quality (SSB), 94-104
auroral propagation, 83-85
AutoSeq, 131
baluns, 58
beam antennas, 66-71
Berry Smulders, PJ4BZL, 83
Bob Locher, W9KNI, 7
Butternut HF6V antenna, 65, 139-140
Callum McCormick, M0MCX, 65-66
Cecil Goyder, 2SZ, 14
Charles Wilmott, M0OXO, 25
Charlie Newton, G2FKZ, 85
Christo Hristov, LZ2HV, 115
Clinton B DeSoto, W1CBD, 14
Club Log, 16-18, 21-23
Col McGowan, MM0NDX, 87
Cushcraft, 66
delta loop antenna, 67-69
digital voice (DV), 35
digital voice keyer, 48-50
Dimension 4, 120
dipoles, 52-58
DNR (digital noise reduction), 50
Don Field, G3XTT, 12, 85
doublet antenna, 56-57
DSP (digital signal processing), 50
DX Code of Conduct, 113-114
DX Commander antenna, 65-66, 140
DX Summit (website), 74, 87-88, 106
DX-World (website), 86-87
DXCC (DX Century Club), 13-16, 19

DXNews.com, 87
equipment criteria, 38
eSSB (extended SSB), 100-101
F2 propagation, 72-74, 82
fan dipole, 56-57
'Fox & Hound' (F/H), 122, 135-136
Frank Bell, 4AA, 14
frequency vs wavelength, 9-11
front panel displays, 37-38
FT4, 115, 118-119, 136
FT8, 5, 7-8, 115-137
   ...ADIF log file, 136-137
   ...audio filter, 121-122, 137
   ...computer requirements, 120-122
   ...logging contacts, 126-127, 133-134
   ...power, 128-129
   ...receive levels, 122
   ...Tx5 free-form message, 137
FT8 Operating Guide, 8, 120-121
G5RV / ZS6BKW antennas, 58-59
gain figures, 70
Gary Hinson, ZL2IFB, 8, 120-121
grey-line propagation, 76-78
ground-plane antenna, 60-61
Guglielmo Marconi, 14, 59-60
HamCAP (propagation prediction), 90
headsets, 96-98
Heinrich Hertz, 9
Hexbeam antenna, 71, 140
HF (high frequency), 8-12
HF SSB DX Basics (book), 5-6, 50
horizontal polarisation, 51-52, 62
Hugh 'Cass' Cassidy, WA6AUD, 13
Hy-Gain, 66
Ian White, G(M)3SEK, 104
Igor Chernikov, UA3DJY, 115
inverted-L antenna, 62-64
inverted-V antenna, 55-56
IOTA (Islands on the Air), 20-21, 138-139
Istvan 'Pista' Gaspar, HA5AO, 25

INDEX

James Watson, M0DNS / HZ1JW, 89-90
Jamie Williams, M0SDV, 107
Jari Perkiömäki, OH6BG / OG6G, 91
Joe Taylor, K1JT 5, 7, 115
John Anning, NU9N, 100-101
JTDX, 115-116, 118, 121-122, 126, 135
K-index, 74
Kees v Zuilen, PA7TWO / M5TWO, 120-121
lag, 121-122, 133
long-path propagation, 79
LoTW (Logbook of The World), 15, 18-20, 25
Mauro Pregliasco, I1JQJ, 87
microphones, 95-98
Mini DXpeditions for Everyone (book), 140
monitor facility, 48
'Most Wanted' lists, 17-18, 138-139
MSHV, 115, 117, 136
multi-answering protocol (MSHV), 136
NCDXF International Beacon Project, 92
N1MM+ Logger, 139-140
nets and lists, 109-111, 142
Network Time Protocol, 120
noise blanker, 47-48
OPDX Bulletin, 87
OQRS (Online QSL Request Service), 25
Paul Herrman, N0NBH, 74
Perseverance DX Group, 25
Philipp Springer, DK6SP, 97
power output (transceiver), 42-44, 128-129
propagation (on each band), 72-85
propagation prediction programs, 89-92
Proppy (propagation prediction), 89-90
QRP DXing, 111-113
QRZ.com, 24, 105
QSLs, 18, 23-25
quad loop antenna, 67-69
RadCom propagation predictions, 88-89
radials, 60-61, 66
Radio Auroras (book), 85
Radio Propagation Explained (book), 74

receiver performance, 38-39
RSGB band plans, 75
RSGB FT4 contests, 136
RSGB Propagation Studies
  Committee, 89-90
SDR (software defined radio), 36-38
Short-Path Propagation from UK
  (propagation prediction), 90
Skip Tx1, 127-128
sloping dipole antenna, 55-56
solar cycle 25, 5, 72-73
solar flare, 85
speech processing, 102-104
split frequency operation, 47, 104, 106-109,
  126, 129-130, 141-142
Sporadic E (Es) propagation, 80-83
SSB generation, 29-32
SSSP propagation, 83
Steve Franke, K9AN 5, 7, 115
Steve Hunt, G3TXQ, 71
Steve Nichols, G0KYA, 90
Tedd Mirgliotta, KB8NW, 87
TEP (Trans-Equatorial Propagation), 83-84
The Complete DX'er (book), 7
The Daily / Weekly DX, 87
The Magic Bands (book), 12, 85
Tim Beaumont, M0URX, 25
Trans World Radio Bonaire, 27
transmission audio tailoring, 98-100
transmission bandwidth, 100-101
tuning in SSB, 32-35
twin / dual receivers, 46-47, 108-109
Valeria Gualerzi, IK1ADH, 87
vertical antennas, 59-67
vertical polarisation, 51-52
VOACAP (propagation prediction), 90-92
waterfall, 29, 37, 125-126, 129-130, 136
'working by numbers', 105-106, 142
working the DX, 104-111
WSJT / WSJT-X, 7, 115-116, 122, 135